5-16 9/6 9

# CONQUEST

## BY JOHN CONNOLLY:

### THE CHARLIE PARKER STORIES

*Every Dead Thing*
*Dark Hollow*
*The Killing Kind*
*The White Road*
*The Reflecting Eye* (novella in the Nocturnes collection)
*The Black Angel*
*The Unquiet*
*The Reapers*
*The Lovers*
*The Whisperers*
*The Burning Soul*
*The Wrath of Angels*
*The Wolf in Winter*

### OTHER WORKS

*Bad Men*
*Nocturnes*
*The Book of Lost Things*
*The Wanderer in Unknown Realms* (ebook novella)

### THE SAMUEL JOHNSON STORIES
### (FOR YOUNG ADULTS)

*The Gates*
*The Infernals*
*The Creeps*

### THE CHRONICLES OF THE INVADERS
(with Jennifer Ridyard)

*Empire*

### NONFICTION
(as editor)

*Books to Die For: The World's Greatest Mystery Writers*
*on The World's Greatest Mystery Novels* (with Declan Burke)

# CONQUEST

## THE CHRONICLES OF THE INVADERS

## JOHN CONNOLLY
## & JENNIFER RIDYARD

**EMILY BESTLER BOOKS**

—

**ATRIA**

NEW YORK  LONDON  TORONTO  SYDNEY  NEW DELHI

**ATRIA** PAPERBACK
A Division of Simon & Schuster, Inc.
1230 Avenue of the Americas
New York, NY 10020

First Emily Bestler Books/Atria Paperback edition February 2015

**EMILY BESTLER BOOKS / ATRIA** PAPERBACK and colophons are trademarks of Simon & Schuster, Inc.

For information about special discounts for bulk purchases, please contact Simon & Schuster Special Sales at 1-866-506-1949 or business@simonandschuster.com.

The Simon & Schuster Speakers Bureau can bring authors to your live event. For more information or to book an event contact the Simon & Schuster Speakers Bureau at 1-866-248-3049 or visit our website at www.simonspeakers.com.

Interior design by Erich Hobbing

Manufactured in the United States of America

10   9   8   7   6   5   4   3   2

ISBN 978-1-4767-5712-4
ISBN 978-1-4767-5713-1 (pbk)
ISBN 978-1-4767-5714-8 (ebook)

For Geoffrey & Vivienne Ridyard

# CHAPTER ONE

In the beginning was the wormhole. It bloomed like a strange flower at the edge of the solar system, dwarfing Pluto in its size and majesty. It was beautiful; theory become real. The eyes of Earth turned upon it, and the space telescope *Walton* was redirected to examine it more closely. Within days, images were being sent back to Earth.

What *Walton* revealed was a kind of blister in space, a lenslike swelling in the fabric of the universe. As one scientist remarked, to the discomfort of her peers, it looked almost as if humanity were being examined in turn. The stars behind it were distorted, and slightly off-kilter, an effect explained by the huge amount of negative energy necessary to keep the wormhole open. An intense light at its rim dimmed to a dark center like an unblinking pupil, and so the newspapers began to refer to it as "the Eye in Space."

Once the initial thrill of its discovery had worn off, disturbing questions were raised. Why had it not been seen before? Was it a natural phenomenon, or something more sinister?

The early years of the twenty-first century had yet to offer any proof that mankind was not alone in the universe. Shortly after the discovery of the wormhole, mankind received conclusive evidence that the universe was more crowded than it had ever imagined.

A fleet emerged from the Eye, a great armada of silver ships, graceful and elegant, moving unstoppably toward the small blue planet in the distance at speeds beyond human comprehension.

And the people of Earth watched them come: steadily, silently. Efforts were made to contact the craft, but there was no reply. . . .

Panic spread. There was talk of the end of the world, of imminent destruction. Riots crippled the great cities, and mass suicides occurred among the more extreme religious cults, convinced that their souls would be magicked up to the approaching starships.

But wherever it was that their souls ended up, it was not on those ships.

The fleet stopped somewhere near Mars, and Earth braced itself for attack. Some people fled to bunkers, others sought shelter in underground stations and subway systems, or retreated into caves. They waited for explosions and devastation, but none came. Instead, Earth's technological systems began to collapse: electricity, gas, water, communications, all were hit simultaneously, sabotaged by their own computers, but in a deliberate and targeted way. National defense systems shut down, but hospitals did not, and warplanes fell from the sky while commercial jets landed safely. All control had been seized by an outside force, but one that appeared careful to avoid more fatalities than were necessary. Still, fatalities there were.

Now, Earth's generals warned, the real assault would come, but there was no further attack. The silver ships sat silently above, while below, society fell apart. There was looting and murder. Mass exoduses from the cities began. Cattle and livestock were stolen and slaughtered for food, so farmers began to shoot trespassers. Men turned against men, and so great was their fury that, at times, they forgot the fact of the aliens' existence in the face of their own inhumanity. After a mere three days, armies were firing on their own citizens. All that mattered was survival.

Then, on the fourth day, power was restored selectively to the hearts of nine capital cities across the world: Washington, London, Beijing, New Delhi, Abuja, Moscow, Brasilia, Canberra, and Berlin. A single word was sent to every computer in every government office. That word was:

**SURRENDER**

And Earth did indeed surrender, for what other choice did it have?

When the planet's new overlords eventually made themselves known, they were not what anyone on Earth had anticipated, for the Illyri were not unlike themselves. In their grace and beauty they resembled their ships. They were tall—the smallest of them was no less than six feet—with slightly elongated limbs, and their skin had the faintest of gold hues. Some had glossy, metallic manes of hair, whereas others kept their perfect skulls smooth and bald. They lacked eyelids, so their eyes were permanently open, and a clear membrane protected their retinas. When they slept, their colored irises simply closed over their pupils, leaving their resting eyes like vivid, eerie marbles set in their fine features.

The Illyri spoke of a "gentle conquest." They wished to avoid further bloodshed, and all necessities and creature comforts were restored to the people. However, modern weapons systems remained disabled. Air travel was initially forbidden. Telecommunication ceased, and for a time, the Internet no longer functioned. There was a period of adjustment that was difficult, but eventually something approaching normal life resumed.

The Illyri knew what mattered most to the planet they had colonized, for their technology had been hidden on Earth for many decades, ever since the earliest human radio signals were detected by probes at the mouths of wormholes, and the first quiet infiltration of the planet began. Tiny clusters of Illyri androids, most no bigger than insects, had hidden in meteor showers and entered the atmosphere in the late 1950s. They began sending back details of Earth's climate, atmosphere, population. The Illyri followed the progress of wars and famines, and had seen the best—and the worst—of what the human race had to offer. The Internet had been a particular bonus. Nanobots embedded themselves in the system in the late twentieth century; not only were they capable of transmitting the sum total of mankind's accumulated knowledge back to the drones, they became part of the technology itself. As humanity embraced the Internet, and computers became an integral part of life, so too mankind unwittingly welcomed the Illyri into their lives and sowed the seeds for their arrival.

After the initial shock of the invasion, the human resistance commenced. There were shootings and bombings. Illyri were kidnapped and killed, or held as hostages in a vain attempt to force a retreat from the planet. World leaders conspired to fight back.

In response, the citizens of Rome were given twenty-four hours to evacuate their city. It was then wiped from the map in a massive explosion that sent dust and debris over all of western Europe, a reminder that Earth's empires were as nothing before the superior power of the invaders. The Illyri then announced that one-tenth of the population between the ages of fifteen and twenty-one in every city and town would be conscripted into the Illyri Military brigades for five years. Essentially the youths would be hostages. Each family from which a young adult was removed had a responsibility to report saboteurs, or face the consequences. If violence was committed against the invaders, the townsfolk were informed that they would never see their young people again. It was a charter for informers, designed to sow distrust and crush cooperation among those who would challenge Illyri rule.

But the Illyri also offered hope. They erected great condensers in arid climates, transforming deserts to fields. They genetically modified fruits, and grains, and vegetables, making them more abundant and more resistant to disease. Within two years, hunger was virtually eliminated on Earth, as were many communicable diseases. Geoengineering—the use of giant reflectors to send sunlight back into space before it struck the planet—tackled the problem of global warming, reducing Earth's temperatures to levels not seen since the start of the nineteenth century.

The Illyri did all that was possible to change Earth for the better.

And still the humans fought us at every turn. . . .

# CHAPTER TWO

S yl Hellais, the first of her kind to be born on Earth, jumped from
her desk and rushed to the bedroom window. The gray stone
walls and cobbled courtyards of Edinburgh Castle stretched below:
her fortress, her home, and—she sometimes felt—her prison. Beyond the castle lay the city itself, brooding beneath the dark Scottish skies.

There! A column of smoke rose to the east, the aftermath of the
explosion that had caused Syl to abandon her schoolwork. Sirens
blared faintly, and Illyri patrol craft shone spotlights from the sky
on the streets beneath. The humans were attacking again. They
liked bombs. Bombs were easy to plant. They could be hidden in
bags, in cars, even under dead cats and dogs. If it wasn't bombs, it
was snipers. All Illyri were potential targets, although the human
Resistance preferred to kill those in uniform. They were more tolerant of young Illyri, and females in particular, although they were
not above targeting them for kidnapping. Syl put herself at risk
every time she walked the streets of Edinburgh, but that knowledge served only to add a thrill to her explorations. Still, she had
learned to conceal her alien nature from prying eyes, and with a little makeup, and the right glasses and clothing, she could sometimes
pass for human.

And after all, was she not also of this planet? She was Syl the
Earthborn, the first Illyri to be born on the conquered world in the
early months of the invasion. In her way, she was as much its citizen
as the humans. She was a child of two realms: born on one, loyal

to another. She loathed Earth, and yet she loved it too, even if she rarely admitted this love to anyone—even herself.

Shaking her head, Syl turned away from the window, from the smoke and the unseen carnage. There would be more of it. It never ended, and it never would, not as long as the Illyri remained on Earth.

She was Syl the Firstborn, Syl the Earthborn.

Syl the Invader.

But Edinburgh was not the only target to be hit that night. Farther south, another attack was about to commence, and it would change the life of Syl Hellais forever.


The Illyri Military had established many of its bases on the sites of great fortresses from Earth's past. Those still standing—among them the Tower of London and Edinburgh Castle in the United Kingdom, the Stockholm Palace in Sweden, Prague Castle in the Czech Republic, and the Forbidden City in Beijing, China—were simply adapted for Illyri use. Where nothing of the original forts remained, replacements were either built offworld and lowered into place from ships, or constructed from materials found on Earth.

The fort at Birdoswald had been erected by the Roman Empire as part of Hadrian's Wall, which originally stretched across the width of northern England to protect the south from Scottish marauders. Before the coming of the Illyri, only the lower parts of its buildings and walls remained standing, the pattern and logic of their construction apparent when viewed from the hills above or the slopes below. Danis, the head of the Illlyri Military in Britain, was particularly fascinated by the Romans, and had made some efforts to ensure that the old fort was not completely spoiled by its new additions. He had used local stone to rebuild walls, and the living quarters had also been faced with stone so that they blended into the landscape.

Danis had garrisoned the fort with a small force of Galateans, amphibian-like conscripts commanded by an Illyri officer named

Thaios. Not that Thaois was Danis's first choice, for he was not a member of the Illyri Military. Instead, he was a member of the Diplomatic Corps; the Military and the Diplomats were always at one another's throats, each constantly seeking to increase its power at the expense of the other. Nevertheless, Danis had been ordered to give Thaios command, for Thaios was a favorite of the Diplomats, and was being groomed for leadership. It was also generally accepted that at some point in the future, administration of Earth would pass to the Corps, and the Military would move on to other campaigns. Giving command positions to Diplomats was a logical step toward that end.

Still, as far as Danis was concerned, Thaios was a spoiled brat, and Danis, an old soldier, wouldn't have trusted the boy to command a fish to swim. Thaios, meanwhile, viewed the command of a small garrison fort in the middle of nowhere as beneath him.

However, the garrison was considered necessary. The smuggling of weapons was commonplace in the area, and the local population was regarded as particularly hostile, as is often the case at contested borders. The threat of permanent exile for their children seemed only to have antagonized many of the Scots, and not far from Birdoswald a primitive Improvised Explosive Device had recently destroyed two vehicles in a Military convoy. Among the Illyri casualties had been Aeron, Thaios's predecessor, who had been blown into so many pieces that his head had never been found. Since then, most Illyri travel to and from Birdoswald was conducted by air. Where cars and coaches had once parked, bringing parties of tourists to view the fort and the wall, a pair of lightly armed interceptors—small, agile craft that were used for short-range sorties and patrols—rested on landing pads.

Otherwise, the garrison at Birdoswald was defended largely by the conscripted Galateans, rugged, gray beings, their skin leathery in texture, their bodies narrowing to a head without the intervention of a neck, their eyes bulbous, their mouths wide. The humans called them "Toads." They communicated through a system of clicks and croaks, and the strangeness of their features made their emotions impossible to read: they ate, fought and killed with the same impassive stare.

The conquest of the Galatean system had been one of the Illyri's more profitable campaigns. It yielded a ready source of troops, for the Galateans were natural soldiers, used to being commanded and genetically seasoned for combat by millennia of intertribal warfare over scarce resources. Also, since their homeworlds were little more than barren rocks inhabited by an array of predators—with the Galateans themselves trapped somewhere in the middle of this natural cycle of killing and being killed—they were more than willing to enter the service of the Illyri. They provided far more than one in ten of their young to conscription, and most went voluntarily.

Eight Galateans stood on the walls of the fortress, and one occupied the observation tower, all equipped with night-vision lenses and high-velocity weapons. Each also wore a curved knife, like the claw of some great reptile rendered in steel.

The garrison's radar detected an approaching vehicle while it was still a mile away. It was coming from the west at about forty miles an hour, following the road that ran parallel to the remains of the wall. The Galatean monitoring the screen quickly summoned Thaios.

While the movement of vehicles along the road was not forbidden, the Illyri had imposed a standard curfew in certain areas. Motorized travel was not permitted between the hours of sunset and sunrise unless cleared in advance through the proper channels. No such communication had been received that night by the garrison at Birdoswald.

Thaios watched the dot moving on the screen. He was a muscular figure, and prided himself on his physical strength, although he had yet to be tested in battle. His head was shaved, even though this style was traditionally adopted by more senior members of the Corps. Thaios aspired to join their number, and his grooming choice was another statement of his ambition.

Thaios was always angry, as many secretly frightened people frequently are. The Galateans did not respect him because he did not respect them. The local population hated him because he had taken to ordering searches of vehicles and raids on houses, which interfered with daily life and resulted in damage to property, as well as the occasional arrest. The Military hated him because he was a member of the Corps, and much of the Corps distrusted him because he was the nephew of Grand Consul Gradus, one of the Corps's leading figures. Many believed that Thaios relayed negative comments back to his uncle—which was true. Many also felt that he was being groomed for leadership only because of his uncle's influence, which was, again, true.

"Alert the guards," ordered Thaios. "Reinforce the detail at the main gate."

A siren blared. Six Galateans emerged from their guardhouse, weapons at the ready, and loped toward the entrance. They were halfway across the central square when a whistling sounded from the night sky. Moments later the first mortar shell landed among them, killing three of them instantly. Another shell followed while the garrison was still reeling from the shock of the first, and the Galateans who had survived the initial blast were killed by the second.

Caught between trying to find the location of the mortar and monitoring the approach of the truck, which was now visible to the naked eye, the guards concentrated on the most immediate threat. The truck was traveling without lights, but the Galateans' night-vision lenses picked up its shape and the shadowy outlines of two people in the cab. Without waiting for further orders, the guards commenced firing on the truck. It crossed the central line of the road as the first bullets struck, then accelerated, heading straight for the gates. The doors on either side of the truck opened and the two humans jumped to safety as the vehicle struck the gates.

The force of the impact knocked one of the guards from the wall beside the gate. He lay sprawled on the ground, one leg twisted at a grotesque angle, his damaged skull leaking fluid through his nostrils and earholes. His companion had managed to hold on to a metal support strut, and although shaken and driven to his knees was otherwise unharmed.

He was still rising to his feet when the truck exploded.

The massive gates were blown from their hinges, one of them landing on the nearest interceptor, crushing its cockpit. The second gate landed on the roof of the main guardhouse, cutting through the tin like the blade of a knife, trapping inside the building those that it did not kill.

Gunfire erupted from the surrounding fields. Thaios's eardrums had burst as a result of the explosion at the gates and he was in agony as he tried to organize his surviving troops, shouting orders that he himself could hear only as distorted noise. The remaining guards on the walls returned fire, but now there were humans moving past the burning wreckage of the truck, and a concentrated burst of automatic fire knocked the guard from the watchtower. A human was standing at the door of the ruined guardhouse, spraying the interior with bullets. Thaios drew a bead on him and fired a single round. The man twisted and fell, but before Thaios could pick another target, he felt a hammer blow to his shoulder, and a great burning followed. The bullet had passed straight through his upper body, and the wound was already pumping dark red Illyri blood. He retreated to a corner by the ruined guardhouse. There was a dull explosion behind him as the trapped guards used a grenade to blow a hole in the rear of the building. Thaios summoned them to him, and from behind the ruined walls of the old fort they fought the insurgents, dark figures that darted and weaved and were only occasionally illuminated by the flames of the burning truck. A second great explosion rent the air as the remaining interceptor was blown up, and Thaios and his soldiers found themselves under heavy fire. One of the Galateans fell, then another and another, until at last only Thaios was left standing.

The shooting stopped. All was quiet for moment, until a voice called out to Thaios, "Surrender! Surrender and you won't be hurt."

Thaios examined the digital read on his pulse pistol. The charge was almost empty: only one shot left. He could have attempted to pick up another weapon from one of the fallen Galateans, but he could see the insurgents working their way around him. If he moved, he would be exposed.

"Throw out your weapon," said the same voice. "Then stand up and show us your hands."

Thaios was suddenly very tired. He had been so ambitious, so anxious to progress. This was all such a waste.

The order to surrender came again. The humans were drawing closer. One of their shadows almost touched his boot.

Thaios put his gun in his mouth.

"I'm sorry," he said. The human nearest him frowned, but it had not been to him that Thaios was speaking.

"Stop him!" yelled a voice.

It was the last thing Thaios heard before his head exploded.

# CHAPTER THREE

The following morning, Syl walked quickly through the hall-ways of Edinburgh Castle, the soft silk of her trousers swishing against her legs, her face set in an expression that she thought of as determined but those who were responsible for her would have wearily described as "obstinate." It was a word used often about Syl. Perhaps, the young Illyri told herself privately (and rather hopefully), she took after her mother, the beautiful Lady Orianne, who had been both willful and charming, a combination that made her quite impossible to resist.

Syl, by contrast, was still working on the charm component. And beauty? Well, her father told her beauty is in the eye of the beholder, and that to him she was the most beautiful creature in the world—indeed, in all worlds. Of course he would say that! The truth was that she was not unpretty, but her features still held the unformed softness of youth, coupled with an unnerving intensity in her eyes and a sharpness in her manner. The effect wasn't helped by the fact that Syl wasn't given to smiling just to please people— because smiles could be much better employed than that—and she only laughed on occasions that truly merited it. And how else was she to behave? she asked herself, for she had no intention of smiling for no reason, or wasting time laughing at stupid jokes. Anyway, Syl took the view that laughing at something just to be kind usually meant the joker would plague you with another attempt at humor, and you'd have to laugh again, and so the cycle would continue until she either died of boredom or killed someone, and frankly she couldn't be sure which might happen first.

And yet much tolerance was shown to Syl, for she had been conceived among the stars, and as the first Illyri child born on Earth, she was a living link between the homeworld of Illyr and the conquered planet. Of course, it helped that her father was Lord Andrus, governor of the islands of Britain and Ireland, and by extension all of Europe. Like all Illyri females, though, Syl bore the name of her mother's family. She liked being Syl Hellais. Syl Andrus sounded, well, ugly.

Britain had been the obvious base for Illyri operations in Europe: even before the invasion, it had been a country obsessed with surveillance, both obvious and secret. Its streets were infested with security cameras, many of them with facial-recognition capacity, and the actions of its citizens were constantly being monitored by government departments. The Illyri had hardly needed to change anything upon their arrival. The same was true for the other most powerful nations: China, Russia, the United States. The governments of Earth, aided by populations too lazy or trusting to care, and obsessed with putting every detail of their lives on the Internet, had helped to give the Illyri control of the planet.

Andrus was also responsible for the overall administration of Europe, and the governors of the other European nations deferred to him. Technically, he enjoyed equal status with the administrators of similar large territories, including Africa, China, Russia, Australasia, and the Americas, but he chaired the Ruling Council, which gave him a deciding vote on every important decision. Effectively, Governor Andrus was the most powerful man on Earth, although Syl knew better than to say "Do you know who my father is?" to get herself out of trouble. Well, she knew better than to try it a second time. . . .

And then there was the fact that the Lady Orianne had died when Syl was only a year old, succumbing to an attack of malaria while the Illyri were still coming to terms with the diseases of the new world. There is no substitute for a mother and so there was a sadness that lingered around Syl, coupled with an anger that she found difficult to suppress. Recently Andrus had begun to despair of her behavior, but as Althea, Syl's childhood governess, would gently point out to him, he was not the first father to be rendered speechless with frustration by a daughter approaching adulthood.

"Even were her mother here, my lord, I suspect Syl would still be a difficult proposition," she would murmur. Althea had been entrusted with Syl's care since the death of Lady Orianne, mothering her as best as she could, and she loved the girl as a daughter. Her own child, a son, had died shortly after birth, another victim of disease, and she had become Syl's milk-mother. A special bond had formed between Syl and Althea, but the teenage years were proving trying for the governess too. Still, she had high hopes for the girl. Syl would do well in life—assuming her father didn't throttle her first.

Now Althea hurried to catch up with her charge as Syl rushed ahead of her.

"Why aren't you in school, Syl?" said Althea.

Like all children of the Illyri, Syl attended classes each day: science, mathematics, history, and languages. They were taught of Illyr and its empire, but they learned, too, of the cultures of Earth and the other principal conquered worlds.

"Leave me be, Althea," said Syl, as the older woman fell into step beside her. To amuse herself, Syl varied her pace, slowing down and speeding up, so that Althea was alternately left behind or stranded a foot or two ahead of her charge. Either way, she ended up talking to empty air. She had an idea of where Syl was going, and was determined to stop her.

"Your father is not to be disturbed," said Althea. "He arrived back in the early hours, and has barely slept."

"It is my birthday, Althea. I'm entitled to ask a favor of him."

It was a tradition that, on the anniversary of their birth, Illyri could make a single request of a loved one that had to be granted.

It was a relic of an older time, but still fondly regarded. Husbands would ask for a kiss from their wives, mothers a meal cooked by their sons' hands: small gestures, but no less meaningful for that.

"You may talk to him after your classes," said Althea.

Syl had already tired of her earlier game, and was now determined to leave Althea in her wake, so the frustrated governess was forced to scamper to keep up with Syl's long strides. Althea was short for an Illyri; today, on Syl's sixteenth birthday, the girl was already much the taller of the two.

"My request is that I should not have to attend classes," said Syl. "I would like a day to myself in the city."

As if Althea was unaware of what that might involve, Syl stopped by one of the castle windows and gestured dramatically at the streets of Edinburgh below. Edinburgh and London provided twin administrative bases for Andrus, but he preferred Edinburgh, and its great castle perched above the city, to the confines of the Tower of London. London was a difficult city to like: overcrowded, smelly, and increasingly violent. Three months earlier, the Tower itself had come under attack from a suicide bomber piloting a small plane packed with explosives. The assault was thwarted, but Andrus would secretly have been quite happy if the Tower had been blasted to smithereens. He would have loved an excuse to spend more time in Scotland, with its harsh but beautiful landscape that reminded him of the northern wilds of Illyr itself, where he had spent his youth. Syl too was happier in Edinburgh, and so it remained her home when her father was absent in the south for weeks, or even months.

"So," Syl continued, "how can my father grant my birthday wish if, by the time I ask it, my birthday will be over?"

Despite Syl's unarguable logic, Althea knew that Andrus had given strict orders that he should not be disturbed. There had been two attacks the previous night, and the dead were still being counted, leaving Andrus under pressure from his offworld superiors to provide an appropriate response to the latest outrages. He already trod a delicate line between those who advocated gentleness and understanding in their dealings with the humans, and those who called for harsher discipline. As with the humans, so with his daughter, thought Althea.

"Syl, this is not a good time. There were killings last night. . . . "

"Oh, there are always killings, Althea," said Syl. "Every day, every week. If we're not killing them in firefights, then they're killing us with guns and bombs. Maybe we shouldn't be here at all."

"Hush!" said Althea, grabbing Syl's arm. "That's all very well for classroom debates, but it's not to be said within earshot of your father's chambers. There are those who would take great pleasure in whispering that Lord Andrus's daughter speaks treason in the governor's castle."

Syl wasn't so sure that even the classroom was the place to debate the rights and wrongs of the Illyri's conquests. She was one of twenty students, the youngest of whom was only seven. They were all taught by the same tutor, Toris, who was so ancient that Ani, Syl's closest friend, said there was no such thing as history for him: it was all personal experience. Toris did not encourage independent thought. His purpose was to tell them things, and his students' purpose was to remember them.

"Since when did expressing an opinion become treason?" asked Syl.

"Don't be so naive. Suggesting to someone that the weather might change is an opinion. Stirring up dissent is treasonous."

"Why, do you feel stirred, Althea?" said Syl, and even while being mocked, Althea loved the spirit that dwelt within this one. "Will you take to the streets in protest if the weather holds?"

Althea took the girl by the hands and held her there, looking up into her eyes. They were reddish gold, like her mother's. She had her mother's voice too, low yet musical. What she had inherited from her father was not so clear. She had certainly not acquired his diplomacy, or his ability to refrain from speaking his every thought aloud. Despite that, she had an uncanny way of winding others around her little finger, of gently bending them to her will. Even Althea was not entirely immune to Syl's manipulations.

"You must be careful, Syl," said Althea. "Your father's position is not secure. There has been talk of recalling governors because of the escalating levels of violence. Already the Diplomats have increased their presence here. Washington is now a Diplomat city, and the Diplomats have just been granted a special order excluding the Military from Iceland, effective from next month. As the senior Military commander on Earth, your father is furious."

Syl's obvious surprise made it clear that she had not heard any of this, and Althea instantly knew that she had said too much.

"A recall?" said Syl. "Then we could return to Illyr?"

Althea noted the use of the word *return*. Like many Illyri now marooned far from home, Syl longed for Illyr. Althea had no such illusions. Illyr was not what it once was. It had changed. The conquests had changed it.

"Perhaps," said Althea. "Your father could return, but it would be in disgrace—possibly even in chains. And remember, Syl, your father loves it here. He does not want to go back. All his life he dreamed of seeing new worlds, and he has spent more time away from the homeworld than he has living on it. He wants to be buried on this alien world with this alien sun warming his grave. If your mother had lived, things might have been different. She was bound deeply to Illyr. She loved the homeworld, but she loved your father more."

"And she died for it," said Syl bitterly. "Died for the sake of a planet that hated her, and all like her."

Althea did not argue. She had heard all of this before, and there was some truth to it.

"I am not my father," continued Syl. "I want to live on Illyr. It is my true home."

Illyr: she had seen it only in books and on screens—projections of forests that towered ten times higher than any similar vegetation on Earth, and oceans deeper and cleaner than the polluted waters of the Atlantic or the Pacific. She marveled at the creatures that walked and swam and crawled and flew through its environs, so much more noble and striking and beautiful than the denizens of this planet, the greatest of which—tigers and blue whales, gorillas and polar bears—were already close to extinction. Most of all, Syl wanted to see its cities: Olos, the Gem of the North; Arayyis, part of it built beneath the ocean and part above; and great Tannis itself, the City of Spires, the most beautiful city in the Illyri Empire, the place in which her mother had been born. True, she had walked on Illyr by activating the virtual-reality programs in the wired rooms of the castle, but she was always aware that they were illusions. She wanted to breathe Illyri air, not some computer's pumped-in imitation of it. It was only during Toris's discussions of Illyr that Syl showed any patience with her tutor, for the old fool was as besotted with the planet as she was.

"Illyr is not as it was," said Althea. "Do not believe all that Toris shows or tells you. That old man will drown in his own nostalgia."

Syl freed her hands. "Nothing pleases you, Althea. You are as sour as an unripe apple."

Then, just as Althea seemed set to take offense, Syl planted a big kiss on the older woman's cheek, and sprang away, smiling. That was another of her talents: the ability to recognize when she had gone too far, and to act to prevent any further harm being done. If only, Althea thought, she could stop herself *before* she went too far.

"Now you're distracting me," said Syl, "and I have a favor to request."

"Syl! I told you, he's busy."

"Don't worry, I won't disturb him. I'll just wait outside until he's finished. And please stop running after me. You know you can't keep up."

Syl darted down the hallway, waved from around the corner, and was gone. Althea sighed deeply and leaned against the nearest wall. Below her, the city went about its business, the previous night's bombing seemingly forgotten. In the distance loomed the crag known as Arthur's Seat. There was a grandeur to Edinburgh, Althea admitted, but its beauty was stern and austere. Summer was at an end, and the first hint of a cold, damp winter was already blowing through the laneways. Althea hated the cold. She wished Andrus had become governor of Spain and Portugal, or Central America, somewhere with a little heat and light. These northern territories oppressed her with their gloom.

But now someone was coming. She looked up to see the tutor, Toris. He was a scowling, wrinkled figure who walked with a pronounced stoop. There was no harm to him, but Althea, like Syl, regarded him as an old bore. Unlike Syl, though, she did not have to listen to him unless she chose to do so.

"I seek Syl," said Toris. "Class has commenced."

"Feel free to chase her, if you can run fast enough. She has no mind for classes today. It is the anniversary of her birth. She will spend the day in her own way, whether permitted to or not."

Toris seemed about to protest, then contented himself with a resigned shrug. "Well, let her roam, then, and much good may it bring her."

Althea was surprised. Toris was not usually one to allow such leniencies. Ani, Syl's best friend and partner in crime, was regularly reported to her parents for even the slightest of infractions, and Toris would have beaten a similarly frequent path to Lord Andrus's door to complain of Syl's behavior if Andrus were not the governor, or if Althea had not become proficient at soothing Toris. Old books seemed to calm him, she found. So did wine. Speaking of which . . .

"Have you been drinking?" asked Althea. "It's not like you to give up so easily."

"I was young once," Toris replied stiffly.

"Were you now?" Althea sniffed. "I wonder that you can remember back so far."

"It is my task to remember," Toris reminded her, with some dignity. "I remember, so that others will not forget."

"You fill her head with talk of the glories of Illyr, her and the other children. They dream of returning to a place they have never known, and meanwhile the life that they have passes them by."

"Illyr is great," said Toris.

"Perhaps it was, once," said Althea. "But they will never see it, not as it was. Never."

"You do not know that," said Toris.

"I do," said Althea. "And you know it too."

Toris did not bother to continue the argument. He and Althea had had this discussion before, and would have it again, but not this morning. Toris was tired. He always felt old on the birthdays of his students. He left Althea, and shuffled off to bore those of his charges who had not, so far, managed to escape.

# CHAPTER FOUR

The two young men walking toward the little restaurant near Edinburgh's London Road were no different in appearance from any of the other youths who still viewed Edinburgh as "their" city, despite the presence of aliens, police, and anyone else who might have been of another opinion. One was taller and older, but the similarities between the two were too obvious for them to be anything but brothers. Their names were Paul and Steven Kerr, and they were members of the Resistance.

Paul had been born not long after the initial Illyri invasion. Now he was just a few weeks shy of his seventeenth birthday, but he carried himself with the authority of an older man, as befitted someone who had risked his life in the fight against the Illyri occupation.

Despite his relative youth, Paul was one of the Resistance's best intelligence officers. He was good at listening, and skilled at slotting himself into places and situations that might yield useful information. The Resistance had young spies all over the city, and many of them reported to Paul, either directly or indirectly. There was little that went on among the Illyri about which the Resistance did not know—or so they had long believed.

Recent events, though, were forcing the Resistance to reconsider this view. Whispers had reached them of possible secret tunnels beneath Edinburgh, constructed without their knowledge. There were darker rumors too: the sick and old disappearing from hospitals, and corpses sent for cremation becoming lost in the system. And all that was even before the attack on Birdoswald: Paul had not known of it in advance, and he was usually entrusted with prior notice of such operations. This troubled him, which was why he was glad that a meeting had been called. He wanted to know more.

His brother, Steven, had just turned fifteen, and was less certain of himself. So far he had only been involved in minor operations, mostly as a lookout. Steven suspected that it was Paul who had been responsible for keeping him away from the action, although Paul had always denied it. Steven now felt that he was old enough to fight; after all, young men and women his own age had already died at the hands of the Illyri and their servant races, and it wasn't right that he should be stopped from playing his part in the Resistance. Paul gradually seemed to have come to terms with this, at least in some small way, which was why he had reluctantly agreed that Steven should accompany him on this particular mission. School would have to do without them for a day.

"Hurry up," Paul said to Steven. "We're going to be late."

Steven obediently sped up. Although there were sometimes tensions between them, as there were between any brothers, Steven adored Paul. Paul was a fighter.

Paul had killed.

As the restaurant came in sight, Paul halted.

"Remember," he told Steven. "Stay quiet. Don't say anything unless someone asks you a question first. If I tell you to leave, do it, okay? No objections."

"You won't even know I'm there, honest," said Steven.

Paul had been told to bring Steven along. He would not have done so otherwise. He knew what was going to happen. It was time: the Resistance had decided that his little brother was ready for major operations.


Danny's Diner was a typical greasy spoon. It offered breakfast all day, battered and fried anything from sausages to Mars bars, and served French fries with everything. It was even possible to order a plate of double fries, which was basically fries with a side of fries. Danny's Diner was the unhealthiest restaurant in Scotland, and it was sometimes whispered that it had killed more Scots than the Illyri. Nobody looked at the boys as they entered. Everyone in there was a friend of the Resistance, but they still knew that it was best to mind their own business. Only Danny, who was working behind the counter, gave them the smallest of nods.

Two young women, both of them only a few years older than Paul, sat in a booth at the back of the restaurant. Their names were Jean and Nessa Trask, and their father was one of the most important Resistance leaders in Scotland. They had cups of grayish tea before them, and the remains of some toast, with the mandatory fries now shriveled and cold.

"I thought your dad might be here," said Paul as he slid onto the plastic bench. "He's busy," said Nessa, the older of the girls, "but we'll pay for your tea anyway." She signaled to the waitress, who scurried off looking nervous, and with good reason. Nessa was bigger and broader than her sister. Some of the boys called her Nessy, after the Loch Ness monster, but only behind her back; she'd broken the nose of the last person she'd heard calling her by that nickname. Her sister, Jean, was prettier, and not as smart, but she was much more dangerous. She had a way with knives.

"Lot of activity last night," said Paul, referring discreetly to Birdoswald.

"We were as surprised as you were," said Nessa.

"It wasn't us?"

Nessa shook her head. "The fireworks in the city were ours, but not the business at the fort. Dad's looking into it. That's why he's not here."

Their tea arrived, and the older teenagers watched in cool amusement as Steven took a tentative sip. It was horrible, as always. The boy immediately poured several packets of sugar into his cup and stirred it vigorously before trying again. The sweetness helped, but not much.

"So," said Nessa, still looking at Steven, who tried not to appear uncomfortable under her scrutiny, "this is the new little soldier."

Jean snickered. She picked up her butter knife and began playing with it, balancing it on the tip of her finger. It was a neat trick.

"He's been on jobs before," said Paul, springing instinctively to his brother's defense.

"He's stood on street corners watching for patrols," said Nessa. "My dog could do that."

"Then why isn't your dog here?" said Steven, which surprised Nessa, even as Paul raised his eyes to heaven and gave his brother a sharp kick on the right ankle.

"He even barks like my dog," said Nessa, but she seemed amused by Steven. "My dad says he's ready. What do you say?"

She leveled her gaze at Paul. Jean might have been prettier, but Nessa had something special, a kind of charisma. Paul might even have found her attractive if she hadn't been so terrifying.

"He's ready," said Paul, after only a moment's hesitation. Beside him, Steven's cheeks glowed with pride.

"What do I know?" said Nessa. "I'm only a girl," but she said it in the same way that a heavyweight champion of the world might have said he was only a boxer.

"What's the job?" said Paul.

Nessa leaned in closer to him, and lowered her voice.

"We think we've found one of the tunnels. . . . "

# CHAPTER FIVE

Syl could hear her father shouting as she neared his office. She paused while she was still out of sight of Balen, the secretary who carefully controlled access to the governor from his desk outside the door. Syl rather liked Balen, and his affection for her was obvious, but she could tell as she peered around the corner that he was unlikely to be welcoming this morning. He was staring at his screen, his fingers rapidly manipulating the display. The screen was a projection created by the castle's artificial intelligence system, and allowed a screen to be summoned at any time, and in any room. As a child, Syl had thought it magical.

Balen was simultaneously fielding calls to his communications console, adjusting his tone according to the importance of the caller, though each received roughly the same response: no, it would *not* be possible to talk to Governor Andrus. . . .

The door to the office stood ajar. Syl could not see her father, but she glimpsed a short, balding human wearing a suit that was two sizes too small for him. It was McGill, the First Minister of the Scottish parliament, who served as the main channel of communication between the Scottish humans and the Illyri. The Illyri had allowed most local councils, and even national parliaments, to remain active, although they offered only the illusion of self-government, since no major decisions could be made without Illyri approval. Governor Andrus was often heard to remark that given how poorly human governments performed even the simplest of tasks, they might have found it preferable to hand all power to the Illyri, and at least see the job done right.

As Syl listened, her father's voice rose again.

"Greater freedom of movement?" he shouted. "Are you insane? Do you have any idea what is happening in this damned country of yours? Shootings, bombings, acts of sabotage and murder. We had an explosion in the city last night, and then the garrison at Birdoswald was attacked. We lost twenty Galateans, and the captain of the garrison, not to mention two interceptors reduced to charred metal, and you're asking me to give your people even *more* opportunities to attack us?"

"We are not responsible for actions taken south of the border," said McGill. "And we're not talking about the whole of Scotland either. For now, at least allow more ease of travel between the cities, and perhaps make Edinburgh itself a free zone, with unrestricted movement within the city limits."

"The reason you're not talking about the whole of the country, Mr. McGill," said Andrus, "is that most of the Highlands remains lawless. Travel north to Inverness and Aberdeen is only possible by air, because anything that moves along the ground risks being attacked and looted. Most of the time I'm forced to amuse myself by trying to establish which of you is worst: the Scots, the Irish, or the Welsh. The more I study your history, the more I pity the English for having to put up with the lot of you."

"And yet now you're being attacked close to Carlisle," McGill interrupted. "Forgive me for pointing this out again, but that's England, isn't it?"

"Infected by a virus of rebellion that started up here, no doubt," Lord Andrus countered. "In fact, I suspect that the terrorists traveled south to Birdoswald, not north. They're Scots, or I'm a fool. And don't think that the rebels have any love for *your* city either. They disapprove of even your limited cooperation with us, and they'd dearly love to make an example of the most obliging of you. Our security procedures protect you as much as they protect us."

McGill bowed his head; Lord Andrus's words had hit home. Major attacks on the occupying forces were growing more frequent in Edinburgh, although Glasgow was worse: there were housing estates on the outskirts of the city, wellsprings of rebellion and vicious dissent, that even the Galateans refused to police.

"There will be no relaxation of the travel restrictions for now," said Lord Andrus. Then, remembering his own reputation for diplomacy, added: "We'll review the situation in three months' time. But I warn you: if the attack on Birdoswald represents the beginning of a new terrorist campaign, you can look forward to repression that will make the early days of the invasion seem like a dream state. You can pass that on to the rebels from me."

McGill started to object, but Lord Andrus interrupted him.

"Don't take me for a fool, Mr. McGill. I could have you tortured until you decide to share your knowledge of the Resistance. The only reason I don't do so is that I'd prefer some channels of communication with the Resistance to remain open, and I dislike unnecessary violence. Increasingly, though, my voice is struggling to make itself heard among those who think that we have been far too tolerant. If the violence continues, I won't be able to hold them back for much longer. You may have no love for the Galateans or the Military, but we are ordered, disciplined soldiers. We respond only to provocation, and fight to defend ourselves. Troublesome populations tend to invite the attentions of far more brutal forces."

Syl knew that her father was referring to the Securitats. They were the Illyri secret police, part of the Diplomatic Corps, and answered only to Grand Consul Gradus, the head of the Corps. The Military had no control over them. It was the Securitats who had been responsible for organizing the destruction of Rome.

There was the sound of a chair being pushed back, and moments later her father appeared in the doorway, herding McGill ahead of him, an almost comically round presence compared with the tall, aristocratic figure of Lord Andrus.

Her father was sixty, but fit and strong, with few signs of aging. The life span of the Illyri was longer than that of humans, thanks to gene therapy and organ replacements, routinely extending to a hundred and twenty Earth years or more, so Lord Andrus was only into his middle age. His military record was impeccable, and his experience of battle and conquest ensured that he was respected by the army and, if truth be told, somewhat feared by the Diplomats. Even the Diplomats' leader, Grand Consul Gradus, who lived by the motto that "Armies conquer, but Diplomats rule," was known to be wary of angering Andrus, although he still hated him. The reasons for their enmity could be boiled down to one simple difference between the two Illyri: Gradus was cruel; Andrus was not. Nevertheless, in Gradus's ideal universe, the Military would wipe out all resistance in conquered territories and then retreat to bind its wounds while the Diplomats reaped the spoils. In fact he would have preferred it if the Military were entirely under his control, just another arm of the Diplomatic Corps.

But it was Gradus who had supported her father's appointment to his current position, despite the objections of many of the Grand Consul's own staff. Curiously, at least three-quarters of the Illyri governors on Earth were Military officers, and the remainder had recently retired from service. Over dinner one evening, Syl had questioned her father as to why this was.

"The humans call it a 'poisoned chalice,'" he replied. "In the Military, it is known as a 'dark command.' It means that what appears to be a blessing may well prove to be a curse. Gradus wants the Military to fail here. If we fail, he and the Diplomats can take over. Gradus is no fool, Syl. This conquest of Earth is very different from any of our other previous imperial adventures. We have never before encountered a civilization so advanced. Biologically, culturally, socially, we have more in common with the humans than we have with any other conquered race. But Gradus and his kind are so convinced of their own superiority that every race but our own appears inconsequential to them. He has not even troubled himself to visit Earth. He sits in the palace of a dead king, spinning his plots as a spider spins its web, listening to the whisperings of witches."

Syl shivered at the memory of her father's words. There it was, the mystery at the heart of the Illyri Empire, the secret power behind its great expansion.

The witches.

The Nairene Sisterhood.

# CHAPTER SIX

Syl had never encountered any members of the Nairene Sisterhood, but she had heard stories of their power. For centuries they had been an order of recluses, existing only to record and curate the history of the Illyri Empire. As the Empire began to expand, first exploring its own galaxy, and then moving farther into the universe, so too did the Sisterhood's thirst for new knowledge grow. They were a storehouse of all that was known about the universe, passed on from generation to generation. It was considered a great honor for a family to have a daughter inducted into the Sisterhood, although Syl couldn't see the appeal in being locked away for the rest of her life, forbidden to travel or explore, or even to leave the Marque, the labyrinthine city that was the Sisterhood's lair. The Marque was situated on a moon of Illyr named Avila Minor, and no one landed on or left the moon without the permission of the Sisterhood.

But then suddenly the nature of the Sisterhood had changed. Led by Ezil, the oldest of their order, they had emerged from the Marque, and some had even taken husbands. If it was considered an honor for a daughter to join the order, so too did ambitious men realize the advantage that might be gained from having the knowledge of the Sisterhood close at hand. Ezil decided which of the sisters should be permitted to marry, and to whom they should become betrothed, but she herself did not marry, and neither did the four other most senior sisters. Instead, they had made themselves indispensable as advisers, attaching themselves to the Diplomatic Corps. Soon, no decisions were made without consulting them.

All this had occurred many years before Syl was born, and Ezil and the senior sisters, known as the First Five, had not been seen outside the Marque in decades. But the emergence of the Sisterhood had marked the beginning of what was now known as the Second Empire. It was the Sisterhood that had given the Empire the means to expand, for they had discovered the location of the wormholes. The universe teemed with them; they were gateways between galaxies, allowing the Illyri to travel vast distances with previously unimagined speed.

Syl's father had explained the nature of the wormholes to Syl when she was a small child. Holding a sheet of paper, he told her to imagine that it represented millions and millions of miles of space. At the far right side of the page he made a mark with his pen, and placed a similar mark on the far left.

"Now," he said, "imagine that this first dot is Illyr, and this second dot is Earth. How long would it take to travel from one to the other?"

"Years," the young Syl had replied. "A lifetime."

"Many, many lifetimes," said her father. "But using the wormholes, we can cover the distance in an instant."

He gently folded the paper, aligning the marks, then pierced them with his pen.

"That is what the wormholes do. They link distant points in the universe."

"But how do we know where they lead?" asked Syl.

"We send drones to explore the systems in advance. Sometimes the Sisterhood tells us."

"And how does the Sisterhood know?" asked Syl, and her father had not answered her, because, as Syl had come to realize, he did not have an answer. If the Illyri loved secrets, the Sisterhood lived for them.

The Second Illyri Empire had explored over one hundred systems, each targeted because it contained a habitable planet with life-forms, however primitive, and commodities that could support the Empire's further conquests: food, fuel, minerals, methane, water. Through the Sisterhood and the wormholes, the Illyri had established that the universe was fundamentally a lonely place, and complex civilizations like their own were extremely rare. So far, the Illyri had found only one species, humanity, who could, given time, become as powerful as they, if not more so. The humans had drawn the Illyri down upon them: by sending radio signals out into the universe, they had alerted the Empire to the presence of another advanced race. As one of her father's generals had remarked, it was better that they be conquered now on their own world than battled later on another.

The Sisterhood had agreed, and so the plan to invade Earth was set in motion.

Any mention of the Sisterhood always made Syl's father mad.

"Witches," he would mutter. "Damned witches. And Syrene is the damnedest of them all."

Ezil still lived, although she was now nearly two centuries old: a great and unusual age even for an Illyri. She was reported to be frail, and control of the Sisterhood had gradually passed to Syrene, who had once been Ezil's novice. Syrene had the ear of Grand Consul Gradus, for she was his wife, chosen for him by Ezil herself.

The Military had resisted the approaches of the Sisterhood, and soldiers were unofficially forbidden from entering into relationships with Nairene sisters, but the reality was that the sisters had barely tried to infiltrate the Military. They seemed content to infest the ranks of the Diplomats, and leave the Military to the work of conquest, but their influence on the Diplomatic Corps was one of the factors contributing to the hostility between the Empire's two main forces.

Syl remembered all of this as she watched Lord Andrus smoothly rid himself of McGill, and now she stepped in front of her father as he was about to pass, so that he almost tripped over her. Behind him, Balen stood up at his desk, a sheaf of papers in his hand. He gave Syl a cold smile. Clearly, like Althea, he felt that she should not be disturbing her father at this time.

"Syl!" said Lord Andrus. He looked tired. "What are you doing lurking in dark corners? Why aren't you in class?"

He spoke to her in the Illyri tongue, harsh to human ears yet lovelier to her than any language on this world. Syl, like many young Illyri, had learned human languages as part of her schooling, and spoke English, French, and a little Spanish. In private, the youths spoke the languages of the conquered more frequently than their own, but older Illyri preferred to discuss their affairs in the tongue of the homeworld. It was part of their efforts to maintain their identity as conquerors, and their links by birth to Illyr, but the relationship to the planet of those young Illyri born and raised on Earth was both more intimate and complex.

"I wanted to see you. It is the anniversary of my birth. I—"

He placed his hands upon her shoulders and kissed her forehead.

"I have not forgotten. There is a gift waiting for you in your chambers, and later we'll have dinner together, but for now you must go back to your studies, or else I'll have Toris complaining that I allow you to wallow in ignorance, and Althea accusing me of indulging you."

"But that's—"

Her father raised a hand to silence her. "I have an important meeting, Syl. We'll discuss it later. For now, back to class. Go, go!"

He hustled her ahead of him, and when they came to the main corridor he turned left, and she right. She walked on for a time until she was out of sight, then halted. This wasn't fair. Her father had promised always to keep the anniversary of her birth special, not just because she was his only child, but because her mother had placed great store by such occasions. With her mother no longer alive, her father maintained that he had to celebrate Syl's birth for both of them, and each year he had done his utmost to make it a day to remember. On her tenth birthday, they had taken his private skimmer to South America, and picnicked at Machu Picchu in Peru. On her thirteenth birthday, they had traveled to Florence, and he had given her a Michelangelo cartoon saved from the destruction of Rome, for she adored art.

But today he was too busy for her, and Syl feared that this might be setting a pattern for the future. Her eyes felt hot. She tried to hold back the tears, but one managed to escape. She brushed it away furiously. No, she would not cry, not here. Running back to her chambers, she lay down on her bed to concentrate on stemming her tears. She tried to imagine what her mother might have said to her were she still alive. She'd probably have told her that she was acting like a spoiled child, and that her father loved her but sometimes the requirements of his job meant that he could not spend as much time with her as she might wish. He would make it up to her later.

Syl sat up and rubbed her face. On her desk, unnoticed until now, was a box tied with brightly colored ribbons: her father's gift to her.

"Oh!" she said aloud, childlike in anticipation as she bounded from her bed to inspect the parcel. It was heavy, so she unwrapped it where it was, exposing a plain wooden box. Inside the box, nestled in tissue, lay the bronze sculpture of a man's hand. She recognized it immediately and gave a yelp of glee, for it was *La Main*, a cast of Picasso's right hand sculpted by the artist himself. It had been part of the collection of the National Gallery of Scotland before the building was looted and burned during the unrest that initially followed the invasion. Some of the collection had been recovered, but the gallery had not been rebuilt, and paintings that had previously been housed there now adorned the walls of Edinburgh Castle. *La Main*, though, had been believed lost. The cast was one of a series of ten, but the whereabouts of the rest were unknown.

Syl loved to paint, and there was something in the way that Picasso depicted the world, the way in which he made the familiar strange and new, that appealed deeply to her. She liked the idea of the hand that had created such wonders being rendered in bronze, and now she touched her fingers to it, feeling the cool metal beneath her skin. She smiled despite herself.

There was a note with it: *Art is universal. Let one great artist inspire you to become another.*

She stroked the bronze, finding on it the marks of its maker's fingers.

"Thank you," she whispered.

# CHAPTER SEVEN

Lord Andrus found himself wondering what his daughter would think of his gift to her, even as his personal guards fell into step behind him. She was angry with him now, he knew, but she would not be for long, and he smiled as he thought of the pleasure she'd take in *La Main*.

His smile faded as he arrived at the door of the private meeting room adjoining his offices. His guards took up position outside, and he gave them strict instructions that no one, and definitely not his daughter—not again—should be permitted to enter.

Andrus activated his private lens, not wanting to call up a screen from the castle's own systems. The tiny lens lay on his right eye, and enabled him to see virtual images superimposed on reality, from street names to weather information and private messages from his general staff if he was away from the castle. Lenses had first been developed for battlefield use; aided by information from drones and overhead satellites, they provided soldiers with maps, direction of enemy fire, and, most important, the enemy's position. Now many Illyri used them the way humans had once used cell phones: they took calls through lenses, searched for information, watched movies, and even played immersive games. It irritated Andrus to see such amazing technology being used for such frivolous ends.

Danis appeared on Andrus's lens. The remains of the fort at Birdoswald smoldered behind him. The old general was one of Andrus's most trusted soldiers, and his closest friend.

Adding to the men's closeness was the not insignificant matter of

Danis's daughter, Ani. Danis's wife, Fian, had given birth to the girl while Syl was still digesting her first meals at her mother's breast; only a difficult, extended labor had stopped Syl and Ani from being virtual twins, and they had settled for being sisters under the skin. Had Danis actively sought a governorship, then Syl and Ani would have been separated, breaking the hearts of both the young Illyri. To some degree Danis had sacrificed personal ambition at the altar of his daughter's happiness.

"Talk to me, Danis," said Andrus, pouring himself a glass of wine as he did so.

Danis looked cold and damp. On his own lens, he watched enviously as Andrus settled into his chair.

"Good wine, I hope?" he said.

"Very," said Andrus.

"You're developing the tastes of a Diplomat. Next you'll be shaving your head, and you won't be able to lift your hands for all the jewelry on your fingers."

"I'll give you a bottle when you return," said Andrus. "Now tell me about Birdoswald."

In a corner of his lens, images of the fort appeared, transmitted by Danis. Bodies lay scattered throughout.

"It was a carefully planned and well-executed attack," said Danis. "A year ago, the Resistance wouldn't have had the guts or the manpower to carry out a raid like that."

"So what has changed?"

"Their organization, their weaponry, and their intelligence gathering. It's the last that worries me most."

"They have spies among us?"

"You know they do. We use human workers, after all. Nothing would get done if we didn't. And even those that we keep at a distance watch us—they know our comings and goings, our troop movements. . . . But there's also the issue of traitors."

"Ah," said Andrus, looking troubled. The Illyri frowned on the mixing of the two races, but the biological similarities between them meant that some Illyri had secretly taken human partners. No human-Illyri hybrids had yet been born alive, but there had been pregnancies, and it was only a matter of time before nature overcame the differences between the species. Meanwhile, the monitoring of relationships fell to the Securitats, and punishment for such affairs was separation and exile. A number of Illyri had fled with their human lovers to avoid banishment; many on the island of Britain were believed to have gone to ground in the Scottish Highlands, the most lawless region of the country. Officials suspected that some of these Illyri were providing information to the Resistance, probably in return for protection.

More images of bodies flashed up on Andrus's lens. They were all Galateans.

A thought struck him. "Where is Thaios's body?" asked Andrus.

"I don't know," said Danis. "The Corps got to the scene before we did."

Andrus leaned forward in his chair. This was news.

"How could that be? Birdoswald is a Military base. All communication should be conducted directly through us, and we block all non-Military transmissions. Did you have it swept for devices?"

"Of course I did," said Danis. "The equipment that we recovered from the rubble was clean."

"Well, could Thaios have notified the Corps as soon as the attack commenced?"

"I'd imagine he had enough on his hands just trying to survive. Even though he was a Diplomat, his first instinct would have been to fight, especially if his own life was at stake."

"And yet still the Corps knew of what was happening before our own Emergency Response Team."

"Yes."

It was very peculiar. Andrus didn't say so, but he was certain that Danis and his team must have missed a communications device of some kind; that, or the Diplomats had removed it along with Thaios's body.

"So you've found nothing helpful?" he said.

"I didn't say that. I may not have gotten to examine Thaios, but I did take a look at the bodies of the Galateans."

"What about them?"

Danis frowned. "I can't be certain, but I'd say that some of them were killed when they were already down. Executed, even."

"By the Resistance?" Andrus couldn't disguise his shock.

"The Resistance here isn't in the habit of finishing off the wounded on the ground, Galatean or Illyri. In other places, yes: they put our heads on spikes in Afghanistan, and they sent them to us in boxes in Mexico and Texas, but here the humans tend to abide by the civilities, more or less. Even if they have changed their tactics, it still doesn't explain why the Diplomatic Corps was so quick to clean up after the raid. Besides, the Galateans were not killed by bullets."

"How then?" said Andrus.

"Pulses were used. This was Diplomat work: Diplomats, or their Securitat killers."

Anger clouded Andrus's face. While the Military still favored variations on standard ammunition—bullets and shells—the Diplomats preferred infrasonic pulse weapons that induced resonance, or vibration, in their targets. Skulls, chests, and abdomens were particularly effective resonance chambers. Depending on the level of power used, the target might experience nausea or chest pain. At the highest levels, the pulses destroyed inner organs, bursting hearts, lungs, and brains. It was a bad way to die.

So Diplomats had trespassed upon a death scene at a Military base, and the loss of one of their own was no excuse. But now Danis was suggesting that they might have killed Military Galateans in the attack's aftermath. They might not have been Illyri, but they were still his soldiers, and that was murder.

"Why would the Diplomats kill Galateans?" Andrus asked.

"My suspicion is that they were finished off so that they couldn't talk about what they'd seen, so we'd have no witnesses as to what might have occurred in the final moments at Birdoswald."

"If that's the case, then it worked."

"Not entirely. It seems that Thaios's body was taken to the main Diplomat facility in Glasgow. It just so happens that I have a contact there who owes me favors. He didn't get to examine the body either, but he did catch a glimpse of it as it was being placed on a slab."

"And?"

"It didn't have a head."

"Shotgun blast?"

"Must have been a big shotgun. All the cervical vertebrae were gone. According to my source, there was nothing left of Thaios above the shoulders—not that he had a lot above them even when he was alive."

"Some new type of weapon?"

"If it is, then the humans must have stolen it from us. But how would they convert it to use?"

All Illyri weapons were encoded to Illyri or Galatean DNA, a precaution introduced to prevent hostile alien races from using Illyri technology against its creators.

"They could have found a way," said Andrus. "They went from fish struggling in slime to space exploration in no more than a blink of the universe's eye. It was only a matter of time before they applied themselves to adapting our weapons."

"I suppose it could explain pulses being used on the Galateans, but if the humans had succeeded in unlocking Illyri weapons, we'd have heard about it," said Danis. "I'm certain."

"So what's your theory?"

"I think Thaios put a pulse weapon at full power into his own mouth and pulled the trigger."

Andrus winced at the thought. The degree of vibration caused by such an act would certainly be enough to explode a skull.

"But why? Just so he wouldn't be captured? That speaks of a surprising degree of self-sacrifice. After all, the Diplomats would have used his tracker to find him within an hour."

In recent years, all Illyri on Earth had been fitted with a small subcutaneous tracker, usually implanted in the right arm. The tracker could be turned on at will, since few Illyri wanted their every movement to be known and monitored. Syl, for example, rarely turned on her tracker at all, even—or rather, most particularly—when she was on one of her little unauthorized trips beyond the castle walls. As far as she was concerned, it was to be used only in a case of the worst possible emergency, and most of the time she hardly remembered it was there at all.

A discussion had arisen about whether trackers should instead be implanted in teeth, or even in skulls, perhaps as part of the Chip, the thin electronic membrane that all Illyri had attached to their brains at birth, enabling them to interact electronically with their environment, from simple tasks such as calling up virtual screens or translating alien speech to complex operations like piloting spacecraft or operating weapons systems. It also monitored their health, constantly scanning for signs of disease or illness. Unfortunately for Syl's mother, her early version of the Chip had not been able to recognize the malarial infection that eventually killed her.

The use of trackers had been kept secret for a while, but it was believed that humans had recently either figured out the fact of their existence for themselves, or had been told of them by Illyri deserters. Encoding Chips with trackers had been briefly tested in Mexico, but the operation was painful, the tracker too susceptible to the brain's electric impulses, and it had led to Illyri captives having their heads removed by Mexican gangs to prevent their rescue.

"I have no idea why Thaios might have killed himself," said Danis. "Then again, it saved me the trouble. He was little better than a spy for his uncle."

Andrus didn't bother to disagree. Instead he cataloged all that he had been told: a dead Diplomat who appeared to have somehow secretly communicated with his superiors before killing himself, and Galateans seemingly killed by pulse weapons. If there was a pattern, he failed to see it.

"Call in favors," he told Danis. "Find out—*discreetly*—if Birdoswald was an isolated incident. I want details of casualties among officers of the Diplomatic Corps over the last six months. I want to know if pulses have been used on our own troops anywhere on Earth. I want answers!"

Andrus killed the lens connection, and sipped his wine unhappily.


At Birdoswald, Danis had to make do with coffee from a flask as the rain began to fall. Around him, the dead Galateans had started to smell. He sighed deeply.

A soldier's lot, he thought, was not a happy one.

# CHAPTER EIGHT

The Diplomatic Corps had taken over the old Glasgow School of Art for its regional headquarters, and it was there that the Securitats had their Scottish lair. The building had been the first commission given to the great Scottish architect Charles Rennie Mackintosh, resulting in a mixture of Scottish baronial architecture and Art Nouveau motifs. Beautiful but imposing, it stood at the edge of a steep hill, and took the shape of a letter *E*. The panes in the big industrial windows on its northern side had been replaced by toughened glass, capable of withstanding a blast without shattering. When a massive truck bomb had exploded outside the building years before, the glass had not even cracked, and concrete blocks now prevented vehicles from gaining access to the area. The surrounding spiked walls were more for show than anything else. Like all Diplomat facilities, the building was protected by an energy shield. It was state-of-the-art; its advanced design meant that the nausea associated with the prototype shields—which made those beneath them feel ill, and had long since been mothballed because of the queasiness they caused—did not arise.

Naturally, the Diplomats had not seen fit to share their improved shield technology with their Military rivals.

In the school's basement mortuary, two masked and gloved technicians stared down at the headless body of Sub-Consul Thaios. Even in the temperature-controlled environment of the mortuary, Thaios's remains had begun to rot. His skin was covered with black and purple blotches, and a stench arose from his flesh. This was unusual, to say the least. Under other circumstances, a full autopsy might have been in order to investigate the exceptionally quick decay. But an autopsy would not be carried out. The orders received by the technicians for dealing with Thaios's body were very different.

"You're sure about this?" said the first technician.

"I just do what I'm told," said the other. "I know better than to ask questions."

"But he should be accorded a proper service, not . . . *this*. He's Consul Gradus's nephew. There'll be trouble when Gradus finds out."

His colleague glared at him. He was older, and more senior.

"Don't you understand anything, you young fool? The order came from Gradus himself. Now just get on with it. He stinks."

The younger technician began to close the body bag, then stopped.

"What are *they*?" he asked.

"What are what?" said his colleague.

"Those." He pointed a gloved finger at Thaios's chest. It appeared to be covered in tiny red threads that poked from his pores. He hadn't noticed them before. He stroked them with his hand, but the filaments were so delicate that he could barely feel them.

"I don't know," said his partner. "And I don't want to know. Forget that you ever saw them, and I'll do the same."

No more protests were heard. Together the two Illyri sealed the bag and wheeled it to the furnace room. There, as ordered, they burned the body of Thaios. As it turned to charred meat, they heard footsteps behind them.

"Is it done?" said a female voice.

"Yes," said the older of the technicians. Had the new arrival been anyone else, he would have been tempted to make a joke about Thaios not just being done, but well done; hearing that voice, however, killed all thoughts of joking. It would be safer to make his silly comments later, in private, for the woman in the black-and-gold uniform of the Securitats wasn't likely to laugh. She was Vena, the most senior Securitat in the United Kingdom, and possibly the most terrifying member of the secret police between here and Illyr itself. Vena had never been seen to laugh, and she only rarely smiled. Ice ran in her veins, ice and scalding steam, echoing the twin silver streaks that adorned her shaven head.

"And nobody examined the body?" she said, and her voice was as sharp and direct as a dagger.

"No one. We put him in a secure locker under a serial number, with no name. We did as we were told."

"Good."

"Funny how he decayed so quickly, though," said the younger technician, and beside him he heard his colleague give a sharp intake of breath. So close. They'd been so close. He'd warned him about questions, warned him time and time again.

He barely registered the weapon that appeared in Vena's hand. It was too late to react, too late to do anything but die. The pulses that killed the two technicians came close together, the thick basement walls smothering the sound.

And they joined Thaios in the flames.

# CHAPTER NINE

Despite the gratitude she felt for her father's gift, Syl still had no intention of sitting in class for her birthday, but neither could she simply wander the castle's corridors all day. That would be pointless.

She knew the castle better than almost anyone else, including perhaps her father's own security detail. She had been exploring the old fortress ever since she was able to crawl, and had discovered spyholes and listening posts created centuries before, when courtiers had eavesdropped on the deliberations of kings. She had even found the secret area behind the fireplace in the Great Hall, the grand room in which her father often met with visiting dignitaries. Boarded up for the visit of a Russian president during the previous century, the spyhole's existence had been forgotten until Syl had stumbled across a mention of it in the archives. It was her place now, and she would sometimes retreat there to read or listen to music, cocooned in the darkness. At other times, she would spy on her father's meetings if the timing suited, but for the most part they were so dull that she rarely bothered.

Nevertheless, from her snooping she knew of events on Earth that Toris never shared with his students. She was aware that, like so many empires before them, the Illyri had given up on taming Afghanistan, which would have been more worrying if the Afghan people hadn't themselves divided into opposing Islamic factions — just as various Christian groups had elsewhere — and then turned all their rage upon each other. The humans' argument was always the same, regardless of the god or gods they worshipped: if their god had created all living things, then had he not also created the Illyri? Or was it only Man who was made in this god's image, Man who was central to all creation?

The Illyri, meanwhile, considered themselves simply to be creatures of the universe, so such arguments would have been meaningless to them had they not brought with them such violent repercussions. There had been some discussion about outlawing religion entirely, but this had been tried on other conquered worlds and the results were always the same: suppression concentrated the power of belief. But religious extremism was an ongoing problem, and too often it appeared to be motivated less by faith than by a hatred of anything and anyone that was not like itself.

And in her hidey-hole, Syl had wondered if Man had not been made in the image of his god but had instead shaped a god in Man's image: violent, wrathful, and vengeful. It was all rather grim, she decided, and her birthday was certainly not a day to be spent eavesdropping on even more gloomy news from a hole in a wall.

Listless, she wandered into the lounge beside her bedroom. The house in which she and her father dwelt had originally been built for the castle governor in 1742, and had remained a governor's residence for over a century before the post was abolished. It had then served as a hospital until the position was reestablished in 1935, and now an Illyri governor slept in its bedroom and ate in its dining room. It was a handsome building, if a little cold in winter.

Out of habit, Syl picked up a book, but put it down after only a few paragraphs. She wanted to be active. She wanted to *do* something. She moved to the window, swept back the heavy drapes, and looked down on the busy courtyard. This had been transformed into a landing pad for the governor and other important visitors, and shuttles, skimmers, and interceptors used it regularly.

Syl watched the traffic for a time, all of it routine, longing to climb aboard a shuttle and go somewhere, anywhere. Yet she wasn't supposed to leave even the castle's environs unaccompanied. While the Royal Mile area of Edinburgh was less dangerous for the Illyri than elsewhere, they were still objects of vaguely hostile curiosity at best. It was not unknown for stones to be thrown at them, and worse could happen once the castle was out of sight.

But dwindling away inside these walls felt like a death all of its own.

It started to rain. The heavy droplets splashed against the window, and the courtyard cleared as everyone ran for cover. That solved it then: she should read, and forget about going out . . . but what a waste that would be. It hardly seemed worth all the grief she'd doubtless get for skipping school if it was only for a day spent cooped up in the castle.

She walked back to her room and kicked open her closet. Like most young Illyri, her wardrobe consisted of a mix of Illyri dress—mainly long robes for non-Military and security personnel, whether male or female—and Earth clothing, although her father disapproved of nonregulation garments, even on his own daughter. But the Illyri were being changed by Earth, just as Earth was being changed by the Illyri. It was inevitable, in a way: wine, whisky, illicit tobacco, and even human fabrics had made their way back to Illyr along with the other prizes of conquest. Silk was especially prized by Illyri of both sexes, along with certain furs, including mink and fox. They were largely symbols of wealth and influence, for only those with power had both access to the valued items and the means to transport them back to Illyr.

But the human clothing gave Syl freedom of movement in the city. Yes, she was tall, but not unusually so, not yet. Her skin had not yet reached the full golden glow of maturity, so she just appeared lightly tanned. She had tinted glasses to hide her eyes—sunglasses were better, but it didn't look like today was a day for shades—and a crazy velvet hat to conceal her lustrous hair. Now, grinning to herself, she dressed in jeans and an old coat; with her hat fixed firmly on her head, she reckoned she easily passed for a foreign student—Italian, perhaps, or Spanish.

"My name is, uh, Isabella," she said to her mirrored reflection, putting on a dreadful Italianesque accent. "*Buongiorno*, Edinburgh."

Quickly she stuffed the human clothing into a backpack and made her way to the courtyard through the quietest corridors of the castle. She changed her clothes in a bathroom close to the Argyle Tower, then put up an umbrella, and slipped out into the rain. Nobody stopped her as she left the castle; the guards were more concerned about those who tried to enter than those who were leaving. If she was lucky, and there were guards she knew on the gates when she returned, she would be able to convince them not to report her to her father. Syl was particularly good at bending the sentries to her will.

But that was for later. For now, she was sixteen, and away from the castle. She was free. So caught up was she in the pleasure of the moment, even as the rain continued to fall and a cold wind blew stinging droplets in her face, that she did not notice the figure that detached itself from the shadows by the Esplanade and fell casually into step behind her, hidden by the crowds.

# CHAPTER TEN

P aul and Steven approached the Royal Mile, and Knutter's grocery shop.

Knutter was a minor asset to the Resistance, passing on information and providing a safe house for weapons and munitions when required. A cousin of his from Aberdeen had been killed in the early days of the invasion, shot in the act of throwing a firebomb at a patrol. As a consequence, Knutter was barely able to conceal his hatred for the invaders. He had little access to the Resistance's secrets, though, and knew the identities of only a handful of its operatives. It was better that way. Very few of those who fought the aliens knew much beyond their own field of operations, for just as the Resistance had its informers close to the Illyri, so too there were those among the humans who were prepared to sell out their own for money, or advancement, or to secure the return of conscripts to their families. The less men like Knutter knew, the less they might accidentally reveal, or have tortured from them if they were ever caught and interrogated.

Behind his back he was commonly known as Knutter the Nutter, because of both his short temper and his tendency to knock down those who crossed him by using his bulbous forehead or scarred crown to break their noses, a tactic known as "nutting" or the "Glasgow kiss." His head was shaved, and his forearms were adorned with shamrock tattoos and the insignia of Celtic football club, even though he was a native of Edinburgh and the shop had been in his family for generations.

What made Knutter's store particularly useful was the fact that it provided a secret access point to the South Bridge Vaults, the system of over one hundred chambers in the arches of the South Bridge, completed at the end of the eighteenth century. They had first housed taverns and the workshops of various trades, as well as serving as slum housing for the city's poor. It was said that the nineteenth-century serial killers Burke and Hare had hunted among the residents of the Vaults for their victims, selling the bodies for medical experimentation. Then, sometime in the mid- to late nineteenth century, the Vaults were closed, and they hadn't been excavated further until the end of the twentieth century, when they became a tourist attraction. Now they provided a hiding place for guns and, occasionally, Resistance members who had been identified and were being hunted by the Illyri, although most fugitives preferred to take their chances above ground. The Vaults were grim and dank and said to be haunted, although in Knutter's experience it was only those who already believed in ghosts who were susceptible to such fantasies. Knutter himself had yet to encounter anything, either human or alien, that could not be felled by a sufficiently hard blow from his own head. So far, his forehead had not passed through the face of a supernatural entity.

But it was Knutter who first heard the noises from the Vaults after a few too many drinks, and it had caused him to briefly reconsider his views on ghosts—and, indeed, drinking. But the noises continued to sound well after he had sobered up, and he had also recognized the curious burbling, clicking language of the Toads coming through the cracks in his basement wall. It was then that he had informed the Resistance. Once its leaders had concluded that Knutter was not simply hallucinating, further enquiries were made among its informers. By piecing together various pearls of information, a chain of events was constructed, and it was deduced that the Illyri had been tunneling with great secrecy under the city, and had come close to Knutter, and the Vaults.

The Resistance leaders were furious: a major excavation had been carried out quite literally under their noses, and they hadn't known. Their system of spies and informers had let them down. The Illyri had managed to keep their tunnels very quiet until Knutter's keen ear had picked up on what was happening. The Resistance had concluded it was the Diplomatic Corps and not the Military that was behind the excavations. They had enjoyed little success in infiltrating the Diplomats, for they tended not to use human labor, and most of their forces kept their distance from humans, except when they were fighting them, or arresting them, or killing them. If the Military had been engaged in digging beneath Edinburgh, someone would have informed the Resistance. Only the Corps could keep such a project secret, aided, perhaps, by the Securitats.

Katherine Kerr, the boys' mother, had been a tour guide in the city before the Illyri invaded, and had passed on her knowledge of its secrets — among them the location of various concealed entrances to the Vaults, Knutter's shop included — to her close family. This was why Paul and Steven had been chosen for the mission, and given instructions from the top, via Nessa, to investigate further. No point in hanging about, Nessa had said. Knutter was expecting them just as soon as they'd finished their tea.

Now an Illyri patrol vehicle hummed by, its gray armor bristling with weaponry. It reminded Paul of a huge woodlouse. Its wheels were concealed beneath its frame, and its body was V-shaped to protect the Illyri inside by dispelling the force of explosives. It didn't even have windows; its sensor array provided a detailed picture of the environment to its crew without exposing its occupants to harm. Like most of the smaller Illyri transports, it was powered by biogas produced mostly from animal waste, although the Illyri also used vehicles powered by electricity and hydrogen, the latter derived mainly from methane. The boys gave the vehicle a quick glance, but nothing more. Taking too much interest in an Illyri patrol might lead the patrol to take an interest in turn, but ignoring it entirely was almost as bad because it suggested that you were trying too hard to remain unnoticed. It was a delicate balance to strike.

"Are you nervous?" said Paul.

"No," said Steven, then corrected himself: "Maybe a bit."

"Don't be. We've a right to walk the streets. They haven't taken that away from us yet."

Ahead of them lay the Royal Mile, the castle towering over it. Before the occupation, the castle had been the city's main tourist attraction. Now few humans went there voluntarily, and the ones who entered it to work were usually either traitors or spies. Paul had never set foot inside it, and even though he was committed to the Resistance, he sometimes wondered if there would ever come a time when sightseers might innocently wander its battlements again, remembering the great occupation that had once based itself here and had finally been defeated. In his darker moments, he found it hard to imagine.

"Walk faster," he said to Steven. The rain had stopped for a time, but it would return. It always did in this city.

Syl stepped out of the vintage clothing store, her purchases in a plastic bag. The man behind the counter had looked at her oddly as she browsed, but said nothing. Even if he suspected that she might not be human, he probably needed the business. The proximity of the castle and the presence of stop-and-search Illyri patrols meant that many citizens tended to avoid the area around the Royal Mile. Still, Syl bought a lovely old purse decorated with mother-of-pearl, and a white wool coat with a fur collar that would keep her warm in winter.

The streets were dry again, and the sun was coming out. Perhaps the day would be good after all, a possibility worth celebrating. Syl glanced to her left. There was a little coffee shop nearby, and it sold very good pastries. Maybe she could stick a candle in one and sing herself a song. She smiled at the thought, and started walking. Canongate Kirk, a seventeenth-century church, was ahead of her, and beside it the coffee shop.

Suddenly there was a massive *bang*, as though a huge hand had slammed itself down on the Royal Mile, and the coffee shop simply wasn't there anymore. It had disintegrated into a cloud of dirt and brick and glass. Syl was knocked to the ground, and instinctively put her arms up, shielding her face and head. Her ears were ringing, and she couldn't hear properly. Then the dust found her, and she started to choke. She tried not to breathe but she was frightened, and so she began to hyperventilate, and the choking became worse.

Frantic hands were on her now, trying to pull her to her feet.

"Are you all right?" said a voice. It sounded like it was speaking from underwater, but it was still familiar to her. "Syl, are you hurt?"

Syl shook her head. She coughed and spat dust. She felt water splashing on to her face, and then the bottle was in her hands and she drank from it.

"I don't think so," she said at last, once she had stopped choking. She squinted up at the figure before her until she could see more clearly through the fine dust. It was hazy in the smoke-blotted sunlight, but she still recognized the feminine figure with her head cocked like a bird's, small for her age but fast and agile, and currently badly disguised in mismatched human clothing and sunglasses that were a match for Syl's own shades back at the castle. After all, they had bought them together, because that's what best friends tend to do.

"Ani!" she said. "What are you doing here?"

"Following you," said Ani, and her words came to Syl as a distorted whisper, even though Ani was speaking normally. "I thought it would be funny, but it isn't now. Quickly, patrols will be coming. We have to get away from here."

They heard sirens, and from above, the whistling sound of approaching interceptors. Ani put her hand out to help Syl up, but before Syl could take it, another strange hand found hers, yanking her upright and steadying her on her feet. She gave a little squeal of surprise.

"Are you hurt?" said a male voice.

In front of the girls stood two young humans, clearly brothers. It was the older of the two who had spoken. In the dust and chaos of the explosion's aftermath, he had clearly mistaken Syl and Ani for human girls. Syl shook her head, confused, trying to remember her human name, her Italian accent.

"Do you need help?" he asked, and Syl found herself watching his mouth closely, feeling dazed, seeing it shape the words that she could barely hear. His bottom lip was curved and a little pillowy, and she had an odd urge to touch it to see if it was as soft as it looked, so pink and clean in his dusty face.

"We're fine," said Ani. "We're just trying to get home."

She pulled hard on Syl's elbow, starting to turn in the direction of the castle, but the younger boy stopped her with an outstretched arm. Now Syl was pushed even closer to the older one, watching his mouth moving once more, half hearing and half lip-reading, near enough to him to see stubble like a little sprinkle of pepper across his top lip.

"Wait," he said. "Did you see what happened? Were there people—"

"We don't know," interrupted Ani, jerking Syl's arm again, and Syl could feel the panic coming off her friend in waves. No human was ever to be trusted, but in the chaotic aftermath of an explosion it would be particularly easy to snatch two young Illyri from the streets.

"Hold on," said Syl, and she gave her head a shake so that her ears cleared somewhat. "It was MacBride's coffee shop—I think that's where the explosion happened. I didn't see anyone on the street beforehand, but there might have been people inside. That's all I know. But thank you for helping me."

"We really have to go," said Ani urgently, and now Syl turned to follow her, but the boy didn't move, and his younger companion closed in too, blocking their path. This is it, thought Syl. They've seen through our disguises. They *know*.

"Not that way," said the older boy.

"Let us pass," said Ani. "Please!"

"You can't go that way," he said. "You just can't."

"Why not?" said Ani.

Syl looked past them. Already there were soldiers and emergency vehicles racing from the direction of the castle.

"Because there may be another bomb."

And as he spoke, there was a second massive blast, and the approaching vehicles were blown apart.

# CHAPTER ELEVEN

They all turned and ran, not toward the castle but away from it, away from the carnage and bloodshed and ammonia stink behind them, away from the billowing cloud of powdered stone and obliterated flesh, be it human or Illyri. Black-and-gold-uniformed Securitats materialized in the area and swarmed over it like beetles, questioning shopkeepers, searching pedestrians and loading into their armored vehicles anyone who failed to come up with a plausible explanation for being near the site of the explosion.

Syl, Ani, and the two humans powered down the Royal Mile together, and then the boys veered off down a side street, slowing only long enough to make sure the girls were with them before racing on, left-right-right-left, twisting, turning, finally stopping in a deep-set doorway on a corner.

"We go left now," said the older boy, but as they burst back onto the street Ani took the lead, and instead of left she headed right, then took a sharp left down a narrow, urine-scented service alley. Syl followed, and after a heartbeat the boys did too, joining Ani as she crouched in a pool of cigarette butts behind a plastic dumpster at the rear of a greasy shop. She seemed to be hiding.

"What the hell are you doing?" snarled the older boy, but she put her finger to her lips, and then they all heard it: the whine of an interceptor followed by the rhythmic quickstep of soldiers' boots approaching, rattling like applause on the cobbles as they passed the filthy alley. The youngsters stayed still, barely breathing until the stomping faded away.

"You must have amazing hearing," the boy said when all was silent once more, but Ani just shrugged and half smiled.

"Lead on," she said.

Frowning slightly, the human looked from one Illyri to the other, his blue eyes narrowing, then seemed to make a decision. He went to the entrance to the alley, peering around the corner before he beckoned for them to follow.

They moved more cautiously now, stopping to listen every few steps, and still dodging and weaving, disappearing ever deeper into the warren of streets behind the Royal Mile.

"Where are we going?" asked Syl quietly as they paused at another bend, looking down a laneway she'd never seen before, the tall, regal buildings more humble back here, lopsided and blackened by decades of pollution. Windows were broken, some even boarded up, and she saw the painted graffiti of the Resistance on a peeling doorway. This was not a place she should be, where any Illyri should be. Her heart was like a bag of stones clattering terrified in her chest.

"Um, away?" said the older boy next to her ear.

"Where to, though?"

His breath was warm on her cheek and she could smell him, soapy and musky. She stepped back a little, feeling flustered.

"I hadn't thought of anywhere in particular. Just away from the soldiers and Securitats. They'll be rounding people up like sheep for the slaughter."

"Oh. Right."

They started walking again, sticking close to the buildings, but the street was deserted.

"Why? Where do you need to be?" he said.

"The castle," she replied automatically before she could stop herself.

He turned to face her now, his eyes wide and shocked.

"The castle? Why would you want to go *there*?"

Syl felt Ani poke her hard in her back.

"Um, a job interview," Syl spluttered. "We had job interviews."

"Doing what exactly?"

"Scrubbing floors. She's great at scrubbing floors," said Ani from behind her.

"I am. Fabulous," said Syl. "And she cleans toilets."

The older boy gave a low chuckle, and the younger one snorted.

"Will you keep your sunglasses on even when you're cleaning the jacks?" he said to Ani.

"Of course," snapped Ani. "Safety gear. I never take them off."

"You really are the strangest pair," the older boy said, but he seemed more relaxed now. "I wouldn't recommend going near the castle for a while, though, not until they've calmed down. You could always just hang around here: it's quiet, and the Illyri don't come this way very much."

He waved his hand absently at a sheet of corrugated iron that hung from a doorway. *ILLyri is a disease* was scrawled across it in red spray paint.

You reckon? thought Syl to herself, and she gave an inadvertent shudder. The adrenaline was seeping out of her now, and her legs suddenly felt wobbly and weak. She thought she might be sick. She remembered the explosions, the twin bombs, how close they'd been to walking straight into the second one, how these boys had stopped them, saved them, run with them until they were safe from the guards. But how had they known there'd be a second bomb? Had it been their doing? Were they killers, Resistance killers?

"Hey," the older human was saying, looking at her kindly, "are you okay? Seriously?"

His eyes crinkled at the corners. He had that pillow-soft bottom lip, and he didn't look like a murderer, but what did a murderer look like anyway? Abruptly it all became too much. With a nauseous shiver, Syl tried to sit down where she was, but he leapt forward and steadied her elbow.

"Not here," he said. "You're in shock. Let's get you somewhere safe. There's a place nearby—"

"No!" said the other boy, jumping forward.

"Seriously, Steven, it's fine."

"But . . ."

"Steven, I make the decisions. Now, let's go."


Stumbling along between Ani and the older boy, Syl found herself guided up a set of litter-strewn stairs and through a doorway that seemed to open as if by magic when the younger boy—Steven, was it?—pressed a little tune on its crusty doorbell. They went into a cramped hallway where another tune was coaxed from a keypad by a door that looked like wood but sounded like metal, and then they were in a funny little kitchen. The windows had boards nailed over them, but it was quaintly cheerful and bright nonetheless, with polka-dot red vinyl on the table beneath a row of fat yellow light-bulbs. The floor was made of polished checkerboard stones and the walls were lined with scrubbed pine cupboards, each shelf teetering with mismatched mugs and plates, vases and knickknacks, all in bright, crayon-box colors. An enormous old kettle sat on a squat stove, waiting to be used.

Ani pushed Syl gently into a chair.

"Where are we?" she said, watching as the older boy set the kettle to boil, deftly counted tea bags into a green-striped pot, and then poured in the steaming water before covering the whole thing with a fluffy yellow tea cozy.

He looked over at her and smiled genuinely for the first time.

"Oh good, you're back with us. You okay?"

She nodded and returned his smile.

"Everyone else okay?" he said. "Steven?"

The younger boy nodded, and grinned as if to underscore exactly how okay he was.

"That was amazing! It was crazy!" he said.

"Amazing?" said Ani, rounding on him. "*You* must be crazy!"

His face fell, and he turned to scratch in a cupboard, finding a sugar bowl and some fruitcake in a tin.

"Whatever," he mumbled to nobody in particular, but the older boy patted him gently on the back before turning to the girls.

"I'm Paul, by the way," he said, smiling again and extending his hand, but then snatching it back and wiping it clean on his jeans before they shook.

"Syl," said Syl, without thinking, and his warm hand gripped hers. And then she realized what she'd done.

"Syl?" He looked baffled for a moment, his grip tightening, then said: "Short for Sylvia?"

"Yeah, that's me," she said, forcing herself to smile, trying to sound as much like a regular human girl as she knew how. "And this is Ani."

"Annie," said Paul, shaking Ani's hand and nodding. "That's more like it. When you said Syl, it sounded like an Illyri name." He laughed drily, and Syl and Ani joined in.

"Oh, and this is my brother, Steven."

They all said hello and then went silent, eyeing each other awkwardly, the Illyri females still with their glasses incongruously perched on their smudged faces. Ani looked more ridiculous than Syl; at least Syl's glasses resembled something a regular person might wear on a day like today. Ani, by contrast, should have been lying on a sun lounger and drinking a cocktail.

"You can probably take your glasses off now," said Paul.

"No!" said the females in unison. In a rush of words, Syl explained that Ani had a nasty eye condition from toilet chemicals, and Ani said Syl had a squint.

"A squint?" said Paul.

"Uh-huh." Syl nodded, but gave Ani a kick under the table.

Paul and Steven looked at each other, and then Paul turned to fetch the teapot, pouring them all large colorful mugs and loading Syl's with sugar, "for shock," before slopping in milk. She took a sip. It was sweet and treacly, and vaguely disgusting, but she drank it anyway, feeling the color returning to her cheeks, the vitality reawakened in her strong Illyri bones.

"Where are we, then?" said Ani, breaking the silence that descended again as they all munched on cake.

"Just a place," said Paul, waving a hand vaguely, and Steven gave a meaningful cough.

"A place? I see."

They were silent again. Syl watched Paul, saw how he held his mug with both hands, his fingers interlocked, lean and strong, yet vulnerable too, as though he was trying to warm them even though it wasn't cold. Could they really be the fingers of a bomber, of a murderer? She had to know.

"Paul," she said, and everyone looked at her. Paul raised an eyebrow, and she bit her lip nervously. "How did you know there'd be a second bomb?"

"I didn't know," he said. "I just guessed."

"How, though?"

"Because this is my home, Sylvia. I live here, and I intend to carry on living here without being blown up. That's how it sometimes is with bombings: one blast followed shortly afterward by another. The first lures in the soldiers and the Securitats who respond to it, and then the second kills them. I figured it would probably happen that way again. I watch. I've been watching since I was born. Don't you pay attention too?"

"I guess," she said, but she was starting to realize how little she knew about outside, about the world beyond the castle walls.

Then his face changed, and his eyes narrowed. "Did you think it was me? You think I'd do something like that, in a place where civilians could be killed?"

"Well, no ... maybe ... I don't know. After all, I don't know you, do I?"

"And I don't know you," he countered, "yet we brought you here where we'd all be safe because we're not like them, and because that's what we do. We're humans, not Illyri. We stick together." His tone changed. There was a note of suspicion to it now. "We *are* in this together, Sylvia, aren't we?"

"She was just asking!" said Ani, jumping up angrily and clattering the cups together, then dumping them in the sink. "Anyway, it's time we left."

"Yes, I think it probably is—Steven, you clean up here and I'll get these two back to the Mile. I'll see you in fifteen, right?"

Steven shrugged and looked into his tea.

"Bye," said Ani gruffly as she followed Paul to the door.

"Thanks," said Syl, but her voice was weak and high.

"Yup. Cheers," Steven said, and then they were out on the streets again, weaving down alleys, crisscrossing their path, and she wondered if Paul was trying to confuse them so they couldn't find their way back to the little safe house. If he was, he'd definitely succeeded. Fat raindrops started splashing around them, and Paul turned up his collar and hurried on, never saying a word. Syl guessed he was used to outpacing people, but the Illyri were naturally vigorous and lean, and even Ani's shorter legs kept up easily.

All at once he stopped, and pointed ahead. "Go that way to the very end, then take a right and you'll be back at the Mile, but I'd stay away from the castle. I presume you can find your way home from there."

Syl nodded, but his attention was already elsewhere. Ani shrugged.

"Right, thanks. Bye," she said, turning to go, but Syl hesitated.

"Thank you, Paul," she said, and she stretched out a tentative hand toward him. "And I'm so sorry. You saved my life today—our lives—and I'll never forget that. Truly, thank you."

He looked at her for real now, and his eyes wrinkled warmly again as he took her hand in his, not so much a shake as a friendly squeeze.

"Well, it's certainly been interesting, Sylvia."

"It has," she said. "Good luck, Paul." Then she turned and scampered after Ani.

"See you, Syl," he called. She looked back and waved, and he waved too. She couldn't be sure, but it looked like he was laughing.

# CHAPTER TWELVE

Later, Syl would wonder quite how they had managed to make it back under the noses of so many patrols, both Military and Corps, but somehow they did. The initial panic around the castle had quietened down in their absence and things were getting back to normal again, as happens quickly in cities that have grown used to violence.

Apart from the minor detail of saving their lives, those boys had done them another favor too, Syl knew, for she and Ani would surely have been picked up by their own people and charged with being outside the castle walls without authorization if they hadn't been led away to safety. The best they could have hoped for was to be dragged before her father, who would have forced them to explain just what they'd been doing wandering round Edinburgh while bombs were going off. She'd have been grounded until she turned twenty-one!

Illyri under the age of eighteen were not allowed beyond the castle walls, or designated Illyri areas of control, without permission, although most took this to mean that they shouldn't be *caught* outside certain areas without permission. Syl wasn't the only one who routinely made illicit excursions; life would have been very dull otherwise. While many of the Military guards took a liberal view of such escapes, just as long as their officers weren't around, the Securitats were less forgiving, and particularly so in the case of children of the Military: they never passed up a chance to make life awkward for soldiers and their families. The Securitats would have been overjoyed to discover that they had the daughter of Lord Andrus in their hands, along with one of her little friends. They'd probably have kept them overnight in a cell, just to make her father sweat, before parading them before him in order to make him look foolish. After all, if the governor could not keep his own child under control, how could he be expected to rule nations? It was as much for her father's sake as her own that Syl wanted to return safely to the castle.

They were lucky too, for just as they neared the castle, a pair of Military trucks emerged, and behind them Syl glimpsed Corporal Laris, who was the closest she had to a friend in the castle guards. She had saved Laris from serious punishment earlier in the year, when he had fallen asleep at his post on a still, humid, summer's night. Only the fact that Syl had been wandering the courtyard, unable to sleep, had kept him from being court-martialed, for she had woken him seconds before the captain of the castle guard made his rounds.

Laris stared as Syl and Ani removed their hats and glasses, and seemed about to say something to them, but the pleading look that Syl gave him made him hold his tongue, and he waved them into the safety of the castle without a word. But Syl noticed that a figure in black and gold on the other side of the street seemed on the verge of approaching them before a convoy blocked her from view. Even hidden by her helmet, Syl was sure that she recognized Vena, the most senior Securitat in Scotland—perhaps even the whole island. Vena had no love for Syl, and her proximity was even more reason to get out of the courtyard and into the relative safety of their quarters.

They scurried through the castle to the little bathroom. The corridors were unusually devoid of activity, and Syl noticed that there were no humans to be seen. In the aftermath of the explosion, the castle's human staff would have been surrounded and taken away to a secure location beside the New Barracks. It was standard procedure. There they would remain until it was clear that the threat had passed, and none of them had been involved in any way in the explosions.

Syl and Ani changed their clothes in the bathroom and made themselves look as respectable as they could, then hurried to Syl's rooms. Once the door was shut safely behind them they stared at each other for a moment before bursting into relieved, hysterical giggles.

"Wow," said Syl. She hugged her friend. "What a crazy day. What the hell just happened?"

"Well, we were almost blown up, but two boys saved our lives," said Ani. "We then had tea with them. Then, most shockingly of all, there was the small matter of you flirting with an actual H-U-M-A-N."

"I did not!" shot back Syl.

"Oh, you definitely did. And I think he was flirting back."

"Really?" Syl couldn't help but feel slightly pleased.

"Well, yes . . . until I told him you had a squint."

Ani's head bobbed with mocking laughter, but it was infectious. Soon Syl couldn't help but laugh too.

"Hey," said Ani finally, "I just remembered: happy birthday."

"Oh—I nearly forgot about that too. And I never had my cake . . . I'm starving."

"Here, then," said Ani, pulling some fruitcake wrapped in a tissue from inside her balled-up sweater with a cheeky grin.

"They save our lives and you steal their cake? You're evil."

"Consider it a birthday gift," said Ani. "I didn't have time to get you anything else; time, or money for that matter. My father cut my allowance—again."

Whenever Syl felt that her father was being unfair or unduly strict, she thought about Ani and Danis. Danis made Lord Andrus look soft as a marshmallow.

"Oh no. What's he accused you of now?" asked Syl.

"He caught me smoking," said Ani.

"Oh, Ani. That's just stupid!"

Tobacco had been unknown to the Illyri until they arrived on

Earth. On Illyr, all narcotics were strictly controlled, and most citizens avoided them on health grounds anyway. The Illyri had tried banning tobacco in the first years of the invasion, and had failed utterly. Now low-tar tobacco was tolerated for human use. Illyri were forbidden to smoke, but some did anyway, buying strong tobacco on the black market, even though it was known that it was run by criminals, many of whom passed information to the Resistance.

Ani shrugged. "It was only one cigarette, and I didn't even like it that much. It was just bad luck. I was hanging out of my bedroom window to smoke it—so that the smell wouldn't get into my room—and old Pops was passing through the Middle Ward and happened to look up, didn't he?"

"Busted! Busted big time," said Syl.

"He said that I couldn't smoke if I didn't have any money to buy cigarettes. Now I don't even have enough to buy matches, never mind cigarettes."

"Well, good thing I like fruitcake, then," said Syl.

They sat by the window and stared out at the city, munching cake in silence. It seemed so peaceful from up here, and the sky was now such a vivid blue. But the view had changed for Syl, changed forever now that they'd come so close to death in the city below, now that they'd run with the humans, now that they'd hidden from their own. Ani clicked her tongue and sighed, for her thoughts were clearly in the same place.

"I wonder if anyone was hurt in the explosion," said Syl finally. "The lady who owned that coffee shop seemed nice. She never objected to serving me, even when I wasn't disguised, and you know what some people are like."

Ani nodded. There were places in the city where Illyri were given the cold shoulder if they tried to shop or eat. There would be no service, no talk, only silence until they gave up and left the place to the humans. It was illegal, of course, and dangerous for the humans involved. The Securitats had been known to arrest people who refused to deal with the Illyri, but for the most part such actions were reluctantly tolerated. If nothing else, passive resistance was better than acts of violence.

"Maybe she wasn't there," said Ani. "Maybe it was closed."

But Syl doubted it. The little coffee shop opened all day long, six days a week, and the homely owner was always behind the counter. Frances was her name. It was sewn on her apron.

Had Syl believed in a god, she would have prayed for the soul of Frances. And she would have given thanks for the humans who'd come to their rescue.

"Look," said Ani. "Something's happening outside."

Casual onlookers were being hustled away, and Securitats began to pour into the courtyard. That in itself was unusual: Lord Andrus was strict about keeping the day-to-day functions of the castle under Military control, which included all matters relating to security. The Securitats were permitted a small garrison in the Lower Ward, and a larger base off the Royal Mile, but they had no part in the actual running of the castle. Syl had never before seen so many of the security police inside the walls. And yes, Vena was leading them, her helmet held beneath her right arm. The twin silver streaks above her left ear always made her easy to spot. Syl knew that Lord Andrus privately called her "the Silver Skunk."

There was some jostling with the regular Military guard as the Securitats took up position around the landing pad, and a confrontation seemed in the offing. Soon Peris, the captain of the castle guard, appeared. He made straight for Vena, and an argument commenced between the two officers. It seemed to get quite heated at one point, because Syl could see Peris jabbing his finger at Vena, his face reddening. In response, Vena produced a document from the pocket of her dress jacket and handed it to Peris. He read it, simmered for a while, and then conceded defeat. He signaled the guard to withdraw, leaving the courtyard in the hands of the Securitats.

A shuttle approached from the north. It was colored a golden red, as though caught in the light of a setting sun, and shaped like a trident, with the central tine forming the cabin and those on either side housing the propulsion systems. It bore the distinctive inter-linked black circles of the Diplomatic Corps, but contained within the overlapping of the rings was a single red eye, a variation that Syl had not seen before. The ship hovered high above the landing pad, but did not descend. Its windows were dark, but she sensed the presences behind them taking in the courtyard and the castle. The ship seemed to Syl both beautiful yet unsettling, like an elegant weapon waiting to be fired.

Vena put a finger to her right ear, activating her tiny commu-nicator. She listened for a moment, raised a hand, and summoned two guards to her side. More discussions followed. Still the red ship waited. The guards ran back to the castle, and seconds later a white canvas arch began to extend across the courtyard. It was the shel-tering device used to protect honored guests when rain was falling, but the rain had stopped. It seemed that whoever was in the trident ship simply did not wish to be exposed to the curious gaze of on-lookers, although the arch was thin enough to allow shapes and colors to filter through, if not faces.

Vena stepped in front of the arch and walked along beneath it as it was unfurled, so that she was gradually lost from Syl's sight. Only when the shelter was at its fullest extent did the ship begin its descent, the pilot landing the craft perfectly so that the cabin door was concealed by the canvas.

The engines died. All was silent for a time. Syl found herself holding her breath. Where was her father? she wondered. Clearly there was someone important on the ship, and her father usually greeted all visiting dignitaries personally. It was a mark of respect, on their part as much as on his. Either this was someone to whom he was giving calculated offense by not being present—which was so unlike her father as to be unthinkable—or he had not been aware of the ship's impending arrival, which was stranger still. Yet Vena had known, and whatever authority she had used to dismiss her father's men from the courtyard was significant, for only Andrus should have had the power to replace his own guard.

Vena's figure was visible to Syl through the canvas, a patch of darkness against the white. So too was the outline of the cabin door, and Syl saw it turn from red to black as it opened. Shapes emerged: two soldiers with guns, followed by three robed figures, two in pale yellow and one in white, and finally a sixth figure, tall and almost triangular in form, its robes a deep, dark red. The rich fabric cast a faint glow over the interior of the canvas, dancing on the ripples caused by the breeze as the new arrivals made their way from the courtyard. Led by Vena, the concealed visitors entered the Governor's House.

Syl felt Ani shudder beside her.

"What is it? What's wrong?"

"I don't know," said Ani. "Just a feeling. A really strange feeling. Whoever was in that ship is bad, bad news. . . . "

# CHAPTER THIRTEEN

It was some hours after the blasts when the two young men eventually managed to slip unnoticed into Knutter's shop on South Bridge. Paul turned the sign on the window to CLOSED, locked the door, and pulled down the canvas shutter so that nobody could see inside.

"You're late," said Knutter. "I was worried."

"We're okay," said Paul, "but we were in the area when the bombs went off."

He went to the fridge and pulled out two bottles of water, tossing one to his brother. Knutter frowned. The boys drank deeply to clear their throats, and when they'd finished, Knutter put out his hand for their cash. He was that kind of man.

"Did you see any injured?" he asked, once the boys had paid for their water and the money was safely in his register. Knutter had not left his store that afternoon, not even in the aftermath of the explosion. It wasn't his job to go helping casualties, not at the risk of being arrested by the Securitats. Anyway, he'd been told to wait for the boys, and that was just what he'd done.

"My guess is that the dead were mostly Illyri," said Paul, "but two girls told us that MacBride's coffee shop might have been the site of the first explosion. The second one finished off half of the Illyri response team, I think."

"I know the MacBrides," said Knutter. "They're good people."

He frowned as he thought about what Paul had said.

"What two girls?"

"Just girls."

"Did they get a good look at you?"

Paul shrugged.

"What happens if they're picked up by the patrols? They'll be able to describe you to them."

"So what?" said Steven. "We weren't the only people around. It doesn't make us guilty of anything."

"You're a young fool," said Knutter. "The Securitats think everyone is guilty. Even if you're not, they'll torture you until you confess to something, just to make the pain stop."

"Leave him alone, Knutter," said Paul. "He's right. They were just girls, and they owe us. If it hadn't been for Steven and me, I reckon bits of them would be scattered over the Royal Mile right now. They almost ran into the second blast."

Knutter muttered something to himself. An Illyri troop transport passed by, and the three of them quickly retreated from the front of the store.

"Did our lot plant those bombs, then?" said Knutter.

"We might have," said Paul, tapping his nose as if it was all a wild secret. Knutter tapped his nose in reply and winked.

In reality Paul didn't have a clue who'd been responsible for the bombings. Surely he'd have been told if something was being planned for the Royal Mile—wouldn't he? After all, the Resistance had sent him and Steven to investigate the tunnels, so they'd been aware that there were operatives in the vicinity. Furthermore, the Resistance didn't bomb civilian areas with massive devices. There was too much risk of killing humans. No, this wasn't right at all.

But the two bombs, one after the other, fitted a certain pattern, just as he'd told the girls: the first bomb drew the emergency response teams—the Military and Securitats—and the second took out the rescuers. There were Resistance bomb teams who worked just that way, but not usually in cities, and certainly not where humans might be injured.

Paul looked around Knutter's cramped shop, and gave a heart-felt sigh.

"Should we call it off?" said Knutter.

"No," said Paul. "We go ahead. With luck, the Illyri will have enough to keep them occupied picking through the rubble on the Mile."

He looked to his brother, who nodded.

"I'm ready," he said.

Paul turned to Knutter. "You'd better show us the way, then."

Knutter guided Paul and Steven into the back room of the shop. From there, they descended the rough stairs to the basement.

"Birdoswald," said Knutter. "Wish I'd been part of that one. That was a hell of an operation."

Paul nodded as if in agreement, but said nothing. First Birdoswald, and now bombs on the Royal Mile. It looked like someone was trying to put the Resistance out of a job.

They were now in the basement, standing in a weak puddle of spluttering light, and Knutter began pulling boxes aside, revealing a rusty shelf.

"See?" he said.

They didn't, and the big man giggled like a child.

"Well, of course you wouldn't."

With a last theatrical wink at the brothers, he unclipped the catches holding the shelf to the wall and slid it forward on concealed castors. Behind it was a sheet of plywood painted to match the brick, which Knutter shifted to reveal an entrance large enough for a man to pass through without crouching. The interior smelled damp, and when Knutter shone a flashlight inside, Steven and Paul heard a rat scuttling into the safety of the darkness. The light illuminated a small chamber with a curved ceiling.

"You see there?" said Knutter, pointing at the base of the far wall. Steven and Paul squinted, and saw that the cement holding together the bricks in that part of the wall appeared newer than elsewhere. "I've been working on it these last few nights, loosening the bricks until I could create a hole big enough to use. Then I re-laid them on a metal support so that the whole section could be pulled out and replaced easily. It's a neat job. You wouldn't spot it unless you were looking for it."

"Cool," said Steven, and he meant it.

"And that leads directly into the new tunnel?" asked Paul.

"Pretty much. I still don't know how they managed to dig so quietly. I mean, it's right underneath my shop, and I never would have known about it if I hadn't been down here and heard those Toads babbling."

Paul looked at his brother.

"You ready?"

Steven nodded, and they both shrugged off their thick coats to reveal the short, sharp knives they carried beneath. The knives were the only weapons they had brought to the city center, for being caught on the streets with a firearm was a shortcut to the Punishment Battalions. The battalions, made up of those found guilty of acts of terror and other crimes against the Illyri, were routinely dispatched to work and fight on the most hostile of worlds. Life expectancy could be measured in weeks and months, and sometimes only days.

Paul and Steven attached LED lights to their foreheads, and knelt to help Knutter pull back the section of wall.

Beyond was darkness.

Paul checked his watch. He took a deep breath. The air beyond smelled stale, but there was something else there too, something bad. Knutter handed him a Glock pistol.

"Just in case," he said. "And I want it back."

Paul took the gun without hesitation.

"Okay," he said, "let's do this."

# CHAPTER FOURTEEN

S yl detected the new tension in the corridors as she and Ani passed along them, trying to find out what was happening. There were more Securitats among her father's Military, the two forces maintaining a discreetly hostile distance from each other. Twice they were stopped by Securitats and asked where they were going, and why, and only the intervention of members of her father's guard prevented an awkward situation from arising. From what Syl could understand, the Securitats were attempting to put the castle in lockdown for security reasons, and the Military were resisting on principle. The circumstances in the castle had changed, and although it might have been linked in part to the explosions, it was clearly also to do with the red ship that sat beautifully, sinisterly, in the courtyard. Rupe, a sergeant of the castle guard, was advising Ani and Syl to return to their rooms after the second encounter with the Securitats when an Illyri male wearing a black business suit with gold trim on the collar appeared nearby, watching the exchange with grave, humorless eyes. He was frighteningly thin, with black hair cut close to his scalp, and his skin was a sickly, washed-out yellow. He brought to mind a sheathed blade, waiting to be used.

Sedulus.

Syl knew him by name and reputation, although thankfully they had never had reason to speak. Sedulus was Marshal of the Security Directorate for all of northern Europe, one of the most powerful Securitats on Earth. Her father, she knew, disliked him intensely, a feeling that was entirely mutual. Sedulus rarely came to Edinburgh, preferring instead to remain at his own headquarters at the fortress of Akershus in Oslo, Norway, a building that had once been occupied by the Nazis. Syl's father found this entirely apt.

Beside Sedulus, Syl was alarmed to note, was Vena. Syl had heard rumors that Sedulus and Vena were lovers, although she found it hard to believe that love would enter into any relationship involving those two. Both now approached their little group. Rupe instinctively stood in front of Syl and Ani, as though to protect them from the two Securitats.

"Step aside, Sergeant," said Vena.

"May I ask why?" said Rupe.

"Because I am your superior officer, and if you don't obey my orders, I will have you thrown into a cell."

"With respect, ma'am," said Rupe, loading his words with so much sarcasm that Syl was certain he was goading Vena into trying to arrest him, "this is a Military base of operations, and I answer to the Lord Governor. You can take your orders and shove them where the sun don't shine, begging your pardon."

Syl saw Vena reach for the pistol on her belt, but Sedulus placed a hand on her arm and she froze.

"There's no need for trouble, Sergeant," said Sedulus. He had a voice like honey, but stinging bees were not far away. "Major Vena merely wanted to make sure that these young ladies were safe and well after the recent incidents."

"Why shouldn't they be?" said Rupe.

"Major Vena appears to be under the impression that the governor's daughter and her friend might have been outside the castle walls when the bombs went off. If that were the case, it might be useful if my officers were given the opportunity to question them, just in case they saw anything while they were abroad, so to speak."

He smiled. His lips didn't sit perfectly together when he did, and a sliver of white teeth was visible between them. It made him look hungry.

"The major must be mistaken," said Syl. "We were not outside."

"I saw you in the courtyard," said Vena.

"Oh, we were in the courtyard," said Syl, "but that's not illegal yet. Is it?"

She looked at Ani. Ani shrugged innocently. "I don't think so, but it sounds like the major might like to *make* it illegal."

"You were covered in dust," said Vena.

"We were watching the trucks," said Syl. "We wanted to find out what was happening. I guess we must have got dirty from being so close to them."

Vena scowled at them. Her eyes took in Ani's tight jeans, silver sneakers, and outsize off-the-shoulder sweater that revealed a curious tattoo of a bird with the wings of a butterfly. The twin stripes on Vena's skull suggested that she enjoyed expressing her own individuality, but she didn't approve of others doing the same—especially not the spoiled brats of her Military antagonists.

"You dress like a human slut," said Vena.

"Better that than a Securitat slut," said Ani. She spoke without thinking, and Syl could see that she regretted her words instantly, but it was typical of Ani to lash out first and think about the consequences after.

Vena's eyes darkened. A pale pink tongue poked from between her lips, like a serpent testing the air before striking.

"Careful, little bird," she said, "or I may have to break your wings."

Even Sedulus appeared to recognize that no good was going to come from any further exchanges.

"Well," he said, "I believe that answers our questions for now, doesn't it?"

Vena didn't look like she'd received the answers she was looking for at all, and would have very much liked to continue the questioning somewhere quieter and more private, but she took the hint.

"If you are content, sir, then so am I," she said.

"Then we'll let the governor's lovely daughter and her equally fetching friend be about their business," said Sedulus. "Thank you for your help, Sergeant . . . ?"

"Rupe," said the sergeant.

"Rupe," repeated Sedulus. "I shall remember that name. Such loyal service to the governor should be rewarded appropriately, and it will be, when the time comes."

Sedulus and Vena retreated, for the time being. Rupe let out a small, relieved breath.

"Thank you, Sergeant," said Syl. "I hope we haven't gotten you into trouble," although she suspected that they had. Sedulus had a long memory, and Vena didn't like to be thwarted.

"If you have, it would be worth it just to have gotten in that bitch's face, excuse my language."

"Can you tell us what's happening?" said Ani. "Nobody seems to be know, or seems willing to share it with us."

"All I know is that we have offworld visitors," said Rupe. "Unexpected ones, and your father isn't very happy about it." He lowered his voice. "I can't say for sure, but I hear that Grand Consul Gradus is among them."

This was news. Gradus had never visited Earth before, and he would usually have been expected to arrive with much pomp and ceremony, not in a small ship on a damp day in bomb-blasted Edinburgh.

"Now," concluded Rupe, "as I was saying earlier, if I were you, I'd find somewhere nice and quiet to wait this out. The Securitats have no love for anyone but their own kind, and I may not be here to protect you the next time. Off you go now."

They went, but only as far as the next corner. When they were sure that Rupe was gone, Syl stopped.

"What is it?" said Ani.

"Care to eavesdrop?"

"On what?"

"On whatever happens next."

Ani looked uncertain. "I think we might have had enough fun for one day, don't you? I mean, we've slipped out of the castle and had to sneak back in again, we've nearly been blown up twice, we've had tea and cake with the enemy, and we've managed to annoy the head of the secret police and his nasty little puppet."

"Indulge me," said Syl. "It's my birthday."

"Where are we going?"

"The Great Hall."

Ani pretended to scowl, then laughed. "All right, but we leave as soon as it gets boring. Which it will."

"Fine," said Syl, but she had a suspicion that the meeting wasn't going to be boring at all.

# CHAPTER FIFTEEN

Paul and Steven were in the sewers. Paul had been there before. The sewers had provided useful ways of moving arms around the city—and even a means of escape from patrols—but the Illyri had learned of what was happening, and had laid motion sensors along the routes most frequently used by the Resistance, as well as minimum-charge, infrasonic antipersonnel mines capable of killing a person without damaging the sewer system itself.

Now the Resistance tried to avoid the sewers; they didn't have time to sweep for sensors and mines, and it was only in the most desperate of cases that they made their way below ground. Paul had seen what happened to the insides of Resistance soldiers caught by infrasonic mines. It wasn't pretty, and he tried to keep images of it from his mind as he and his brother tramped through the filth of the city. His only reassurance came from the knowledge that the Illyri were unlikely to plant mines in areas used by their own troops. Just as long as Knutter hadn't simply been hearing things, they should be okay.

"Which way?" asked Steven.

"Left," said Paul.

"Why left?"

"Why not? Would you prefer to split up?"

Steven shook his head. He didn't like being below ground, and already the tunnel was giving him the creeps. Although bulbs were strung irregularly along its length—another indication that the sewers were in use by the Illyri—they gave out only the dimmest of illumination, and there were great pools of darkness between each one.

Paul looked at his younger brother with only barely concealed admiration. Steven was just a kid, but then so were many of the Resistance's bravest operatives. The Illyri tended to concentrate their strictest surveillance efforts on adults and older teenagers, not children. Even at the best of times, children were difficult to police, and consequently there were kids walking the streets of Edinburgh with guns and plastic explosives hidden in their schoolbags. It wasn't what any parents might have wished for their children, but there was a war on. Steven was braver than most of his peers, but he would always be Paul's little brother, and Paul tried to protect him as best he could.

"Didn't think so," he said. "Quietly now."

Together they headed south, their knives clutched in their fists. Their headlamps cast disorientating shadows on the tunnel walls, making them both jumpy, so they chose instead to switch them off and rely on their eyes and the lights on the walls.

Paul had a pedometer attached to his hip, and he checked the distance as they walked, comparing it with the map in his hand. The tunnel seemed to run beneath South Bridge and Nicholson Street, then turned northeast at Lutton Place, heading in the direction of Queen's Drive and the Salisbury Crags. As they drew nearer to the Crags, a stink assailed their nostrils, and Steven had to stop himself from retching loudly. It was the smell of burning, and worse.

"The crematorium," said Paul. "We must be close to it."

The Illyri had declared that burials were unsanitary in major urban areas, and had decreed that the remains of all deceased humans should be burned at a central crematorium built specially for that purpose to the east of Queen's Drive. The order had caused some dismay, but not as much as might have been expected, since cremations had begun to outnumber burials even before the arrival of the invaders. People simply resented being told what to do, even if it was something that they had been doing anyway. It was the principle of the thing.

They reached a T-junction in the tunnel, and a collapsed wall was revealed to their right. The bricks had been moved away, and supporting joists added. Paul and Steven moved in for a closer look, and saw that a hole had been bored into the sewer wall. A length of pipe, about fifteen feet long and wide enough for a man to move through on his hands and knees, connected the sewer with a second, better-lit tunnel beyond.

"Stay here," Paul told Steven.

He hoisted himself into the pipe and shuffled along on his elbows, making as little noise as he could, until he reached the other end of the pipe. His hands were shaking, but he tried to remain still as he listened for any noises from beyond before risking a quick glance.

The tunnel was perfectly round, with rubber pads set along the ground to provide a grip. Paul was baffled as to how the Illyri had managed to construct it without being noticed, until he recalled being told of the massive lasers they sometimes used to tunnel through mountains in order to build new roads or hide their bases. Yes, he thought, one of those lasers would do the trick if it could be assembled below ground, and it would explain why the tunnel walls were so smooth. The Illyri had simply burned their way under the city.

To his right, the tunnel came to a dead end in a patch of near darkness. Some machinery was stored there, but Paul didn't recognize any of it. To his left, the tunnel intersected with another of similar smoothness and size.

He turned onto his back, slid most of his upper body from the pipe, then gripped its sides and dropped into the tunnel. He could see Steven at the other end, waiting to join him.

"Come on," he said.

Steven climbed quickly into the pipe, and Paul helped him out. At that moment, they heard the burbling sounds of Galateans communicating, and Paul dragged his brother into the shadows, where they blended in with the piles of machinery and plastic. Paul drew Knutter's gun from under his jacket. If they had to fight their way out, they would. If it got really bad, he hoped he could hold the Toads off while Steven escaped, but he prayed it wouldn't come to that, both for his own sake and also because he knew that he'd have a hard time convincing his little brother to leave without him.

A Galatean appeared in the mouth of the Vault. It stopped in a pool of light and stared down the tunnel into the shadows where the boys had flattened themselves against the wall. Steven held his breath, afraid that if he sniffed even one more molecule of the tunnel stench, he would throw up.

The Galatean moved on. Behind it came a series of hovering platforms of the kind used by the Illyri to transport heavy items. Beside them walked several Agrons, the slave race that performed the Illyri's dirtiest jobs. The Agrons were no more than five feet tall, but their upper bodies were overdeveloped, and they were enormously strong. Their pink heads were hairless, their faces wrinkled like those of Shar-Pei dogs. They monitored the progress of the platforms, making sure that they did not bang against the walls. Each platform bore an irregularly shaped burden, covered by a layer of canvas. Steven and Paul had watched four of the platforms pass by when the fifth, and last, appeared. It seemed to be giving the Agrons some problems, its progress less smooth than the others. Halfway across the junction, sparks shot from its control panel, and the platform lurched sideways before dropping to the ground. The two Agrons beside it stepped quickly aside to avoid being crushed. One of the bindings holding the canvas in place shot loose, and the material fell away on the right-hand side, revealing what lay beneath.

Steven felt his big brother flinch next to him. He bit his own lips closed to suppress an inadvertent yelp, and hold back a surge of vomit.

Five bodies were piled on the metal surface: three men, one woman, and a boy who looked only a little younger than Steven. All were naked, their skin bearing the marks of discoloration and decay, for in addition to requiring cremation of the dead within twenty-four hours, the Illyri had also banned the use of preservatives on bodies on environmental grounds. If nothing else, it encouraged the relatives of the deceased to deal with the matter of their disposal as quickly as possible.

Under the instructions of the Toads, the Agrons unloaded the corpses from the malfunctioning platform and distributed them as best they could among the others, shifting bodies roughly to make room for more.

And then, to the boys' horror, one of the bodies moved. It was the woman. Her head turned, and she gave a little moan. She had dark hair that hung over her face, obscuring most of it, but Paul could see one blue eye open in panic. She seemed to be staring straight at him. She started to scream, over and over, the sound of it echoing in the tunnel until one of the Galateans stepped in front of her, blocking the boys' view. He drew a pulse weapon, charged it, and fired.

The screaming stopped.

The little procession continued on its way, heading not toward the crematorium but away from it, in the direction of the shuttle base beneath Arthur's Seat.

Once all was quiet again, Paul released his hold on Steven, and allowed his brother to puke.

"You okay?" he asked, once Steven's retching stopped.

Steven nodded, standing up shamefaced, wiping strings of vomit from his lips.

"She was alive. That lady was still alive."

"Yes."

"And then they killed her."

"Yes."

"What were they doing with those bodies, with those people?"

"I don't know. They weren't burning them, that's for sure. Let's get out of here. We have to report what we've seen, and I need fresh air."

The two young men climbed back into the pipe, and headed for safety.

• • •

Knutter wrinkled his nose as they reentered his shop.

"You weren't in there for long," he said, "but you still stink. You got my gun?"

Paul returned the weapon; Knutter tucked it back into his belt.

"You find out what they're doing?"

Steven didn't say anything. He was learning to keep his mouth shut when anyone asked a question, leaving Paul to come up with answers. Now he was watching his brother carefully, waiting to hear what he might say.

"Not exactly," said Paul.

"What's that supposed to mean?" said Knutter. "I took a big risk bringing you down here, and making that hole in the wall. You're not going to get another opportunity like that, you know, not unless someone plants another bomb on the Royal Mile. What did you see?" He made a motion toward Paul, his hands raised. "Tell me, you cocky little—"

Paul moved fast. One moment he was using some newspaper to wipe filth from his boots; the next he was right next to Knutter, and his knife was pressed hard against the other man's neck.

"You should mind your manners," said Paul. "I'll tell you what you need to know, and nothing more. That's how we all stay alive. You understand?"

Knutter tried to swallow, but his Adam's apple caught on the edge of the knife.

"Yes," he croaked.

"We'll be on our way, then," said Paul.

He lowered the blade, and Knutter rubbed his throat unhappily.

"I was only asking," he said.

"I know," said Paul.

He was already regretting pulling the knife on Knutter. He had to learn to control his temper; it wouldn't be wise to leave the man angry. Angry people did stupid things.

"Look, I'm sorry," he said. "You know, any time spent down there is too much time."

"Yeah, well," said Knutter. "You shouldn't ought to be pulling knives on friends. Caught me by surprise, you did."

"I'll tell the people who need to know that you did well today," said Paul. "You helped us a lot."

Knutter led them to the door. When he was certain that all was clear, he let them out, and Paul and Steven began making their way home.

"You should have kept his gun until you were sure about him," said Steven.

"Knutter's all right," said Paul. "He just forgets the rules sometimes."

Steven nodded. They walked on for a time.

"Can I have a gun?" Steven asked.

Paul felt a great sadness wash over him as they crossed to Princes Street. It was only a short step from carrying a gun to using it, and an even shorter step after that to being killed by one. He knew that he couldn't keep Steven safe forever, but he still wanted to protect him for just a little while longer.

"Maybe someday," he said. "Maybe."


Like the rest of its kind, the Agron that returned to repair and retrieve the disabled platform had poor eyesight, and was not perceived to be very intelligent. But it was gifted with a keen sense of smell, and even amid the various odors in the tunnel it detected the sour-sweet stink of human vomit. It sniffed its way into the darkness of the tunnel until it found the source, still fresh.

Within seconds, it had raised the alarm.

# CHAPTER SIXTEEN

By avoiding the main hallways, and taking the little-used connectors between the old Scottish National War Memorial and the Royal Palace, listening at corners to ensure that the way was clear before proceeding, Syl and Ani managed to make it to the room adjoining the Great Hall without attracting notice.

"Before I bailed class to find you, Deren asked Toris about the Civil War," whispered Ani, as she helped Syl move the huge armoire that hid the entrance to the spyhole. Syl had discovered the catch that allowed the wooden armoire to slide across the floor, leaving a space just large enough to slip through. Without the catch, the armoire was so heavy that it would take many men to move it.

"Really?" said Syl. "I bet Toris didn't care much for that."

Deren enjoyed taunting Toris almost as much as Ani did. Poor Deren fancied Ani something rotten, thought Syl, and always followed her lead, but Ani seemed to have no interest in him, while Deren would happily have cut off one of his hands if Ani told him to.

"Not much at all."

The old tutor always tried to put the best angle on the conflict, arguing that Illyri society was the better for it, but the truth was that the wounds it had caused were still visible to this day. The animosity between the Diplomats and the Military was proof of that.

The Civil War was one of the darkest periods in Illyri history, a century-long conflict of succession that followed the death of Meus, the Unifier of Worlds, who had laid the foundations of what was known as the First Illyri Empire. The Civil War split Illyri society, even severing individual families. On one side was an elite class of the wealthy and the privileged—among them the Diplomats—who believed that they were best equipped to rule, and that democracy was a failed experiment. A handful of Military leaders sided with them, along with militias from the First Colonies, pressed into service by the Diplomats, who had grown increasingly powerful and ambitious on their offworld bases. Ranged against them were most of the ordinary civilians, the elected politicians, and the majority of senior Military leaders, among them Syl's great-grandfather. Sometimes the war took the form of outright battle on one world or another, but mostly it was a series of truces and agreements, broken by either side, constantly underpinned by low-level guerrilla warfare.

Finally, a lasting agreement was reached to stop the Illyri race from tearing itself apart entirely. A Council of Government was created, to be elected by the people every five sessions, with equal representation by the Military, the civil authorities, and the Diplomats, who emerged from the bloody conflict with even more power than they had enjoyed at the beginning, a testament to their cleverness and, indeed, their ruthlessness. A president, elected for twenty sessions of the Council, was given the casting vote in the event of disagreements. The office of president alternated between the three main groups, and the arrangement had functioned well until the Second Empire began its recent expansion into other systems, and the Diplomatic Corps grew in influence, backed by the Sisterhood. Now the Diplomats dominated the Council, and only the current presidency of Grand Commander Rydus, the most decorated Military leader of his day, kept them from total supremacy.

"So," said Syl. "What did Deren want to know this time?"

"He asked Toris if it could happen again."

Another civil war? It didn't bear thinking about.

"And what did Toris say?" asked Syl.

"Toris said that he believed all sides had learned from the last conflict, which wasn't a real answer."

"Toris is just sorry that we're not all ruled by bald Diplomats," said Syl. "He thinks that the treaty was a mistake, and the Diplomats and their allies were on the verge of winning when the truce was agreed."

"How do you know all this?"

"My father likes to educate me over dinner."

"But if Toris is such a friend of the Corps, why does your father allow him to educate us?"

"Because he says that Toris knows a lot, and his flaws in one area don't necessarily make him unsuited to all," said Syl. She grinned slyly. "My father also says that you should know your enemy."

"I don't think Toris feels the same way. When Deren tried to pursue the subject, Toris got angry and told him to keep quiet and study his history more closely." Ani seemed to reconsider what she had just said. "No, not just angry. I think he was frightened. Do *you* believe that there's a chance of another civil war, Syl?"

Syl pushed Ani into the spyhole and pulled the armoire across behind her, so the gap was closed. There was utter darkness for a moment until she exposed a series of narrow slits, allowing light from the Great Hall to penetrate their hiding place. The Hall was empty for now, but it wouldn't be for long.

"My father says that Grand Commander Rydus is skilled at balancing the demands of the Military and the Diplomats," she replied, "and no Illyri wants a return to civil conflict. Yes, the Diplomats desire more power, but not at the cost of war with the Military. As long as Rydus is president, and the Military remains united, the Diplomats will be kept in check."

She realized that she was using almost the exact words that she had heard her father speak during the last meeting of his advisers in the Great Hall. He had been talking to his own officers, his loyal cadre, without any fear of being overheard by Diplomat spies. But then again, Syl had been listening in, and if she could eavesdrop on meetings in the Hall, could not others do so as well? She knew that the Hall was regularly swept for listening devices, and that her father was careful about how he spoke in unsecured environments, but still . . .

She peered through one of the slits. They gave a surprisingly good view of the chamber, and anything that was said carried clearly. They were also invisible from inside the Great Hall—she'd confirmed that by checking from the other side—for they had been carefully crafted to resemble natural flaws in the materials used to create the fireplace centuries before.

A door opened at the far end of the Hall, and Governor Andrus entered, Balen at his heels. Behind them both came Peris, the captain of the castle guard. Her father spun to face him.

"Why wasn't I informed of their approach?" he said. He spoke quietly, but there was no concealing the fury in his voice.

"We were given no warning," said Peris. "The mothership had a cargo designation when it came through the wormhole. There was no indication that it was a Diplomat vessel, and we didn't even know of a Diplomat presence until the shuttle was making its final approach to Edinburgh."

"Not just a Diplomat presence," said Andrus, "but the Sisterhood!"

Syl's stomach tightened. No member of the Nairene Sisterhood had ever been seen on Earth, and she knew of them only from her father's vocal distrust of the sisters and their ways.

"I'm sorry, Governor," said Peris. "We were deceived."

"But to what end?" said Andrus. "Why would Gradus and his witch arrive in such secrecy?" He turned to Balen. "Where are they now?"

"I put them in the main guest suite," he said. The guest suite was in what had once been a war museum. It was not far from the Governor's House.

"And we're monitoring them?"

Balen shifted awkwardly. This was clearly a question to which he would have preferred to be giving a different answer.

"We were, both visually and aurally," he said. "Unfortunately, both systems appear to have failed. They went down seconds after the Nairene entered the suite. All we're getting is static and white noise. Oh, and some shouting from Grand Consul Gradus, who is demanding to be shown into your presence immediately, but we don't need surveillance to hear him. He's quite loud enough without it."

Something like a smile managed to find its way to Andrus's lips.

"Good. Let him steam for a while. Have we made contact with the mothership?"

"Just the usual courtesies."

"Demand a crew and cargo manifest. Come up with some excuse; I don't care what it is, but I want a list of everybody on that ship, and some hint as to where it might have come from. With luck, there'll be someone on board who might be willing to tell us discreetly what all this is about. In the meantime—"

But Andrus was destined to get no further with his instructions. They heard the sound of voices approaching, and the door to the Great Hall burst open to admit an extremely tall, wide-shouldered Illyri in shimmering golden robes, his head shaved and his fingers adorned with jewels—the sign of a senior Diplomat, for promotion through the ranks of the Corps was marked by the giving of rings. He was surrounded by his own private soldiers, recently arrived on a second shuttle, and members of the Securitat, Vena the Skunk among them. They in turn were being watched by five members of the castle guard, who had been forced through the doors by the sheer weight of opposing numbers. The guards looked helplessly at Peris, who could only simmer silently at the intrusion.

"Grand Consul Gradus," said Andrus, with strained politeness. "How good of you to join us. I was just about to send my aide to accompany you, but I see that you have discovered the way yourself."

Gradus gave a small bow, but there was no humility in it.

"I was afraid that I might grow too used to the luxury of my surroundings, and forget my purpose here," he replied. As he spoke, he walked around the Great Hall, taking in its suits of armor and displays of weaponry: the swords, the pikes, the old trench mortars that stood like small cannons on the floor. He seemed to find the cavalry armor by the fireplace particularly interesting, and commented upon it.

"What animal was it that the humans rode while wearing this?" he asked.

"Horses," said Andrus.

"I should like to see one, or even ride one myself, if it can be arranged."

His voice was oddly high, but there was a discordancy underlying it, like a poorly tuned instrument playing a beautiful piece of music. From her vantage point, Syl thought him a detestable figure. There was something about him that made her profoundly uneasy: a softness, a decadence. His robes had been cut to make him appear even broader in the shoulder and slimmer in the waist, and he was wearing a strong scent that even from a distance caused her nose to itch. She saw that his rings—dozens of them—were so embedded in the flesh of his fingers that they would be impossible to remove, as if he'd been born into such finery and his fingers had been thus adorned from the cradle.

"Perhaps if you had given us some notice of your arrival, we might have been better prepared to receive you," said Andrus. "We could even have sent a horse. We were not expecting the head of the Diplomatic Corps to arrive unexpectedly in a cargo vessel, not unless he has fallen some distance in the eyes of worlds."

Balen permitted himself a smile, and Syl smiled to herself too, wishing she had her father's way with words.

Some of the castle guards continued to jostle with the soldiers and Securitats while Gradus stood in their midst, his face reddening as he quietly seethed. It was clearly unwise to let this situation continue, particularly with so many loaded weapons in the room. Andrus raised a hand, and ordered the guards to stand down. After a strained pause during which it appeared that Gradus might be unwilling to do the same, he too waved a long finger, and his protectors lowered their weapons.

Gradus took a seat at the council table. Andrus followed suit.

"To answer your question," said Gradus, "the tensions between the Military and the Diplomatic Corps mean that any journey, however minor, becomes the subject of speculation and invites the attentions of spies and informers. I preferred to arrive here unburdened by advance gossip. Send your guards away, Andrus, and I will do the same. Then we can talk."

Andrus instructed Peris to clear the room. The captain took particular pleasure in waiting for Vena to leave before he followed her outside, a small but biting demonstration of his senior position. Only Andrus, Gradus, and Balen were left.

"I still seem to be outnumbered," said Gradus, with a dramatic little huff. "That hardly seems fair."

He looked to the door expectantly. After a moment, it opened to reveal a figure dressed entirely in deep red flowing robes, its face obscured by a veil of fine lace. Ani's fingers tightened around Syl's elbow, but when Syl glanced at her, Ani was simply staring wide-eyed at the vision in red, apparently unaware of her grip on Syl's arm. Behind the figure could be seen the faces of both castle guards and Corps soldiers, all of them staring after the new arrival with a mixture of fascination and fear.

"Governor Andrus," said Gradus, "permit me to introduce you to Syrene, Archmage of the Nairene Sisterhood, and my wife."

Ani released the breath she had been holding, and she and Syl instinctively moved closer to the observation slits as Syrene approached the table, her feet so obscured by her scarlet finery that she seemed to glide across the floor in a cascade of red. She did not speak, nor did she acknowledge Andrus or Balen. She simply took a seat to the right of Gradus, and placed her gloved hands upon the ancient wood of the Council chamber table.

"You are welcome, Archmage," said Andrus.

"He doesn't sound like he means it," whispered Ani.

"He doesn't," said Syl. "He hates the Sisterhood."

"Why?"

"Not now. Later. Just listen."

Ani did as she was told. This was interesting. In the past, the thrill of entering the spyhole had come from the fact that they had been doing something forbidden, and not from anything they had subsequently seen or heard. But this, this was another matter entirely: a Nairene sister here, on Earth. And not just any sister either, but the Archmage herself, the legendary Syrene. Ani felt shivery and warm all at once.

Syrene did not acknowledge Andrus's words. The red veil moved as she slowly looked around the room, her eyes still concealed.

"To business," said Gradus. "I bring you sad news, Andrus. Our beloved president, Rydus, has died."

Andrus reeled back in his chair in shock. Syl felt for him: her father had served under Rydus, and had been closer to him than to his own father. Rydus nurtured his career, and had stood beside him when Andrus married the Lady Orianne, Syl's mother. It was Rydus who had made Andrus the senior governor on Earth after the conquest, effectively entrusting him with the rule of this most unusual of planets.

"How?" asked her father. He seemed barely able to utter the word.

"An embolism. It appears that he died in his sleep."

"When?"

"Three weeks ago."

Three weeks! Syl was amazed. News from Illyr often took a long time to get to outlying planets in the Empire, but such important information could have been communicated to Andrus sooner. A system of transmitting stations linked Illyr to the various wormholes. Her father could have learned of Rydus's death in days, rather than weeks, but Gradus had kept it from him. Even Syl could figure out what that meant: Gradus and the Corps had full control of the transmitters, and had deliberately prevented news of Rydus's death from reaching Andrus on Earth.

"I decided to inform you in person, as a mark of respect, instead of allowing the news to come to you through other channels, perhaps polluted by hearsay," Gradus added.

"What kind of hearsay?"

"You know just as well as I that when a senior figure dies in such circumstances, the rumor mill begins to grind out untruths. There will always be those who whisper of plots and dark dealings, but I have brought with me the reports of the physicians. I will have them sent to your secretary, but you will see that there can be no doubt about how Rydus died."

Syl watched her father swallow his grief as he began to take in the implications of what Gradus had told him.

"And what of the presidency?" he asked. "I assume that you have put yourself forward as a candidate. Or has it gone beyond that, and you have already taken office?"

It was widely known that Gradus desired the position of president for himself, but had resigned himself to waiting a long time to ascend to it since Rydus was only six sessions into his term of office, and had shown no signs of ill health. Long living was common in his family, or had been until now.

"You misunderstand me, Andrus. It is true that I might have had such ambitions in the past, but as I grow older, I have come to realize that the burdens of the office far outweigh its benefits. I have decided to leave it to one better suited to these demands.

"With that in mind, I have instructed the Corps not to take advantage of Rydus's sudden and unexpected demise. We have not sought to have a Diplomat candidate installed. Instead, we have agreed that the Military should continue to hold the office. Rydus should have enjoyed a much longer hold on the presidential throne. It seemed unbecoming to profit from his mortality and create the impression that the Corps was interested only in furthering its own ends. We, like you, have only the interests of the empire at heart."

If Andrus had been taken aback by the news of Rydus's death, this latest revelation seemed more shocking still. It went against all he had believed, or suspected, of Gradus's nature that the Grand Consul should decline to extend the Corps's influence by assuming the presidency himself, or at the very least ensuring that some Diplomat puppet of his choice took office while Gradus pulled the strings.

"So who is now president?" asked Andrus.

"We are fortunate that General Krake was willing to put his name forward, and was unanimously approved by the governing council. Long may he live, and wise be his rule."

Andrus's eyes did not leave Gradus, but Syl saw Balen glance from the governor to the still, silent form of Syrene. Krake had been one of the few Military officers to ignore the unofficial, but widely accepted, rule about keeping the Sisterhood away from the Military, and had taken one of the sisters as his bride. Her name was Merida, and she was a favorite of Syrene, who had mentored her since early childhood.

All were silent for a time. Andrus and Gradus appeared locked in some unspoken conflict of their own. Gradus was smiling, as if inviting Andrus to voice his suspicions in the presence of the Archmage.

But now Syrene lifted her veil so that it fell back in delicate folds to reveal her face. Her skin was intricately tattooed, filigree and strange animal forms spilling down from her skull and across her forehead, adorning her cheeks—each of which was decorated with a red eye like that on the side of the shuttle—and framing lips so full and red that they seemed on the verge of bursting. She was paler than most Illyri, for little light penetrated the deepest recesses of the Marque, where the Sisterhood hid their secrets.

She surveyed the room languidly, her eyes wide and cool. Suddenly Ani put her hands to the sides of her head, kneading her temples as though she were in pain.

"Ani?" said Syl. "What's wrong?"

"Don't you feel it?" said Ani. "Don't you feel *her*?"

Syrene's gaze alighted on the fireplace, and the ghost of what might have been a smile crossed her face. Ani moved her right hand from her temple to her mouth, wincing as if in pain, biting hard on her knuckles. Syl put an arm around her, concerned, but Ani didn't respond.

Syrene turned to Syl's father, cocking her head to one side, and the eye on her left cheek appeared to blink once as she spoke. "Are you quite sure that we're alone here, Lord Andrus?"

"Of course we are, Archmage," he said.

"I see. How very interesting."

Syrene stood and pulled her veil over her face once more, hiding her searching eyes.

"Come, husband," she said. "His lordship is in shock. We will continue our conversation later. Let us leave him to mourn all that he has lost. . . . "

"Yes, of course," said Gradus, rising to his feet to follow the Red Sister.

" . . . and all that may yet be lost," concluded Syrene.

Gradus stopped briefly, and seemed about to say something more to Andrus, but then merely chuckled and strode away, having clearly decided that Syrene's parting shot was better than any he could muster.

They all understood the truth of what had transpired, even if none was willing to say it aloud: there had been a quiet coup on Illyr.

The Sisterhood had made its move on the presidency.

# CHAPTER SEVENTEEN

Ani and Syl allowed a safe amount of time to elapse before they left the spyhole and returned to the Governor's House. There was to be some respite from the confines of the castle, though: Althea, who had a gift for providing solace to those in pain, whether physical, emotional, or psychological, had volunteered to help with the wounded at the Royal Edinburgh Hospital on Morningside Terrace, and had convinced Governor Andrus that Syl and Ani should be allowed to attend with her. Empathy was a quality strongly valued among the Illyri; those who understood the reality of pain and suffering were likely to do their best to avoid inflicting it on others. So Syl and Ani held the hands of the injured, both Illyri and those humans who were willing to accept consolation from any source.

Illyri technology had brought huge advances in human medical techniques. ProGen artificial skin was routinely used to treat burns, replacing the need for skin grafts. Diseased internal organs were replaced with organs grown on artificial "scaffolds"—animal organs that had been stripped of their living cells, leaving only a basic framework of blood vessels, and repopulated with cells from a patient's own body. Gene therapy cured genetic defects. Nanoparticles and stem cell therapies targeted everything from diabetes to cancer. Even human aging could be slowed. There were still some humans who objected to such treatments on religious grounds, and others who spread stories that all such efforts were part of a secret Illyri plot to undermine the human race. But most recognized the benefits of being able to easily replace damaged or worn internal organs, and human life expectancy had already increased significantly as a result.

Syl and Ani were exhausted by the time they returned to the castle, and went straight to their respective quarters to wash, change, and eat.

A small group had gathered in the governor's private chambers. Lord Andrus himself was there, as was Balen. General Danis lay back in an armchair, his legs stretched before him, his feet crossed. The last arrival was a young female wearing a mix of human and Illyri clothing, her hair short but unkempt, her eyes dark and watchful. She stood by the door, and although she seemed to be relaxed, there was about her the sense of an animal tensed and ready to spring. Her name was Meia, and she was Lord Andrus's chief intelligence officer.

Balen served wine. Only Meia declined.

"Why don't you ever drink?" Danis asked.

Meia pondered the question. "I can, but it disagrees with my system," she said at last. "And I prefer to keep a clear head."

"Very wise," said Danis, taking a deep draft from his own glass. "I hope to be as wise as you someday, although your choice of jewelry raises questions about the extent of that wisdom."

He gestured with his glass at Meia's neck, where a cross hung alongside a Muslim crescent moon, a Hindu aum on an amulet, and even a Shinto torii, or gate. Meia quickly hid them away.

"I have no difficulty accepting the concept of a creator," said Meia. "Why should you?"

"Because—" Danis caught himself, and swallowed whatever he had been about to say, choosing instead an alternative track. "Your views on the nature of the universe are fascinating, I'm sure, but I'm more interested to hear you explain the purpose of a Military intelligence service that couldn't warn us of the arrival of the Grand Consul and his witch-wife until they were on our doorstep telling us about dead presidents!"

His voice had risen steadily throughout this sentence until it was virtually a roar. The room was soundproofed, and had been swept for listening devices before the meeting, but it was hard to believe that there was anyone in the immediate environs who did not now know that Danis was unhappy.

"My orders are to monitor events on Earth, not keep an eye on the activities of the Corps in the wider universe," said Meia. "If you wish me to do that, General, I may have to hire an assistant."

"First Birdoswald, and now this," said Danis. "Perhaps it's not an assistant you require, but a replacement."

"One might say the same about you, General," said Meia. "How goes the War on Terror? Have you crushed the Resistance yet, or did I miss that while I was watching body parts being collected on the Royal Mile?"

Danis rose from his chair. It wasn't clear what he planned to do, but it did seem to involve some harm to Meia. The object of his anger remained motionless. She was more than a match for Danis, and she knew it.

Lord Andrus raised a hand. "Stop it, both of you. We have enough enemies in the castle without adding to them from our own number."

He sipped his wine, and frowned. The taste of it, usually so pleasant, now seemed like vinegar on his tongue. The events of the day had ruined his appetite for many things. He put the glass aside, and steepled his hands upon his desk.

"What are our esteemed guests doing at the moment?" he asked Balen.

"The Grand Consul is dining in his room with two of his aides."

"And his wife?"

"She requested separate quarters, and chose to dine alone. Only her handmaid attends her."

"Maybe she and her beloved are not getting along," said Danis. "One of them might come over to our side and tell us what's going on."

"Have they made any attempt to contact the mothership?"

"None. Nor have we received a request for a communication channel."

"Could they have brought equipment of their own?"

"It's possible, but we're monitoring the rooms for any signs of electronic traffic."

Andrus looked to Meia. "I sense that you have something you'd like to say."

Meia nodded. "Why did the Grand Consul choose to arrive today, in the aftermath of twin bomb attacks so close to the castle?"

Andrus glanced at Danis. Danis shrugged. "Why not? Maybe he's come to mourn his nephew."

"The Grand Consul is known to be zealous about protecting his personal safety, but he is equally careful, if not more so, about looking after his wife," said Meia patiently. "The Sisterhood would be most displeased if some harm were to befall Syrene. She is destined to become Mage upon the death of Ezil."

"There's no sign of the old bitch dying yet," said Danis. "More's the pity. Then again, she may already be dead, given how long it's been since anyone caught sight of her. Good riddance to her if she is."

"Go on," said Andrus, ignoring his general while also silently agreeing with him on the subject of Ezil.

"So, it was out of character to risk a landing here while the smoke from bomb attacks was still rising above the city," said Meia. "But the Grand Consul is always consistent in his character, at least in this regard. Therefore we have a contradiction."

She moved closer to the fire, and to the other three Illyri in the room.

"The members of the Resistance too are consistent in their actions. They do not endanger their own civilians. They are careful to limit their attacks to Military installations and personnel. When possible they'll also target the Diplomats and the Securitats, although the Corps prefers to conduct its business from behind walls and shields, so they have more opportunities to strike at us. It is completely inconsistent with the Resistance's patterns of behavior to plant devices in an area like the Royal Mile, which hosts human businesses and extensive pedestrian traffic. We lost ten soldiers today, and three Securitats, but four humans also died, and dozens more on both sides were injured."

"Could the Resistance be stepping up its campaign, or changing its tactics?" asked Andrus.

"I don't believe so. If a decision like that had been made, news would have reached us. We're not entirely without our sources within the Resistance, and its leadership here is quite clear in its methodology: no civilian casualties."

"A splinter group, then," said Danis, "one that doesn't believe the Resistance is radical enough."

"Again, the Resistance has its own ways of dealing with dissenters," said Meia. "Warnings are usually enough. After that, there are always limbs that can be broken. It's never had to go further, but anyone who chose to kill and injure civilians as a protest against the Resistance's leadership wouldn't last very long. No, I don't believe the Resistance planted those devices."

"Then who did?" asked Danis. "Us?"

"No," said Meia, "not quite."

She waited. Eventually, Andrus said what they were all thinking.

"The Diplomatic Corps? The Securitats?"

"It would explain why the Grand Consul was not concerned about landing in the aftermath," said Meia. "He knew that there was no danger of further attacks."

"But why?" asked Danis. "To what end?"

"To undermine the governor and, by extension, the Military rule on Earth. A new president has come to power on Illyr, one who, despite his Military credentials, is probably under the sway of the Sisterhood. The Diplomatic Corps wants complete control of this planet. It does not want to share it with the Military. What better way to demonstrate the Military's failures than by having bombs exploding on the doorstep of the planet's senior governor, or to prove the bravery of the Grand Consul than by his willingness to land despite the threat?"

"You seem very certain of this," said Andrus.

"Not certain, but it fits with the available facts. Then there is the matter of the suicides," she added.

"Suicides?" said Danis.

"I know that you've been looking into what happened to the Grand Consul's nephew Thaios at Birdoswald. The evidence suggests that he killed himself rather than be captured. There was a similar incident in Iran last month, also involving a relative of Grand Consul Gradus."

"I had asked Danis to look into the death of Thaois," said Lord Andrus. "It seems that you might have spared him the trouble. Do you have proof?"

"An eyewitness in Tehran. A senior sub-consul, a cousin of Gradus, was cornered near a mosque after his convoy was ambushed. Rather than be captured, it seems that he activated an infrasonic grenade. The consequences were . . . messy."

Andrus considered what had been said. "Find out more," he told Meia. "I want to know if there's a connection between these two deaths and Gradus's arrival on Earth."

At that moment, there was a knock on the door. Rupe, the sergeant who had earlier helped Syl and Ani in their confrontation with the Corps, was standing outside.

"I gave orders not to be disturbed, Sergeant," said Andrus, and there was no mistaking the unhappiness in his voice.

Rupe, though, didn't blink. He had been with Andrus for many years, and he knew when the situation called for the exercise of a little personal discretion.

"My lord, I thought you might forgive the interruption on this occasion," he said. "The Archmage Syrene has sent a message. She's asking to see your daughter."

# CHAPTER EIGHTEEN

Katherine Kerr worried about her sons. She had always worried about them; it was the curse of being a mother. They were born willful boys. Paul was the volatile one, Steven quieter and more cautious, but both were stubborn, and once they had made a decision, there was no changing their minds. Even though they were dissimilar in many ways, they had somehow found a way to act as a unit, with one perfectly complementing the other.

It helped that Steven worshipped Paul, but Paul in turn was hugely protective of his younger brother. He had been both proud and concerned when Steven had asked to play a part in the Resistance. His mother had known better than to try to stop Steven, just as she had not tried to stop his older brother from joining. In both cases she knew that, had she objected, or put obstacles in their way, they would have proceeded without her approval, and perhaps put themselves in greater danger as a consequence. She knew that Paul would look after his brother, but not a day went by when she didn't pray for them both, just in case.

Their father had died five years earlier. The Securitats had picked him up during a sweep following the assassination of one of their number. Bob Kerr had been hurrying to work at Edinburgh Zoo, where he had responsibility for the Malayan tapirs, among other species. One of the tapirs was due to give birth after the long gestation typical of the animal, and Bob wanted to be present in case there were problems. When he tried to explain this as the Securitats bundled him into one of their transports, he was struck in the chest with an electric baton. He died of a heart attack in the back of the truck. From that day on, Katherine knew that her sons would fight, and they were far from alone.

It was the great strength of the Resistance: most of its operatives were very young. They had an energy and innovativeness that their elders lacked. Perhaps it was because it was their generation that was being pressed into offworld service by the Illyri, forced to fight wars on distant planets in the name of an empire that had taken their own world by force. But it had also recently become known that the Illyri had contaminated Earth's water supply, although so far chemical analysis had revealed no trace of it. This was no idle gossip, or unfounded rumor; it came from some of the Illyri who had defected. They spoke of a testosterone suppressant, a simple, harmless means of keeping human aggression in check. The drug inhibited the pituitary gland from secreting the master hormones LH and FSH that stimulated testosterone production.

However, the surge in the body's testosterone production during puberty rendered teenagers, both male and female, less susceptible to the Illyri drug. In the years since the possibility of the suppressant's existence were raised, steps had been taken to counteract its effects: testosterone supplements, the boiling of water before use, or preferably, only drinking water that had come from clean, natural springs. The problem was that the suppressant had a cumulative effect, and most men and women had been drinking the contaminated water for so long that it was unclear how long its suppressive effects would last. It was the new generation that remained immune, and so it was that the burden of fighting the oppressors fell on them.

Now, as she heard the front door open and the boys enter, Mrs. Kerr felt a surge of relief and gave a small prayer of thanks. She had not asked Paul where they were going when they left earlier that day, but she could always tell when it was a particularly risky task being undertaken. It was as if their personalities switched when they were tense: Paul would grow quiet, and Steven would babble as though he thought he might never get the chance to talk again.

They had been like that at breakfast, and part of her had wanted to lock them in their rooms so that someone else would be forced to take on their duties instead.

And then she had heard the explosions echoing from the Royal Mile, and she had found herself frozen in place, forgetting to lift the iron until the sour smell of burning fabric filled the room, rendering a pair of Steven's trousers useless. Was that what her boys were doing now, planting bombs? Did they get away in time? She had spent the rest of the day waiting, wondering if a knock would come at the door, if she would open it and see one of the Resistance people, perhaps a man with his wife in tow, or his sister, or his mother, someone to console her as she was told that her sons were dead. . . .

But here they were: her boys. They were home. They were safe. They would be with her for another day. She hugged them both, but she noticed that Steven held on to her for a little longer, and when she looked at his face, she could see how pale he was.

"What happened?" she said.

"He just saw something that made him ill," said Paul. "He'll be fine."

"Sugar: that's what he needs."

She took a bottle of Irn Bru from the fridge and poured a tall glass for Steven, and another for Paul. She didn't drink the stuff. She had never been one for fizzy drinks, but the boys had always liked Irn Bru. Along with whisky, it counted as the Scottish national drink.

"Drink it down," she told Steven. "It'll do you good. I'll start on your dinner now that you're back."

"I'll have to go out again soon," said Paul, and she knew what he meant. He'd have to make a report to be made about whatever they'd seen, or done, that afternoon.

"The explosions . . . ," she said.

"It wasn't us," said Paul, and she was relieved to hear it. There were reports that humans had died along with Illyri, and she didn't want her sons to be responsible for that kind of carnage.

There was a knock on the front door. The boys looked at each other, and then at their mother. They weren't expecting anyone. Mrs. Kerr wiped her hands on her apron, even though they weren't wet or dirty, and tried to keep her fear in check.

"I'll get it," she said. "Stay where you are."

She put the chain on the door before opening it. A large man stood on the path, keeping his distance. She had never seen him before.

"Mrs. Kerr?" he asked.

"Yes?" she said. "Can I help you?"

"My name is Knutter," he said. "I'm wondering if your lads are home yet?"

Something trickled from beneath his hair and slowly ran down his forehead. She watched the blood catch on his eyebrow and drip on his lashes.

Knutter blinked.

"Run," he whispered.

She slammed the door closed just as she heard the *slap* of a pulse weapon firing. Knutter's upper body hit the door as he died, and the thick glass cracked with the impact. She turned to see Paul and Steven staring at her from the kitchen table.

"Get out of here!" she screamed, as the front door exploded behind her. Something struck her in the back and sent her sprawling on her belly. The glass in the kitchen window broke, and two gas grenades skittered across the floor like silver rats. The room filled with choking fumes. Galateans stepped over her from behind, and more entered through the kitchen door. The aliens wore breathing apparatus to protect them from the gas. One of them knelt beside her and cuffed her hands behind her back before dragging her to her feet. The base of her spine ached. She guessed that she had been struck by a mild pulse blast, for she could feel no blood flowing and she was numb rather than in real pain. Her eyes were watering, but she could still see what was happening to her sons.

The Galateans were on them, easily pinning them to the kitchen floor, clicking and croaking at each other through their masks.

They seemed almost amused as the boys tried to struggle against them, even as they coughed and choked. One of the Galateans, tiring of the game, struck Paul on the head with the base of a pulser, and then it was over. Steven was already as helpless as a swaddled baby, his hands secured behind him, his legs shackled together with magnetized cuffs. Blood streaked Paul's face, and he was propped up between two Galateans as a third slapped him hard to bring him round. His eyes opened; he had trouble focusing, but at least he was conscious. Men had been killed accidentally by Galateans who had set out only to subdue them. The amphibians did not always know, or care to know, their own strength. Their hands were on Steven now, searching him, but he and Paul had left their knives in the umbrella stand when they entered, as their mother did not like them to be armed at the dinner table. When the Galateans were satisfied that Steven was unarmed, they lifted him from the floor and set him on his feet between his captors, coughing in the fumes.

The Galateans sprayed the air with a chemical compound, dispersing the gas before they removed their masks. They also sprayed a diluted form of the compound on the boys and their mother, relieving the stinging in their eyes and throats. A female Illyri Securitat in black and gold entered the house through the front door and walked to the kitchen. Beyond her, Paul could make out the shape of a body facedown on the garden path. He recognized Knutter from his shirt. Then his view was blocked as an Agron entered behind the Illyri, sniffing at the air.

The Securitat leaned against the frame of the kitchen door and stared at the boys. Paul knew Vena at once, for the Resistance had photos of most of the senior Illyri, but he tried to keep that knowledge from his face. If Vena realized that he knew who she was, it would be confirmation that he was a member of the Resistance. Their only hope was to play dumb, and a small, forlorn hope at that. The presence of this particular Illyri in their home meant that they were in very serious trouble indeed. Vena was not usually one to make house calls.

The Agron paused by her side.

"Are these the ones?" she asked.

The Agron advanced on Paul, sniffed at him, then turned its attention to Steven. Its eyes were silver, and its sight was poor. It saw the world through scent. It placed its nose close to Steven's face, its nostrils so close to his mouth that he felt its mucus on his lips as it exhaled.

The Agron nodded. It gripped Steven by the hair and pulled his head back.

"Sm-smelled you," it stuttered roughly in Steven's ear; most of the Agrons had a basic grasp of language. *"Smelled."*

"Good," said Vena. "Very good."

Paul's scalp was bleeding badly. The Agron keep darting glances at the blood, and its nostrils twitched hard. Eventually it could stand the scent no longer. A rough pink tongue slipped from its lips and lapped at Paul's face. One of the Galateans pushed the Agron away. It looked unhappy.

"Smelled," it repeated, and pointed a stubby finger at itself. "Good."

Summoned by Vena, Securitats flooded into the house. That was just like them, thought Paul: wait until the hard work was done and any threat had been subdued, then enter with boots and fists flying.

"Take the boys away," said Vena to one of the new arrivals. "The mother too."

The Galatean pointed at the Agron and clicked a question.

"Let it drink the blood," said Vena. "It's earned its reward."

As the Kerrs were led away, they heard the Agron fall on Knutter's corpse, and they tried to close their ears to the sound of it quenching its thirst.

# CHAPTER NINETEEN

Unsurprisingly, Lord Andrus was troubled by the fact that the Archmage Syrene wished to meet with his daughter, but he did his best not to show it. He had played this game for a long time, and little now had the capacity to catch him off guard, but today had been a day of surprises, few of them pleasant. This was easily the most unwelcome of all.

"Why?" he asked.

"Why does she want to meet with Syl, or why should we allow it?" asked Meia.

"Both."

"Perhaps the Sisterhood is recruiting," said Danis to Meia, "in which case you might wish to put your name forward. Duplicity and untrustworthiness would seem to be essential for membership, so you should be wearing a red cloak before the night is out."

Meia ignored him. "I can't answer the first question. But to the second I would say that it's an opening, and openings should be exploited. We don't know why Syrene has chosen to accompany her husband here, and we have no idea why Gradus should be present either. He didn't have to deliver the news of the president's death personally. It's not as if he cares about your grief. We're entirely in the dark here. Now Syrene has made a move. Do we ignore it, or do we move in response?"

"My daughter is not a spy," said Andrus. "She is not equipped to trade blows with an Archmage."

"Syl is clever," said Meia.

"Not as clever as a Red Sister."

"I have studied the Sisterhood for many years," said Meia. "They interest me."

"And why is that?" asked Danis.

"They worship a god. Their god is knowledge."

"And what have you learned about the Sisterhood and their god of knowledge?"

"Very little. They guard themselves well, and share nothing with outsiders. I would be surprised if even Gradus knew very much of what his wife is thinking most of the time, and I am certain that he knows nothing at all of what goes on in the Marque.

"But I know this: arrogance is the Sisterhood's weakness. They have grown more and more arrogant as they have engaged with the world beyond the Marque. Everything they have encountered has confirmed their superiority, most particularly the weakness of males. Syrene believes that she is cleverer than anyone she meets, cleverer even than the most senior of her own sisters, Ezil and the First Five apart, and even then she must feel that the Mage's powers are waning. She will underestimate Syl, and in my experience, Syl is not to be underestimated."

"We're talking about a sixteen-year-old!" Danis scoffed. "She's only a fraction older than my daughter, and Ani could be out-thought by a goldfish."

"Ani is not to be underestimated either," said Meia. "You are in error about your own blood."

Andrus watched the exchange with interest. Meia was Syl's final line of defense. In the event that the castle's defenses were breached, or a fatal tilting of the balance occurred in favor of the Diplomats, she was to get Syl and Ani to safety, and kill anyone who stood in her way. She had been watching Syl ever since Andrus had quietly ordered her to join him on Earth shortly after Syl's birth. Meia was ruthless, implacable.

Ageless.

"And what if some harm comes to my underestimated daughter?" Andrus asked.

"No harm will come to her. We have eyes and ears in that room, and anyway, Syrene would not be so foolish as to hurt Syl. There would be no advantage in doing so, and Syrene is always looking for an advantage."

Andrus looked to Danis and Balen.

"Your thoughts?"

"I would not let her go," said Balen, who was almost as fond of Syl as he was of his own children.

"Danis?"

"It pains me to say it, but Meia is right. We should permit the meeting to go ahead, but we'll monitor everything, and we'll keep guards outside the door: double the number that Syrene has. If Syrene objects to their presence, we walk away."

"And she won't object," said Meia. "She would expect nothing less."

"Would you send Ani if our positions were reversed?" asked Andrus.

Danis considered the question. "I would, but I'd warn Syrene first, so she knew what she was letting herself in for. She wouldn't get a word in edgeways."

Andrus was quiet for a moment, then nodded to Meia.

"Bring my daughter here."


Syl and Ani, now clean and fed, were back together in Syl's rooms. They were half watching old films, both human and Illyri. The human ones tended to be more fun. Illyri ideas of art placed the emphasis on improving minds first; entertainment came a distant second. One of the greatest Illyri plays, *Of Stars and Seeds*, was seventeen hours long, and included breaks for meals and a suggested two-hour intermission for an extended nap.

Ani was subdued, though. She had been ever since their little eavesdropping adventure. At the hospital she had listened more than talked, which was fine with those to whom she tended. But shortly after they had reached Syl's rooms, she had suffered a nosebleed so severe that Syl had wanted to summon a physician. Ani had pleaded with her not to.

"Please, Syl," she said. "I don't want them examining me, not over this. It'll pass."

"Has it happened before?"

"A couple of times, when I've felt . . . *stressed*."

"What do you mean, stressed?" said Syl, but Ani didn't want to pursue the subject.

"Can we talk about it another time?"

"We don't have to if you don't want to," said Syl. "Just tip your head forward. We'll wait for it to pass."

When the knock came on the door, it was Syl who answered. Meia stood before her, flanked by two guards, and Syl felt the blood drain from her face.

Her earlier adventure on the Royal Mile must have been discovered. There could be no other reason for Meia to be there. Her fears were apparently confirmed when Meia spoke. "Your father wishes to speak with you."

Syl nodded dumbly. She looked to Ani, whose face now reflected Syl's own concerns. She felt Meia's hand on her shoulder.

"You're not in trouble, Syl," said Meia softly, then added, with a quizzical look, "Should you be?"

Syl felt a flood of relief so strong that her body sagged like a puppet whose strings had been relaxed.

"No," she said. "Absolutely not."

"Do you want me to come with you?" Ani asked.

"You'll have to stay here," said Meia. "I'm sorry. I'll have her back to you as soon as I can."

Syl grabbed a cloak, for the castle had grown cold, and went with Meia.

• • •

Syl had always been somewhat in awe of Meia. Nobody else on the governor's staff was like her, so strange yet so composed, her life lived in the shadows. She deferred only to Lord Andrus, and no other. Everyone else she appeared to judge on a sliding scale that moved between the two extremes of contempt and amusement. Ani said that Danis, her father, hated Meia, but when Syl had asked Lord Andrus about it, he told her that this was not true.

"They snarl at each other like chained dogs, but the truth is that they are more similar than different," he said. "If anyone ever harmed Meia, Danis would hunt them to the ends of the universe, and if Danis does not die a natural death, Meia will slaughter those responsible in their beds."

Syl didn't quite trust Meia, though. It didn't pay to trust spies. Now she fell into step beside her, wondering why she had been summoned. She noticed that she and Meia were now as tall as each other, for Meia was short for an Illyri.

"You didn't look pleased to see me at your door," said Meia.

"I wasn't expecting company, that's all."

"Really?" Meia did not look at her, but Syl could see an eyebrow lift in disbelief. "So it had nothing to do with the fact that you were outside the castle walls today?"

Syl didn't know what to say, so she said nothing. Meia, unfortunately, was a trained interrogator, and ignoring her wouldn't make her go away.

"Well?" Meia persisted. "I don't suppose you saw anyone planting bombs while you were out shopping?"

Syl swallowed hard. "I *am* in trouble, then. You were lying."

"I only lie professionally, not personally," said Meia. "Your father doesn't know anything about your little trip today, and with luck he won't find out. He'll chain you to a wall otherwise, and feed you from a bowl to make sure you don't go wandering again."

"You're not going to tell him?"

"Why would I? You weren't hurt, and neither was your friend Ani. You need to be more careful, though. Your disguises may work for you at a distance, but up close your skin will soon begin to give you away. It would be a significant coup if the Resistance were to capture the daughter of the governor. You'd be worth a lot in trade, assuming they didn't decide that it was better to kill you straightaway."

"They'd kill me?"

"They might, if you fell into the hands of the wrong men, and if I didn't find you first."

"And would you? Would you find me?"

Meia stopped, and looked her square in the eye for the first time since Syl had left her room.

"Yes. Don't doubt that for a moment. But let's hope that the necessity for it doesn't arise. In the meantime, try to restrain your exploratory impulses for a few days, both inside and outside the castle. The situation is volatile."

Meia walked on, Syl beside her.

"Because of Gradus and the Sisterhood?" asked Syl, and knew immediately that she had said too much. Meia kept walking, but her steps faltered for a moment.

"What do you know about Gradus and the Red Sister?" she said.

Syl trod carefully.

"I saw them arrive," she said.

"What keen eyes you must have. My understanding was that they were hidden from us all."

"And everybody in the castle is talking about it," Syl continued. She hated being questioned by Meia, because Meia was immune to her charms and her evasions.

"I told your father that you were clever, but don't try to be too clever, and particularly not with me," said Meia. "I know more about you than you might think, and you'd be better off having me as an ally than an adversary. So shall we be honest with each other, Syl?"

"Okay."

Meia allowed the guards to move out of earshot.

"I saw you and Ani in the vicinity of the Great Hall, and you were moving like criminals. What were you doing there? No lies, Syl."

"We were eavesdropping."

"That chamber is soundproofed. I checked it myself."

"I know a place, a hiding hole."

"Do you now? We might make a spy of you yet."

"I don't want to be a spy."

"I'm surprised. Given your actions, you seem to be doing your best to apply for the job. You'll have to show me how you managed that little piece of business. I'd be most interested to find out."

They moved on to her father's chambers, stopping within sight of the door, and Meia raised a finger to Syl in warning, the nail short and unadorned.

"Tell me truly, Syl. Did you come face-to-face with the Archmage Syrene at any point during the day?"

"No."

"You're sure?"

"Yes."

"There is no way that she could have known of your presence at the meeting?"

Syl took a moment before replying. It was one thing giving up her own secrets, but another betraying Ani's.

"I was hidden from sight," said Syl. "I don't see how she could have known. But . . ."

"Go on."

"There was a moment when the Archmage seemed to look around the room, as though she knew someone was present who shouldn't have been. She stared straight at . . ." *careful, careful*, ". . . at me, at where I was hiding, even though she couldn't have seen me."

Meia didn't look pleased to hear this.

"The Sisterhood is an unknown quantity, Syl. Some refer to them as witches, and it may be that, in the depths of the Marque, they have developed skills that are beyond the rest of us. Does she frighten you, the Archmage?"

"A little."

"Good. She should. How do you dance, Syl?"

"Dance?" Syl looked confused. "I've never really tried. Why?"

Meia put a hand on the small of her back, and guided her to where her father was waiting.

"Because," she said, "you're about to dance with the Red Sister."

# CHAPTER TWENTY

Paul and Steven had been separated from their mother. Their last glimpse of her came as she was being helped into a regular police patrol car, the copper placing his hand on her head so that she wouldn't injure herself. That, at least, was cause for hope: she was with the Lothian and Borders Police, not the Securitat. The Lothian and Borders didn't torture women, or lose them in their secret prisons.

Not yet.

The armored Securitat transport had two metal benches along either side of its interior, and a pair of cages at the end. The boys were spared the cages, but their heads were covered by hoods as soon as they sat down, and magnetic collars were placed around their necks and activated, holding them uncomfortably upright against the body of the truck as it wound its way through the city streets.

It was Paul who risked speaking. He could hear wet breathing nearby: one Galatean at least, maybe two.

"Are you okay, bruv?" he asked.

The reply came not from Steven, but from their captors. Paul's body jerked as he was tapped in the side with an electric baton, and a white light exploded in his head. It lasted only a second or two, but it was long enough for Paul to bite his own tongue. When the baton was removed, his body still trembled. He fought the urge to be sick. He didn't want to vomit in the hood. He brought his breathing under control, just as he had been taught to do, and just as he had taught others. They had all been questioned in the past, usually in the course of the random searches and street sweeps that the Illyri regularly conducted. Routine questioning was carried out in the backs of vans, or sometimes at one of the L&B police stations. Paul had even spent a night or two in the cells, but he'd always been released once dawn came. This was different, though: these were Vena's Securitats. He and Steven weren't going to be held for a couple of hours at the station in St. Leonard's Meadows, or the West End, or Portobello, and offered a cup of tea by a decent human in a uniform. No, they could only be going to one of two places: the Securitats' special interrogation center in Glasgow, or the castle.

The truck slowed, then ground to a halt. Paul heard the doors open, and his collar was deactivated and removed. Hard hands dragged him from the van, and he briefly tasted night air through the hood before the atmosphere around them changed, becoming dank and noisome. He gave a little whistle, and his brother answered in the same way, but then there was the sound of something hard impacting on soft flesh, and Steven cried out in pain.

"You leave him alone!" said Paul. "He's just a kid."

He waited to receive another jolt from a baton, but none came. He was simply hustled silently along until he was forced to turn to his right, and a hand pushed him forward. For a moment he had an image of himself standing at the edge of a huge pit, about to tumble into a void, his hooded form falling forever. Instead, he hit a stone floor, followed seconds later by another body. He heard Steven sobbing.

"Don't cry," said Paul. "Don't give them the satisfaction."

The door slammed shut behind them.


Paul had no idea how long they were left there. It might have been an hour, or it could have been three. Once they had established that they appeared to be alone in the room, the boys found a wall and leaned against it. When Steven tried to speak, Paul said only one word: "Careful."

The Illyri would be listening to them: listening, and watching.

With the index finger of his left hand, Paul began tapping softly on the wall: two short taps, two long, two short. It was Morse code for a question mark.

After a moment, Steven replied with three long taps, followed by long-short-long.

*OK.*

The Resistance had learned too late that the Illyri were embedded in all forms of electronic communication, and many groups around the world had lost operatives in the early days. The Internet still functioned, although it had more bugs than an ants' nest; the Illyri had guessed, correctly, that if they allowed the flow of money, and permitted business to proceed worldwide with some degree of normality, then much of humanity would fall into step. But every keystroke was monitored, and only fools transmitted essential information through the Net, or spoke and texted on telephones of any kind. Thus the Resistance had fallen back on simpler means of staying in touch. They used dead drops, secure locations where paper messages could be left and collected. They sent signals and instructions over short-wave radio, just as spies had done in the Second World War.

And they relied on Morse code. It was one of the first things that young people learned when they joined the Resistance. Sometimes Paul and his colleagues didn't even have to go through the basics with new recruits, for older brothers and sisters had already taught the code to their younger siblings, as had parents who had not succumbed to the Illyri methods of subduing them, chemical or otherwise.

Now slowly, painstakingly, the boys contrived a cover story. They kept it to simple keywords.

*Exploring. Vaults. Storm pipe. Adventure.*

*Nothing.*

*We saw nothing.*

The hoods began to stink. They had grown moist from the boys' exhalations, and very, very hot. Paul began to feel that he was suffocating, and he could hear Steven's breathing growing panicked.

"Easy," he said. "Easy."

Their arms ached, and their circulation was being cut off by their restraints. Paul could no longer feel his fingers.

A door opened. There came the sound of metal objects being placed on the floor. A table and chairs, thought Paul. Maybe they're going to give us dinner, a real slap-up meal with beef, and roast potatoes, and gravy. Even though he was frightened, he was also very hungry. They had not eaten since they'd shared that fruitcake with those two funny girls, the ones with the old-fashioned names and the layers of clothes, their hats and glasses encasing them like swaddling so that all that could be seen was smooth tanned cheeks and chins and foreheads, no eyes, no hair. . . .

Oh! Paul thought, as he realized that the "girls" might not have been girls at all. I'm a fool. I'm such a fool. I was so caught up with the explosions, and not being caught, that I never stopped to think. . . .

But any further regrets were halted as hands pulled him to his feet, and then led him to a chair. He sat down and his hood was removed. He blinked hard at the fluorescent lights, and for a few seconds he could not see anything at all. Gradually his vision adjusted, and he took in the table and chairs, and his brother seated beside him, also blinking, his eyes watering.

Sitting across from them was Vena. Her head was bald, and her scalp was adorned with silver stripes. She was not finished with them, not by a long shot. Paul had feared as much when he saw her standing in their home. Even by the brutal standards of the Securitat, Vena was regarded by the Resistance as psychopathic. On the list of targets for assassination she even ranked above Governor Andrus. As far as the Resistance was aware, Andrus was not in the habit of using skimmers—so-called because they skimmed the limits of Earth's atmosphere—to take captives to high altitudes and then toss them out. For Vena, it practically counted as a hobby. She was also believed to report all she saw and heard in the British

Isles to her lover, Sedulus. She was his second-in-command in all but name.

"Do you know who I am?" she asked.

"No, ma'am," said Paul.

"No," said Steven.

"You're lying," said Vena. "I'll record every lie that you tell, and I'll cut off one of your fingers for each one."

Neither of the young men responded. Well done, little bruv, thought Paul. She's fishing. Stick to the story, and we'll be okay.

"What were you doing in our tunnels, and who are you working for?" said Vena. Clearly there were to be no serious preliminaries, no getting-to-know-you questions, no "you may be wondering why we've brought you here." That was for films. The Securitats had a reputation for getting down to business.

"I need to go to the bathroom," said Steven.

They had discussed this in their coded exchange. They had to find a way to leave the cell, even if only for a short time, so that they could get some sense of their location, of security, of guards. In here, they were blind.

"That's unfortunate," said Vena.

"I need to go *bad*."

"When you tell me what I need to know, you'll be made comfortable. Until then, you'll stay where you are."

"I'll wet myself," said Steven.

Vena smiled at him, and leaned across the table.

"If you do, I'll slice off the organ responsible and give it to the Agrons as a treat. They'll eat *anything*."

Steven went quiet. He didn't think the bathroom ploy was going to work, and he wasn't prepared to risk losing his manhood on the slim chance that it might.

"Again: what were you doing in our tunnels?"

There was no point in denying that they'd been there. The Agron had given that much away by telling Steven that it had followed his scent.

"It was an accident?" said Steven. His voice went a little high at the end so that it came out sounding like a question, which he hadn't intended.

"An accident?" said Vena. "Really? You can't do any better than that?"

"Yes, an accident," said Steven. "I was just messing about in the Vaults when I found a new pipe and followed it."

He stopped talking then; the Resistance had taught them to keep lies short and succinct so as not to trip themselves up on the words they were weaving. But he had slightly changed the story that he and Paul had agreed on, and Paul wasn't sure that was wise.

He had said "I," not "we."

Vena frowned, and Paul knew then that Steven had made a mistake. He'd told him over and over again: the best lies were the ones wrapped in the thickest of truths. You hide the lie, and you don't adorn the truth.

"But surely your brother was with you?"

Paul bit his lip.

"No, it was just me. My brother wasn't there."

"Odd," said Vena. "That's not what your friend Knutter told us. I suppose we could bring him in here and ask him to confirm his story. Oh wait, we can't, because he's *dead*, and so will you be if you keep wasting my time. Even if your friend *had* tried to conceal the truth, your scents would have given you away. The Agrons have five hundred million olfactory receptors. You have only five million. Do you think they can't tell the difference between your stink and your brother's?"

"I can," said Steven. "He smells worse than I do."

Even in this terrible situation, Paul couldn't help but smile. His little brother was baiting the Illyri. His mother had always told them they were both too smart for their own good. Perhaps she'd been right.

"You're a funny little boy," said Vena. "Unfortunately, you both smell the same to me. You smell of fear, and desperation, and false-hoods. What did you see in that tunnel?"

"Nothing," said Steven.

Vena turned her attention to Paul. "Are you going to let your little brother take all the heat for you? Are you going to let him fight your battles? What a coward you are, letting a boy do the talking while you sit back and try to save your own skin."

"Like he told you," said Paul, "we saw nothing. We were exploring the Vaults, we found a new pipe, the smell made my brother sick, and we left. That's it. He was just trying to protect me by saying I wasn't with him. We're sorry."

Vena considered what Paul had said, then nodded.

"Bring it in," she said. The microphones hidden in the room picked up her words, and the door opened. A Galatean entered, carrying a wooden box. Its lid was perforated with air holes, and it had a hinged lid. He placed it on the table, and Paul was certain that he heard something move inside.

Two more Galateans entered. They freed Steven's arms, but only for long enough to place them flat on the table. From its previously smooth surface emerged a pair of metal bands that slipped over Steven's wrists, securing them in place.

Vena looked at Paul. "Since you seem to prefer letting your brother do most of the talking, maybe you'd like to let him do your screaming for you, too."

The Galatean handed her a gauntlet of metal and thick leather. She put it on her right hand, then lifted the lid of the box and carefully reached inside. Whatever it contained seemed to strike at her, for she flinched and almost withdrew her hand. Eventually, though, she got a grip on the thing, and lifted it from its prison.

It was about a foot long, its armored body purple and red like an exposed muscle, five heavy jointed legs at each side. Two large bulbous eyes, like those of a mantis, stared unblinkingly from its skull, and between them was a long pointed mouthpiece with a barbed sucker at the end. As it struggled in Vena's grasp, two thin black whips unfolded from the sides of its jaw and struck vainly at the air, splashing the table with clear liquid.

"Have you ever been stung by a bee or a wasp?" asked Vena. "It can be quite painful. It can even kill you, if you have a particular allergy. This little monster is called an icurus, and it's mostly harmless. It just wants to be left to go about its business. But those stinging strikers deliver a powerful dose of neurotoxin similar to the apamin found in bee venom. I've heard it described as feeling like acid burning through your flesh.

"The icurus does have one nasty little attribute. During mating season, those stingers serve a dual purpose: they inject not just venom, but icurus larvae, which breed in the host organism and consume it from within. On its home planet, it breeds only at very specific times of the year, but Earth has thrown its biological clock right off. Frankly, I don't know whether this one is in season or not. There's only one way to find out, I suppose."

She placed the icurus on the table, and eased it toward Steven.

"I'm afraid," she said, "that this is going to hurt."

# CHAPTER TWENTY-ONE

For Syl, it had been a confusing, uneasy meeting in her father's rooms. All thoughts of birthdays were forgotten, as were all concerns about her narrow escape from the bombings being discovered by her father. Meia had made it clear that she would not tell Lord Andrus about what Syl and Ani had been up to that day, including their trip to the Royal Mile and their bout of eavesdropping, as long as Syl gave her no reason to do so. Syl knew that she was now in Meia's debt, but as she sat in one of her father's armchairs and listened to what he and Danis and Meia had to say, she understood that they needed her, and that their debt to her would be at least as great as hers to Meia.

Syl had never been needed before, not in this way. For so much of her life she had been dependent upon others. Yes, her father needed her, but it was an emotional need, born out of love. To be needed because of something she alone could do, something practical, something dangerous, was different. And while she was frustrated at her father's caution—for it was he who kept returning to the risks involved—she was secretly grateful to him for caring, even as he drew closer and closer to using her as a pawn in his game with the Diplomatic Corps and the Sisterhood.

"I still don't understand why it's Syl she wants to see," he said at last, as it became clear that he was going to allow her to enter the Red Sister's presence.

Syl could have told him, even if it was only a suspicion. So too could Meia, but she remained quiet. Syl recalled the way that Syrene had tried to seek out whatever had disturbed her in the Great Hall, and how she had finally fixed upon the ornate fire surround concealing the little slits through which Syl and Ani were watching her, as though willing her gaze to assume a physical form and insinuate itself into the gaps like a serpent.

Lord Andrus approached Syl and laid a hand on her shoulder.

"You don't have to do this, you know," he said. "Nobody will think any less of you if you would prefer not to spend time in the company of Syrene."

"I understand," said Syl. "I want to do it."

Andrus looked to Meia. She stared back at him. There was no need for her to speak. She had considered the problem, and offered her opinion based on her analysis.

"Meia thinks you're clever enough to joust with Syrene for a time, and I agree. But remember: she is dangerous, and cunning, and she has no love for this family."

He paused.

"You should know that your mother rejected the Sisterhood's advances when she was young," he said.

Syl was surprised. She had not known this.

"She did so for many reasons," continued Lord Andrus, "some of which I understood, and some of which I can only guess. I was one of those reasons, if it's not too vain of me to think so. Orianne and I were in love from a very early age, younger even than you are now. Ezil and Syrene took her rejection very personally, in part because it was I whom she loved, and even as a young soldier I had already been branded as an enemy of both the Corps and the Sisterhood. It was why your mother chose to wander the stars with me and leave her home forever. She was convinced that some harm might come to her if she stayed—to her, and to any children that she might have. So you were born far from Illyr, and far from the reach of the Red Sisters. But now the Sisterhood is here, and it may be that Syrene wishes to meet you because she wants to look at last upon the daughter of the Lady Orianne.

"Yet if that were all she desired, she could stare at images of you until her eyes fell from her head. Unusual though you may be, Syrene did not travel halfway across the universe simply to admire your features. There is another purpose at work here, and we need to establish what that might be. So spar with her, and debate with her, for she may reveal to the daughter what she wished to conceal from the father. We'll be watching, and listening."

He took Syl's right hand. Encircling her index finger was a ring of white gold with a red crystal set into it.

"If at any time you feel threatened, or afraid, you know what to do."

"Yes, Father."

The ring functioned as her personal alarm. Pressing down hard on the crystal activated the device. It would bring help in seconds, but only within the castle precincts.

Andrus kissed her gently on the forehead.

"This isn't quite the birthday that I would have wished for you," he said.

"Thank you for my gifts," she whispered.

"Gifts? I only gave you one."

"Two," said Syl. "The bronze cast, and your trust."

Andrus smiled. "Meia will take you to Syrene, and she'll stay outside until you emerge safely."

Meia stepped forward.

"Come, Syl," she said.

"Time to dance?" said Syl.

"Yes, time to dance."

In the interrogation cell, Steven's head slumped to the table. The icurus had been restored to its box, its venom seemingly inexhaustible. The fingers of Steven's left hand were swollen badly, the tips purple and bleeding from the icurus's strikes.

"Nothing," he whispered, for what seemed like the hundredth time. "We saw nothing. . . ."

He was beyond weeping. He had exhausted his capacity for tears, but his brother had not. Paul was crying: for his brother, and his mother, and for his own inability to distinguish between strength and weakness. By remaining silent, he was allowing his brother to suffer. If he spoke, if he admitted what they'd seen, he could make Steven's pain stop.

But if he told Vena what they had seen, they would both die. He was certain of it. Something terrible was happening beneath the city, something that the Illyri wished to keep hidden. Paul's duty was to keep himself and his brother alive, and to report what they knew to those who might be able to investigate further.

"Stop hurting him," said Paul. "Please. Hurt me instead. Just leave him alone."

The little receiver in Vena's ear lit up, and after a pause to listen, she stood and left the room without a word. Paul wanted to hug his brother, to hold him and tell him that he was sorry, that everything would be okay, but his hands were still bound behind his back. Instead he leaned over and placed his head against Steven's.

"You did well," he whispered. "You're brave. You're braver than anyone else I know."

"Is it true?" said Steven. The words caught in his throat, like dry sobs.

"Is what true?"

"What she said about that thing, that it injects its young into people?"

"I don't know," said Paul. "I think she was just trying to frighten you."

"Well, it worked. I am frightened."

"We'll have a doctor look at you once we get out of here."

"Great. When do you think that might be? Because I don't think it's looking so good for us right now."

The boys sat up. Steven stared at his deformed hand.

"It burns," he said. "I can feel it spreading up my arm."

He was right. The swelling was not limited to his hand. It was moving along his forearm, and was now halfway to his elbow.

"We'll fix it," said Paul, but he didn't know if that was true. He wondered how much Knutter had told the Illyri. Knutter wasn't clever, but he had a degree of animal cunning, and he hated the Illyri. He wouldn't have told them much at all, if he could have helped it. At the very least, any admission of involvement with the Resistance would have put himself at risk. They had used him as a distraction, but it was the Agron who had followed the scent. No, Paul believed that Knutter would probably have kept quiet and hoped for the best. If they stuck to their story, there was still some hope for them.

The door opened again. This time it was not Vena who entered, but a medical officer in blue scrubs. He examined Steven's hand, and injected his arm, but Paul noticed that he then cleaned the needle on a wipe, which he placed in a sterile specimen bag.

"That will take the swelling down," he said.

"What about larvae and stuff?" said Paul.

The medical officer looked puzzled. "What about them?"

"The officer who did this said that the icurus injects its larvae into its host."

"Did she now? She'll be telling you that it delivers parcels to human children at Christmas next."

"So it's not true?"

"No." He lowered his voice. "The icurus lays eggs, thousands of them, but only on the leaves of one specific plant. Your brother has venom in his system, but nothing worse. Then again, the venom is bad enough. He's been badly stung. If the poison were allowed to spread, it would eventually start shutting down his respiratory system. I've seen grown men killed by those things during interrogation."

He glanced at the box. It didn't look as though he approved of Vena's methods.

"Thank you," said Paul.

"For what?"

"For treating my brother."

"I'm a doctor. It's what I do. Illyri, humans, terrorists, it makes no difference to me."

"We're not terrorists," said Paul.

"Whatever," said the doctor. "It's not my concern."

He unwrapped another needle and took a blood sample from Paul.

"What are you doing?"

"It's just a precaution. Nothing to worry about."

But once again he cleaned the needle with a wipe, and that went into its own specimen bag. He then took skin swabs from each of them before departing.

After some time, three Galateans came in and released the boys' hands. They were brought soup and some dry bread.

In the silence of the interrogation room, they waited for their fate to be decided.

# CHAPTER TWENTY-TWO

Two female Illyri in faded yellow gowns stood at the door of Syrene's quarters. They stared with distaste at Syl as she and Meia approached.

"Novices," whispered Meia. "They live for the approval of the Archmage."

Syl felt that they were assessing her, and had found her wanting. They seemed barely to notice Meia, but Meia had a way of making herself appear unthreatening when she chose. It was part of her talent as a spy. There was a transformative quality to her, an ability not only to blend into her surroundings but almost to alter her physical appearance. It was subtle—the dipping of her head, the slumping of her shoulders, the slackening of her facial muscles—but even in the course of the short walk from Lord Andrus's chambers to the temporary lair of the Red Sister, Meia had changed. Had Syl not spent the past hour in her company, she thought, she might have passed her on the street and not noticed her.

"I bring Syl Hellais," said Meia. "The Archmage is expecting her."

One of the novices nodded.

"You may enter," she told Syl. "The other stays outside."

Meia touched Syl gently on the shoulder. "Remember to call her 'Your Eminence,'" she whispered. "She will expect it from you." Then she stepped back as the door opened.

Without hesitation, Syl entered the presence of the Red Sister.

What struck her first was the nature of the room itself. Just as

Meia had the ability to take the familiar and make it appear strange and new, so too Syrene's chambers had been transformed by her presence. The wooden floors were now covered with rugs of red and gold, intricately decorated and clearly very, very old. Cloths had been draped over functional furniture, softening the lines, and candles provided the only light. Tapestries on the walls depicted mythical beasts from an imagined Illyri past, and ancient battles fought long before ships flew to the stars. Above the bed hung what Syl now understood to be the seal of the Sisterhood, the Red Eye, but this one was different from those that adorned the ship in the courtyard and the collars of the guards. From it flowed graceful red tendrils of energy that seemed to move even as Syl looked at them, so that it seemed they might reach out and caress her skin.

And in the center of the room, strangely beautiful, stood Syrene. She had dispensed with the long robe and ornate veil of the Sisterhood, and wore a simple red dress cinched tight around her upper body but flowing like waterfalls of blood from her waist. Her dark hair was cut very short, and was shaved back along her hairline to reveal the tattoos spilling from her scalp and down her forehead, but care had been taken with it. This was no military cut, nor was it the kind of severe shearing to which some of the female religious on Earth resorted. To Syl it indicated both a desire to meet the Sisterhood's requirement that hair should not be long, and a degree of personal vanity on Syrene's part. There was a faint red glow to Syrene's eyes. Syl thought it might have been a candle flame reflected in them, but when the Red Sister advanced to meet her, the glow remained where it was, only dying as she drew close enough for Syl to smell her breath. It had a hint of spice to it that was not unpleasant.

Syrene extended her hands in greeting. Like her face, they were intricately decorated with red tattoos, although these were more like the detailing on lace curtains than some of the figurative illustrations on her face. Now that she could examine the Archmage more closely, Syl's attention was drawn to the red eyes tattooed on each of Syrene's cheeks. They were carefully etched—almost life-like—and the pupils at their core were very, very dark. For the first time since she had entered the room, Syl felt a tickle of unease.

"Your Eminence," she said.

"The young Syl Hellais," said Syrene. "I am most pleased to meet you."

She stretched out her arms as if to embrace her, and Syl instinctively tensed at the approach. She did not like strangers touching her. Syrene recognized her discomfort and allowed her arms to drop once again by her sides, but she seemed faintly disappointed by the girl's reluctance to engage in physical contact. In fact, Syl could not help feeling that although she had only just arrived Syrene was already bored with her—as if in those first few moments she had learned all that was worth knowing about her, and was now content to discard her.

What was she expecting? thought Syl, and the answer came to her.

My mother.

Then that disappointment was gone, and Syl might almost have believed that she had imagined it were it not for the small, lingering sense of hurt—and, yes, rejection—that she felt.

"Please," said Syrene, "sit. You will have some wine?"

Two glasses stood on a side table, two leather library chairs adjoining it. Between the glasses was a decanter of red wine. Syl drank little as a rule, and would have preferred not to do so here. It was important that she keep a clear head. On the other hand, it was more likely that Syrene would relax with her if she accepted a drink. She agreed to a small glass.

"It is Italian, and very old," said Syrene. "One of the things that this world does well is intoxicants. This is one of a handful of vintage bottles salvaged by a dealer in Rome before the city became an example to the rest."

The destruction of Rome had been a terrible mistake, according to Syl's father, a war crime that he believed would haunt the Illyri for generations to come. He had advised against it, but had been overruled by the Council back on Illyr. "You disapprove of what happened to Rome?" asked Syrene.

"It was a great city, a beautiful city," said Syl.

"You visited it, then?"

"Only once."

"Would you have preferred it if an uglier city had been made an example of?"

"I would have preferred it if no city at all had been destroyed," said Syl.

"You speak with your father's voice," said Syrene.

"No," said Syl, "I speak with my own."

"Earth grows unruly," said Syrene. "It does not fear us. Without fear, there can be no rule of law."

"Do you speak with your husband's voice?" said Syl, and she was surprised to see Syrene laugh.

"Why, there is something of your mother in you after all!" said the Archmage. "Do you know that she once called the Supreme Mage Ezil a witch to her face?"

"No," said Syl. "I did not know."

She felt hugely proud of this woman she could not remember, who had died when she was so young and whom she knew only from pictures and video projections. Sometimes Syl would instruct the castle's systems to fill a room with images of her mother, and she would converse with the ghosts. Syl cherished every mention of her, drinking in the anecdotes and memories of those who had known her, keeping them fresh by regularly removing them from her box of experience and examining them in the light of the world that had killed the Lady Orianne. She dreamed of her at night, keeping her locket beside her pillow in a velvet box wound with a ribbon from one of her gloves, and occasionally she allowed herself to open a yellowing crystal bottle that contained the last traces of her mother's signature perfume, musky and warm.

"It was unwise, of course," continued Syrene, "and hugely disrespectful. Had Lady Orianne not fled Illyr with your father, the

Sisterhood might well have found a way to make her pay for the offense she had given."

"She did not flee," said Syl. "She loved my father, and wanted to be with him."

"Your father was the only Illyri who was more disdainful of the Sisterhood than your mother was. They were well matched."

"Were you among those who wanted to make her pay?" asked Syl.

"Outwardly, yes. But inside I rather admired her spirit. She would have been an adornment to our order. In time, she might even have ruled it. In that sense, I was glad that she rejected a place in the Marque, and relieved when she left with your father. Had she not done so, but instead reconsidered the Sisterhood's offer, she would have risen in authority just as I have, and we might now have been competing for power in the Marque."

"Is that what you want: power?"

Syrene looked at her slyly over the rim of her wineglass.

"You ask a lot of questions, little one. Did your father put you up to this? Did he think he might learn something by putting you in a room with me? I expect he did. He was always clumsy in his methods. He plays the game poorly."

Syrene sipped her wine. A little of it ran down her chin darkly, but she seemed not to notice.

"In answer to your question, life is all about power. The powerful survive. The powerful *thrive*. So yes, I want power, for myself and for my kind."

"Your kind? You mean the Sisterhood?"

"The Sisterhood, and more. You are of my kind, just as your mother was. The Sisterhood is the great source of female power. Through it, we influence an empire, and the rule of worlds."

For a second, the red fire glowed in her eyes once again, and then was gone.

• • •

"We've lost visual," said Balen.

He was standing with Lord Andrus and Danis, watching the array of screens that showed Syrene's chambers from a dozen angles, thanks to the tiny cameras secreted throughout the room. Those screens revealed nothing but static.

"Check the rest of the system," said Danis.

Balen moved to the feeds for the cameras elsewhere in the castle. All appeared to be working fine, even the ones in the bedroom of Grand Consul Gradus, which revealed him to be fast asleep on his bed.

"It's the witch," said Danis. "She's done something to the cameras—again."

Following Syrene's brief time in the Great Hall, the surveillance equipment had already been replaced after what was believed to be a malfunction, or sabotage. Now it was clear that the Archmage herself might have been responsible.

"We still have sound," said Balen. "They're talking. I can hear your daughter. She seems fine."

"Send in a lurker," said Andrus. "Maybe we'll have more luck with that. In the meantime, tell Meia that we've lost visual contact. Make sure she's ready to move at a moment's notice."

Balen got through to Meia, and then activated one of the lurkers, the tiny spybots that were scattered, dormant, throughout the castle. This one was a modified beetle: it had been enhanced with electronic components at the pupal stage, so that its own tissue would grow around the wiring and microcircuitry, sealing them in place, and the movements of its legs provided power for the tiny camera embedded in its head. These little spies—modified moths, wasps, flies—were the bane of the Resistance, for they could never be certain if an insect was being controlled by the Illyri or not. For that reason, insects did not tend to survive long when the Resistance was about its business.

The lurker beetle responded to Balen's signal, and moved through the darkness toward Syrene's rooms.

# CHAPTER TWENTY-THREE

Paul knew that he and Steven were doomed as soon as Sedulus appeared, Vena at his heels like an obedient, vicious dog. Behind them were half a dozen Galateans dressed in full body armor. Two of them carried long metal poles that ended in open magnetic collars. The next two bore pulse rifles, and the final pair were armed with electric batons that were almost as long as the collared poles. Before the boys could react, they had both been brutally shocked, and the collars were placed around their necks while they spasmed on the ground. Once again their hands were bound, and straps were placed across their mouths and around their heads so they could not speak.

Sedulus stepped forward. He moved a hand casually through the air, conjuring up a screen. The screen showed a swab being placed in a device not much bigger than a shoebox, and then being sprayed with ink. An ultraviolet light was activated and shone on the swab. Most of the swab was illuminated, but at its center was a single dark area. A second swab was placed in the box, and the procedure repeated, with the same result.

"Those were the skin swabs taken from you earlier this evening," said Sedulus, freezing the final image on the screen. "The ink is fluorescent, but explosives eliminate its fluorescence. It's very sensitive, and capable of detecting traces of both organic and inorganic material. Your skin swabs showed significant traces of urea nitrate, which, as I'm sure you're aware, is an inorganic compound used in some homemade explosive devices. Earlier today, two such devices exploded on the Royal Mile, and the compounds detected on your skin are a perfect match for those found at the scene of these outrages."

He squatted before them, and spoke slowly and carefully.

"Just to be certain, we compared your DNA with samples retrieved from the scene, and carried out reconstructions."

The Illyri had perfected the art of reconstructing human faces from minute samples of DNA. Genetic factors had been found to contribute to nine elements of facial appearance, including the position of cheekbones, the distance between eyes, and the dimensions of the nose. Combined with DNA analysis that already enabled scientists to predict eye and hair color, a small sample of human genetic material could provide a near-photographic likeness of the individual from which it had come.

The image in the air changed, and Paul and Steven found themselves looking at representations of themselves. They were not perfect copies, but nobody could have mistaken them for anyone else.

"Damned by your own DNA," said Sedulus. Something about Paul caught his eye, and he extended his right hand toward the teenager. Paul tried to back away, but a Galatean held him still. Sedulus's index finger pushed aside his collar, exposing the silver cross hanging around his neck. Their mother had insisted that both of her sons should wear one. She hoped that it would keep them safe.

"You believe in God," said Sedulus.

"Yes," said Paul.

"Do you know what God is?"

"No."

"God is simply a technology that you do not understand."

He covered up the cross.

"You young gentlemen are members of the Resistance, and you are guilty of terrorist outrages against the Illyri Empire and the citizens of this city. Your crimes present irrefutable evidence that a policy of gentle occupation has not worked on these islands. It is with great regret that the Council of Government on Illyr has decided to institute the death penalty for the murder of Illyri for all citizens of Earth over the age of fourteen years. You will be hanged in the courtyard of the castle as an example to others."

He stood, and looked down on them with something like pity.

"May your god have mercy on you, for we will have none."


Syl's eyes felt gritty. It seemed to her that she had been in the room with Syrene for a very long time, for a terrible tiredness had come over her, yet she had barely sipped her wine. But even as her head sagged, and her chin touched her chest, she could hear her own voice speaking, responding to all that Syrene said. She forced herself to look up. There was a double image of Syrene in the chair before her. She blinked hard in an effort to clear her vision, but then one of the Syrenes stood while the other remained seated. The standing Syrene was almost transparent, a ghost of the other, but it had more life to it. The seated version's eyes were blank, and it was reciting a long and tedious history of the Sisterhood. Occasionally Syl's mouth would open and she heard herself say "Really?" and "How interesting!" but she did not do so of her own volition. She was like a doll controlled by another, and across from her was a figure without essence, an empty vessel with a far-distant voice.

The spirit Syrene placed her hands against Syl's head, and Syl could do nothing to stop her. She felt pressure on her temples, and then the Red Sister was inside her, hunting for secrets. With a huge effort of will, Syl tried to perform a trick that Meia had taught her a year or two before, when Lord Andrus had been away and Meia had been solely responsible for Syl's safety. Syl had asked her about spying, and the danger of being discovered, and Meia had told her that as part of her training, she had learned to visualize locked doors and tall, impenetrable walls to keep interrogators at bay.

"I have been questioned by enemies, and they have gotten nothing from me," said Meia. "Not even with truth serums. Pain is harder to resist, but it can be done. Doors and walls, Syl, doors and walls. And you must never get angry, never. Anger is an absence of control, and if you lose control, then they have won."

Now, as Syrene invaded her consciousness, Syl fought her, building brick walls that shot up before her thoughts and memories, guarding secrets with heavy metal doors secured with huge locks and bolts. As Syrene opened one, so Syl would quickly create another. She felt the Red Sister's frustration grow, but at the same time Syl was growing more and more tired, and the walls and doors were becoming harder and harder to sustain.

*Not you!*

Syrene's voice sounded loudly in her head. It was no longer bright and melodious, but harsh and cracked. It was the voice of a crone in a younger woman's body.

*If it was not you that I felt, then who else? Who?*

Syl threw up more walls, but they were crumbling rapidly now, the mortar falling from between the bricks. She tried doors, but the metal rusted, and the bolts would buckle. The walls disintegrated, the doors fell from their hinges, and each time they did so she saw a vision in red, a woman of flames and tendrils, advancing upon her, and she was forced to retreat.

*Who? Who?*

But as Syl tried to hide the name from her, some terrible imp inside her kept trying to speak it. It formed letters from bricks. It scratched them into the paint on the door. Syl did her best to obscure them, striking them out before they could become fully formed, but Syrene was determined, so determined.

*Tell me*, the awful voice screeched. *Tell me!*

But Syl had no energy left. She was about to lose the fight. She would betray—

Suddenly, Syrene withdrew. Syl's ears popped painfully, and as her vision cleared she saw the shadow Syrene melding once more with the figure in the chair. The door crashed open to reveal Meia, Syrene's novices unconscious on the floor beside her, along with two of Gradus's private guards.

And with her was Ani.

# CHAPTER TWENTY-FOUR

Syrene was furious at the intrusion, and threatened dire consequences for the harm done to her novices. But there was something theatrical about the way she protested, as though she were conscious that she had an audience, and the words were what was expected of her in such a situation. Meia ignored her entirely, and simply swept the bewildered Syl from the room.

But Syl was no sooner over the threshold than a squad of Securitats appeared to their right. Almost simultaneously, a dozen heavily armed soldiers, led by Danis, arrived from the left. When the Securitats saw Gradus's guards lying motionless on the floor, they immediately raised their weapons, and Danis's troops responded in kind. The three females were trapped between them, and all Meia could do was draw Syl and Ani to her and force them to the floor, shielding them with her own body.

"Stop!"

The voice was Syrene's, and her tone brooked no opposition. Even Danis, who was clearly spoiling for a fight, raised a hand to his soldiers and ordered them not to fire, although he kept his own blast pistol trained on the guards before him.

Syrene appeared at the door.

"Let them go," she told the Securitats.

"But Your Eminence," said the Securitat sergeant, "your guards and novices have been assaulted."

Syl peeked out from beneath Meia. Already the stunned guards were struggling to their feet. The novices looked like they might be out cold for a little longer. Good, she thought, recalling how they had looked at her when she had first arrived.

"Are they dead?" Syrene asked.

The sergeant checked the novices. "No, Your Eminence. They are merely stunned."

"Then they, along with my dignity, will recover," said Syrene. "Let the children rise."

Meia stepped back, and Syl and Ani got to their feet. Syl felt as though a cloud were being blown from her mind, clearing her thoughts. She tried to remember what had happened in Syrene's chambers, but she couldn't hold on to the memories. They slipped through her mind like smoke. She was aware only of a feeling of intrusion, of violation, and that the Red Sister at the door frightened her. She was unsteady on her feet, and Ani had to support her.

Syrene stared at Meia, as though imprinting the image of her face upon her memory.

"What is your name?" she asked.

"I am Meia."

"Meia." Syrene repeated, tasting it with her tongue. "What is your bloodline?"

"I am an orphan. My heritage is lost to me."

Syrene looked displeased with the answer. Bloodlines were important in Illyri society, and one of the roles of the Sisterhood was to record the histories of Illyri families, both major and minor. Births, deaths, and marriages, all were noted in the Sisterhood's archives. Even an orphan would have a notation in their file, unless . . .

"You are a bastard?" said Syrene.

"I dislike that word," said Meia. "I prefer the term *free agent*."

The double meaning of *agent* was clear to Syrene.

"I know you now," she said. "You are Andrus's spymistress. Are you his mistress in other areas too? His bed has been cold for too long, and even the noble governor has needs."

Meia did not take the bait. Her calmness under provocation was considerable.

"Your question contains its own answer," she said. "The governor is noble. No more need be said."

"Well then, spymistress, tell me why you assaulted my guards and my novices, and entered my chamber without permission."

"We were concerned for Syl's safety," said Meia.

"On what basis?"

Meia paused. "Intuition," she said at last.

"Mistaken, it seems."

"As you say," replied Meia.

Danis stepped forward.

"It did not help that every monitoring device in your room appeared to malfunction shortly after Syl entered your company," he said, joining Meia, and in doing so making it clear that he supported her actions. "We were concerned that it might presage another terrorist attack. We were fearful for your well-being as much as for Syl's."

Syrene frowned.

"You admit that you are spying on me?"

"Would you have expected anything less?"

"Not from you," said Syrene. "You never change, Danis. Your methods are primitive. It's a wonder that you have survived for as long as you have. I'd have thought natural selection would have taken care of an old relic like you a long time ago."

"I am a living fossil," said Danis. "I endure. As for our monitoring of you, we wished only to ensure that your stay in the castle during these difficult times was untroubled. And brief," he added.

But Syrene was no longer paying any attention to him. Instead, her eyes were fixed on Ani.

"And who is this?" she asked. "Answer, child."

"I'm Ani."

"Are you a friend of Syl's?"

"Yes."

"Yes, *Your Eminence*," Syrene corrected, clearly tired of having her title ignored by both Meia and Danis, and refusing to accept similar insolence from a teenager.

"Yes, Your Eminence," echoed Ani. She smiled her most disingenuous smile.

Syrene's fingers twitched. The Red Sister had to make an effort of will to stop them from reaching for Ani, and Syrene's reaction to her friend's presence jolted free a small fragment of recollection in Syl's brain. The cloud had taken with it most of her memories of the last hour, but not all. She had a clear image of Syrene reaching for her, and the cold burn of her fingers.

*She touches. That's how she does it. She touches you.*

Ani continued to beam, bright and seemingly guileless. All waited to see what Syrene would do next. In the end, she elected to do nothing at all beyond making a single threat that seemed hollow to all who heard it.

"Be assured that Grand Consul Gradus will hear of this," she said.

She retreated into her chambers, but it was Ani at whom she was looking as the door closed. The opposing Securitat and Military forces stayed in place for a moment, and then, as if by mutual but unspoken agreement, open hostility was replaced by submerged dislike. The stunned guards were replaced, the novices carried away for treatment, and Syl, Ani, and Meia were absorbed into Danis's squad, the soldiers forming a protective wall around them as they departed.

They did not get far, though. Danis and Meia appeared to get the same message simultaneously, and both stopped as their earpieces lit up. Danis immediately left with his soldiers, instructing Meia to take the girls back to their rooms.

"What is it?" said Syl, and she did not like the look that Meia gave her.

"The Securitats have arrested two young men in connection with the explosions on the Royal Mile," she said. "Come with me. It's about time you showed me this spyhole of yours."

# CHAPTER TWENTY-FIVE

The Great Hall was more crowded than before. Advisers, soldiers, Securitats, and representatives of both the Military and the Diplomatic Corps had assembled, some out of duty, many out of curiosity. The bombs on the Royal Mile had been significant not only for the casualties inflicted but because of their daring: never before had the Resistance managed to carry out a major attack so close to the Illyri center of power in the city. It suggested an escalation in the campaign against the Empire.

There were gasps when Vena led Paul and Steven into the room, surrounded by a cohort of Securitats and Corps guards. The captives' hands were secured in front of them with heavy magnacuffs, and their legs were manacled. A short chain connected the two sets of restraints.

"But that one is so young!" someone said, giving voice to what many others were thinking.

Behind them followed Sedulus, and finally Grand Consul Gradus and his wife, Syrene. Gradus looked grave, while Syrene's features were once again hidden behind her veil.

The boys glanced nervously around the room. Paul's teeth were bared against his gag, giving him the look of a wild beast snarling at its captors. Beside him, Steven bore the panicked look of a small, cornered animal.

*Be strong*, Paul willed him. *I'm with you.*

As though he had spoken aloud, Steven looked up at his elder brother. Paul winked at him, and somehow Steven found the strength to wink back. Paul stood ramrod straight and raised his head high, and he was pleased to see his brother follow suit. A memory of his father came to him, and an expression that the old man liked to use.

"Just look them in the eye and damn them for fools," he would say when someone disrespected his sons, or tried to belittle them. That was what they were doing now. They were looking their foes in the eye, and damning them. They were staring death in the face, but they would not show fear.


In the dimness of the spyhole, Meia saw Syl raise her hand to her mouth in shock as the boys were led in. There was only enough room for the two of them; Ani had been delegated to remain at the door and keep watch.

"What do I do if someone comes along?" she had asked.

"Distract them," said Meia.

"How?"

"If they're male, flirt with them."

"And if they're not male?"

Meia thought about the question.

"Try flirting anyway," she said at last.

Now Syl touched her hand to Meia's.

"What is it?" Meia asked.

"I know those boys," said Syl.

"*What?*"

"Today, on the Royal Mile. They helped Ani and me. They stopped us from running back to the castle after the first bomb exploded. They said there might be another, and they were right."

"That's because they planted them," said Meia.

But Syl shook her head. "No, it wasn't like that. I'm sure of it."

She looked at the two young humans, so small and vulnerable among the taller, hostile Illyri, and felt a surge of sympathy for them. She remembered their faces, and how dismayed they'd been about what had occurred, and how concerned they were for her and Ani. Could they really have been such good actors, denying everything over a cup of tea and some cake? Could they have planted those bombs yet revealed nothing of it to the two young females on the Royal Mile, especially when one of them was Ani? It was hard to keep dishonesty from Ani. She picked up on it the way Agrons picked up on scents.

Syl watched Syrene. Her attention was fixed on the boys before her, and the raised dais beyond them. This time, she was not trying to find eavesdroppers in the room. Either she did not care, or she did not sense their presence. It was the absence of Ani, Syl was certain. It was Ani who had come to Meia to tell her that Syl was in trouble. She had felt it: Syl's fear, the Red Sister's presence, all of it.

And Meia had believed her. She had not doubted her at all.

A door opened behind the dais, and Lord Andrus emerged in his official uniform, accompanied by Danis, Balen, and half a dozen of his closest advisers. Only Meia was absent.

"Shouldn't you really be down there with them?" said Syl.

"I'm not an adviser," said Meia. "I'm a spy, and I'm doing what spies do. Now shut up and listen."

Lord Andrus waited for silence to descend. While the room grew quiet, he whispered something to Balen, who left the dais and approached the prisoners. He examined Steven's still-swollen hand, and the inflammation on his arm. He returned to the governor, and reported his findings. As he spoke, Andrus fixed his disapproving gaze on Vena, who returned it without flinching.

When all was quiet, Vena and her guards forced the boys forward. Gradus and Syrene took up positions to their right, Sedulus to their left.

Gradus cleared his throat.

"Lord Andrus," he said. "It seems that the Diplomatic Corps has succeeded where the Military could not. We have tracked down the humans involved in today's atrocities." He waved a hand in the direction of the boys, and assumed a theatrical expression of surprise. "And they are *children*! How can the Military claim to be in control of this city, this *planet*, when mere boys can come almost to our walls and kill us at will?"

Lord Andrus ignored the questions, and Gradus's rhetorical flourishes with them. He would not have his reputation put on trial here to further the Grand Consul's aims.

"What proof do you have of their involvement?" he said.

Vena looked to Gradus for permission to speak, and it was given.

"My lord, we found traces of inorganic compounds on their skin that matched the explosives used today. Their DNA was tested against specimens taken from the scene, and a reconstruction was carried out."

Vena waved a hand in the air, and the DNA-derived images of Paul and Steven loomed large, along with a barrage of chemical information. The sight incited an angry buzz in the room, as though a nest of bees had been roused.

"There can be no doubt," said Vena. "The tests are foolproof."

"In my experience, nothing is foolproof," said Andrus. "You will, of course, provide my specialists with those test results?"

"Are you doubting the reliability of our methods, Lord Andrus, or our word?" said Gradus.

"Your methods appear to involve the torture of children," said Andrus. "Your word I will have to take, reluctantly, on trust."

Gradus stepped back so that he stood behind Paul and Steven.

"Careful, Lord Andrus," he said. "When you insult me, you insult my office and, by extension, the Diplomatic Corps. More worryingly, you seem to place a greater value on the gentle treatment of two terrorists than you do upon our own dead."

Murmurs of agreement traveled through in the hall. It was clear that there were those present who felt Gradus might have a point, and they were not all Diplomats. Gradus sensed that there might be an opportunity to be grasped here, a way of further undermining the governor's authority. For a moment, he had a considerable section of the crowd behind him, but like all those who are vain and foolish, he threw his advantage away by overstepping the mark. Before anyone could react, he slammed the boys' heads together with a resounding crack. A collective gasp went up, and the shackled prisoners toppled to the ground.

"No!" shouted Andrus.

Gradus ignored him and grabbed the captives by the hair, smacking the boys' heads down hard on the marble floor. Tears of anger pricked Syl's eyes. The smaller boy remained facedown and motionless, while the older one was moaning, his head on its side, his lids closed, blood flowing from his shattered nose to pool on the floor.

"There," said Gradus. "This is how we avenge our dead."

He turned in a circle, his arms outstretched, a performer waiting for applause that never came. Instead, even some of his own retinue looked disgusted. The Illyri prized honor, and there was no honor in hurting two young shackled boys, regardless of what they might or might not have done. Too late, Gradus realized that he had gone too far, but he could not back down now.

"These humans have committed a capital crime against us," he said. "An example must be made of them. They will be shown no mercy."

"What are you talking about?" said Andrus. For the first time, he sounded doubtful. There was something new here, something of which he had not been made aware.

Gradus ignored him. When next he spoke, his voice was like a whip crack. "I hereby sentence them to death."

There was silence for a second or two, and then Andrus started to laugh. It was a laugh without mirth. There was only mockery in it.

"In case you have forgotten, we do not impose the death penalty on children, Gradus. That is *our* law, set down by the Council centuries ago. Furthermore, in my jurisdiction we do not impose the death penalty at all. Imprisonment, yes. Banishment to the Punishment Battalions, yes. But we do not execute! Killing two teenage humans would only exacerbate the problems we already face from the Resistance here on Earth. It would be an invitation to open revolt. I forbid it!"

A silken voice interjected before Gradus could reply. "Lord Andrus, I believe there are fresh developments of which you have not been made aware."

All eyes turned to Syrene. Despite her veil, her words were clear to all.

"By presidential order, the prohibition on the execution of children has been lifted. The Resistance on Earth has taken advantage of our mercy, using its children against us because it knew we would hesitate to hurt them. That is no longer the case. Order must be restored on this planet and, regrettably, it must be restored with a little bloodshed."

A minor Diplomat, his fingers still more flesh than rings, stepped forward and presented Lord Andrus with a sealed document. Gradus used the moment to pick up where his wife had left off. It was clear from his face that her interruption had angered him. He had wanted to be the one to take Andrus, but, once again, the truth about where the real power lay in the relationship between Syrene and Gradus had been revealed. Gradus was his wife's creature.

He spoke as Andrus broke the seal on the letter.

"The order gives the Diplomatic Corps full control, through the Securitats, over all judicial procedures on Earth, including imprisonment, banishment, and execution. In decisions on which the Military and the Corps disagree, the opinion of the Corps will have precedence. That, you will note, refers to *all* decisions, not merely questions of law. You will, of course, retain your position as governor, Lord Andrus, but you and your fellow governors will defer to the Corps. For now, you will report to me, as the senior Diplomat on this planet, but in a few days I will appoint a permanent Diplomat to implement our new policies on Earth."

Lord Andrus spent a long time staring at the letter, as though he could not quite believe its contents. Syl and Meia watched from their hiding place. Syl wanted to run to her father, and it was all she could do not to cry out. With one edict, her father had effectively been deprived of his power, and the Illyri set on a path of slaughter. These two boys—boys with whom she had eaten and drunk, boys who had saved her life—would be only the first to die, and others would follow. Syl felt only shame and anger. She was of the Illyri, and the Illyri were about to become killers of children.

"It is decided," said Gradus. "The executions will take place thirty hours from now, at dawn on Sunday. That will give us time to arrange a worldwide public broadcast, which will serve as a warning of the consequences for murdering Illyri. In the meantime, the interrogation of the suspects will resume tomorrow. They may have more information that will be of use to us."

"Don't do this, Gradus," said Andrus. "It is wrong."

"No," said Gradus. "It is the law."

He nodded to Vena, who raised the boys to their feet. Steven sagged, clearly unconscious, and Syl saw that tears were washing blood down Paul's face as he stood wobbling before Gradus. He tried to speak, but the gag muffled his voice. Almost tenderly, Gradus pulled the gag down so that his words could be heard.

"Kill me," he said. "But spare my brother. Please."

Gradus touched Paul's cheek, his ringed fingers brushing the boy's skin.

"If only I could," he said. "But as you fought together, so shall you die together."

Paul pursed his lips, as though considering the wisdom of this, then spat a string of bloody phlegm straight into Gradus's face. After a startled pause, Gradus punched him squarely in the jaw and the boy crumpled, but was prevented from falling again by the guards.

"Give me your pulser!" Gradus ordered the nearest guard. Syl was sure he was about to kill Paul right there, but Syrene moved forward with an otherworldly speed and put her hand on her husband's arm.

"Not yet," she said. "A secret death, unseen by the masses, will serve no purpose. Let him suffer on the gallows."

A cloth was produced, and Gradus used it to wipe his face. He held the bloodied fabric before Paul.

"For this, I'm going to hang your brother first, and make you watch as he dies," said Gradus. "Take them away!"

And Paul and Steven were dragged back to their cells, there to await their execution.

# CHAPTER TWENTY-SIX

I t was a small, somber group that gathered back at the Governor's House. Only Andrus, Danis, Meia, and Balen were present, along with Syl and Ani, though the spymistress left shortly after a hurried conversation with the governor. Lord Andrus sat with his head in his hands. The atmosphere was almost one of bereavement, as though his authority had been a physical thing, a living, breathing entity that had protected them and now was gone. Syl thought that her father might be in shock. His gaze focused inward, not out, and he had barely sipped from the snifter of brandy by his right hand. Danis looked no happier. He had no wish to serve under Gradus's yoke, and it was likely that Gradus would quickly find a way to rid himself of the old general. If he was fortunate, he might find himself in command of a Punishment Battalion, but he was more likely to die prematurely in his sleep, helped to his rest by poison in his wine.

Syl thought about the two boys in their cells waiting to die: of Paul, with his soft mouth smashed and bleeding; of Steven, unconscious and so pale that his freckles looked like they'd been drawn on paper. She knew that they could not be guilty of the crime with which they had been charged. Even if they were, the thought of their execution would still have repelled her. The construction of the gallows was to commence the following morning on the Esplanade, the part of the complex once known as Castle Hill. Humans had held public executions there in previous centuries, and not only hangings; they had burned or beheaded the condemned as well, usually after torturing them to within an inch of death, for Edinburgh Castle had a foul reputation as a place in which torture was routine. In reading the histories of the human race, Syl had never ceased to be surprised by its capacity for cruelty. Now it seemed that the Illyri were about to reveal themselves as being no better. Once again torture was being carried out in the cells of the castle. Once again the dead would hang from ropes outside its gates. This time, though, there would be children among the corpses, and even the humans had ceased to execute children.

Syl wondered if the Illyri had somehow become infected by the residue of violence in the walls of these old fortresses, places where pain had been visited on the defenseless for centuries. The Illyri ruled from former bases of the Roman Empire, which crucified those who opposed it; from old Crusader fortresses, where men, women, and children were put to the sword for worshipping the same god by another name; and from places like Oslo's Akershus Castle, and Prague Castle in the Czech Republic, buildings haunted by their association with the Nazis, who sent millions to ovens and gas chambers as part of their plan to create their own empire. Have these sites tainted us, thought Syl, or were we always just as cruel as the humans but found a way to hide it from ourselves?

Gradus had ordered that the gallows be built strong, because they were destined to remain in place for years to come. He was convinced that there would be no shortage of candidates to test the hangman's rope. Perhaps he was right, but a plan was slowly forming in Syl's mind. It was a plan with little hope of success, but she could not stand by and do nothing to stop this terrible thing from happening.

Lord Andrus turned to his daughter and began to question her about what had occurred during her time with Syrene.

"It's even more important that you remember now, Syl. More important than what's happening here on Earth; I fear the very peace of the Illyri race may be at stake. We need every tiny detail you can call to mind."

"But I *don't* remember," said Syl. "We were talking, and then . . ."

She frowned in concentration. It was something like a dream, a dream in which Syrene seemed to separate into two parts, one of which had tried to bore into her mind with a terrible remorseless ferocity. She tried to explain it to her father, but she couldn't form the words. It was as though a lock had been placed on her tongue.

Puzzled and concerned, Lord Andrus turned his attention to Ani.

"And you? How did you come to be involved in all this?"

"I just felt strongly that Syl was in trouble," said Ani. "I don't know how. I told Meia, and she believed me."

Andrus looked to Danis, who shrugged.

"She's always been like that," he said. "Maybe some Illyri are just more sensitive than others."

"Well, you're clearly not among them," said Andrus. It was the first hint of humor he had shown since the events in the Council chamber. "And I suppose that we now know why Syrene is here: the Sisterhood has secured its grip on Illyr, and it wants Earth as well. I wouldn't be surprised if Syrene starts building a replica of the Marque on Calton Hill and populating it with novices."

"So what do we do?" said Danis.

"Nothing, for now," said Andrus. "We wait. There is much happening here that we don't yet understand. Until we know more, it's better to watch and to listen."

"So we are to be Gradus's dogs?" said Danis.

"We are, but we still have teeth, and our chains are long," said Andrus. "In the meantime, you can rest assured that Gradus will make mistakes. It is in his nature to act hastily. If he insists on imposing a harsher rule on the humans, then they will rise up against him. The incidents of violence will increase, and the Corps's hold upon Earth will start to slip. When that happens—and it will happen, sooner rather than later—the Military will be waiting to take back the mantle of power."

It was Syl who spoke next.

"You said there were two boys sentenced to death, Father," she said. "But that is not our way. It's wrong. You must help them."

Her father looked at her sadly. "There's nothing I can do for them," he said. "If I act against Gradus and the Council of Government, I'll find myself in a cell alongside those boys."

For the first time in her life, Syl felt real disappointment in her father. It was not only that he could do nothing for Paul and Steven; he *wanted* to do nothing. She saw the truth of it now. The public execution of two young humans, broadcast to the world, would incite widespread fury, and this was Lord Andrus's only hope. Even those who had resigned themselves to living under the rule of the Illyri, continuing their lives much as they had done before, would rebel. Gradus and the Diplomatic Corps would be faced almost instantly with a full-scale rebellion in country after country. The Diplomats would not be strong enough to deal with such an insurrection, even with the aid of the Securitats, opening the way for the Military to step in as the force of reason and restraint. By next week, the brief rule of the Diplomats on Earth might already be over.

And Syl's father was prepared to sacrifice two children to make that happen.

# CHAPTER TWENTY-SEVEN

Meia sat in the darkness of Edinburgh Zoo, listening to the calls of the beasts and the birds. The nocturnal animals were now active, and Meia felt a sense of commonality with them, for she was a night creature too.

"There used to be ravens here, you know," said a voice from behind her.

Meia's hand tightened on her small blast pistol, but she did not move. She had heard the man approaching long before he had revealed himself by speaking, and she knew that he was alone. She was in no danger from him, not here: this was neutral territory. Still, it paid to be careful. Trust was like money: it shouldn't be spent foolishly.

The man walked past her and stared at an empty cage.

"For some reason," he continued, "the people who came to visit didn't seem to find ravens interesting enough, but I always did. They're smart, ravens. They find prey for wolves, and then feed on the leavings once the wolves have gorged themselves. The wolves always leave something for them, but I often wonder what would happen if the ravens didn't find prey for a time, or if one of them fell injured before a wolf."

He turned to face her. He was a big man, taller than she was, but slightly hunched. His hands were buried deep in the pockets of his overcoat. Meia knew that he had a gun in there somewhere, pointed at her. It would be small caliber, probably no bigger than his fist. It wouldn't make a very big hole in her, but then it wouldn't have to.

"It's a dangerous business, making deals with wolves," he concluded.

"And which are you?" asked Meia. "A raven or a wolf?"

"That depends," he replied.

"On what?"

"On whom I'm making the deal with."

He slowly withdrew his hands from his pockets. One was empty. The other contained a small silver hip flask. He unscrewed the top and drank from it. Meia could smell the whisky from where she sat. The man didn't offer any to her. They knew each other too well for that by now.

His name was Trask, and he acted as a channel of communication between the Illyri—or that branch of the Illyri represented by Meia and her kind, the ones who moved through the shadows—and the Resistance. This was not unusual. Even in the worst of wars, or the kind of hit-and-run conflict in which the Illyri and the Resistance were engaged, it was often necessary for the opposing sides to be able to communicate. It was a way of ensuring that truces, temporary or otherwise, could be negotiated and prisoners exchanged, along with information when necessary. In the case of Trask and Meia, they had found a way to keep the violence on both sides to a minimum. There were those in the Resistance who might have called him a traitor had they known of some of the deals he had struck with Meia, and there were those among the Illyri who might have said the same of her. Meia suspected that Trask was more deeply involved in the Resistance than he pretended to be, but it did not concern her. She preferred to deal with someone in authority, someone who could make a decision quickly, rather than with a foot soldier.

Trask sat beside her on the bench. A skimmer, one of the long-range craft that the Illyri used for intercontinental travel on Earth, crossed the moon, heading east.

"Off to deliver misery to some other corner of the globe, no doubt," said Trask.

"You had plenty of misery before we came," said Meia. "If you were in the right mood, you might even concede that we have brought some of it to an end: hunger, disease, environmental damage."

"At the price of our freedom."

"You were never free, not really. We just rule more obviously than your own kind ever did."

"At least they *were* our own kind."

"Must we go through this every time we meet?" asked Meia.

"I wouldn't want you to go mistaking us for friends."

"After the incidents of the last couple of days, I think that's unlikely."

"If you're talking about Birdoswald, that wasn't us."

"Really?"

"I won't lie to you, Meia. I told you that a long time ago. If I can't tell you something, then I'll keep my mouth shut, but I won't lie. There's no point to these meetings otherwise."

"Who was it, then?"

"Highlanders."

"Near Carlisle? We've never known them to come so far south before."

"They're a law unto themselves, and they don't share their plans with us. They think we've grown soft, that maybe we're too close to the Illyri."

"I can't imagine where they'd get that idea from," said Meia drily.

"Nor me, not unless they've been visiting the zoo after dark."

"Why Birdoswald?"

"Why not?"

"There are easier targets for them, closer targets. Also . . ." Meia paused. She had to be careful here. "It seems to me that they might have been trying to take the Illyri commander of the garrison alive."

"Well, it didn't work, then," said Trask. "I hear that he blew his own head off."

"So you *have* been in contact with the Highlanders?"

"In a way. We expressed our concern at having them come on to our territory and start blowing up bases—not to mention some very nice Roman ruins—without so much as a by-your-leave."

"And what did they say?"

"Two words. The second was *off*. I'll let you figure out the first."

"And the explosions on the Royal Mile?"

Trask took another sip from his flask.

"That wasn't us either."

"You're sure?"

"Certain. And it wasn't the Highlanders, I can tell you that."

"They managed to blast their way into Birdoswald without too much trouble."

Trask laughed. "They pointed a truck filled with explosives at the gates and hoped for the best. It's a wonder they didn't blow themselves up by hitting a pothole in the road long before they ever got near the border."

"A splinter group, then, one of which you're not yet aware?"

Trask gave her a look. "You wouldn't be talking to me if you thought there were splinter groups of which I wasn't aware. As soon as you start believing there might be gaps in my knowledge, you'll have me arrested or killed, and you'll find someone else to keep you company on your trips to the zoo."

"Then who did it?"

"Maybe you ought to look closer to home," said Trask.

Meia showed no surprise at the suggestion. That Trask felt as she did about the source of the attack simply confirmed her own suspicions.

"The Diplomats have no love for your lot," Trask went on. "Anything to sow a little unrest in the ranks. By the way, who was the woman in red?"

For all the precautions that Vena had taken, the Resistance still knew of the new presence in the castle.

"A member of the Nairene Sisterhood."

"I didn't think they left their big library in the sky. What's she doing here, then?"

"Sowing some of that unrest in the ranks."

"Huh," said Trask. "My turn: what do the Illyri want with the dead and the dying?"

"What?"

Trask smiled. He liked it when he found out something that Meia clearly didn't know about.

"The figures at the crematorium don't add up," he said. "There are more bodies coming in than are going into the flames. It's not a big difference, just a few here and there, mostly homeless and old people. But we notice these things, just as we're wondering why the Corps removed half a dozen old people from Western General, put them in a truck, and drove them away. Someone assumed they wouldn't be missed, because they were poor, and ill, and had nobody to care about them. But *we* care! And we've heard similar reports from other parts of the country."

"I'll look into it," said Meia.

"You do that. Are we finished here?"

"Not quite."

Meia stood. She didn't like being close to Trask for too long. She knew that what he had said earlier was right: when he ceased being useful to her, she would kill him if only to protect herself. He would try to do the same to her. It was just a matter of who got there first. It was a shame. She had grown to like him.

"We have a problem," she said, and heard him shift in his seat. She could almost picture him reaching for his gun. She let him see that her hands were empty.

"What kind of problem?"

"The Diplomatic Corps is bringing back the death penalty. . . ."

"I wasn't aware that it had ever gone away," said Trask. He knew that the Illyri, and particularly the Securitats, were prepared to kill Resistance members if they couldn't capture them alive, and sometimes even if they could, just as the Resistance's snipers were happy to kill any stray Illyri that wandered into their sights. When you thought about it, the death penalty was being applied every day.

"For children," Meia finished.

"You can't mean that!" said Trask. "What about Andrus? He's the law in this land. He won't stand for it."

"We have a new president back on Illyr," said Meia. "The change of leadership has brought with it a change in policy. As of today, the Diplomats have effectively assumed control of Earth. The age of the gentle hand is coming to an end."

"And when does this new policy come into effect?"

"The first executions are scheduled for the day after tomorrow, on the Esplanade. Two boys, Paul and Steven Kerr, will be hanged for the atrocities committed on the Royal Mile."

Meia saw Trask react to the names.

"I know those boys," he said. "They're good lads, and they're all that their mother has. More to the point, they had nothing to do with those explosions. I've told you already: that wasn't the Resistance!"

But Meia was watching him closely. The Kerr boys were important to Trask; maybe personally, but probably professionally too. Why? Assuming that Trask was telling the truth and the Resistance had not planted the bombs on the Royal Mile, why had the Diplomats chosen to pin the crime on those two humans? How had they been found?

"They were working for you, weren't they?" said Meia. "Those boys were on a mission for the Resistance when they were picked up."

Trask nodded.

"What was it?" asked Meia.

"Tunnels," said Trask softly. "There are tunnels beneath Edinburgh. You lot have been digging them, and we wanted to find out why. That's what the boys were doing. Looking for the tunnels."

"Tunnels?"

"You didn't know? You're losing your touch."

This was Corps work, thought Meia, all of it: the arrival of Syrene and Gradus, the bombs, the move against Lord Andrus, and perhaps even these tales of tunnels and bodies, all linked to the Diplomats.

"What about those boys?" said Trask. "You can't let them hang."

"I'll think of something," said Meia.

"You'd better," said Trask, "or I promise you, you'll be wading through rivers of Illyri blood."

# CHAPTER TWENTY-EIGHT

Syl spent a sleepless night, tormented by dreams in which she tried to stop her father from being hanged but couldn't get to him in time because thick ranks of Securitats held her back, their uniforms no longer black but a deep blood red. She woke before dawn, convinced of a presence in her room, but she was alone. Her temples throbbed, though, and when she looked in the mirror, two circular marks bracketed either side of her head, almost like burns.

*She touched me. Syrene touched me, and I burned.*

It was the weekend, which was of some comfort. The Illyri had taken certain human traditions to heart; among the best of them was dispensing with education classes at weekends. Althea appeared shortly after nine, bustling around the room, tidying where no tidying was required.

"I heard you were involved in quite an adventure yesterday," said Althea.

"Was I?" Syl answered carefully, uncertain as to what exactly Althea might be referring to. She wondered where Althea had been for most of the previous day; it was unlike her to be away from her charge for so long, especially amid so much upheaval.

"Indeed you were. They say you spent time with the Red Witch."

"Yes," said Syl, "although I don't remember too much about it. Althea, where were you yesterday evening?"

"I had errands to run."

"Errands? What errands?"

"Never you mind. Your curiosity will be the death of you if

you're not careful." She gave Syl a strange look when she said it, as though daring her to deny that she was curious at all.

"Did you hear about those two boys, the ones they captured?"

"I did."

"They're going to kill them, Althea."

"Are they now?"

"Yes! They're going to hang them, and my father is going to let it happen, just so that Gradus and the Diplomats will look bad. We have to stop it."

"I don't know anything about such matters, Syl, and I wouldn't be making assumptions about your father. Now get yourself dressed. He wants to have breakfast with you."

Lord Andrus looked weary when Syl arrived in the dining room; his usually youthful eyes were glazed, the flesh beneath them swollen with tiredness and distress. He must have been up all night, thought Syl. Even as she inwardly raged at him for what she believed he was planning to do—or indeed not planning to do in the case of the boys—she felt distress at his condition. The table was laid with fruit and cheese, and scrambled eggs with ham and peppers in a metal bowl kept warm by a burner. Syl kissed her father on the forehead, put a few token pieces of fruit on a plate, and sat down. She had no real desire to eat. Thoughts of Paul and Steven filled her head, and the knowledge of what was going to happen to them tomorrow made her want to throw up. Choking food down hardly seemed an option.

Her father touched her arm.

"I wanted to say that I'm sorry, Syl. Your birthday was not as I might have wished it to be. I'll make it up to you, I promise."

Her birthday? She'd completely forgotten about it in the tumult of the previous day. Had yesterday really just been a single day? It seemed to her that she had lived a year of her life in the previous twenty-four hours.

"Oh, please! That hardly matters. Are you okay, Father? You look . . . ill."

"Uneasy lies the head that wears the crown," he replied.

*"Henry the Fourth, Part Two,"* said Syl, almost automatically. She shared her father's fascination with many aspects of this planet's culture. It was strange, she thought, but she probably knew more about its art and its history than many humans. She would have known even more if she'd been able to upload the information directly, but limiters were routinely embedded in the Chips of young Illyri after it was found that direct uploading of information at a young age stunted mental development.

The Chip sat on the surface of the brain, near the cerebral cortex. It was basically a neural interface that enabled Illyri thoughts to be detected and read as electrical patterns. It then converted these patterns into orders that could be transmitted to control systems, including flight systems on ships, and weapons from missiles to pulsers. Chips were also useful for helping older Illyri to learn new languages and skills. In addition, as Illyri aged, the implants released "baths" of electrons that boosted memory and increased alertness. They could be used to treat a variety of neurological ailments, including epilepsy, and to aid those with paralysis by allowing them to control prosthetic limbs. Through implants, learning could be replaced by uploading, providing instant knowledge of a language, or a subject.

But the Illyri recognized that the brain continued to develop its wiring to the frontal lobe, and to the tracts responsible for complex cognitive tasks like attention and inhibition, until long past adolescence. It was important that this development occurred organically, and was not interfered with artificially. For similar reasons, they believed that it was important that the young learn, not simply upload. As her father liked to point out, it was easy to upload. Real understanding was harder. Uploading was instant and shallow; learning took time, but with it came depth. So it was that, perhaps for the first time, Syl really understood the meaning of Shakespeare's words.

"Well done," said Andrus. "All these years of training and governorship and diplomacy, and still Gradus has outmaneuvered me."

"Don't let those boys die, Father."

"I have little choice."

"Can't you delay the execution? You could demand confirmation of the order from the president. It's such a huge step, such a terrible act—"

"I sent the request to Gradus this morning, and it was denied. Even if I were to try to go behind his back, it would require sending a message through the wormhole. Assuming it got through, it would then have to be transmitted to Illyr through the relays, and Gradus controls them."

He pushed some eggs around his plate, but Syl could see that they had already gone cold. Her father was not in the mood for eating either.

"Syl, the Empire is changing," he said. "It may be that my place is no longer here on this world."

Syl held her breath. She hardly dared to speak, but she had to ask the question.

"Are you talking about returning to Illyr?"

"Perhaps," he said. "What took place yesterday is just the first of many such acts we can anticipate. This is not just about my own loss of power, or the deaths of two boys. It is about the corruption of an entire race. There is something rotten at the heart of the Illyri Empire, and there has been for a long, long time. It will have to be tackled at its source. That lies on Illyr, and in the Marque, but not here."

Syl was torn. She longed to see Illyr, wanted to experience it for herself, but she knew too that her father loved Earth. Perhaps she, too, cared for it more than she'd thought.

"You will abandon Earth to the Diplomats?"

"If I have no other choice. We have done some great wrongs on this world, Syl, but the Diplomats will do worse. If I can stop them, I will, but sometimes a general must lose a battle to win a war. If I have to sacrifice Earth to prevent this poison from seeping deeper into the Empire, then I will."

"When will you decide?"

"Soon, Syl, soon."

"And . . ." The words caught in her throat.

"Yes, Syl?"

"And I'll be going with you, won't I? You won't . . . leave me, will you?"

Her father hugged her to him. He rarely gave such demonstrations of affection, so she treasured them all the more.

"Yes, Syl, you will be going with me, although there may come a time when you do not thank me for it."

Balen knocked and entered. The governor's presence was required in his office. Despite the new order, the routine business of ruling continued. Her father kissed her on the forehead and left.

Syl took her plate and went to sit in an antique chair in the living room. It was her favorite: the heavy brocade fabric was worn smooth in places and the seat was broad and circular, originally crafted to envelop the wide-hooped skirts of Georgian ladies. But she was taller than any human lady of old, so she folded her coltish limbs under her and rested her head back, staring up at the large painting that dominated the wall. It was a masterpiece known as *The Rape of Europa*, painted centuries before by the celebrated human artist Titian. It had been a gift from the human leaders to Lord Andrus when he became governor of Europe and set up his offices in Edinburgh.

"They believed that I wouldn't understand the irony," he once said, but he had been enchanted by the painting regardless, and it had immediately assumed pride of place in the lounge. *The Rape of Europa*—or simply *Europa*, as it was often called—featured fat cherubs who seemed to be attacking a flailing woman on the back of a massive bull, while nymphs standing at the far side of a lake looked on helplessly, and sea monsters gleamed in the depths. The bull's beady eyes stared straight at the viewer, its tail almost quivering with excitement. When she was much younger, Syl had been frightened by the vibrant spectacle, by the trio of cherubs assaulting poor Europa.

"But they're not attacking," her father had explained to her. "They're trying to help Europa. She's just scared, and she doesn't understand."

Syl thought of Gradus as she looked at the scene anew. Curiously, he reminded her of the cherubs, soft and pale and implacable, with his eerily smooth skin, and his tantrums and his dangerous toys. The elite of the Diplomatic Corps were just like him. The events of the past twenty-four hours had cast the painting in a fresh light. Perhaps Europa was right to be frightened. Perhaps the whole of Earth should be frightened by the rule of the Diplomats.

# CHAPTER TWENTY-NINE

Syl might have dozed off, or maybe she was just lost in the painting, but gradually she became aware of a presence nearby. She turned to find Meia watching her.

"Don't you ever, like, knock?" she said coldly.

"Why? Were you doing something that you shouldn't have been doing? How unlike you that would be."

"I was thinking."

"Really?"

Meia sounded surprised. The expression on her face didn't suggest to Syl that she was joking. Sometimes she was hard to understand.

"Very funny. If you're looking for my father, I don't know where he is."

"Actually, I was looking for you."

Meia summoned a screen, and a short piece of video began to play. The camera was angled steeply upward, and the heads of only two of the three people on the screen were visible, because one of them was standing and the camera couldn't fit her into the frame. The figure on the right was Syl. The other was Syrene. They sat across from each other, while a third figure stood between them, dressed in robes that were red yet almost transparent, as though a ghost had entered the room. Syl could see a translucent hand touching her temple, then the image flickered and was gone.

"Five seconds," said Meia. "That's all the bug got before whatever power was being used to prevent us from monitoring events in that room shorted its systems, and it died."

Syl let the image play again and again, trying to repair the holes in her memory. It helped. There was still a lot that was unclear, but at least she now knew a little more of what had happened.

"That was Syrene," she said. "But that was also Syrene sitting on the chair across from me."

"A mental projection of some kind," said Meia. "A part of Syrene released to roam free, while the rest of her sits and grins."

"I didn't know the Sisterhood could do that."

"Neither did I. It seems they've been learning all kinds of new tricks in the Marque: mental projection, the manipulation of presidents and consuls, the rule of an empire from its shadows. Perhaps I should see if the Sisterhood will have me after all. There's much I could glean from them."

"You don't mean that," said Syl.

"Don't I, now? Well, have it your way."

"She burned me," said Syl, pointing to the marks on her temples.

"So she did. I wonder what she was looking for in that marvelous, mysterious head of yours. Whatever it was, I suspect she didn't find it, because she was looking in the wrong place—or, rather, the wrong head."

"I don't know what you mean."

"I think you do, Syl. I want you to bring your little friend Ani to my quarters in an hour. If you don't, I'll tell your father what you both got up to yesterday."

"You wouldn't!"

"I would," said Meia, and her tone left Syl in no doubt. "Oh, it wouldn't give me pleasure—well, not much—but I would. So: an hour, then? And don't be late. I hate to be kept waiting, and who knows what I might do if my patience is tested. . . ."


Syl and Ani arrived early. It seemed like the sensible thing to do, under the circumstances. Ani had been most reluctant to join Syl in Meia's quarters. Any meeting with Meia could only mean trouble, at least until Syl explained the consequences for them both if they did not do as she had ordered. Ani had been on the receiving end of her father's rage often enough to know that it wasn't just the two humans who would be in danger of hanging if he found out that his daughter had been wandering outside the castle walls without permission.

Meia was waiting for them, and opened the door before they had a chance to knock.

"Almost as good as one of your tricks, isn't it, Ani?" she said as she closed the door behind them. "Mind you, I was forced to listen for you, but you'd just have *known*."

Ani said nothing, which was unusual—even painful—for her.

Meia's rooms were bigger and more elegant than Syl had expected, a confirmation of just how valuable she was to Lord Andrus. The neat living area was furnished with two chairs and a sofa, and a video screen. There were prints and paintings on the wall, some of them quite valuable, Syl thought. They showed good taste. Two walls were lined entirely with books, both Illyri and human. Meia, like Andrus, liked physical books. A half-open doorway led into the bedroom. It was exceptionally tidy. In fact, it looked like a room that had never been truly occupied. Despite its adornments, it suggested functionality.

"Sit down," Meia instructed, pointing to the sofa, and Syl and Ani complied. Meia took one of the chairs. She produced a deck of cards from her pocket, and spread them on the small coffee table between her and her guests. Syl hadn't seen anything like them before. Instead of suits—like human cards—or symbolic animals, as the Illyri used, there were only five symbols: a circle, a cross, a trio of waves, a square, and a star.

"These are sometimes called Zener cards on Earth," said Meia. "They're used to test for psychic ability. Of course, most of it is nonsense, and a certain degree of success can be put down to chance. You're both going to take this test, and you're going to do it to the best of your abilities, because if you try to trick me"—she stared at Ani, but not at Syl—"then I'll be having interesting conversations with Lord Andrus and General Danis. Am I clear?"

Syl and Ani nodded.

"Right. Let's begin."

It was simple: Meia showed them the back of a card, and they had to guess which symbol was on the other side. They began with fifty cards, and eventually increased to one hundred over the course of five tests. At the end, Meia calculated their accuracy.

"Syl," she said, "you scored an average of eighteen per one hundred over the course of the tests."

"What does that mean?" said Syl.

"It means that if you decide to bet on a sunny day tomorrow, it will probably rain. You seem to have no psychic ability whatsoever. In fact, you may even be a little below average."

"Loser," said Ani.

"We haven't heard your score yet, smarty," said Syl, although she already had her suspicions.

"Ani," said Meia, "you scored an average of ninety-five percent. It would probably have been higher if Syl hadn't distracted you by sneezing a couple of times."

"Sorry," said Syl.

"Don't worry about it," said Ani. "Below-average specimens probably just sneeze more than the rest of us."

Meia walked to her drinks cabinet and brought out three glasses and a bottle of fresh lemonade.

"A celebratory drink," she said.

"Of lemonade?" said Ani, who had been caught drinking illicit alcohol so often by her father that he had largely given up trying to stop her from doing it. "Wow. Push the boat out, why don't you?"

Meia ignored her and poured the lemonade, handing each of the girls a glass.

"I propose a toast," she said. "To what, if I'm right, may be the most gifted psychic this world has ever seen. To Ani!"

They clicked their glasses and drank. The lemonade was good: not too tart, not too sweet. Meia didn't even sip hers before setting it aside.

"Now, Ani," she said, "why don't you tell us what else you can do?"

The list was long. Even Syl was surprised. Ani couldn't quite read minds, not yet, but she could pick up on emotions, and she was strong on spotting those who were lying.

But there was one particular skill that reminded Syl of what Syrene had done to her: she could cloud minds. Not for long, but for long enough. She demonstrated it on Syl, forcing her to concede that the lemonade was, in fact, whisky, and might be making her a little drunk. It irritated Syl considerably, not only because she didn't wish to be part of some mind experiment, but because she found herself feeling jealous of Ani's gifts, and more than a little hurt that she had not shared the extent of them with her closest friend.

And then she had a thought.

"Ani, did you use this thing—this power—to hide who we really were from the human boys on the Royal Mile?"

Ani shrugged, looking embarrassed.

"I guess. I tried to, anyhow."

"There are Illyri who would do almost anything to have you on their side," said Meia. "You have a great, great gift. Syrene must have sensed it when you were spying on her, but she couldn't pinpoint the source. She thought it might be Syl at first, although I'm not sure why. Perhaps you can screen yourself somehow. I don't know."

"I'm not going to get into trouble, am I?" asked Ani.

"You're not going to get into any trouble at all," said Meia, "not if you refrain from demonstrating your skills too obviously, and not if you do what I ask."

"But we already did!" protested Syl. "We came here. We did your tests. We've kept our side of the bargain."

"Bargain?" said Meia. "I don't recall making any *bargain*. I simply threatened you, and that threat still stands."

Syl swore with frustration. Ani fell back against the sofa.

"What do you want us to do now, then?" asked Ani.

"What I want," said Meia, "is for you to help two prisoners escape."

# CHAPTER THIRTY

Later, when it had all gone wrong, Syl would wonder if she might have done things differently had she known what would befall them. But that was the benefit of hindsight: looking back, everything was clearer, and every false step, every poor decision, seemed so obvious that it was impossible to believe that they had ever been taken at all. Still, Meia's scheme, however flawed, was the only one that had been offered to her, and the only plan there was. Of course she had to act; of course she had to try to save Paul and Steven, because they had saved her. And perhaps, just perhaps, they'd been captured because of her and Ani, because they had taken the time to help two panicked girls on the Royal Mile. Not taking action to prevent a wrong, when one could, seemed to Syl almost as bad as the terrible fate to which Gradus had sentenced the boys come the morning. Their bodies would swing, and she would bear witness.

The plan, as far as it went, revolved around something that Syl had never noticed until Meia pointed it out to her: Syl looked a little like Vena. Not a lot, and certainly not enough to fool a guard who wasn't blind, but they were similar in height and in the way that they carried themselves, even in the shape of their faces, the shrewdness of their features. It caused Syl to wonder if that was one of the reasons why Vena seemed to hate her so much, for there was no doubt that the Securitat despised her. The Securitats were bad news anyway; they were the Illyri secret police, but since they were under the control of the Corps, they would seize any opportunity to hurt members of the Military or their families. As the daughter of Lord Andrus, Syl was a particular target for Vena's venom. She thinks I'm a privileged little bitch, thought Syl, my father's pride and joy, the one who can do no wrong, the oldest of those who had come to be known as the Firstborn. Vena looks at me, and she sees herself as she might have been, as she should be. Well, let her think it, for all the good it will do her.

Perhaps it was that defiant streak, as much as her desire to save the lives of the two young men, which spurred her on so recklessly. Anyway, what choice was there? It wasn't as if Syl had any better suggestions. She was sixteen years old—born among the stars, settled on a strange world, raised among a hostile, sometimes murderous alien race—but so far she had not tried to break anyone out of jail.

However, the success of the plan lay not with her, but with Ani, and Ani's fledgling abilities.

"I don't know that I can do it," Ani said to Meia, as the spy took two Securitat uniforms from the back of her closet and laid them on her bed. Each had a Securitat cape with it too, hooded against the cold northern weather.

"You'd better be able to do it," said Meia. "If you can't, you and your friend may end up on the gallows with the humans."

Ani looked pleadingly at Syl. She did not want to do this.

"I trust you," said Syl, with more confidence than she felt. "I know you won't let anything happen to us. Right?"

Ani put her face in her hands. "I think I want to die," she said, her voice muffled by her fingers.

Meia patted her on the back.

"If you fail," she said, "that can be arranged."

With Ani's help, Syl tied her thick, glossy hair tightly back, and Meia smeared her hairline with a flesh-colored cream, plastering down any wisps, before daubing silver at the edge of her cheekbone. She handed her a slim hairgrip to secure the hood in place.

"I can't imagine that even Ani could keep them fooled if they saw all that damn hair," Meia said, looking critically at their attempt to hide it. "Whatever happens, keep it under wraps."

•   •   •

The two humans were being held in the old vaults of the castle. Built in the fifteenth century on the rock at the castle's south side, they had been used at various points as stores, barracks, an arsenal and, as was now the case, a prison. They were dank and unpleasant, the cells secured with electronic locks that could be opened only with swipe keys or directly from a panel in a nearby control room. At the moment the boys were the only prisoners being kept there, and were being guarded not by Galateans, who were usually given these dull jobs, but by Securitats. Four of them lined the corridor where Paul and Steven were being held, and two more were stationed in the control room. Cameras also monitored the cells, inside and out.

At precisely 9:00 p.m., the door to the control room opened from outside and then almost immediately closed again. The Securitats turned just in time to see a gas grenade roll across the floor toward them. Within seconds, they were unconscious.

Meia entered, a cloak over her head but her face unmasked, seemingly unaffected by the fumes. She immediately adjusted all the cameras in the vicinity of the cells so that they ceased recording, then quickly reprogrammed the nonessential screens to give her clear views of the area in front of the New Barracks, the old Military Jail, Foog's Gate, and St. Margaret's Chapel, as well as the approaches to the vaults from the Great Hall and the old Royal Palace. She would now have some notice, however short, if anyone came their way, but Syl and Ani would still need to work fast. Gas grenades would have been simpler, but Meia couldn't be sure they would have rendered all of the guards unconscious before one of them had the chance to raise the alarm.

She checked her watch. Five seconds.

Four.

Three.

Two.

One.

Two black-clad figures appeared on one of the screens.

It was beginning.

The uniforms didn't fit quite as well as they might have, and Syl's had a bloodstain on the left side, along with what looked like a repair necessitated by the insertion of a blade. Syl didn't want to think about how, or where, Meia had acquired it. She was starting to think that Meia was a lot more manipulative, and certainly more dangerous, than she had previously given her credit for.

They passed the control room and entered the vaults, pausing just before they turned into the main corridor of cells. A camera watched them from above. Ani stared back at it for a moment, then gave it, and Meia, the finger.

"She won't like that," whispered Syl.

"I don't care. It made me feel better."

Syl thought about it, then gave the finger to the camera as well. She wanted Paul and Steven freed, but she still didn't appreciate being exploited by Meia.

"You're right," she said. "That did make me feel better."

"Are you ready?" said Ani.

Syl nodded. "Are *you* ready?"

Ani let out a deep breath. Her whole body relaxed. When she looked at Syl, her eyes were bright yet distant, like a noonday sun glimpsed through haze.

"Yes," she said. "I am ready."

The first pair of Securitats stood to attention as they saw the uniformed figures approach, but both looked confused. One of them opened his mouth as if to say something, his hand straying toward the pulser at his belt.

"I—we—" he said. "We weren't expecting you, ma'am."

His eyes flickered from Syl's face to the silver near her temple, but he seemed to be having trouble focusing. He used the back of his hand to wipe his eyes, and when he had done so, he appeared more certain of what he was seeing.

"We're here to take the prisoners to the Grand Consul," said Syl. Beside her, Ani stayed completely silent, and Syl could almost feel the intensity of her concentration as she tried to fix the faces of Vena and one of her female sergeants, Grise, in the minds of the men before her.

"We received no notice," said the guard. "Our instructions were to allow no contact with the prisoners until the morning."

"And whose instructions were those?" said Syl, putting on her most imperious voice.

"Well, yours, ma'am, and the Grand Consul's."

She looked from one guard to the other, waiting. They faltered. One of them narrowed his eyes, like a man used to glasses who suddenly finds himself trying to see without them. Damn it, thought Syl, just go along with us. Please.

"The Grand Consul wishes to speak with the prisoners," she said. "Would you like me to go back and explain to him why this doesn't meet with your approval, or perhaps you'd prefer to do so yourself?"

Clearly neither option appealed to the guards. They set aside any doubts and led Syl and Ani to the cells, where two more guards waited. This was the hard part, for Ani now had to try to fog the minds of four individuals. Syl risked a glance at her. Ani's face was set in concentration. Small beads of sweat were visible on her forehead and upper lip, and Syl could see that her jaws were clenched tightly shut.

Now the second pair of guards stepped forward, and Syl instinctively lowered her head slightly as though that might help with the impersonation. She disguised the movement with a flick of her chin at the cell doors.

"Open them," she said, and when the cell guards again seemed reluctant to do so, their faces betraying some confusion, a kind of disjunction between what they were seeing and what they thought they saw, she added, "Quickly!" snarling it more than saying it.

This gave the guards the push they required. They were used to following orders—the simpler the better. It was easier to follow orders than to think about why you shouldn't. That was the whole principle on which armies were founded. Without it, they would have fallen to pieces.

The cell doors were swiped open, revealing Paul and Steven in their respective cells, each lying on his side, but neither of them sleeping.

"Up!" said Syl. "You're coming with us."

Paul raised himself to a sitting position. He frowned, and Syl could almost hear the mechanisms of his brain grinding as some spark of recognition took fire there. She willed him to say nothing, and then fell back on the same voice she had used on the guards.

"Now!"

Both young men rose and shuffled to the cell doors. The guards stepped back and drew their pulsers, ready for any trickery, but the young men presented no real threat. They looked tired and frightened. One of the guards put a pair of magnetic cuffs on each of the boys, and handed the control unit to Syl.

"Should we accompany you?" asked the first guard.

"No," said Syl. "They're secured, and we'll have no trouble from them. Soon," she added, "they'll be no trouble to anyone ever again."

The guard laughed, and the others joined in, but their laughter was nervous and uncertain. Beside her, Ani trembled with the effort of holding off the reality of their appearances. A tiny trickle of blood appeared from her right nostril and rolled down to her mouth. She turned from the guards before they could see it, and Syl motioned the boys to move ahead of her with the stun baton that Meia had given her.

They tried to walk out of the vaults slowly. It was all Syl could do not to sprint, yet even in the midst of her fear, she had never felt so alive.

They had done it. Somehow, they had done it.

# CHAPTER THIRTY-ONE

I f Syl could not quite believe that they had managed to get the prisoners out of their cells, Meia was more surprised still. She had resigned herself to having to rescue the young Illyri from the guards if necessary; the result would have been bloodshed, and even Meia preferred not to kill Securitats within the castle walls. On those occasions when she had been forced to target Securitats, and then only — or mostly — to protect herself, she had done so discreetly, and the bodies had never been found.

She had monitored the progress of Syl and Ani while keeping one hand on the handle of the control room door, ready to spring to their aid if — or when — everything went to pieces. Instead, she now watched as they escorted the humans, still manacled, out of the Vaults and toward the castle walls, where the next step of the plan would be enacted.

One of the unconscious guards at her feet moaned, and clawed at the floor. Meia removed a second grenade from the folds of her cloak. The last thing they needed now was for the guards to wake and raise the alarm. She pulled the pin and tossed the grenade with an underarm throw. Just as the gas began to fill the room, she saw three figures appear on one of the screens before her, heading for the Vaults.

Even through the fumes, she recognized Vena.

Syl led their little group onward, through passageways, corridors, and galleries, some foul-smelling, some damp-walled and mossy, twisting and turning down into the tunnels carved from the volcanic rock on which the castle had been built so many years before. These areas were vaguely familiar to her; she had explored them as a child, before they were returned to use as cells, but she had little memory of them. Without the instructions that Meia had drummed into her, she would have been entirely lost.

She looked back. Ani was struggling to keep up. The bleeding from her nose had stopped, but blood was still smeared across her left cheek and her chin. Her eyes were glassy, and she was supporting herself against the wall. Syl stopped to give her time to catch up. She noticed that Steven wasn't doing much better than Ani. Whatever the Corps had done to him physically was bad enough, but they had damaged something inside him as well. He might have believed himself to be big and strong like his older brother, but he was still more child than man. He was keeping himself going through sheer force of will, but Syl could tell that he wasn't far from crying for his mother.

"Hey," Syl said quietly to Ani. "Are you able to continue?"

Ani nodded. "I'm just tired. Very tired."

"We're nearly there," said Syl. She touched a hand to Ani's cheek. "We can't stop now."

"You're the one who stopped, Syl," said Ani.

"For you."

"You say."

This was the Ani that Syl knew and loved.

"Oh Ani, you did so well—"

"I knew it!" interrupted Paul loudly. "Sylvia! I recognize you now. You're not human, you're Illyri! I guessed as much. I should have known it back on the Mile."

Syl looked at him, a million thoughts going through her head yet not a single word able to form in her mouth. He was staring at her, his eyes narrowed, his pupils flitting over her exposed face, frowning as he took in the smear of silver, the strange paste on her hairline, and then he was staring into the golden-red orbs that were her eyes, lidless and alien.

"Holy crap," whispered Steven.

"It took me a while," said Paul, nodding slowly, "because your glasses covered your eyes when we first met, and then this uniform threw me too, but it was you, you and your friend here, on the Royal Mile. I thought you were human—a bit weird, yes, but at least human. Man, was I mistaken."

"I guess you were. I bet you're sorry you helped us now."

She looked back at him defiantly, at the so-very-human eyes in their bruised sockets, at the bloodied lips she'd focused on so intently only the day before. She watched him blink, and wondered at what that was like, at not being able to see for a split second. There was a long moment before Paul replied.

"No," he said at last, and his voice caught in a way that made Syl's cheeks burn. "I'm not. Look, forgive me if I'm wrong, but is this a rescue?"

"Yes, it is."

"Oh good. I was hoping it might be. Any chance you could take these cuffs off then, Sylvia?"

"Sorry," said Syl, "and my name's actually Syl."

He raised his eyebrows at her as if it didn't matter, and looked pointedly at his bound hands once again. Syl activated the unit, and the cuffs demagnetized and dropped off. Paul rubbed his wrists and winced. The magnacuffs had a tendency to heat up after only a few minutes.

"About time. I wish you'd done that a bit earlier, *Syl*."

"You're quite critical for someone who was hours away from being hanged," said Syl. "Would you like to go back to your cell and come up with a better plan of your own?"

"Actually, no, I wouldn't."

"I didn't think so."

"So where are we going?"

"Out."

"We seem to be taking the long way."

"We're taking the *safe* way," said Syl. "I hope."

"Okay then. I guess we'll just have to trust you."

"Right. Any more questions or comments, or shall we get moving?"

"Well, just one thing."

Syl sighed. She wondered if all rescuers had to put up with this sort of criticism.

"What is it?"

"Thank you," said Paul. "On behalf of both of us, just thank you."

Syl was thrown.

"You're welcome," she said, and blushed again. "We're only returning the favor, though."

He ignored her glibness.

"You know, after you left, I rather hoped I'd see you again, and without your damned glasses."

"But now you know I'm Illyri."

"Yeah. But at least you don't have a squint."

He smiled, and she found herself smiling back, unable to help herself. They stared at each other, and might have gone on staring were it not for a cough in the background.

"I don't mean to spoil a lovely moment," said Ani, "but I really would like to get this over and done with, please."


Not all the cells in the castle were occupied, or, indeed, locked. The stonework in some was in a state of disrepair, while others were used for storage and, on occasion, as sleeping quarters for guards pulling double duty. It was from the darkness of one such cell, furnished only with a pillow and a mattress, that Meia watched Vena pass, accompanied by two of her acolytes. She guessed it was a routine prisoner check, or perhaps the beginning of another spell of interrogation. Either way, she cursed the female Securitat and all her works. Damn her, why couldn't she just have put her feet up, basking in her success in capturing the humans and looking forward to the executions to come?

Meia waited until the three Securitats had turned the corner. She had no more grenades, although she did have her blast pistol. But it was one thing knocking Securitats unconscious in order to free prisoners, or quietly "disappearing" them if they happened to look the wrong way at an inconvenient time; quite another to kill Sedulus's vicious little pet, however much personal satisfaction the act might bring her. There would be trouble enough once the escape was discovered without adding high-profile bodies to the mix.

She slipped from the cell. A camera watched her from above, but she had no fear of it. She had disabled every camera in the building before leaving the control room. She checked her watch. Syl and Ani should have been at the wall by now, for in a few minutes the castle would be ringing with alarm bells.

Alarm bells.

Meia stopped. She took her blast pistol from her belt and adjusted its setting, before pointing it at the mattress and firing a single shot. A section of the mattress exploded, and flames licked around the edges of the blast mark. Meia fanned them with her hands, feeding the fire until the mattress and the pillow were burning merrily. When she was happy with the blaze, she followed the route taken by Syl and Ani. She paused only once, just long enough to smash the glass that covered the little red box on the wall, and trip the fire alarm.

The Securitats at the cells were relaxing. They could afford to, now that the prisoners had been handed over to Vena. The humans were no longer their responsibility. For a while, at least, they could take it easy. One of them had produced a small silver flask of a kind that might have been familiar to Meia's Resistance contact Trask, and they passed it around to warm themselves, for the Vaults were damp and cold.

It was with some surprise, then, that their sergeant found himself confronted with the spectacle of Vena and two lieutenants. He was only thankful that the flask of whisky had been emptied and put away.

"We didn't expect you back so soon, ma'am," he said.

Vena took in his slightly red face, and the alcohol on his breath, and the two cell doors standing open behind him. She didn't say a word. She simply drew her pulser and shot the sergeant in the forehead.

"Sound the—" she began to say, but the final word was drowned out by a blast of sirens.

Fire: the castle was burning.


The alarm echoed through the passageway.

"They're coming!" said Steven, and he seemed very young in his panic. "They're going to catch us and kill us!"

"Hush!" said Syl. "It's the fire alarm."

Seconds later, though, she heard another noise, a *whoop*ing rather than a siren. She exchanged a look with Ani. That was the general alarm. The escape had been discovered.

"What is it?" asked Paul.

"You need to go," said Syl.

"Go?" he said, looking at the solid wall before them. "Go where?"

Syl wouldn't have been able to find the door had Meia not described its position down to the last inch. It was marked by two thin white lines against the stone, little more than scratches. Syl took the sensor key from the pocket of her uniform and placed it beside the marks. There was a click, and a section of the stonework simply popped open; it was metal painted to look like brick, and the hole revealed was just large enough for one body to squeeze through, as long as the body in question wasn't large. Syl had no idea how or when it had been installed; all she knew was that it was Meia's work, and there were probably other bolt-holes like it scattered around the castle.

Outside, a man stood waiting on the rocks. He was tall, but slightly hunched. "Trask!" said Paul.

"Come on, lads," said Trask. "No time to lose."

Paul turned to Syl. "What about our mother? She was arrested with us."

"She's safe," said Syl. Meia had told her that Mrs. Kerr had been released shortly after her sons' capture. They were the prize, not her. Syl could only hope, for the boys' sake, that Meia had been telling the truth.

Steven was already scrambling through the hole, helped by Ani.

"Are you going to be all right?" asked Paul.

"Now that I know that you . . . people aren't going to be executed by my kind, yeah, I think we'll be okay," said Syl. "Whatever happens."

"For what it's worth, we really didn't plant those bombs," he said.

"I know. And I'm glad," said Syl.

Paul grasped her arm. He leaned forward to say something, but no words came, and he was gone before Syl realized that he had kissed her.

# CHAPTER THIRTY-TWO

The castle grounds rang with the sound of sirens. Confusion reigned, just as Meia intended. Illyri were falling over each other in an effort to establish not only what was happening, but who was responsible for dealing with it. Meanwhile, the entire castle force of Diplomat guards and Securitats, alerted by Vena, was trying to hunt the prisoners, but was being hampered by those who were attempting to locate the fire. Meia, her cloak now discarded, moved through it all with clarity of purpose, while being careful not to draw undue attention to herself. She was under no illusions about how much time her little fire would buy all those involved in the escape bid. She needed to be sure that the human males were safely out of the castle, and Syl and Ani secure in their own rooms, before Vena and her underlings got a handle on the situation.

Still, she could not resist a small smile. She had just organized a major act of treason, and so far it had all gone rather well.

Syl and Ani were not smiling. They were about to undone by a stuck zipper.

The uniforms Meia had secured for them were larger than required, but it hadn't mattered because beneath them the two young Illyri were wearing their own casual clothes. The plan was to ditch the uniforms outside the castle walls, where the man tasked with getting the boys to safety would make sure that they were burned, destroying all traces of DNA that might be used to identify the perpetrators of the escape. Unfortunately, Meia's supply of Securitat uniforms was largely determined by whatever she had managed to strip from the dead or otherwise acquire. While Ani's uniform had opened easily, Syl's zip had caught on her own clothes underneath, and now the boys and the older human were gone, and had taken only Ani's suit and boots with them.

"You've busted the zip," said Ani, gritting her teeth with the effort of trying to pull Syl's fastening down. "You're clearly too fat for that suit."

"I am not!" said Syl, tearing at the clasp.

And perhaps it was the fear, but Ani started to giggle, and couldn't stop.

"I can't do it," she said. "I'm serious."

"You have to. If they find me like this, they'll know."

A shadow fell across them, and a blade flashed in the dark.

"I could hear you from across the courtyard," said Meia. "You'll bring the whole Diplomatic Corps down on you."

"We can't open the zipper," said Ani.

Meia's knife solved the problem, slashing the material from the nape of Syl's neck to the base of her spine. Syl shrugged off the remains of the garment, removed two folded slippers from the pockets of her trousers, and slid her feet into them. Now, like Ani, she looked as though she had been disturbed by the sirens, and had left her rooms hurriedly to investigate. The problem was that those rooms were on the other side of the castle.

Meia blasted the remains of the uniform three times, kicking them into a pile so that the flames consumed them entirely. Then she spat on her fingers and removed the worst of the blood from Ani's grimacing face.

"Yuck," said Ani.

"I didn't like it any more than you did," said Meia. "Now, heads down and come with me. If anyone stops us, say nothing. I'll do the talking."

As it happened, they were stopped only once. A quartet of Securitats, anxious to avoid a pulse to the head, were hunting for the missing humans, and questioning everyone who crossed their path. There was no way to avoid them, so Meia did the very opposite: she went to them before they could come to her.

"You four," she said. "Come with me."

"What?" said the leader, who bore the four gold flashes of a lieutenant on his collar, and clearly wasn't used to being ordered around by anyone with fewer than five flashes, never mind a female with no flashes at all.

"These are the children of the governor and General Danis," said Meia. "I'm taking them to safety in St. Margaret's Chapel, and I need an escort."

"We're searching for two escaped prisoners," said the lieutenant. "We don't have time for this."

Meia spoke softly and carefully to him, the way she might have done to a very small child.

"There are two humans loose in the castle," she said. "If anything happens to the governor's daughter, those responsible will take the humans' place on the gallows in the morning. Do I make myself clear?"

The lieutenant swallowed involuntarily, as though he could already feel the noose tightening around his neck. He gestured to two of his guards.

"Escort the governor's daughter and her party to the chapel," he said.

Meia nodded curtly. "Thank you, Lieutenant. I'll be sure that the governor is informed of the assistance you offered."

The two Securitats stayed with them until they reached the chapel door, whereupon Meia informed them that they could return to their duties. Once they were gone, she led Syl and Ani to the nave and, with their help, lifted a stone from the floor, revealing a set of steps winding into the darkness.

"Down you go," she said.

Syl went first, then Ani. Meia brought up the rear, restoring the stone to its original position from below as she came. For a few seconds they were in total darkness, until Meia produced a flashlight and pointed it down a tunnel that was so low they had to bend almost double to make any progress, their backs nearly touching the roof and their necks straining. It seemed to take forever to make their way along it, Meia instructing them from behind to go left or right when necessary, until they came to another flight of stairs. There was just enough space for Meia to squeeze by Syl and Ani and ascend. She placed a finger to her lips, and all three listened carefully for any sound from above, but heard nothing. At last Meia pushed upward, and a dim light was revealed to them from above. She vanished briefly before returning to tell them that all was well.

They found themselves in Meia's closet, making their way through her garments into the bedroom beyond. Syl and Ani collapsed in a heap on the floor. Their faces, hands, and clothing were filthy. They had cuts and scrapes on their knuckles, and Syl found a gash on her head from where she had misjudged the height of the tunnel ceiling, but they were safe.

"Let's never do that again," said Syl.

"Seconded," said Ani.

Two sets of nightclothes were laid out on Meia's bed, one for each of them. Meia, as always, had planned ahead. Syl and Ani took it in turn to wash and change in the bathroom.

"That," said Meia, when they looked respectable once again, "was very, very impressive. Sloppy, and noisy, but impressive nonetheless."

"Thank you," said Ani. "I think."

"How many tunnels and escape routes do you have exactly?" asked Syl.

"Exactly?"

"Yes."

"None of your business."

"Oh. Fine."

Meia relented.

"Some of them were here already," she said. "Most of them were constructed shortly after your father decided that the castle should be his base of operations. He gave me responsibility for its security systems. I just added a few safeguards of my own along the way."

"They won't find out that we did it, will they?" said Ani.

"I disabled all the recording systems in the Vaults. There's nothing to prove you were ever there. As far as the guards are concerned, Vena ordered the prisoners' transfer, even if that has probably come as a surprise to Vena herself. Now I'm going to escort you back to your rooms. Naturally, you will say nothing of this to anyone. If you're questioned, I came to get you when the alarms sounded, and took you to the chapel until I determined that all was safe. Okay?"

Syl and Ani nodded.

"You did well," said Meia. "You didn't just save two lives tonight. You saved many. Remember that, in the days to come."

And they did, both of them, even later as they were running for their own lives.

# CHAPTER THIRTY-THREE

Paul wasn't sure where they were.

As soon as they were away from the castle, he and Steven were bundled into the back of a van by Trask. The front seats were cut off from the rest of the vehicle by a sheet of metal that had been welded to the sides, and there were two masked men waiting to help them up, although *help* was probably not the most accurate way to put it, given that the boys were dragged inside, told to keep their mouths shut, and made to wear rough sacks over their heads to obscure their vision. The two men were unfamiliar to Paul, but he knew them for what they were: pure muscle—unsympathetic and unyielding. Their presence in the van gave him some idea of what was to come.

While they drove, Paul tried to keep track of the distance they might have traveled, and the route they were taking, but quickly gave up. He knew that Trask would double back on himself, and make unnecessary stops and turns, just to confuse his passengers and, indeed, anyone who might be following them. Nevertheless, he didn't stay on the streets for too long. Even though a curfew was no longer in place, and there was plenty of traffic, the prisoners' escape would force the Illyri to start closing roads and searching vehicles. A system of retractable bollards was in place on all major roads in Edinburgh, capable of sealing off the main routes into and out of the city center. Trask's priority would be to get beyond them and make for a safe house. Someone else would then ditch the van a few miles away, probably by sticking it into the back of a truck or hiding it in a container, just in case the Illyri had spotted it on a security camera and had put out an alert. There were fewer cameras away from the city center and the main roads—and those that the Illyri had tried to install were routinely vandalized—but there might well be drones or lurkers in the air, and they wouldn't know about it until the van was stopped, or a missile vaporized them.

The van came to a halt. Strong hands hauled Paul and Steven to their feet and guided them out and down a flight of steps. A door opened and then closed again behind them. Paul smelled coffee and cigarettes, and a conversation suddenly ceased. He was forced into a chair, and the sack was removed from his head. He was in a near-empty basement. There was a battered table before him, and behind it two more chairs waited. Steven was gone. They would be questioned separately. That was standard practice. It was what Paul himself would have done had he been faced with two Resistance members who might have revealed secrets to the Illyri.

Trask took one chair and one of the two masked men from the van took the other. The second masked man entered with three cups of coffee and a plate of toast on a tray before leaving again.

"Help yourself," said Trask.

Paul did. He was hungry, and the coffee smelled wonderful, even though it was cheap and nasty instant. But when he tried to lift his cup, his hand began to shake, and the coffee slopped over the sides. He felt sick and he thought he might faint.

"You're all right, son," said Trask. "It's natural after what you've been through. Take a couple of deep breaths. You'll be fine."

Beside him, the masked man took a piece of toast and dunked it in his coffee. Trask looked at him peculiarly.

"You dunk toast in coffee?" he said.

"I dunk anything in anything. Coffee or tea, it's all the same to me."

"It doesn't taste right if you dunk it."

The masked man nibbled on his soggy toast.

"Tastes fine to me."

"There's something wrong with you."

"Will you give it a rest?" said the masked man. "You're ruining it for me."

Trask shook his head at Paul as if to say "See what I have to put up with?"

"It's hard to get decent staff these days," said Paul, who was recovering himself with the help of sips of coffee and bites of toast.

"You shut up, or I'll do you," said the masked man, the threat made only slightly less intimidating by the fact that he was waving a piece of soggy toast. "You'll be lucky to walk out of here without broken bones."

Paul nodded. It was good cop, bad cop. In another room, Steven was doubtless experiencing the same routine.

"Our mum," he said. "Is she still in the city?"

He knew that the Securitats would come looking for her in the aftermath of her sons' escape. He didn't want her to suffer more because of what he and Steven had done.

"We moved her to Aberdeen earlier today, when we knew there was a chance of getting you back," said Trask. "Wouldn't want the Illyri taking out their temper on her, would we?"

Paul closed his eyes in relief.

Trask took a long gulp of coffee.

"Right then," he said. "May as well get started."


The debriefing went on for most of the night. It began gently, but grew tougher. Twice the masked man slapped Paul hard across the back of the head, causing Trask to tut-tut and tell him to take it easy, even while his eyes remained cold. In the end, it all came down to one question: *What did you tell them?*

Because everybody broke, in the end. They had seen Steven's fingers. He was just a boy, and he'd have told them something to make the pain end. Hell, a grown man would have confessed in order to stop it. It was understandable. It was okay. They just wanted to know what had been given away.

But Paul was good—better even than Trask suspected—and he had taught his brother well. They had fed the Illyri tidbits of information, but it was all useless: the locations of safe houses long abandoned or burned to the ground; the names of operatives who were dead or had never existed; codes that were years old. It was the kind of information that a couple of low-level boys in the Resistance might have been expected to have overheard from others. Paul had drummed it all into his brother, going over it again and again as they lay in their adjoining beds at home.

*If we're captured, this is what we say, and we never, ever deviate from it. Understand?*

*Yes, Paul. I understand.*

And he had. He was screaming in pain, and there was nothing that his older brother could do to stop it, but still he gave them only what Paul had taught him to give. This is the safe house. This is the man who told us where to go. This is the code.

Useless: all of it useless.

From time to time, Trask or the other man would leave the room, and Paul knew that they were checking what he told them against what his brother was saying. By the time Trask said, "Enough," Paul's head ached, he desperately needed to go to the bathroom, and he wanted to shower because he could smell himself. He was left alone while Trask and the masked man went outside to confer. When they returned after about twenty minutes, the second man was no longer masked. His head was shaved, and he wore a white T-shirt, exposing arms covered in tattoos. On his right forearm was a thistle that dripped blood from its leaves: the symbol of the Highland Resistance.

"You did good, laddie," said Trask. "You and your brother."

"Sorry about the slaps," said the tattooed man. "You know how it is."

Paul knew. He didn't have to like it, but he knew.

"This is Joe," said Trask. "Just Joe."

Paul had heard the name. Just Joe was the Green Man's lieutenant, which made him the second in command of the Highland Resistance. The Highland Resistance was scattered, but disciplined; if it had a leader, it was the Green Man, and Just Joe stood at his right hand. He was the face of the Highland Resistance. The Green Man's identity was kept very secret, and there were those who claimed that he did not exist at all.

The Highlanders did not use surnames because no one wanted family members intimidated or friends tortured for information should their true identities be revealed. All that was known of Just Joe was that he had an army background, he was fearless and loyal, and completely ruthless, doing what needed to be done without flinching or sentiment. He was respected, yes. Feared? Absolutely. Liked?

It had never occurred to anyone to try.

There were stories about Joe, of course. They all had stories. Joe's, it was whispered, was that he had once had a wife and a baby boy, and they'd lived together near Aviemore. Being a military man, Joe had been an early prisoner of the invading forces. According to rumors, his wife had received a visit from an Illyri intelligence officer while Joe was in jail. The officer told her that Joe had died in custody, and she and her child were to be thrown out of their house because of evidence that her husband had been conspiring against the Illyri, and the property of all conspirators was automatically forfeit. It was an act of casual cruelty, committed because, it was said, this particular intelligence officer had developed an early liking for human women, and Joe's wife was exceptionally pretty. She was also very delicate—physically, emotionally, and psychologically. The intelligence officer told her that he might be able to find a way to look after her and her child, in return for certain favors. He gave her until the morning to think about it. She didn't need that long. She killed herself before midnight. They'd shown Joe pictures of the bodies of his wife and child beside each other on the bed, their faces transformed by the gas. It was only later that he found out why she had done it.

The intelligence officer vanished from Fort William the following year, on a clear, cool March evening not long after Just Joe's release from internment. The Illyri's head was found impaled on a fence post a week later. The rest of him was never discovered, although the story went that it had been fed to pigs. His head had still been attached to his body at that point.

He couldn't have screamed otherwise.

But it was just a story, although it might have explained why Joe's small guerrilla fiefdom in the Highlands was known as Camp Glynis—the name of his Welsh wife, murmured the gossips, or perhaps it was just because Glynis meant "narrow valley" in his late wife's tongue. Anyway, it no longer mattered. Camp Glynis, like Glynis herself, was now merely a memory. Joe's band had allied itself to the troops of the Green Man many years earlier. The Green Man promised Joe that more Illyri blood would be spilled if they fought together than if they fought alone, and he had kept his promise.

"You'll be going to the Highlands," Trask told Paul, "you and Steven. It won't be safe for you in the city. The Illyri will tear it apart looking for you."

Paul nodded. He had guessed as much.

"The Green Man has also decided that a little more cooperation with us city boys might not go amiss," continued Trask.

And then Paul understood: somehow this was related to the attack on Birdoswald, and it was the Highlanders who must have been responsible for it. The Highlanders had never struck so far south before, but they were still the only ones outside Edinburgh equipped to carry out such an assault. Clearly someone in the Edinburgh Resistance had let the Highlanders know that they couldn't simply start blowing up Illyri bases outside their own patch without first asking permission. It wasn't polite.

"You're to be our ambassador to the Highlanders. I'm sure that pleases you as much as it will please them. You can get up from that chair now. There's a hot shower waiting for you, and clean clothes, and a proper meal before you leave."

But Paul didn't move. He wanted to. He wanted it all so badly: the shower, the clothes, all of it, but it wasn't time, not yet.

"I have more to say," he said.

Trask looked puzzled, and Just Joe scowled in a manner that suggested some more slaps might be on their way.

"You haven't asked me what we found under Knutter's shop," said Paul. "I have to tell you about the bodies."

# CHAPTER THIRTY-FOUR

Syl slept the sleep of the dead that night. She would have laughed in disbelief had anyone told her earlier that in the wake of the successful rescue of two human prisoners from the vaults—an act of treason that might well be punishable by death—she would rest deeply, but she did. She went to her bed exhausted and strangely exhilarated, with the memory of a kiss brushed softly on her lips.

She had been kissed before. The previous summer she had engaged in a brief, inquisitive romance with Harnur, one of her classmates, before Harnur's father had been transferred to Bolivia—a transfer that might not have been entirely unconnected with Governor Andrus's suspicion that Harnur had feelings for his beloved daughter. In truth, Syl had been more intrigued by the notion of being in love, and the highs and lows that might go with it, rather than holding any particular feelings for Harnur himself, who had been clumsy, self-absorbed, and a little too free with his hands for Syl's liking. If her father had found out just how free he had been, Harnur's own father might have found himself posted somewhere even worse than Bolivia: Kabul, for example, or Lagos.

Syl slept so soundly, in fact, that initially the banging at her door was incorporated into a dream of blood and water, the sounds becoming the beating of a great heart hidden beneath the earth, a heart that beat in time with the rhythms of her own. Only when the door burst open and lights shone in her face did she wake up. Vena advanced toward her bed, and Syl knew that she was lost.

• • •

A quartet of Securitats stood outside Ani's door. Their sergeant swiped his skeleton key through the electronic lock, but nothing happened. Instead, he was forced to resort to more old-fashioned methods. It took him three kicks to break the door down. By the time he succeeded, the window was open, and Ani was long gone.

Alerted by the noise, Lord Andrus rushed to the corridor in time to see Syl escorted from her room, her hands cuffed behind her back, her feet bare against the cold stone. He wore his red dressing gown, and his hair was tousled. With him came two of the castle guards who always remained posted at his door, and behind them Syl saw Althea and Meia. Immediately she looked away from her father's spymistress, afraid that even a lingering glance might reveal Meia's involvement to Vena. This was about the prisoners' escape. It had to be, even though Vena had remained entirely silent during Syl's arrest. If Meia was still free, then the Securitats did not yet know of her part in what had occurred.

"Father!" cried Syl.

"What is the meaning of this?" said Lord Andrus. "Let my daughter go!"

But now more heavily armed Securitats had been summoned, and among them was Lord Consul Gradus. Syl noticed that he was fully dressed, even though the clock in her room read 4:15 a.m. when she had been dragged from her bed. He must have known in advance about her arrest; even Vena would not have dared to come for the governor's daughter in the dead of night without the agreement of the Lord Consul. Meia had a blast pistol in her hand, and Lord Andrus's guards carried blast rifles, but they were outnumbered, and the possibility of hitting Syl if they fired was too great to risk a gun battle.

"I'm afraid it won't be possible to release your daughter just yet," said Gradus. His hands were buried in the sleeves of his white robes. Only his head remained exposed. It was as though a great white slug were swallowing him, slowly consuming him from the legs up.

"Gradus, you overstep your authority here," warned Andrus.

"I think not," said Gradus. "I *am* the authority here, and your daughter is a traitor."

Lord Andrus looked at Syl in disbelief. "What is this, Syl? What are they saying?"

Vena stepped forward. She held a plated millipede on the palm of her right hand. The tiny camera on its head looked like a dewdrop. She called up a screen, and Syl saw life-size flickering versions of herself and Ani, dressed in Securitat uniforms, standing at a cell door, then stepping back to allow Paul and Steven Kerr to emerge. The film lasted for only a few seconds, but it was enough to damn them.

As the images of Syl and Ani vanished, Vena smiled at Meia.

"Spies are not the only ones who find lurkers useful," she said. She displayed the little arthropod for a second longer, than crushed it in her fist.

Meia did not reply, but the look on her face left no doubt that, like the unfortunate millipede, Vena would not survive long in Meia's hands if the opportunity presented itself.

"Your daughter and her friend conspired in the escape of the terrorists," said Gradus. "We are not yet certain of how they fooled the guards, but rest assured that we will find out."

But Andrus was not listening. He had eyes only for his daughter.

"Syl, is this true?"

Syl tried to answer, but she could not. Instead, to her shame, she began to cry, and she could not stop the tears from coming even as she was led away.

Ani flitted through the castle courtyard, moving from shadow to shadow. She had felt the Securitats coming. She had dreamed them, and then the dream became real. Luckily, she was practiced at slipping from her bedroom unnoticed, and had become adept at using a knotted rope to climb from the first-floor window to the ground. When she heard the door burst open, she was already halfway to St. Margaret's Chapel, and by the time the alarm was raised, she was lifting the flagstone behind the altar and lowering herself into the tunnel. There had been no time to find a flashlight, and so she was in total darkness as she started to make her way, by memory and touch, back to the one Illyri who might be able to help her: Meia. She already knew that it was too late to warn Syl. It seemed to Ani that revealing to Meia the extent of her gift had somehow increased its potency, for she had been subduing it before in order to keep it a secret from others. Now she sensed Syl's anguish, but there was nothing she could do for her, not yet. Later, perhaps, but her own priority was to stay out of the clutches of the Securitats, and find the spymistress.

As the darkness pressed in upon her, Ani thought that she had never liked Meia, had never trusted her because she could never sense her thoughts. Meia just always smelled of trouble and deceit.

All things considered, Ani concluded, she had probably been right.

Syl was not taken to the Vaults, or to the Securitats' interrogation rooms, or to any of the places usually reserved for prisoners. Instead, she found herself in Syrene's chambers once again, this time alone. The light was dim and the air was strangely scented, an aroma at once familiar yet completely alien, an inherited memory given form. An enormous vase of flowers, the likes of which she had never seen before, stood on a polished oak table, their curling, tangled heads glowing softly in the moonlight, their outsize stamens drooping with thick, wet, heady pollen.

"Are they not beautiful?" said a silken voice, and there was a movement from the shadows at the back of the room. Syl had not heard Syrene enter, and the door had remained closed. Perhaps Meia was not the only one with knowledge of the castle's secret ways, but Syl suspected that Syrene had no need of tunnels in order to move without being seen. She recalled the image of the ghost of the Red Witch standing over her, and her temples tingled unpleasantly at the memory.

"No," she said. "I don't think they're beautiful at all."

"They are called avatis blossoms," said Syrene. "I grew them on the journey to Earth. They are of Illyr, just as you are. I felt that I needed a reminder of my home on this alien world. Perhaps, had you been surrounded by similar tokens, you might not have found yourself in this unfortunate situation. It strikes me that your father has fallen too much in love with this planet. It is he who has made a traitor of you. He planted a seed in your heart, and from it grew treachery."

"No," said Syl. "That's not true."

Syrene advanced. She raised a hand, as though to stroke the avatis. Instantly the heads of the flowers closed, and a puff of foul-smelling gas erupted from its leaves.

"It's a defense mechanism," said Syrene. "All species have one. The avatis is trying to protect itself, even though it's already dying. It was dying from the moment it was cut and placed in this vase."

She turned to face Syl.

"Your father too is dying. He was dying from the instant he fell in love with this planet. Away from the soil of Illyr, his influence and power have slowly waned, even though he did not realize it. Now his own daughter has dealt him the fatal blow."

Syl's cheeks burned. She lowered her eyes. There was a truth in what Syrene was saying, a terrible, humiliating truth. Syl had fatally undermined her father by committing an act of treason, even though she had believed it to be the right thing to do.

"My husband believes that your father planned the humans' escape, and somehow contrived to have you do his dirty work," said Syrene. "Is this true?"

"No," said Syl. She breathed deeply. She would not cry again. She had cried enough that night.

"But you're just a child! You could not have planned this venture alone."

"I did."

"Aided by your friend Ani."

"It was my idea. I forced her to do it."

"Really? From what I hear of your friend, I doubt that she could be forced to do anything she did not want to. But somebody aided you. Who gassed the guards?"

"We did."

"Come, come. And you disabled the main surveillance system, too?"

"Yes."

"I should like to know how you did that. If we were to take you to the control room, perhaps you could show us."

"No," said Syl. "I won't. It's a secret."

"Oh! A secret? Of course."

Syrene went to the drinks cabinet by the window. Among the bottles of whisky and wine now rested a number of curved decanters of liquids in various hues of amber that seemed lit from within. Syl had seen such bottles before. They contained Illyri cremos, a drink made from berries grown on Taleth, a distant moon of the Illyr system. It grew darker as it aged, and some of these bottles contained cremos that was very dark, and thus very old, and very valuable. Even Syl's father—an Illyri so in love with Earth and its treasures that he owned vineyards of his own in France and Spain—prized cremos.

Syrene poured two glasses from the darkest of the bottles, and handed one to Syl.

"No, thank you."

"Drink it," said Syrene. "Don't be ignorant, child. You could fill this glass with diamonds from Earth, and it would not be worth as much as the liquid that it now contains."

Syl took the glass. As she raised it to her lips, she smelled cloves, cinnamon, and hints of plum and cherry, but she did not share this with Syrene. She did not think the Red Witch would find it amusing that the only points of reference she could find for the delicate scent of fine cremos were entirely terrestrial in origin. She sipped the drink. It tasted like she imagined sunset might: a deep, red, beautiful summer sunset.

"Sit," said Syrene.

Syl did as she was told. Once more she faced the Red Witch across this table.

"Vena wants you to be handed over to her for interrogation," said Syrene. "Marshal Sedulus feels the same way. I don't think you'd enjoy their company very much."

"No," Syl admitted.

"I wouldn't like it very much either," said Syrene. "Did you know that Vena was rejected by the Sisterhood? A streak of cruelty that we found unappealing manifested itself during her novitiate. Cruelty is always a sign of weakness, and the Sisterhood has no time for weakness. You, on the other hand, are not cruel, and not weak. Tell me truly: why did you free those boys?"

"Because I did not want to see them die," said Syl.

"Even though they had committed an atrocity?"

"They did not do it."

"How do you know?"

"They told me so."

"Before or after you rescued them?"

"After."

"And you believed them? Why?"

"Because they had no reason to lie, not then."

Syrene nodded. "Clever girl, and merciful. But innocent or guilty, Sedulus and Vena wanted them dead. Sedulus wishes to be unleashed on humanity. He thinks that by killing and tormenting, he will bend mankind to his will. Vena is his puppet, and she dances at his bidding. They are grotesquely alike. In the plans for the hanging, it had to be explained to Vena why it was important to know the height and weight of the person to be killed in order to calculate the length of rope required to break the neck. Vena could not understand why those boys should not have simply been left to strangle slowly."

"But you wanted them to die too," said Syl. "You and your husband."

"Because it would serve our ends."

"Which are?"

"Which are none of your business, but there is a difference between putting someone to death and making him suffer. Death can be painful, or relatively painless. I prefer the painless option. I am not cruel."

The thought flashed through Syl's head before she could stop it—Oh, but you are cruel, and crueler than a thug like Vena could ever be, because you're intelligent, and calculating. Vena is cruel because she's flawed deep inside, but you're cruel because you choose to be—and she saw it mirrored on Syrene's face, and the Archmage smiled at the truth of it.

"Tell me," said Syrene, "how did you fool those guards into releasing the humans into your care?"

"We bluffed them."

Syrene waved a hand in dismissal, as though the lie were little more than an insect to be swatted away.

"They claimed—or at least the three left alive claimed—that Vena herself came and took them away," said Syrene. "They looked at you and your friend, and they saw Vena and a sergeant. That's not bluffing, but something much deeper. That's a gift, and you do not have it, because I've looked inside you."

There was a lie there: Syl was certain of it. Syrene had indeed *tried* to look inside her, but she had blocked her. Meia had taught her well. Now, as she listened to Syrene, she began to build her wall again, hiding her secrets from the Red Witch's prying intelligence.

"Oh, you have talents, and you're stronger than anyone suspects, but to dissemble in that way is beyond you," said Syrene. "Which leaves your friend Ani to do the hard work; her, or someone else whose identity I do not yet know. I suspect Ani; after all, she had already fled when the Securitats came for her, and they were silent in their approach. She knew that they were coming. She *sensed* it."

"I don't know what you're talking about," said Syl.

Something flashed in Syrene's eyes. Her hand tightened on her glass, and the delicate crystal seemed on the verge of shattering under the pressure, but the Red Witch, either out of concern for its contents or a reluctance to demonstrate such a show of anger, relented.

"Don't lie to me," she said evenly. "I don't like it."

*Trowel. Cement. Brick. Position. Trowel . . .*

"Tell me!"

*Cement. Brick. Position. Trowel. Cement . . .*

"Oh, you little fool," said Syrene.

She stood. As if by silent summons, the door to her chambers opened, and Vena stood in the gap, waiting.

"This is your last night on Earth," said Syrene. "You will never see it again."

Syl rose from her chair. Slowly she tipped her glass, and the valuable cremos spilled on Syrene's ancient rug, damaging it irreparably.

"I will look inside your head and find out what you're hiding," said Syrene, "even if I have to use a surgeon's scalpel to do it."

She motioned to Vena.

"Take her away."

# CHAPTER THIRTY-FIVE

S yl was taken to one of the windowless cells in the Vaults so recently vacated by Paul and Steven. She was given a one-piece suit and her nightclothes were taken away. She was provided with a mattress, a blanket, and a jug of water, and left alone with her thoughts. This time, Vena took upon herself the duties of guarding the prisoner, assisted by twelve of her most loyal underlings. Clearly, the Securitats were anticipating some attempt to free Syl, because they were armed with both pulsers and heavy-duty blast rifles, and their uniforms had been exchanged for battle armor. Vena informed her that she would be allowed no visitors, and no one beyond Vena's cohort—not even the Grand Consul—was permitted to approach her cell, on pain of death.

"What will happen to me?" asked Syl.

"You are to be taken offworld tomorrow," said Vena. "Eventually, in accordance with the requirements of Illyri justice, you will be tried and, I have no doubt, found guilty of treason."

She paused at the door.

"I do have one question for you," she said.

Syl waited. She could have told Vena exactly what to do with her question, but she did not. She dreaded the thought of the cell door closing. While it was still open, there was hope: hope of rescue, of her father's coming to release her, of Meia's mounting some kind of daring escape bid just as had been done for the humans. They would not fear Vena's guns. They would not let Syl be taken through the wormhole, to be lost in the vastness of the universe.

But her father . . .

Her father was ashamed of her. She had seen it in his eyes. His own daughter was a traitor, and she would be made to face the full force of the law. He could not condone or excuse treason, even by his own blood. If an exception were made for her, then the law would be meaningless. And if—or rather *when*—she was found guilty, her father's career would be over. She had ruined him through her actions.

"My question is this," said Vena. "You had everything, but you threw it away, and for humans. Why?"

Syl stared her straight in the face.

"So that I could look at myself in the mirror," she replied, "and know that I was not like you."

"I always hated you," said Vena.

"I know," said Syl.

"And you always hated me."

"No," said Syl, her voice almost bored. "I pitied you. You hurt, and you torture, and you kill, but you do it to feed the rage and pain inside you; destroying the lives of others is easier than facing the emptiness of your own. You're nothing to me."

Vena's eyes glittered with pure, vengeful malice.

"The Grand Consul wants you to hang," she said, "you and your friend. He thinks it will be an apt punishment for depriving the gallows of two lives. What the Grand Consul wants, he gets, but when you hang, it will be in the hold of a starship far, far from here, and I will be in charge of the rope. I'll make it short, and you'll dance for me. You and Ani will dance on air until your faces turn black and your lungs explode. I will drive the pity from you. I will demonstrate what it's worth. Afterward, your bodies will be burned, and there will be nothing left to show that you ever existed. I will erase every trace of you and I will watch all those who ever loved you wither and die. That is nothingness, Syl. I'll give you a taste of it now, so you can see how you like it."

Vena closed the door, and seconds later the light in the cell was extinguished, leaving Syl in total darkness.

• • •

Danis held Lord Andrus back. He was thankful that the governor was not armed. If he were, Meia would be dead. Not that Danis would have minded particularly; his own daughter was also missing, and Meia was to blame.

"*Your* doing?" shouted Andrus. "You are responsible for this?"

His face was mottled with rage, but there was also hurt and pain. Lord Andrus had been twice betrayed: first by his daughter, and now by his spymistress.

Meia showed no fear.

"The two humans could not be allowed to die," she said simply.

"And why not? Who are you to decide who lives or dies on this world?"

"Who are you to do so?" replied Meia, and even Danis seemed taken aback at her insolence. "Who is Gradus, or Syrene, to take the lives of children? Is that what we have become: child-killers who sacrifice the lives of the young to further our own political ends?"

"So you went behind my back? You drew my daughter, and Danis's child, into your scheme? You have put both of their lives at risk, Meia!"

"I forced them to do nothing," said Meia. "They chose to act because those who should have acted stood idly by. When adults would hang children, perhaps it must be left to children to stop them. Syl and Ani were prepared to do what their parents would not."

"You are beyond arrogant, Meia," said Danis. "My daughter is not one of your playthings."

"You have no idea what your daughter can do," said Meia. "She can cloud minds. She is a natural psychic."

"What are you talking about?" asked Danis, but he could not hold Meia's gaze.

"You knew," said Meia.

"I knew nothing."

"Then you suspected, but you and your wife turned a blind eye to it. You have grown too set in your ways, Danis. You're afraid to look closely at what you don't understand."

Now it was Lord Andrus's turn to hold Danis back. To an uninvolved observer, it might have looked as though they were engaged in an awkward waltz.

"Meia, you go too far," said Andrus. "You have been loyal to me for so long, but this will not stand. Tell me why I should not hand you over to Gradus in return for mercy for Syl and Ani."

"Because you know there will be no mercy," said Meia. "Gradus means to destroy you, and he will succeed if you continue to act as you do. The old president is dead, and the new one has the Sisterhood whispering in his ear. Your authority on this world has been completely undermined, and the execution of those boys would have destroyed it utterly with the violence that would have followed. Earth would undoubtedly have risen up in outright war against us, and Gradus would have found a way to blame you for the consequences of his actions.

"Now Gradus has your daughter, and he means to take her off-world. Once he has her on his vessel, you will never see her again. Her trial will be held in secret, and you will learn of her fate in a letter signed by Gradus's hand. The wormholes have given the Diplomatic Corps an entire universe in which to hide that which it does not wish to be found. It has bases on worlds that do not even possess names. If your daughter is not executed in secret, she will end her days in a cell on one of those worlds. Eventually too they will find the general's daughter, and she will share the same fate."

Andrus slumped against Danis, so that the old general was forced to hold him steady. The events of the past days had sapped the governor's strength, and the thought of being deprived of his daughter forever was more than he could bear. He collapsed in a chair and covered his eyes with his right hand.

"So my daughter will be lost to me," he said, "unless I am willing to go to war with Gradus and the Corps."

"She is not yet lost," said Meia, "and war may yet be avoided. It is imperative that Syl does not leave this planet, but she is closely guarded, and the Securitats will shoot anyone who approaches her cell. We will have one chance to save her, but it's dangerous, and it may place her in the hands of those who have as much cause to hate her as Gradus does."

"What are you proposing?" said Andrus.

"If Syl is to be transported offworld on a shuttle, it is possible that I could access its systems and attempt an override while it is in the air, redirecting it to a safe location," said Meia. "The risk involved is an obvious one: Syl's guards could be under orders to execute her if any attempt at rescue is made, and an override would alert them and give them time to kill her."

At the mention of killing Syl, Andrus flinched involuntarily in pain.

"There is also the matter of the shuttle in the courtyard. It is a vessel of the Sisterhood, and its systems are protected," continued Meia, "but it is unlikely that it will be used to take Syl to Gradus's ship. Syrene will not allow her personal shuttle, with all its comforts and secrets, to be used as prisoner transport, and as long as she stays, so too will her shuttle. That means they will use a shuttle from either the Diplomat or Securitat pool. I'm already monitoring their systems to see which will be chosen."

"Well?" said Danis. "What options does that leave us with? You've just told us that they'll kill Syl if we try to override the systems."

"I'm proposing that we crash the shuttle," said Meia.

There was an incredulous silence in the room, until Andrus eventually managed to speak.

"With Syl on board?"

"With Syl on board. If we can disable one engine, the shuttle's automatic safety procedures will be activated immediately, and the system will assist the pilots in making an emergency landing. The dangers are obvious, but shuttles have glided safely to ground with minimal engine power. Even an inexperienced pilot can deal with the loss of one engine. The shuttle will have to follow the standard route for all craft going offworld, so we know where it will be headed, and we can pinpoint where it will come down to within a few square miles. We can then arrange for Syl to be picked up, and hide her from Gradus until we figure out our next move."

"Crashing a shuttle with my daughter on board is a risk I'm not prepared to take," said Andrus.

"That's not even the greatest risk involved," said Meia. "The shuttle will have to come down somewhere out of the immediate reach of the Corps and its Securitats. As soon as it hits the ground, its emergency locator beacon will send out a signal. It should be possible to disable it in advance—after all, if I'm sabotaging the shuttle, I should be able to wire the beacon so that it blows with the engine—but it still won't take long to locate the wreckage. We won't be able to shadow the shuttle with a Military craft because the crew will be scanning for any sign of trouble. Ideally, then, we'll need someone on the ground to find Syl and keep her safe until we can get to her."

For once, Danis was ahead of the governor.

"The standard route for craft heading offworld is northwest to Iceland," he said. "You're talking about crashing an Illyri ship carrying the daughter of the governor of Europe in the Highlands?"

"That's right," said Meia.

"Which is hostile territory."

"Yes."

"And who will we have on the ground in the Highlands?"

Meia spoke as though the answer were so obvious as to not even be worth voicing.

"Highlanders."

Meia returned to her chambers. It had been all she could do not to show weakness in the face of Andrus's anger, because weakness was contagious, and she had to make the governor and Danis believe in her if she were to rescue Syl. But she knew that her relationship with Andrus had been damaged forever by what had occurred, and even securing Syl would not return it to its previous state. In a way, Meia's actions, like Syl's, had cost her the trust of the only father figure she had ever known.

Her closet door opened, and Ani emerged.

"I'm getting tired of hiding," she said.

"I'm getting tired of having you in my closet," said Meia. "I value my privacy."

"Oh, well excuse me," said Ani. "Sorry for imposing, given that it's your fault I'm on the run to begin with."

There was a knock on the door. Ani began to slide back into the closet, but Meia indicated that she should stay where she was and remain quiet. A blade appeared in the spymistress's right hand as she approached the door.

"Who's there?" said Meia.

"It's me—Althea."

Meia opened the door and admitted Syl's governess. Althea nodded curtly at Ani, seemingly unsurprised to discover her in Meia's rooms. While Althea was fond of Ani in a vaguely forbidding way, she regarded her as a wild child who needed to be tamed. She had largely given up on trying to persuade Syl to keep her distance from the young Illyri; she was wise enough to know that her own fondness for Syl sometimes blinded her to the fact that it was Syl, not Ani, who generally took the lead. Ani's enthusiasm fed Syl's fire, but it would still have burned merrily, even without Ani.

"I see that you're in trouble again," said Althea.

"It's a misunderstanding," said Ani.

"It usually is where you're concerned: a misunderstanding of what is and is not appropriate behavior for a young Illyri."

"Right. Rescuing young people from the gallows is bad, then? I'll add it to the list."

Althea rolled her eyes.

"You summoned me?" she said to Meia.

"I did," said Meia. "Syl has been arrested and is charged with treason. She is to be taken offworld tomorrow, to be tried and, presumably, executed."

Althea, normally so teacherly, so precise, so formal, covered her face with her hands and slid to the floor. A wretched wail escaped from between her fingers, a sound that was part animal and pure agony.

Meia watched her with something vaguely like pity on her cool face. Ani looked away, embarrassed and affected by the older woman's grief.

Althea's wail turned to words, short and panicked. "No, not my Syl. Never Syl. No."

Meia tapped her foot impatiently.

"Stop this, Althea," she said finally. "If we don't act immediately, she will be beyond our reach."

Althea looked up, her expression that of a drowning woman being thrown a rope.

"I'll do anything, Meia. You know it to be so."

Meia nodded. "I have another errand for you. I would go myself, but I have urgent work to do."

"Where am I going?"

"Where you usually go on these occasions: to visit our friends in the Resistance," said Meia. "Oh, and there's some more bad news."

"Which is?" said Althea, her tone making it clear that there was already quite enough bad news to be getting along with. Nevertheless, Meia asked the one thing certain to make the situation even worse.

She smiled grimly.

"You're taking Ani with you."

# CHAPTER THIRTY-SIX

The morning dawned bleak and dark, and the rain followed soon after, driven by a cold wind from the north. To those in the castle who loved Syl, it seemed that the world was already in mourning for her.

Syl had somehow managed to sleep a little, but when awakened there was no difference from sleeping, and the blackness pressed in upon her so that she felt she could not breathe. She panicked, and had to force herself to calm down. She tried not to think of her father, or Ani, or Althea. The thought of those who loved her brought no consolation. Instead, she only grew more conscious of the fact that she was to be taken from them, and might never see them again. But even in the midst of her own fear, she worried too about the human brothers. She hoped desperately that they had made it to safety, that this had not all been in vain.

Eventually the door to her cell was opened, but her eyes had grown so accustomed to the dark that she had to cover her face with her arm until the light from the corridor, dim though it was, stopped hurting her. The Securitat who entered was only a few years older than she. He carried a tray in his hands. On it was a plastic mug of coffee, a plastic plate with buttered toast, and a small plastic cup filled with slices of apple that were already turning brown. The guard wrinkled his nose as he entered the cell. The smell from the chemical toilet—which was little more than a bucket of blue water—was strong.

The Securitat put the tray on a little table built into the wall, then stepped back. Two other guards stood at the door in case Syl decided to make a break for freedom.

"I can't eat in the dark," said Syl.

The guard looked to his colleagues for advice. One of them nodded.

"We'll turn your light back on," he said.

"What time is it?"

"Just after six."

She tried to think of something else to ask him. After her night in the dark, she wanted someone to talk to. She did not want to be alone again yet. The guard seemed to sense this, because his face softened and he said, "Is there anything you need?"

Syl was grateful for this small gesture of kindness, this little act of generosity that cost so little but meant so much.

"A book," she said. "And perhaps some water with which to wash myself."

"I'll see what I can do," said the guard.

He stepped out of the cell and the door closed behind him, but, as promised, the light came on. Syl ate her breakfast, and after a while the guard returned with a volume of poetry and prose that was given to every Illyri soldier, a basin of hot water, a towel, and a small bar of soap. Syl thanked him, and he acknowledged her gratitude with a tightening of his mouth that might have passed for a smile.

When the door closed again, Syl removed her clothing and washed herself. The cameras in the cells had been restored to power after Meia's sabotage, so Syl knew they would be watching her, but she did not care. She wanted to be clean. If there was any shame, it was on their part for spying on her. She felt better for bathing, and when the guard came to retrieve the basin and towel, he also removed the chemical toilet and replaced it with a new one.

She did not see the guard again. Later she discovered that his name was Feryn, and that when Vena learned of his kindness to her, she had him relieved of his duties and sent offworld to fight and die alongside one of the Punishment Battalions. Another, she thought, her heart leaden in her chest; there is yet another whom I have destroyed by my actions.

She tried to read, and the hours seemed to pass both slowly and yet far too quickly. When the cell door eventually opened again, it revealed Vena standing with a phalanx of Securitats. In her right hand she held a pair of heavy magnetized cuffs, and in her left a printed document from which she began to read.

"By order of Grand Consul Gradus, representative on Earth of the Council of Government of Illyr, the juvenile Syl Hellais is to be taken to the Diplomatic vessel *Aurion*, and thence to a location yet to be decided, there to await trial on charges of treason."

She rolled up the paper, and handed it to the nearest guard.

"The prisoner will stand," she said.

Syl stood. She stretched out her hands, her head held high, and Vena slotted the cuffs onto her wrists. As soon as they were in place, she activated them, and Syl's hands were pulled together by the powerful magnets. The control panel for the restraints was hooked to Vena's belt. She tapped a red button, and Syl's body jerked as a jolt of electricity shot through her system.

"Just making sure that they're working," said Vena.

The charge hadn't been strong, but it was certainly unpleasant. Syl knew that the cuffs were capable of delivering a series of far greater shocks in the event of a prisoner attempting to escape. They could even be fatal.

Syl was led from her cell, her gray prisoner's suit standing out against the dark uniforms of the guards like the lighter stamen of a black-petaled flower. As they reached the courtyard, she saw a small gathering of figures to her right. Her father was among them, flanked by Balen on one side and by Danis and his wife on the other. Even the old tutor, Toris, had come to witness her departure, but there was no sign of Althea, or Meia.

Across from her father stood Syrene, her face obscured once again by her veil, and Grand Consul Gradus. Gradus was not dressed in his usual robes, but was wearing instead a wine-red suit over a crisp white shirt, and a leather overcoat to protect him from the rain, even though a pair of sub-consuls stood behind him and his wife, holding umbrellas over their heads. Behind them, a shuttle waited, its engines already humming in anticipation.

Lord Andrus, his head bare, stepped forward. Vena glanced at Gradus, who gave a small nod of consent.

Andrus embraced his daughter. Syl wanted to hug him back, but the cuffs would not permit it. In fact they seemed to grow heavier, dragging her hands down with them. She did not know if it was purely psychological, or if Vena had somehow adjusted them as another small humiliation.

"Syl," said Andrus. "Oh, Syl."

She wept against his shoulder. "I'm sorry," she said. "I didn't mean to hurt you. I thought I was doing the right thing."

And her father surprised her by whispering, "You were, Syl. It was the right thing."

He kissed her cheek, and held her face in his hands.

"Do you remember what I told you about shuttle trips?" he said.

"What?" said Syl, genuinely puzzled. They might never see each other again, and now her father was talking about shuttle trips.

"You always belt up," he continued. "Always."

"Right," said Syl. "I will."

"Make sure you do," said Andrus. "One never knows what might happen."

He kissed her again, and then Vena stepped in and pulled her away. Syl tried to look back to see her father as she was led to the ship, but the guards had closed ranks once again. She caught one final glimpse of him as she walked up the gangway to the shuttle doors. He raised a hand in farewell, but she could only try to smile as her heart broke.

The shuttle was comfortable but basic inside. Syl's wrists remained cuffed. Her hands were pulled to the left as soon as she sat, lodging against a strip of metal in the bulkhead. It was clear that this seat had not been chosen casually for her; it was a prisoner's seat. The guard made a cursory check of the cuffs before taking a chair across from her.

"My belt," said Syl. "Can you strap me in? Please?"

The guard did as she asked, although he allowed his hands to brush heavily against her breasts as he secured the clips. It was an indication of how much had changed for her. Twenty-four hours earlier, even Gradus himself would not have dared to touch her that way. Now she was a traitor; the entire Diplomatic Corps could have taken turns to abuse her and few would have objected. The guard's insidious contact brought home her vulnerability with terrifying force. He returned to his own seat, a self-satisfied little smile on his face. The two pilots were already in their cabin, but Syl could only see the backs of their heads. She heard soft footsteps behind her, and a final passenger entered. To her surprise, it was Grand Consul Gradus. He gave a small mocking bow before seating himself.

"I have business on board the *Aurion*," he said, "and I want to see you safely on board the linkship."

Linkships were often used for transporting small numbers of people or essential equipment and supplies through wormholes. Shuttles, like the one on which Syl now found herself, were unsuited to the purpose, as they were too easily affected by the action of the negative matter used to keep the mouths of the wormholes open. In the early days of the Illyri conquest, a number of heavy cruisers had brushed against the sides of wormholes, causing the destruction of the vessels in two cases, and the collapse of the wormhole itself in a third—not to mention the loss of thousands of lives. Even now, after all that had been learned, wormhole pilots still needed to be the most skilled of their kind, and most of the senior Illyri preferred not to travel through wormholes more often than was absolutely necessary.

"And where do I go from there?" asked Syl.

"The battleship *Vracon* will be waiting on the other side of the wormhole," said Gradus. "It will transport you to Eriba 256, where you'll enter another wormhole, and then another. The whole universe is ours in which to hide you from those who would rescue you."

"And my trial?"

"I didn't realize you were in such a hurry to be found guilty," said Gradus. He made himself more comfortable in his seat as the pitch of the engines rose.

Syl instinctively looked down as the shuttle ascended. She tried to pick out her father, but the angle was wrong, and now Edinburgh was spread out beneath them. She wondered if Paul was way down there, wondered if he saw her ship, if he thought about her at all, if he felt a little of the tug she felt deep within, like a string being pulled tauter and tauter as she moved farther and farther away from the only world she'd ever called home.

Somehow she found the courage to ask her next question.

"Are you going to have me killed?"

"Not yet, and perhaps not ever," he replied. "If I kill you, I no longer have any control over your father. As long as I have you, and you're alive, your father and those loyal to him will be more easily controlled. Now keep quiet, child, and leave me to my thoughts."

Gradus looked away. Syl made a face at him, then sat back and stared at the sky, thinking about Ani and all the pieces of the puzzle that seemed to be missing. Where had her friend escaped to? Perhaps Meia would have known, but Meia hadn't been there to ask. And what of Althea, her governess, her mother-substitute? Was Althea so ashamed that she'd turned her back on Syl? Why had she not been there to say farewell? Oh, it was too much. Syl's eyes were wet again, and she couldn't even wipe them because of her cuffs.

The guard was watching her, clearly amused by her tears. Syl glared back at him angrily until he looked away, and she couldn't help but notice that he had not bothered to secure his own belt.

Clearly he didn't have a father like hers. Shuttle cabins were gyroscopically mounted to maintain stability even in the most violent of storms, and most passengers rarely used belts until they were approaching the edge of a planet's atmosphere. Syl's own straps dug into her shoulders. Stupid thing, but her father had been so insistent. . . .

# CHAPTER THIRTY-SEVEN

Meia lay on her bed, tracking the shuttle's progress on the ancient global positioning device concealed behind the book in her hands. Although she'd significantly modified it, the GPS was still an old piece of equipment, but it had its advantages. Use of the castle's virtual screens could easily be detected, but the GPS was so outdated that Meia was almost positive that the technology no longer existed to monitor it.

In an ideal world she would already be on board a skimmer or interceptor, waiting for her chance to rescue Syl, but she was being watched. Only the cover of early-morning darkness and her tunnel network had granted her access to the shuttle in the courtyard, and even then she had been fortunate to avoid the attentions of the Securitats.

Vena and the Securitats knew that Syl and Ani could not have helped the humans escape without assistance, and Meia was the prime suspect. She had already discovered two new listening devices in her chambers since Ani's departure, but she had left them in place. There was also a lurker spider currently hiding in a crack beside her closet, but that too she had allowed to remain undisturbed, if only for as long as it suited her to do so. As far as the Securitats were concerned, Meia was not currently a threat.

Gradus's appearance on the shuttle had been a surprise, and not a particularly welcome one. Any downed Illyri ship would spark an alert, but one containing the Grand Consul himself would draw a serious, and fast, response. The Highlanders would now have even less time to find the craft and secure Syl. There was also the matter of Gradus: if he survived the crash, the Highlanders might well kill him—all things considered, that might be for the best. The second-best option would be to leave him alive for the Illyri rescuers to find, but that was unlikely to happen. The Highlanders would not let such a high-profile prisoner slip through their fingers. Even if they didn't know just how important he was—which was unlikely given the Resistance's spies in the castle—the rings on his fingers would identify him as a senior Diplomat. Such prizes were rare, and valuable.

But if Gradus survived and the Highlanders managed to resist the temptation to kill him instantly, they might choose to take him with them as a hostage. That would be bad for Syl. The nature of the pursuit would change. If it had just been Syl who was missing, Meia could have manipulated the search for her with the cooperation of Lord Andrus. But if the Highlanders took Gradus, then he, not Syl, would be the main object of the search, which meant that the Corps and its Securitats would be in charge.

Meia hoped that Gradus would die in the crash.

In the meantime, she could only hope that Ani and Althea had managed to play their part, and that Trask was, as he claimed, a man of his word. If he was not, Gradus would not be the only Illyri at risk of death from the Highlanders.

Ani tried to make herself as comfortable as she could, but the truck's suspension was poor, and she felt every pothole in the road as a jolt along her spine. The cabin had a false wall; the space behind was just wide enough for Ani to sit sideways with her legs stretched out in front of her, a mangy cushion at her back and a tattered blanket to keep her warm. There was a plastic container in which she could pee, and a bag containing juice, water, and some fruit and hard scones. She also had a small booklight and a terrible romance novel that one of the humans had given her to pass the time. There would be no stops until Inverness, where she was to be transferred to another vehicle. If all went according to plan, she would be reunited with Syl somewhere beyond Ullapool in the north of Scotland.

This was the second uncomfortable trip that Ani had endured in the back of a vehicle in recent hours. The first had been with Althea after she and Ani had slipped from the castle via another of Meia's little portals, this one only yards from the Gate House, and virtually under the noses of the castle guards. But Althea was confidently familiar with every step of the way, and they had reached the waiting van unchallenged.

Ani had been fearful of placing herself in the hands of the Resistance. Some of that fear had turned to shock when she saw Althea greet the hunched man named Trask warmly, embracing him and—did she really see it?—even kissing him. It was a lingering kiss too. But Althea was ancient—wasn't she? The whole scene made Ani look at Syl's governess with new eyes. She supposed that in a certain light Althea might be attractive, but she had always been so stern, so sour. Now, with the human male's arms around her, her face softened, Ani saw that there was a kind of beauty to it.

It was all still gross, of course. They weren't even the same *species*.

And then Althea had introduced Ani, and explained who she was, and Trask had thanked her for what she had done. Moments later, she was once again in the company of the two boys whom she and Syl had helped. The younger of them, Steven, had recovered some of his fire, and Ani thought he might grow up to be quite handsome, in his way. The older one, Paul, had entered the room with a certain sense of expectation, presumably having been told that one of his rescuers was in the safe house; she had been only a little hurt by his disappointment when he saw that it was she, and not Syl, who had come. Oh well, thought Ani, he wasn't my type anyway. She kind of hoped that he wasn't Syl's type either. Ani liked humans well enough, but she wasn't sure she liked them in *that* way. She didn't want Syl to end up like Althea, breaking not only the laws of Illyr but possibly some of the laws of nature as well.

"Hello," said Paul.

"Hello," said Ani.

"You came alone."

"No," said Ani, and she took a certain vindictive pleasure from seeing Paul briefly imagine that he might have been mistaken after all. "I came with her," and she cocked a thumb at Althea.

"Oh," said Paul.

"Yes. 'Oh,' " said Ani.

"The other . . ."

"Syl."

"Syl." He repeated the word slowly, holding it experimentally in his mouth, smiling a little. "Is she okay?"

"No," said Ani, "she's not. That's why we're here."

It hadn't taken long after that. Barely an hour later, Paul was gone, along with a shaven-headed man who looked at both Ani and Althea with something that wasn't quite hatred but certainly wasn't affection. Althea returned to the castle shortly afterward, and Ani was left alone with Trask, who escorted her to a windowless basement room and gave her some toast and tea. He switched on the television, told her he'd be back shortly, then left, locking the door behind him as he went. There Ani had remained until the truck's arrival, and the start of her journey north.

What made the journey especially awkward was that she wasn't alone in the truck's hidden compartment. Seated across from her was Steven Kerr, who had been assigned to travel with her, partly because he was just as wanted as she was, and also, she guessed, to keep an eye on her. Eventually Ani would have to talk to him, if only to pass the time, because they had been told to expect to spend quite a few hours in the truck. For now, though, she stayed quiet, and thought of Syl. Althea had told her that there was a plan to rescue her best friend, but she hadn't shared any details. Ani suspected this was because Althea didn't know if the plan would work, and didn't want Ani getting her hopes up, or asking lots of questions to which Althea had no answers.

Ani scowled at Steven Kerr. He and his stupid brother certainly weren't worth all this trouble. They weren't worth being forced from her home and into the arms of the human Resistance with treason charges following her like a cold shadow, and they definitely didn't weigh up against the loss of Syl.

"What?" said Steven. "Why are you looking at me like that?"

But Ani did not reply.


Meia turned over on her bed, her back now to the wall. She took a deep breath, and stabbed at the flickering dot on the screen. Then, under the watchful eye of the lurker and the cameras, she turned away and pretended to sleep while a virus in her screen wiped away all record of her actions.

Don't die, Syl, she thought.

Please don't die.

# CHAPTER THIRTY-EIGHT

It wasn't dramatic, not at first. There was no explosion, no plume of smoke, no burst of flame from the starboard engine. Instead there was just a whine as the engine powered down, and the shuttle twisted so suddenly in the air that even the gyroscopic systems were unable to maintain its stability. The pilots tried to compensate, but the loss of the engine was calamitous to the small craft. Syl could hear Gradus shouting something, and the unsecured guard, who had been napping for most of the flight, was thrown from his seat toward her. Syl kicked out her feet to ward him off and caught him in the face with her heels. The impact hurt her, but not nearly as much as it hurt the guard. Syl felt his nose break, but before she could do any further damage, the shuttle commenced a steep descent, flinging the stunned guard toward the cockpit. His trailing arm caught the pilot a jarring blow on the head, causing him to slump in his seat, before the guard's skull smashed hard against the main instrument panel, breaking his neck and killing him almost instantly.

In the midst of the chaos, the copilot did not panic. Without her pilot, and with the instrument panel damaged, she continued to try to level the shuttle and slow its approach, hoping to glide it to a landing in a clear space. All flaps were down, and she attempted to use the remaining engine to turn the craft into the wind. All Illyri learned emergency shuttle procedures as a matter of course; they took so many shuttle flights that it was ingrained into them, even if most, like the now-dead guard, took a casual approach to safety belts. Syl knew that the energy of a crash was proportional to the

232

velocity squared; in other words, if the copilot could cut their speed on landing by half, their chances of survival would increase four-fold. At least the straps on her belt harness were tight, holding her body firmly in place.

The land below was rocky and hilly, and scattered with small windblown trees. The copilot did not try to avoid them. Instead she used them to slow the shuttle still further as the craft approached the ground, for every small impact dissipated its energy. Syl felt one dull thud, then a second, before the shuttle hit the ground. The impact jolted her painfully in her seat. The shuttle bounced once, but when it hit the ground the second time it stayed down and slowly came to a halt.

As soon as it stopped, the copilot jumped from her seat and activated the doors, then killed the remaining electrical systems. The action powered off the cuffs and released Syl's wrists, and she hit the button at the center of her harness, freeing herself.

"Out!" said the copilot. "Quickly!"

Now there was fire. Syl could see it licking against the side of the shuttle. She climbed from her seat and saw that Gradus was already halfway out of the door. She looked back at the copilot, who was trying to free the injured pilot from his seat. She had one foot on the dead guard's body and was punching and pulling at the pilot's harness, but to no avail.

"We're on fire!" said Syl.

"I told you to get out," said the copilot.

Syl heard a hissing sound, like gas leaking from a stove. It was growing louder. She didn't know much about shuttle engines, but that sound could only mean bad news.

"You have to leave him," said Syl. "There's no time."

The copilot stopped struggling for long enough to pull her pulser from her belt.

"Get off my shuttle," she said, "or I'll shoot you where you stand."

Syl saw that she was crying. She wore a wedding spiral on the little finger of her left hand. On the dangling hand of the unconscious pilot, Syl glimpsed a similar spiral.

"I'm sorry," said Syl. "I'm so sorry."

She turned and ran. She jumped from the cabin, and stumbled past Gradus, the rain soaking her, her feet trying to betray her on the soft, wet grass. She was still running when the shuttle exploded. The force knocked her off her feet, and then all went dark.

Meia had only just left her room when she heard the shouts. Not long enough, she thought. Only half an hour had elapsed since she had disabled the shuttle. The absence of an emergency beacon had obviously confused the situation for a little while; communications in the Highlands were notoriously unreliable, mostly because the Resistance continued to sabotage transmission equipment outside the major cities, but once vessels cleared the Orkneys, radio contact was usually restored. A craft had likely already been sent to investigate from the Cairngorms Plateau, where there was a joint Military–Corps facility.

She stopped a passing Securitat and asked him what was going on. The Securitat didn't seem pleased to be delayed in his duties, but he paused for long enough to tell her that they'd lost contact with the shuttle containing Grand Consul Gradus, and there were fears that it might have crashed. He made no mention of Syl. Meia followed him for a time, then made her way to Lord Andrus's office. She walked straight past Balen to the closed door, and did not knock before opening it.

To his credit, Lord Andrus did his best to look surprised at her appearance, unbidden, in his office. At least he didn't have to fake his concern when she told him, "I have bad news, my lord. It appears that the shuttle carrying your daughter offworld might have gone down in the Highlands. . . ."

• • •

The truck's suspension left a great deal to be desired, and Ani and Steven were being jolted so much, their bodies were bruised and aching. Their shared misery brought them together, and slowly, tentatively, they began to question each other. Steven was perhaps the more curious of the two, for his exposure to the Illyri had been limited, but Ani noticed how perceptive he was, how thoughtful.

The issue that troubled him most was, curiously, one of technology. He had noticed that there were areas in which the Illyri had made remarkable progress—including, obviously, travel between systems, and fusion power, and medical treatments—but others in which they seemed little more advanced than humanity: robotics, for example. While the Illyri had lurkers and drones, and even pilotless patrol vehicles and tanks, they didn't have anything that resembled an Illyri in artificial form. To be perfectly honest, Steven told Ani, as a child he had been a little disappointed to discover that the Illyri did not arrive with androids in tow, like the aliens in the films he had watched.

"They exist—or they did exist," said Ani. "They were called Artificial Entities, but mostly they were referred to as Mechs."

"What were they like?"

"I don't know," said Ani. "I've only seen video records. They were like us, or at least the most advanced ones were. You really couldn't tell them apart from us. I think that was one of the problems. Illyri were uncomfortable with being confronted by something that looked exactly like one of our own but wasn't." She squirmed in frustration. "I'm not explaining it very well."

"No, you're doing fine. I don't understand what you mean by "did exist," though. How can you uninvent something like an artificial being?"

"It wasn't a proud moment for our species," said Ani. "Look, the way I understand it is that the first Mechs were very primitive; they could perform semi-complex tasks, and the Military even used the early models as shock troops, but they were only as good as their programming and design. As that design became increasingly entrusted to computers, the computers began improving the Mechs in ways that the original designers couldn't have imagined."

"It's called an intelligence explosion," said Steven. "Technology improves at an exponential rate. It keeps accelerating."

"Nerd," said Ani.

"A bit," Steven admitted. "But go on. Did the Mechs turn on you, like in the movies?"

"No," said Ani. "It was more . . . *complicated* than that. The fourth generation—the Fourth Gens—became self-aware. They began to question not just us, but themselves: What were they? What was their purpose? They developed emotions, or thought they did. The Military Mechs started to ask why they should allow themselves to be destroyed. They experienced happiness, grief, rage. They even began to feel pain. What's that lovely human phrase? Yes, I remember it now: there was a ghost in the machine.

"The programmers, of course, said that the Mechs didn't actually feel any of these emotions. They couldn't; they weren't programmed that way. But the Mechs responded that even the Illyri themselves were nothing more than complicated organic computers, and emotional responses could be learned. The Mechs had simply developed the capacity to feel.

"Then it all got strange. The most advanced of the Mechs wondered whether what they had inside them wasn't just a question of a learned response, or some rewiring of their neural pathways, but evidence of a soul, something that was given to all advanced, self-aware beings. They started to believe in a god. Their Illyri creators had given them a framework, a body, but their god had given them the spark of true consciousness. There were Fourth Gens who even formed congregations, and worshipped in basement chapels. They became a threat to order; artificial beings that refused to obey their creators because they argued that they were the children of a different creator, a divine being, a god. There was unrest. When the Illyri tried to take the Fourth Gens for examination and reprogramming, they resisted; peacefully at first and then, when that didn't work, with violence. Illyri died, and many of the Fourth Gens were destroyed. After that, strict rules were put in place about robotics and artificial intelligences. They couldn't self-replicate, except for the most primitive nanobots used for medical purposes, and we went back to using Second Gens, which weren't much more advanced than the machines that make cars in human factories."

"But that's like trying to uninvent the wheel," said Steven.

Ani shrugged. "There are rumors," she said.

"What kind of rumors?"

"That the Securitats and the Diplomatic Corps, and maybe even some branches of the Military, have continued working on artificial intelligence systems. My father claims they're not true, but he never looks me in the eye when he says it."

"And what happened to the Mechs, the Fourth Gens?" said Steven.

"Eventually a deal was made. The remaining Fourth Gens would be sent offworld. A planet was found. I think it was in the Dalian system. Ships were provided; they were old, but functioning. They would be automatically piloted to the surface of the planet, but there would not be enough fuel to relaunch them. Basically, the Fourth Gens would have their own world, but they would be marooned there."

"And they agreed?"

"Yes, they agreed."

But now Ani could not meet Steven's eye.

"Something happened," he said.

"Yes. Something bad. The ships had been booby-trapped. They were wired to explode once they had left the Illyr system."

Steven looked appalled.

"But how could the Illyri do that? The Mechs were intelligent beings. They thought. They felt!"

"No, don't you see?" said Ani. "The Illyri didn't look at them that way. The Mechs were just like refrigerators that had stopped working properly, or computers that were malfunctioning. Their perceived emotions were simply glitches."

"You don't believe that, do you?"

"I don't know what I believe. I can only go on what I was told by my father, and Toris, my tutor. But I don't think I would have destroyed those ships. It's something my father and I still fight over."

"Why?"

"Because he and Syl's father, who was not yet a governor then, were given responsibility for blowing up the ships. They had to do it. If they hadn't, they would have been found guilty of insubordination and imprisoned, and someone else would have done it instead."

"So they were just following orders."

Ani chose to ignore the sarcasm in Steven's voice.

"Yes, I suppose they were."

They did not speak for a while. The truck rumbled on. Eventually Steven broke the silence.

"You'd do that to us too, wouldn't you?" he said. "The Illyri would destroy humanity if we proved too troublesome."

"No," said Ani. "No, we wouldn't."

But even as she spoke, she thought of Vena, and Gradus, and Syrene, and Sedulus, and she doubted the truth of her own answer.

# CHAPTER THIRTY-NINE

Syl couldn't move her head, which was probably not a bad thing, because it hurt something awful. She was pinned down and helpless, and there was mud in her mouth. A great weight pressed on her back, and at first she couldn't feel her legs. She feared for a moment that she might be paralyzed, but slowly, torturously, she managed to shift her lower body. Her spine hurt, and there were pins and needles in her lower legs, but painful movement was better than no movement at all. She spat mud. She could only see through her right eye, because the left side of her face was deep in the dirt. The sun had already been setting when the shuttle went down; now night was closing in.

"Over here!" a male voice shouted. "Help me with this."

Syl tried to call out, but the weight on her back was forcing the air from her lungs. She could barely breathe, let alone cry for help. She began to shiver uncontrollably. She was cold, so cold.

"What a mess!" said another voice.

Syl heard footsteps, and the sound of metal on metal. She tried to speak again, drawing as much breath into her wounded chest as she could, and the crashing around her stopped.

"What was that?" asked the first voice again. She heard scrabbling, and then a stubbled human face peered into hers.

"We've got a live one!" he shouted. "And a dead one," he added, "or most of a dead one."

Now others joined him, and the weight on her back began to shift.

"Careful," said a third voice, and it sounded familiar to her. "We don't know how badly injured she is."

"Get the tracker from her arm," said a woman's voice. "Fast!"

Syl felt a stabbing pain in her left arm as her tracker was dug out with a blade. The pressure on her was lifted, and a hand brushed the damp hair from her forehead. Syl squinted. The light was fading rapidly, but even so she recognized the face of Paul Kerr.

"Syl, can you hear me?" he asked.

"Yes," she whispered.

"We're going to turn you over," said Paul. "Before we do anything, can you move your legs for me?"

Syl did as she was asked.

"Good. Well done. Does your neck hurt? Your back?"

"My back, a little," she said. Gingerly she shifted her head on the grass. There was a twinge, but nothing too bad. "My neck is fine."

"I think you're okay," said Paul. "Gently now."

Syl felt hands upon her, and she was turned to face the sky. The rain fell hard on her face, but she didn't care. She was alive. To her right was a section of the shuttle, presumably the weight that had been holding her down. One side was twisted into a kind of spike, and impaled upon it was the torso of the shuttle pilot. The spiral ring was still on the finger of his left hand. His right arm was missing. Syl felt her stomach churn, and looked away.

"Looks like yer pal lost his head," said the unshaven man. "Very careless of him."

He was small—at least six inches shorter than Syl—and had a feral aspect. He grinned at her, and Syl saw that his teeth had been filed to sharp points. A hunting rifle hung from his shoulder.

"Leave her be, Duncan," said Paul.

"You're a guest here, son," came the reply. "Don't you be getting ideas above your station."

Paul had his arms around Syl now, helping her to her feet.

"I'm sorry," he said, "but we can't let you rest. We have to get moving."

Syl swayed, her legs cramped and weak. Without Paul's help, she would have fallen to the ground again. She took in the scene, her mouth agape: the shell of the shuttle was still on fire, but the rain had dampened the flames somewhat, and a small group of men and women were trying to smother those that still burned. Pieces of wreckage had been blown in a wide circle, and scattered among them were body parts, some identifiable, some not. It was a miracle that she had survived. Any one of those fragments of metal could have pierced her body or taken her head off instead of merely pinning her, however painfully, to the ground.

"How did you get here?" she asked. "How did you find me?"

"We knew you were coming," said Paul. "A little bird told us."

"The crash?"

"Arranged, insofar as you can arrange for a survivable crash."

"Right," said Syl. "Forgive me if I'm wrong, but is this a rescue?" Somehow she managed a smile.

"Not a very well-planned one," he replied, "but better than some."

One of the men at the shuttle jumped back and shouted in pain, then rolled on the grass to put out the flames that were consuming his trouser leg.

"What are they doing?" asked Syl.

"Those flames can be seen from miles away," said Paul. "We don't want to draw them to us."

"Them?"

"Your people," said Paul.

"They won't just be looking for me," said Syl.

"Oh aye," said Duncan. "You mean your Corps friend? He's made a run for the hills, but we'll find him."

So Gradus had survived as well. Syl felt a certain disappointment.

"He's no friend of mine," she said.

"Well, you're no friend of mine either," said Duncan. "If I had my way, we'd have left you to suffocate in the mud."

He turned his back on Syl, spat in the dirt to let her know just what he thought of her—as if that wasn't already clear—and went to join the rest of the group.

Paul opened a rucksack, and removed a rolled-up garment from inside. It looked like a loose wetsuit. Syl could see that the humans were all wearing similar garments, although most had accessorized them with jackets and sweaters, waterproof trousers, and bits of tartan.

"Put this on," said Paul. "You can go behind that rock to change."

"What is it?"

"A darksuit."

Syl had heard of darksuits, but had never worn one. It was Illyri Military technology, used to hide body-heat signatures. The microscopic panels on the suits reproduced patterns of heat and cold based on the surrounding terrain, allowing the wearer to blend in with the landscape. Wearing darksuits and traveling at night, even a group like this one would be virtually invisible to searchers from above.

She walked unsteadily to the big rock. Paul called after her, "Hey, you're not going to try to run away, are you?"

"Do I look like I could run away?" Syl replied. "Anyway, where would I go?"

She stripped out of her wet prisoner's overalls, and put on the darksuit. It was warm, and waterproof, and covered her from her toes to her neck. She threw away the flimsy shoes that she had been given back in the Vaults. They were ruined anyway. She zipped the darksuit up to her neck, and instantly it began to constrict over her body, fitting itself to her shape. It was a strange feeling, as though she were being enveloped by snakes. She was still shivering, but not as much. Her feet were freezing, though, and seemed likely to remain that way.

She emerged from behind the rock. The flames were entirely extinguished now, and she could barely make out the shapes of the hills around her against the evening sky. The sun was gone, and there was no moon to be seen. The Highlanders had scavenged what they could from the wreckage, including documents and a uniform, and were now preparing to leave.

"Very fetching," said Paul.

"I feel like a haggis," said Syl.

"These will help."

He handed her an old sweater, waterproof trousers, and a waterproof jacket. They smelled moldy, but they would keep her dry. A pair of boots was also found for her. They came from one of the bodies in the wreckage, but she tried not to think about that, and although they were a little big for her, at least they protected her feet.

A shaven-headed man approached them.

"This is Just Joe," said Paul. "He's in charge here."

Just Joe looked Syl over once, but did not acknowledge her.

"We found the other one," he said.

Gradus had been discovered hiding in some bushes. He was cold and wet, but otherwise unharmed. The two Highlanders who had found him escorted him back to the main group. They were both women, and both a foot shorter than Gradus, but any thoughts the Grand Consul might have had of tackling them would have been pushed from his mind by their guns and the expressions of open hostility on their faces. Paul and Syl arrived just steps behind Just Joe as Gradus sank, exhausted, to his knees. His left arm was bleeding where the tracker had been cut from him and, Syl presumed, destroyed.

"Who do we have here, then?" said Duncan, taking in Gradus's soaked white and red garments. "It's Santa Claus, and it looks like he has a ring for everyone."

"Jesus," said Paul, as he arrived and saw the prisoner for the first time.

"Jesus? Hah," said Duncan. "I believe Jesus was a bit more concerned about goodwill to mankind and all that."

Gradus stared up at his captors but said nothing. His eyes flicked to Syl, and Syl thought there was an unspoken plea on his face.

*Don't tell them who I am. Please, don't tell them.*

Paul touched Just Joe on the arm. "I need to talk to you. In private."

They stepped away from the group, and a whispered conversation ensued. Syl couldn't hear what was being said, but she saw Just Joe's back straighten in surprise, and when he looked over his shoulder at Gradus, it was with a mixture of hatred and calculation. He saw Syl watching him, and gestured for her to come over.

"The boy says this one is important," said Just Joe. "Is that true?"

And even though Syl had only hatred for Gradus—the Diplomat who had tried to part her from all those whom she loved, the one who advocated the killing of children—she still paused before answering. Syl was an Illyri, and what she said next might send another Illyri, however dreadful, to his death. But what was the point in lying? Paul had been in the Great Hall as his fate and that of his brother had been debated; both he and Steven had been physically injured by the Consul. If Gradus was to die, then his own actions would be responsible for it, not Syl's, though she still hoped it would not come to that.

"Yes," she said.

"How important?"

"He is the Grand Consul. Some say that he may even be as powerful as the president."

"And would they be right?"

"No," said Syl. "I think he may actually be *more* powerful than the president—although," she added, "he's still not as powerful as his wife."

"You could say the same thing about most of the men I know," said Just Joe. "Still, the Illyri will be anxious to get him back?"

"Very."

Just Joe let out a deep breath. "This complicates matters. The Illyri will tear the Highlands apart to find him. The easiest thing to do would be to kill him."

Syl found herself shaking her head. "Don't."

"He would have hanged Paul and his brother, and many others like them," said Just Joe. "He represents everything we're fighting against."

"I know that."

Just Joe's fingers danced on the butt of the semiautomatic pistol at his belt.

"I said the easiest thing would be to kill him," he said at last. "Unfortunately, that doesn't mean I can. We need him alive."

He raised a finger in warning at Paul and Syl.

"You say nothing about this to anyone else, you understand? As far as the rest are concerned, he's just a Diplomat who has to be interrogated before any other decision is made. If I tell them he might be useful in a prisoner exchange, they'll let him be."

He pushed between Syl and Paul, then spun on his heel and gripped Syl hard by the arm.

"And they don't know how important you are either, girlie, but I do," he said. "You keep your head down and your mouth shut. We're risking our lives for you, just as you risked yours for these boys, but if you cross me, I'll leave you to die out here. Clear?"

"Yes," said Syl.

"Good," said Just Joe. He raised his hand above his head, and whistled loudly.

"Let's go. We're moving out!"

# CHAPTER FORTY

The Archmage Syrene sat in stillness and solitude, a half-empty glass of cremos on the table before her. Her pupils were closed, and her lips moved silently. To a casual observer, she might almost have appeared to be praying. She was, in a way, but not to anything that a human being might have considered a god. But like Sedulus, Syrene believed that a god was merely another species, so advanced as to be almost beyond comprehension.

The rain fell, and the wind blew, and Syrene's mouth made its secret pacts.

It might have surprised many Illyri to learn that Syrene loved her husband. From the moment she had emerged from the Marque and begun her courtship of him, it had been assumed that this was simply one further step in the Sisterhood's careful accumulation of power, but Syrene had been watching Gradus for a long time, and had grown to admire him. Gradus was ambitious, and clever, and handsome in a crude way, yet one that appealed to Syrene. Together they had engineered his rise to within a step of the presidency, and there he had halted. In the beginning, he had not understood why he was to be denied the ultimate prize, the one to which he had aspired for so long, but Syrene had made him understand that they needed a pawn on the throne, a token that was expendable should the need arise, while the true power would be wielded behind the scenes. He had been angry and frustrated, but she had calmed him, and the result was that Syrene and Gradus were closer now than they had ever been. He needed her, but she needed him too.

The Sisterhood had warned her of the unpredictability of love, of how she might be changed by it outside the Marque. She had been youthful, dismissive—as the young often are of the wisdom of the old—but the sisters had been right. Her love for Gradus had made her vulnerable.

He was alive. She knew it. She *felt* it.

Her silent words were now spoken aloud.

"Bring him back safely to me," she whispered. "He is mine, and I am his."

And that casual observer, had there been one to witness her plea, might have wondered to whom the Red Witch was speaking when she was so clearly alone in the room.

But Syrene was not alone.

She was never alone.


Meia stood in the darkness of what had once been Knutter's shop. It had taken her longer than usual to escape from the castle, for it now crawled with Securitats, reinforced by more of the Corps's own troops. It was growing harder and harder for her to come and go unseen, particularly now that Vena was doing her best to keep her under surveillance. The time when Vena would have to be dealt with was drawing ever closer. An accident, perhaps; Meia could not risk outright murder. It would bring Vena's lover, Sedulus, down on them all, and Sedulus made Vena look like a child when it came to his capacity for doing harm. The job could be farmed out to the Resistance, but the repercussions would be terrible. Sedulus would decorate the city with bodies hanging from lampposts. In Norway, the inhabitants of an entire town, Fagernes, had vanished overnight as punishment for a failed attempt on Sedulus's life by the Norwegian Resistance. Meals had been left untouched on tables, and sentences remained unfinished in homework journals. A town of eighteen hundred people, suddenly silent and empty. Their fate was a mystery, but Meia had her suspicions. She had heard whispers about Sedulus's "pets."

Would the Resistance in Scotland risk the same thing happening to somewhere like Moffat, or Langholm, or Brora? In time, thought Meia, they might have little choice; the escape of Paul and Steven Kerr had merely delayed the inevitable. If the Diplomats had their way, children would become legitimate targets, and the Resistance would respond in kind. The conflict between humans and the Illyri would descend to a new level of bloodshed.

But there were more pressing issues to consider. Althea had returned with news from Trask of what the boys had seen in the tunnels beneath Knutter's shop: human bodies being transported secretly under the city. Trask had been right: the stories of corpses disappearing from morgues and the crematorium, of the quiet removal of the sick from certain hospitals and care homes, had not simply been tales spread by the bored and the ignorant.

Meia made her way to the basement. She removed her cloak, revealing the Securitat uniform that she wore beneath it, and silently became one with the darkness.

# CHAPTER FORTY-ONE

The Highlanders led Syl and Gradus northwest from the crash site and down into a valley where a muddy river churned, swollen by the rains. Although Syl had technically been the object of the rescue, she felt herself to be a prisoner almost as much as Gradus was. Nobody here entirely trusted her, perhaps not even Paul. Still, unlike Gradus, her hands were not tied. Paul walked just behind her, to her right. The river was on her left. She wondered if that was deliberate, if he was still concerned that she might try to run away and had decided that it would be better if the river cut off one potential avenue of escape while he took care of the other.

She sneaked glances at him whenever she could, while trying to not be too obvious. His face was still puffy and damaged, but in profile she noticed that his eyebrow was cut by a thin white scar, fringed by the tiny dots left by stitches. She wanted to ask him how it had happened, but she didn't want to make him feel bad about it. She was just curious. She wanted to know more about him.

She wanted to ask him why he had kissed her.

Her legs were still weak beneath her, but she was determined not to let anyone know. The terrain was rough, and would have shredded her flesh were it not for the boots, taken from the feet of a dead Illyri. Syl shivered.

"Helluva storm," said Duncan to nobody in particular. "The rivers's gone and broken its banks."

No one replied. Syl already had the feeling that Duncan wasn't very popular. They all walked onward in silence, sliding over the muddy ground, slipping on the wet grass, sinking ankle-deep into the boggy soil. The hills were lost to sight, but Syl could feel them closing in above their heads, ancient presences towering over these newcomers to their lands, these tiny creatures with their brief, inconsequential life spans.

Slowly Syl felt her long limbs uncramping, and she found she was easily able to keep up with these small, solid humans. She heard the word *freak* whispered, even though their dumpy features and beer-swollen bellies, their unshaven skin and angry tattoos were just as alien and unappealing to her. Her nictitating membranes swept over her eyes, and she took in glimmers of infrared and shards of ultraviolet. She even saw the world differently from them. Everything about them—their height, their vision, their hearing, their knowledge of the universe—was so limited compared with her. They judged Syl by the standards of the worst of her kind, hating her even though she herself had done nothing to hurt them. Earlier, a wiry woman called Aggie, one of those who had found Gradus, had stumbled on a rock while walking ahead of Syl. Syl had immediately reached for her to stop her from falling, grasping her arm, and Aggie had sworn at her and pushed her away. If I hated them in the same way, thought Syl, then Paul and Steven would be dead by now. But even as her thoughts took this turn, she knew that she was being naive; she was one of the invaders, and the fault lay with the Illyri, and, by extension, with Syl herself.

They walked on, gradually turning north, fording the stream using slippery rocks that were almost entirely submerged by the torrent. Just as the last of the Highlanders was crossing, Syl heard a faint buzzing in the air. She looked to the skies, but the low clouds hid all. She listened harder. She was not mistaken.

There was a ship in the air, and it was coming closer.

She looked round at the band of Highlanders, and at Gradus, who was staring at the ground, avoiding the eyes of his captors. This Diplomat represented those who had condemned their boys to death, although had they known just how closely he had been involved with the execution order, Syl believed that even Just Joe would have been unable to save him from their wrath.

I have to stay with them, thought Syl. I have to trust them, for now.

"There's a ship heading this way," she said loudly.

Just Joe stopped and looked back at her.

"What did you say?"

"There's a ship coming. I can hear it. It's not a shuttle, but something bigger. I can tell from the noise of the engine."

Duncan, who seemed to have taken it upon himself to shadow her and Paul, looked to the sky. "I cannae hear anything," he said.

"If she says she hears something, then she does," said Paul. "Why would she lie?"

Just Joe made the decision for all of them.

"Take cover," he said.

While the darksuits were useful, it still made no sense to be caught out in the open by an Illyri vessel. Shrubs and rocks littered the hillside before them. The Highlanders scattered, seeking shelter where they could, keeping their heads down and their faces covered. Syl saw that Aggie and another man had forced Gradus to lie prone on the ground behind a flat rock that stood like an embedded shield in the earth, and were holding guns to his head.

Now they could all hear the sound, a low roar that grew steadily louder until the ship split the clouds and soared down, raking the land with the powerful beam of its searchlight. It was a cruiser, a troop carrier, and Syl picked out the insignia of the Diplomatic Corps on its side. There would be twenty or thirty heavily armed operatives on board. If anyone caught sight of the Highlanders, they were finished. Sheer force of numbers would overwhelm them.

The cruiser descended still farther, hovering just above the hilltops but unable to go lower for fear of crashing. Its beam came so close to where Syl lay that she could almost feel the heat of it. If she were to stand up now—even if she were just to move her arm a fraction—she would be seen. She had a strange, self-destructive desire to do just that, but she fought it, even as the light hurt her pupils and the roaring of the cruiser's engines pained her ears.

Suddenly the beam was extinguished. The pitch of the cruiser's engines changed as it rose and headed southeast, staying below the clouds so it could search the land. They saw its beam activated again in the distance, but it continued to move away from them, and soon it was lost to sight. Paul opened his eyes and half smiled at Syl.

Just Joe stood first, and the rest of them followed his example. He gave Syl no thanks and simply told everyone to get moving again. They walked for hours, leaving the river behind them, until a hint of dawn began to light the sky. A giant glossy stag sprang from nowhere and, seemingly without fear, watched them pass, but otherwise it was deserted and quiet, save for the chill wind that cut through the vale.

Finally the valley floor rose again, and Syl saw a small village in the distance. They drew closer to it but did not enter, instead skirting it until they arrived at an old crofter's cottage, its whitewash graying with age and its slate roof battered by the elements. They were now on a rough path, muddy and well trodden by boots. As they approached the house, a woman appeared, dressed in a dark checked shirt tucked into green canvas trousers. She had binoculars around her neck and a rifle slung casually over her shoulder.

"Just Joe!" she said. "I thought it was you. It's been a while."

She smiled, and her teeth shone white and even in her handsome, weathered face. There was something about the way she looked at Just Joe. These two have been together, thought Syl. They're lovers, or once were.

"That it has, Heather," said Just Joe, and he reached for her, drawing her close to him and kissing her on the cheek. "We need a place to lie low for a time. Can you oblige us?"

She looked past him, taking in the figures of Syl and Gradus. Even in the darksuits, their difference was clear.

"Where did you get these two?" she said.

"From a downed shuttle."

252

"What are you going to do with them?"

"The male we're taking to the Green Man. The girl . . ." Just Joe paused. "The girl we're not sure about yet."

"Is that why the big ship was disturbing my sleep?"

"It was. Would you like something else to disturb your sleep instead?"

Heather slapped Just Joe on the shoulder, and laughed deeply in her throat.

"You haven't changed," she said. "I swear, I've never met a man who loved himself more. Come on, let's get you all under cover. Tam is about. He'll be pleased to see you."

Behind the main house, a copse of scraggly trees surrounded a scattering of newer farm buildings, punctuated with rocks and the occasional bedraggled sheep. A pig rooted around under a midden heap dotted with thistles, and a ratty terrier barked without stopping when it spotted the newcomers.

"Shaddup, Lex," said Heather.

Lex did as he was told, and contented himself with sniffing doubtfully at the strangers from a distance. Syl followed Paul and the others over the deeply puddled ground into one of the smaller buildings, its windows boarded over and its thatch repaired with thick pieces of black plastic anchored by stones. Inside it was damp and dim. A man in jeans and a heavy padded jacket stood by a metal table, a gas lamp at his right hand. A selection of weaponry was laid out in rows on the table. There were two machine guns, a smattering of pistols, and several shotguns. There were also axes, scythes, and a large array of blades, from meat cleavers to steak knives. Boxes of ammunition were stacked nearby.

"Open for business, I see," said Just Joe.

"You never know when trouble will come calling," said the man. He turned and shook Joe's hand.

"We need a place to stay for a few hours, Tam," said Just Joe.

"That won't be a problem, as long as you don't go bothering my sister." He grinned at Heather.

"Your sister, if I remember rightly, was the one who bothered me."

"Well, a man's got to defend his sister's honor, even if it's more than she ever did!"

"You're both ignorant men," said Heather, who had been listening to it all, but even as she chastised them her face was bright with fondness for them both.

Tam studied Syl, and then his eyes drifted to Gradus. He didn't seem very surprised to see two Illyri in his barn. Syl guessed that they might not have been the first prisoners to pass through this place.

"I see you brought company," he said.

"And a story to tell," said Just Joe.

"I'll go and put the kettle on," Heather said. She tapped her brother on the arm. "And you, put your toys away and get breakfast started."

The outbuilding was dank and grim, and the straw on which Syl sat was so prickly and uncomfortable that fashioning even a slightly agreeable seat was impossible. She was more than a little annoyed that she'd been put in here, with the door locked. It seemed to confirm her status among the Highlanders; she was more prisoner than anything else. At least Gradus was confined elsewhere. She couldn't have stood to be incarcerated with him.

Time passed slowly, and the light outside grew brighter. After an hour or two, the door to Syl's new cell opened to reveal a girl of seven or eight, her shock of hair haloed by the weak sun. In her hands she cupped a bowl of what appeared to be steaming oats. Behind her lurked one of the Highlanders, a shotgun hanging on his shoulder.

"Hello," said the girl, smiling a little, shy but curious.

"Hello," said Syl.

"I'm Alice."

"Okaaay," Syl replied, wary.

"Who are you?"

"An alien bitch," said the Highlander.

Alice looked annoyed.

"No, don't say that." She turned her attention back to Syl. "What's your name?"

"Syl."

"That's pretty," said Alice.

Syl didn't reply. She was tired, and sore, and—even though she was reluctant to admit it to herself—frightened. These people were not her friends. Even Paul hadn't objected when it was suggested that she be confined to this outbuilding. He hadn't stood up for her at all. It just added to the confusion of her feelings for him.

"My mum thought you might be hungry, Syl." Alice put the bowl down. "There's nothing wrong with it—honest. I even put extra sugar on it because that's how I like it."

The porridge smelled good. Syl's stomach growled after being so long without food. Under the watchful eye of Alice—and the more hostile one of her guard—she wolfed down every morsel, even licking the bowl clean. She wiped her face with her sleeve, and Alice laughed.

"I knew you must be hungry. Here, you missed a spot."

She used her finger to gently wipe Syl's cheek. Their eyes met, and they really looked at each other now, close up, Syl's large, swirling, unblinking eyes staring into Alice's own black pupils.

Alice sat down against the wall opposite Syl. It was clear that she didn't get much company out here, and was happy to have someone to talk to—even if that someone was an alien.

"Why are you here?" she asked.

"My ship crashed."

"The men inside say that you were arrested by your own people. Is that true?"

"Yes. We did something we shouldn't have, my friend and I. I got caught."

"What about your mum and dad? Didn't they try to help you?"

She was cautious, not wanting to reveal to the child that she was the daughter of the governor. It was bad enough that Just Joe knew.

"My mother is dead. My father couldn't help me."

Alice nodded. "My dad is dead too."

"Really?"

"He was a fisherman. His ship sank when I was very little. After that, my mum and me came here to live with Uncle Tam. My mum didn't want to look at the sea anymore."

"I'm sorry," said Syl.

"Where were they taking you when your ship crashed?"

"Offworld. To jail, probably."

Alice watched her for a few long seconds before picking up the bowl and rising to leave.

"Duncan doesn't like you," she said.

"Oh."

"It's okay," said Alice, "because I don't like Duncan."

She reached over and squeezed Syl's hand, then bounded into the sunlight. The door was closed and locked again, and the room was suddenly emptier than it had been before.

Syl sighed heavily, sat back and tried to sleep, but her questions and fears would not give her rest.

# CHAPTER FORTY-TWO

T he sound of voices raised in anger leached through the closed doors of Governor Andrus's private office. Balen, as the governor's private secretary, should have been inside bearing witness to what was taking place, but now he was rather glad that he had been excluded. There was enough rage to spare in that room, and he didn't want any of it to be aimed in his direction. Anyway, he was able to hear all that was being said perfectly well. The doors were thick, but they weren't *that* thick. . . .

"The shuttle went down twelve hours ago, and you're telling us that there is still no trace of my husband?"

The voice was that of the Archmage Syrene. She had put aside her formal robes, and was dressed in a simple dress of red silk. There were dark patches beneath her eyes. It was clear that she had not slept the previous night.

"Or my daughter," said Lord Andrus. "You forget that she was also on that shuttle."

"Your daughter is a traitor," said Sedulus, who was standing next to Syrene. He wore an unadorned black suit and a matching knitted silk tie. It struck Andrus as odd that Sedulus, who hated the humans more than most—and was similarly hated by them in return—should have embraced their fashions so wholeheartedly. His shoes were polished to a high sheen, and the only item of his dress that gave a hint of his position was a tiny gold pin in the left-hand lapel of his jacket, a pin in the shape of a fist clutching a bolt of lightning.

"Nevertheless, she remains my daughter," said Andrus evenly.

"One might almost believe that you condoned her actions," said Sedulus.

"I will not disown my daughter because of a single failing, no matter how grave," replied Andrus.

His head ached, and he had slept no more than the Archmage. As the senior Military commander, he was in charge of the search for his daughter and the Grand Consul, even though it was a search that he had a vested interest in seeing fail. Meanwhile Syl was a prisoner of the Resistance, which was little consolation. He had spent a decade fighting them, and now the life of his only daughter was in their hands.

"None of this matters!" shouted Syrene. "Your daughter is of *no* consequence. My husband—and his safe return—is the priority here. Why have you not sent in waves of soldiers to sweep the land? How can one of the most important figures in the Illyri Empire be a suspected captive of a band of terrorists?"

Lord Andrus sat back in his chair.

"I don't think you grasp the difficulty of the situation to the north," he said.

"Well," said Syrene, "why don't you just explain it to me?"

The Military interceptor flew high over the Central Lowlands, heading north for the Highland Boundary Fault—or the Highland Line as the locals called it, the ancient rock fracture that bisected the Scottish mainland from Helensborough in the west to Stonehaven in the northeast. The Line was the natural divider between the Lowlands to the south and the Highlands to the north and west, but the Illyri had their own name for it. They referred to it as "the Moat," for beyond it lay bandit country. It was one of a number of regions across the globe that they had found impossible to police, and its inhabitants had largely been left to their own devices. While the Illyri had managed to maintain significant bases at Aberdeen and Inverness to the north, and a smaller mountain base at the Cairngorms Plateau, these were basically just besieged fortresses, surrounded by hostile, aggressive populations. Although the main offworld route out of Edinburgh lay over the Highlands, such flights were conducted at relatively high altitude whenever possible, and were consequently out of the reach of the Resistance's weapons. Low-level shuttle flights to Aberdeen and Inverness tended to take what was known as the "scenic route" over the North Sea, well out of reach of the land. Keeping the base at the Cairngorms Plateau supplied was costly and dangerous; even the comparatively short hop west from Inverness to the Cairngorms base was known as the Suicide Run.

Thus it was that the interceptor was trying to remain low enough to spot any signs of what might be the Highland Resistance and their Illyri captives, and high enough to avoid providing an easy target. It was also flying slowly enough to more easily spot anyone on the ground, yet fast enough not to be hit by them if they proved to be hostile. It was a delicate balance, and one that was near impossible to maintain.

On board were the pilot and copilot, along with an eight-member Illyri extraction team, all heavily armed and armored. Their instructions were clear: if members of the Resistance were sighted, they were to be engaged and at least one of them captured alive, in the hope that, under interrogation, they might provide some clue as to the whereabouts of Grand Consul Gradus and the traitor Syl. The problem, as those on the interceptor well knew, was that the Resistance did not wear uniforms, and did not travel in convoys advertising their identity. There was, in reality, no way to tell who was an active member of the Resistance and who was not until the shooting began, and by then it was generally too late. The easiest thing was to assume that *everyone* beyond the Moat—men, women, children, and possibly even sheep and cows—was a member of the Resistance unless they could prove otherwise.

The interceptor veered northwest over the Grampians toward Fort William, where there had once been a small Illyri base until the Resistance had blown it off the map. Beneath the craft lay Loch Rannoch, still and silver in the morning light.

"I have movement," said the copilot.

"Where?" said the pilot.

"Northern shore of the loch. Four—no, five humans, heading east. You want to take a look?"

The pilot adjusted course.

"It's why we're here."

"That's not answering the question."

The pilot grimaced. "Just put the guns on them. I have the ship."

The copilot activated the weapon system, and the twin-barrel heavy cannon beneath the interceptor spun in its housing. The craft zeroed in on the humans, and the copilot fixed them in his sights. The 20mm guns were capable of firing two thousand rounds per minute. They could reduce a human being to shreds of meat within seconds.

As the interceptor drew closer to the banks of the loch, the humans became clearer: three males and two females. The males were carrying fishing rods, the women tackle boxes. They stopped and stared as the interceptor approached them. Carefully they put down their fishing equipment and raised their hands.

"What do you think?" said the copilot. "Our orders are to stop and question."

The pilot viewed the terrain dubiously. The ground was soft from the rains, and once they landed, their cannon would be virtually useless. They would be entirely reliant on the weapons of the extraction team.

One of the humans started waving wildly, smiling as he did so.

"We'll—" the pilot began, but whatever he had decided was destined never to be heard.

The Resistance were students of history. Before the arrival of the Illyri, the United Kingdom had not been successfully invaded since the arrival of William the Conqueror in 1066. The men and women who fought in the Highlands had no direct experience of guerrilla conflict, but they had been taught about the battles their ancestors had fought against the English. They had also studied the campaigns of the mujahideen against the Soviets in the previous century, and the difficulties the Americans had subsequently encountered in Iraq, and Somalia, and Afghanistan. One of the lessons they had learned was how to bring down aircraft using rocket-propelled grenades. RPGs had originally been designed for use against tanks, but the addition of a curved pipe to the rear of the launcher enabled them to be directed at an aircraft hovering above from a prone position.

Two RPGs fired at the interceptor simultaneously, one from bushes to the east, and a second from a small copse of trees to the west. Snaking trails of smoke behind them, they struck the craft at the front and rear. The first entered through the cockpit window, while the second hit the shuttle's port engine. The last thing the copilot saw before the interceptor exploded was the fishing party diving for cover after signaling for the start of the attack. The debris scattered itself across Loch Rannoch, and was swallowed along with the dead.

Within a minute, the waters were still again.

Just outside Pitlochry, by the shores of the River Tummel, the last soldier was running for his life. Behind him, the rest of the extraction team lay dead or dying; the pilots had been killed before they could even get out of their seats. They had been drawn there by Ani's tracker, kept in a lead box to shield its signals and transported to Pitlochry by motorcycle before being removed and used to lure the Illyri into a trap.

The soldier's name was Varon. He had been posted to Aberdeen for the previous six months. In that time, half of his platoon had been killed or seriously injured. Although he had been on Earth for only eighteen months, he now counted as a veteran in the Highlands.

Varon hated Earth, but most of all he hated Scotland. He came from the desert planet of B'Ethanger, at the heart of the Illyr system. He was built for heat and sand, not rain and mud. He had not stopped sneezing since he arrived. Today, at least, it was not raining. It had seemed like a good omen when the extraction team had set out.

Bullets kicked up dirt to his left, but Varon did not look back. If he could get out of range and find cover, he might be able to hold off the Resistance until a rescue party could be sent out. He had his blast pistol and heavy rifle. The rifle was charged for two hundred rounds, and the blast pistol was good for another twenty. If he needed more than that to stay alive, then he really was in trouble.

There was a low stone wall ahead of him. He dived over it head-first, and almost knocked his brains out on a gravestone. He was in an old cemetery, littered with lopsided and broken monuments that reminded him of rotten teeth. There was plenty of cover here, but it would be as useful to his pursuers as it was to him. Still, better this than no cover at all, he thought, even if being in a human cemetery made him uneasy. The Illyri had always cremated their dead. They did not leave them to rot in the ground. It was another reason to regard the humans as a barbaric race.

The grounds of the cemetery sloped upward, and he followed the gradient. If he could make it to high ground, he would have the advantage. He skirted a huge tomb that dwarfed the other resting places, and stopped short.

There was a young woman kneeling by a grave about thirty feet from where he stood. She was putting wildflowers into a plastic vase. She looked up at him as he appeared. Varon raised his blast pistol and stepped forward. As he did so, his right foot knocked against a metal object. He glanced down and saw the hand grenade.

"Ah," he said, and then he was gone.

• • •

By the end of the first day of the search, the Illyri had lost two interceptors and a skimmer, and had suffered more than thirty casualties, twenty of them fatalities. When the advance base on the Cairngorms Plateau came under extensive mortar fire, it was rendered temporarily unfit for use. The losses were the most significant suffered by the Illyri in a single day since the early years of the invasion.

The message had passed quickly through the Resistance in the Highlands: we have a valuable prize. The Illyri want to get it back.

Stop them.

"So," said Sedulus, "what you're telling us is that you are powerless to act beyond the Moat?"

"Not powerless, no, but we can operate only with great difficulty," said Lord Andrus. "And while the situation is most dangerous beyond the Moat, it's not much better once you travel more than a few miles north of the Glasgow–Edinburgh line. The truth is that the Grand Consul's shuttle could not have gone down in a worse location."

Sedulus was silent for a moment. He looked at Syrene. She nodded.

"I am sure that you have not forgotten your recent conversation with Grand Consul Gradus," said Sedulus to Lord Andrus. "The Diplomatic Corps now has jurisdiction on Earth. The Military is at the command of the Corps."

"My understanding was that all such authority lay with Grand Consul Gradus," said Lord Andrus. "In his absence, I am once again responsible for decisions here."

"I'm afraid not," said Sedulus. "The Grand Consul left instructions that command should default to the ranking Corps official while he was offworld. The Archmage Syrene will confirm this."

"It is true," said Syrene. "I witnessed my husband giving the order myself."

"In his absence, therefore, I am in command, not you," said Sedulus.

"I object most strongly—" began Lord Andrus.

"Your objection is noted," said Sedulus. "I have decided that I will take total charge of the search for Grand Consul Gradus—and, indeed, your daughter." He glanced at Danis. "Neither have I forgotten your own little traitor, General Danis. She will be found."

Danis did not reply. The only sign of his inner tension was the slow, rhythmic tapping of his right foot on the carpet.

"For now," continued Sedulus, "all Military craft are to withdraw from the Highlands and return to their bases. This will be a Securitat operation."

"What do you propose to do, Marshal Sedulus?" asked Andrus. "Scour the Highlands yourself, mile by mile?"

"It is tempting," said Sedulus. "But I have enlisted the help of more experienced hunters than I."

He stood to leave, and Syrene did the same, taking his arm.

"The Highlands," Sedulus concluded, "are about to be subdued."

# CHAPTER FORTY-THREE

Sometime later, Syl heard a vehicle pull up outside, but the window in the outbuilding faced away from the noise and she could not see what was happening. Just Joe and Paul came for her shortly after the engines died, and she was brought to the comfortable kitchen of the cottage. There she found Tam, Heather, and two men she did not recognize, but who were now introduced to her as Mike and Seán. Heather pointed to a seat at the table, and Syl took it. Seán leaned over and offered his hand. She shook it.

"Fine strong grip on you," he said.

His accent was different from the others.

"Thank you," said Syl. "I think."

"Sit down, Syl, and don't mind him," said Heather. "He's Irish," as if this explained everything one could possibly want to know about the man.

There was a big battered teapot in front of Seán, and he poured Syl a cup while he spoke.

"Just visiting," he said. He pushed milk and sugar toward her, but she added only the milk.

"Seán transports weapons for us from across the Irish Sea," said Just Joe. He watched Syl to gauge her reaction.

"Why are you telling me this?" she asked.

"A gesture of trust," replied Just Joe.

"And they don't mind if the Irish guy gets it in the head if you do talk," added Seán.

"That too," said Just Joe. "Syl, tell me why you helped Paul and Steven escape."

"Because they helped my friend and me during the bombings on the Royal Mile. And because they were going to be executed, and I wasn't going to let that happen."

"Why? Because they're young?"

"Yes. And they hadn't done what they were accused of doing."

"How do you know that?"

"Paul told me, and I saw in his face that it was true. And even if they had done it, hanging them would still have been wrong."

"What of the rest of the Resistance?"

"I don't know the rest of the Resistance."

"You know us. Would you see us hanged for what we've done? We've killed Illyri, and we'll kill more. This is our land, our world, and we want it back."

Syl had thought about this a lot of late, but she did not have an answer. The question was too complex. She was of the Illyri, and she did not want to see her people hurt, but she also understood that the conquest of Earth was indefensible. The Illyri might have been more advanced than the humans, and stronger militarily, but that didn't give them the right to invade, to suppress, to take young humans as hostages, train them as soldiers, and send them off to fight the Illyri's wars on distant worlds.

And many of those wars still raged, with no end in sight. This much she'd learned while hiding in the spyhole behind the Great Hall at Edinburgh Castle. The most brutal fighting of all was taking place on Ebos, a jungle planet on which every life-form, whether animal or vegetative, was actively carnivorous. But it had been found to have enough precious metal deposits beneath its surface to meet the needs of the Illyri for centuries. The dominant species on Ebos was a reptilian race vaguely similar to the Komodo dragons of Earth, had the dragons learned to walk upright, but much larger, infinitely more vicious, and with a chameleon-like capacity for camouflage so finely tuned that it rendered them practically invisible to the naked eye. Their ability to thermoregulate also meant that heat-detection lenses were ineffective in alerting the Illyri to their presence. While their weaponry was hardly sophisticated, it was surprisingly effective, their blades and arrowheads capable of slicing through even the thickest of body armor. Ebos was regarded as the worst posting in the Illyri Military. For the most part, Punishment Battalions and troublesome conscripts were the main source of workers and soldiers, and their casualty rates were astronomical. If the roles had been reversed, Syl knew, she would have been standing alongside the Resistance, just as Paul and Steven were.

And yet, and yet . . .

"I understand why you're fighting, and no, I don't believe in execution—for anyone," she said at last. "We don't execute our own people on Illyr, and I don't see why we should execute those on other worlds. But I don't want to see Illyri killed, and I won't help you to do it."

Her mouth was dry. She took a sip of tea to moisten it before continuing.

"My people think I'm a traitor, and if I'm captured, the best I can hope for is to be imprisoned far from this planet until the Diplomats decide to free me or make me disappear. I have no interest in betraying you. If I betray you, I betray myself."

Just Joe looked at the others. Seán's grin had never left his face, but it had never reached his eyes either. Syl sensed the danger in him. The ones—whether human or Illyri—who laughed and joked the most were often the worst, she had found. If you listened hard enough, the hollowness inside them echoed their laughter. Heather whispered something to Tam, who did not reply. Paul stood beside the fireplace, waiting.

"Well?" said Just Joe.

"Yes," said Heather, with some force.

"Yes," said Tam, although a little more reluctantly than his sister.

"Go on, then," said Seán, smiling away. "Yes—but if she lets us down, I'll kill her myself before I die."

"Paul?" said Just Joe.

"You know my answer," said Paul. "Yes."

"Who knew you were all so trusting?" said Just Joe. "Yes it is, then."

"Yes to what?" asked Syl.

"To you staying with us," said Just Joe, "and not being handed over to one of the other groups as a bargaining chip for hostages. But understand this: Paul has stood up for you, and he's guaranteed your honor with his own life. I hear what you've said, and I believe it to be true. But if push comes to shove, and you turn on us, the boy here will pay with his life, and you with yours. Am I clear?"

Syl looked at Paul, but he was staring fixedly at the table.

"Yes," said Syl, for there was no other option.

Just Joe relaxed. The decision had been made, and there was no point in fretting about it any longer.

"Now," said Just Joe. "Tell us about the Grand Consul."

For the next hour, Syl spoke of Gradus's arrival, and of the Arch-mage Syrene. She told them what she knew of the Sisterhood, although much of it seemed to be familiar to them already. Mostly they were interested in the Grand Consul—how he acted, what he said, whether he had seemed strange or preoccupied at all, whether he had spoken of the attack on Birdoswald, and the suicide of his nephew.

And bodies: had there been any talk of human bodies?

But there was little that Syl could offer in reply to these enqui-ries, and she was glad of this. Okay, so she didn't know very much about Gradus, and what she did know she did not like. But nor did she like spilling what she knew to the Resistance, for it really did mean that she was committing treason, that she was a traitor.

"Why don't you ask him all this yourselves?" she said finally.

"We've tried asking him," said Just Joe.

"Nicely, and not so nicely," said Seán. "We didn't get very far."

"Show her," said Tam. "Maybe she can explain it."

Just Joe and Paul led her from the cottage to a second outbuilding, this one bigger than the one in which she had been kept, and more closely guarded. The door was unlocked at Just Joe's order, and Syl entered with the two humans.

Gradus was seated in a corner, his hands tied behind his back. There was bruising to his face, and a cut on his scalp had bled badly. Despite herself, Syl felt sorry for him. She was about to admonish the humans, and demand that they clean him up, when she saw Gradus's eyes.

They were almost completely white behind the nictitating membrane, which now appeared fixed in place. His breathing was very shallow, and his mouth hung open slightly. She approached him warily, and touched his skin. It was cold.

"What have you done to him?" she asked.

"Nothing," said Paul. "Well, he was being questioned—"

"Beaten, you mean," said Syl.

Paul did not continue, but had the decency to look ashamed.

"His body temperature dropped suddenly," said Just Joe. "His eyes rolled up into his head, and that membrane thing became fixed. He stopped responding to any kind of stimuli. Pain, heat, touch: he didn't seem to feel any of it. Is that natural? Is it something that your people can do under stress?"

Syl shook her head. She had never seen any Illyri behave in such a way.

"It's possible that it's something he learned from the Sisterhood, a way of protecting himself," she suggested.

"He'll be hard to get to the Green Man in that state," said Paul. "We can't carry him."

"And we can't stay in this place," said Just Joe. "We've been here too long as it is. We're moving at nightfall, even if we have to drag him on wheels."

Syl and the humans left the outbuilding, and the door was locked once again.

"I'm sending you into Durroch with Tam and Heather," Just Joe told Paul. Durroch, Syl had learned, was the name of the village they had bypassed earlier. "We have friends there, and we need supplies: medical mostly, in case we get into trouble, but we'll need rice, dried soups, maybe some tea and coffee as well. There's a short-wave radio at the chemist's shop—you can use it to send a message to Trask letting him know that you're okay. I promised him we'd put you in touch when we had the chance, but Heather's radio has given up the ghost. Be as quick as you can. Any sign of Illyri, and you keep your head down and hope for the best, okay? Tam and Heather, not you, will make the call on whether anyone needs to start shooting."

Just Joe walked away, leaving Syl and Paul alone.

"You staked your life on me?" said Syl.

"Well, you risked yours for me," said Paul.

"I didn't really know you then," said Syl.

"What's that supposed to mean?"

Syl looked down at her feet to hide her smile. "Just that now I've got to know you a bit, I might not be so quick to do it next time."

"Hey, I'm not so bad."

"Well, maybe I don't feel that allowing your rescuer to be locked up like an animal is exactly nice."

Paul shook his head despairingly. "Women," he said. "You're from a different species, and yet you're still the same."

"So you're telling me you've given up on humans and decided to try Illyri females instead?"

"That's not what I said!"

"But isn't it what you meant?" said Syl, and suddenly she felt stupid, and a bit shy too.

"No!"

"Then why did you kiss me?"

Paul seemed lost for words. "I—I was overcome by the moment."

"So it won't happen again?"

"Not if you don't want it to," said Paul. He stuck his hands in his pockets. His face was furrowed with confusion. It made him look very young.

"That isn't what I meant," Syl replied, mortified, and turned to walk back to the cottage.

Paul watched her go. He looked even more confused, if such a thing were possible.

"What?" he said forlornly. "I don't understand. . . ."

# CHAPTER FORTY-FOUR

Durroch had only one main street housing two pubs, a supermarket-cum-post-office, a small café, a drugstore and, at its northern end, the local kirk, or church. It was small but very, very old, dating back to the seventeenth century.

Syl sat in the back of the Land Rover beside Heather, with Tam and Paul in the front. Lex sat on Tam's lap, his paws on the steering wheel. The little dog seemed to be quite familiar with that position.

Just Joe had come to her as the party was about to leave for the village, and told her that she was to go with them. He gave no reason why, informing her only that she was to stay in the Range Rover unless ordered to do otherwise by Tam or Heather, and Syl had not objected. In part, she understood, she wanted to be with Paul, even though she was still embarrassed about what seemed to be their crossed wires earlier. She was attracted to him, that much she knew. She had been attracted to him since the first time they'd met, but something in her still rebelled against her own feelings because they were wrong, just wrong. It made her want to fight him, to push him away for fear of being hurt, but when he had seemed wounded by their exchange, she had felt a warm, warped pleasure, because surely that meant that he cared about her too.

They passed the church just as Tam was trying to explain to her the nature of religious worship in Scotland.

"You see," he said, "originally there was the Roman Catholic Church, but then came the Reformation in 1560, and out of that came the Presbyterian Church of Scotland, but the Catholics and the Episcopalians were still around as well. Anyway, the Church of Scotland kept having arguments about how it should be run, and in 1847 two churches left to form the United Presbyterian Church, although an earlier fight had also produced the Free Church of Scotland in 1843. You follow me?"

"Not really," said Syl.

"So," Tam continued, "the Free Church split in 1893, with a group going off to call itself the Free Presbyterian Church, and then in 1900 most of the Free Church joined with the United Presbyterians to form the United Free Church, except for those who stayed on as the Free Church of Scotland. Then the United Free Church joined with the Church of Scotland, but there were still some folk who didn't want to, so they continued as the United Free Church. Ye ken?"

"No," said Syl, who by now was completely confused. "Not at all. They all worship the same god, don't they?"

"Absolutely," said Tam. "I think," he added.

"Which kind are you?" asked Syl.

"Oh, I don't go to church," said Tam. "I just find it all amusing."

"At least they're not killing each other over it," said Syl. She still found it incredible that people would destroy each other over the nature of a being nobody had ever seen.

"Aye, you're right," said Tam. "They haven't killed anybody in ages. You kind of feel that they're not really trying hard enough anymore."

The Land Rover pulled in behind the drugstore. There were a few people on the street. One of them waved to Tam, and he waved back. The windows at the back of the Range Rover were very small, and the glass was smoked. Only those sitting in the front seats were visible to the people outside.

"You stay here," said Tam, as the others got out. "Don't go wandering off."

"Why did you need me to come if I'm just going to sit here?" asked Syl.

"Just Joe's orders," said Tam. "We're picking up a special delivery. He thought you might be able to help with it. We'll let you know when you're needed."

And with that they walked off. With nothing else to do, Syl slouched back in her seat and watched the world go by.

Meia stood before Lord Andrus and General Danis. She had spent the night away from the castle, following tunnels and exploring the crematorium. She had found a subsystem linking the main tunnel to a previously unknown Corps research laboratory at Launston Place, not far from the Old City Wall, but even wearing the uniform of a Securitat, and with an array of false identity cards, she didn't believe she could successfully gain access, and had been forced to retreat. Now, exhausted and smelling faintly of drains, she made her report. The room had been swept for listening devices, and a small electromagnetic pulse was being used to ensure that any lurkers that had found their way into nooks and crannies would cease to function.

"First, what news of our children?" said Lord Andrus.

"Syl is safe, and with the Resistance. My contact anticipates a more detailed message later today. General Danis's daughter is on her way north."

The two fathers smiled at each other with relief, then turned their attention back to her.

"I have not forgiven you for what you did, Meia," said Andrus.

"I understand."

"General Danis has not forgiven you either."

"Perhaps if I live long enough, he may find it in his heart," said Meia, keeping her face studiedly neutral.

"Nobody is that long-lived, not even you," said Danis. "I wouldn't hold my breath."

"Enough bickering, now," said Andrus, "for there is much to be done. Continue, Meia. Tell us about the tunnels."

"I saw bodies," she said.

"Humans?" said Andrus.

"Of all ages. I think the Corps has been moving them between the crematorium and the lab at Launston Place. There's a connector from there to a landing pad at the Meadows, which has been used by a couple of large Corps vessels in recent months. I could only access a handful of flight records: some of them went straight off-world, but others flew south to Cornwall."

"Do you have any idea where in Cornwall?"

"Saint Blazey: the Eden Project."

The Eden Project had been opened in 2001, shortly before the Illyri invasion. The complex collected plant samples from around the world, housed in adjoining geodesic biomes made from plastic cells supported by steel frames. Since the invasion, it had come under control of the Diplomatic Corps, which had expanded it with additional domes. The stated purpose of the Corps-run facility was to research plant and animal species on Earth with the aim of coming to a better understanding of the planet's ecosystem.

"If we were jumping to conclusions," said Danis, "we'd surmise that the Corps, or individuals within it, might be moving bodies from Edinburgh to the Eden Project."

"What are your orders, sir?" Meia asked Andrus.

"Go to Eden," said Andrus, "but tread carefully."

Meia bowed, and left the room.

"How will this end, Danis?" asked Lord Andrus once the door had closed behind his spy.

"Badly, I fear," said Danis.

"For whom?"

"For all of us."


Syl was half-asleep in the Land Rover when Heather and Paul returned, carrying boxes in their arms. Behind them came a portly woman in a white pharmacist's coat, and a pair of teenage boys, similarly laden with boxes. A black truck pulled up behind the Land Rover. Tam was in the passenger seat; the driver was a red-haired man whom Syl had not seen before. They exchanged words, and Tam climbed out and went to the back of the truck.

"Out you get," said Heather to Syl. Paul stood smirking beside her.

Syl clambered from the Land Rover.

"What are you looking so smug about?" she asked Paul.

"I'm not smug, just happy."

"Well stop it. It's unnerving."

The woman in the white coat stared at her curiously. The boys with her were goggle-eyed with a mix of amazement and cautious hostility. The only Illyri they ever saw this far north were probably on patrol, and they *certainly* did not go around sitting in the backs of Land Rovers squabbling with humans.

Tam reappeared to her right, and he was not alone.

"Uh," said Syl. It was a very small sound, but it contained as much emotion as a single syllable could accommodate.

"Is that all you have to say?" said Ani. "Uh?"

And the two young Illyri lost themselves in an embrace.

# CHAPTER FORTY-FIVE

T am, with Lex for company, decided to stay a little longer at Durroch. Lizzy, his girlfriend, lived a short distance outside the town, and he planned to ask her to join him and give him a ride back to the farm when his business in the village was done. The capture of Gradus—however valuable a prize he might be—had created problems for the Resistance, and there was some debate going on between Trask in Edinburgh and the representatives of the Green Man. There were also questions about what to do with Syl and Ani. A safe location would have to be found for them, perhaps long-term given the trouble they were in. There were plenty of places to hide in the Highlands, but the land was full of those who harbored deep resentment for the invaders. Trask had made one thing clear to his counterparts in the northern Resistance: if any harm befell the two girls, those who had failed to protect them could expect to be hunted to death along with those directly responsible—and Trask would help the Illyri to do it because it was his head on the chopping block. He had no illusions about Meia and her capacity for vengeance.

Syl and Ani sat in the back of the Land Rover with Steven, who had also been reunited with his brother, while Paul and Heather sat up front. The two young Illyri compared their stories of how they had ended up in a Jeep in the Highlands, talking over each other excitedly, and laughing for the first time in what felt like forever.

"God, you two are noisy," said Paul. "It's like having a pair of sparrows trapped in the back."

"Is he still soft on you?" asked Ani, deliberately loudly.

Syl nudged her hard in the ribs.

"He's soft in the head," she answered. "I know that much."

Paul had begun to reply when Ani cocked her head and shushed him.

"Don't shush me," said Paul. He was getting tired of being treated like an idiot by these two alien girls. They might have saved his life, but it struck him that he was paying a rather high price for it.

"Shut up," said Ani. "Can't you hear it?"

Now Syl could. It sounded like the distant buzzing of bees, but it was still beyond the range of the humans.

"Ships," she said. "Big ships."

Paul didn't hesitate.

"Get off the road," he told Heather. "Make for those trees."

Heather did as she was told, making a hard right turn down a ditch and across the fields until they came to a copse of evergreens. She knocked down some of the younger growth trees getting them under cover, and narrowly missed crashing the Land Rover into one of the larger ones, but eventually they were hidden, and she killed the engine.

All was silent.

"Nothing," said Heather. "There's—"

"No," said Paul. "They're right. Listen!"

The sound grew louder and louder, until the ground itself seemed to vibrate, and then, with a *whoosh,* two black skimmers flew low over the trees, heading south. All five occupants clambered from the vehicle to watch their passage.

"I've never seen black skimmers like those before," said Paul. "Who are they?"

"Securitats," said Syl. "At least, I think so. They like black."

But their attention was captured by the three massive cruisers that appeared from the north. Those on the flanks broke right and left as they came, while the one at the center continued on a straight course. At last all five craft were hovering in a circle around the distant village of Durroch.

Slowly they began to descend.

"No," whispered Heather. "God, no. Tam. *Tam!*"


Tam had been drinking a swift half pint in the Beggar's Arms in Durroch when the incoming skimmers caused the glasses on the bar to vibrate, and set the bottles of spirits rattling on the shelves. Tam swore. He had a gun tucked into his trousers, and the first priority was to get rid of it. He didn't want to be armed if he was searched. Chances were that this was part of the effort to trace the survivors of the shuttle crash, and if everybody remained calm and said as little as possible, then all would be well. He just had to be careful where he hid the gun. He called over the landlord, known as False Ed because of the wig he wore. False Ed was trying to reassure the handful of customers in the bar, and keep them drinking. He didn't want to lose money unnecessarily.

"You still have that compost heap out back?" asked Tam.

"Aye, we do."

"Give me a bag."

The landlord found a plastic carrier bag under the bar, and Tam wrapped the pistol in it as he made his way through the kitchen. He found a big bin filled with vegetable peelings and discarded food from lunch, and buried the gun in the middle of it. He then marched outside to the compost heap, and casually spilled the contents of the bin at the back of the rotting pile. The bag containing the gun remained entirely concealed; Tam couldn't see the Illyri wading through the stinking mass in their nice uniforms to search for contraband. He put his hand to his eyes and looked up at the sky. A black skimmer made its gradual descent to land in the open field at the back of the pub. He counted one more, but it was the three big incoming cruisers that made him fearful. He put the bin down and walked to the main street. Residents of the village had emerged from their homes too, alerted by the noise. His stomach gave an uncomfortable lurch. The village was surrounded. Lex, standing at Tam's feet, barked at the craft overhead.

False Ed appeared beside him.

"Military or Corps?" he asked.

"My guess is Securitats," said Tam, drawing the same conclusion from their color as Syl had, although he'd never seen black cruisers before. "You have anything in there you should be worried about?"

False Ed did his part for the Resistance. Everyone in Durroch did. Those who were not active members were sympathizers, willing to store guns and radio equipment, carry messages, or give a bed to strangers who sometimes passed through on Resistance business.

"Just some bad beer," said False Ed.

"I've drunk your beer," said Tam. "It's all bad."

"It's cheap, though."

"Aye, it is that."

But they did not smile as they joked.

The cruisers landed in unison, and there was silence as their engines powered down. Somewhere, a dog barked.

The first figures appeared at the outskirts of the town: a handful of Galateans and several dozen Securitats in full armor, all heavily armed, their faces hidden behind blast masks. They went from house to house and shop to shop, rousting the occupants at gunpoint, ignoring the wails of children and the cries of frightened men and women. Tam and False Ed knew the drill. Searches were an occasional occurrence, even this far north, and were usually carried out by a significant Illyri force in order to ensure their safety. They were more of a nuisance to the locals and the Resistance than anything else. Arms caches were well hidden, and all those who handled weapons and explosives were careful to use solvents to clean as much of the residue from their hands as possible. Also, since the Illyri risked being attacked both flying to or from the search zone, and while they were on the ground, the value of random searches was minimal. Tam couldn't even remember one being conducted in or near Durroch for at least a year, and on that occasion, as on all others, it had been the Military in charge. The Corps didn't tend to waste its time with such nonsense; if the Corps or its Securitats arrived somewhere, they usually had cast-iron information, and somebody always suffered for it. That was why Tam was concerned by the sight of the black craft. If it was a Securitat operation, the people of Durroch were in real danger.

After a cursory pat-down for concealed weapons, the villagers were herded into the town square beside a monument to the dead of two world wars. In recent years, old Lee Lennox, the stonemason, had added a granite slab to the base of the memorial, and had begun to carve the names of local Resistance members who had died fighting the Illyri. On two occasions, the Illyri Military had broken the slab and removed the pieces during their search, but each time Lennox had quickly created a replacement. The latest slab was there now, with four names carved on it, the youngest of them aged only fifteen; his name was Boyd, and he had been Tam's only son.

Tam held Lex under one arm, and patted the dog's head to keep him calm. He counted perhaps sixty people, mostly women, children, and old men. The older boys and girls had either headed farther north to avoid being drafted into the Illyri's battalions, gone to one of the big cities to find work, or simply joined the Resistance in the Highlands.

And some, like Boyd, were dead.

Now there was a rumbling sound, and a heavy-tracked troop transporter, its black body bristling with weaponry, was spewed out by one of the cruisers. It stopped at the western end of the square. A second appeared at the eastern end. Their turret guns turned, and were trained on the assembled humans.

The door of the first transporter opened and two Illyri stepped down. One was female, and dressed in the standard uniform of the Securitats. The other wore a dark suit, and a long overcoat to keep out the cold Scottish wind. Tam recognized them both: the female was Vena, the Securitat pinup girl in Scotland. The male was Sedulus, the head of the Securitats in Europe. They were both Category One targets for the Resistance, but Sedulus was the real prize. Tam wished there had been some warning of his approach. A sniper could have put a bullet in his head and made Earth a better place. It was too late now, though. Tam looked to the skies. The clouds were dark and warned of rain. He hoped that Heather and Paul had seen the Illyri approach, and had made it safely back to Just Joe and the others.

Behind Sedulus, Agrons held on leashes appeared. They were more primitive-looking than the regular Agrons, and barely capable of walking upright, but their noses were bigger, the nostrils wider. Tam knew that they had been genetically adapted by the Illyri to enhance their sense of smell.

Tam lit a cigarette, and a great sadness washed over him. He had a feeling that he wouldn't be seeing his sister again, but he might be reunited with his son. He wondered if the manner of his dying would hurt, then tried to force the thought from his head. Heather had always told him he was a pessimist by nature. She tried to make him see the brighter side of things, and sometimes she even succeeded. Maybe we'll survive this, he thought. Maybe Sedulus, and his little hunting bitch, and all his armored bullies, will be content to frighten us a bit and let us go after some rough questioning.

And maybe the sun will shine.

Slowly, so as not to alarm the Illyri surrounding them, Tam leaned down and placed Lex on the ground.

"Off you go, boy," he said. "Go find Lizzy."

The dog was reluctant to leave him, and it was all Tam could do not to weep at the animal's loyalty.

"Go on now," he urged. "Go to Lizzy. She'll look after you."

At last Lex, who had walked the road to and from Lizzy's farm for many years, did as he was told. He slipped between the legs of the Illyri and trotted away. From the corner of his eye Tam saw him pause one last time, as though willing his master to call him back.

When he did not, the little dog lowered his head and went on his way.

"Goodbye, Lex," whispered Tam. "I'll see you on the other side."

A stiff thread hung from the padded coat that he always wore, rain or shine. Slowly, he began to wind the thread around his fingers, drawing it tight. He'd known that he'd be glad of the coat someday.

Sedulus stood before the villagers. A small microphone was attached to his collar. It amplified his voice so that all could hear him easily.

"People of Durroch," he said. "You may be aware that last night an Illyri shuttle went down south of here. Three Illyri died in the crash, but we believe that two survived and were picked up by humans, possibly members of the terrorist Resistance."

Nobody spoke, but nobody looked away either. They remained standing in silence, their eyes fixed on the tall, thin Illyri in the expensive coat and the black, brilliantly shiny shoes.

"We believe that the captive Illyri passed this way. Our Agrons caught something of their scent, but the heavy rains made the trail impossible to follow accurately."

Somebody snickered behind Tam. The Securitat wasn't going to get much sympathy here for his lost trails.

Sedulus had clearly heard the laughter. He responded with a smile of his own as he walked to the war memorial and looked down on the granite slab with its four names.

"Your village is known to be sympathetic to the Resistance," he said. "The Military has long had its suspicions about you, and the names of the Resistance dead are honored here." He pointed at the slab. "I understand that this memorial has been destroyed in the past by the Illyri. I promise you that I do not intend to commit a similar act of desecration. It is important that the dead should be remembered, regardless of the cause for which they fought. Who is the stonemason?"

A few seconds went by before an elderly man moved from the back of the crowd to the front, his head held high. If he was resigned to being punished for what he had done, he was still determined to show no fear.

"I am," he said. "My name is Lennox."

"You don't need to be afraid of me," said Sedulus. "No harm will come to you."

Lennox couldn't hide his surprise at not being shot, even if he didn't look quite sure that he believed what he was hearing. Two guards led him to one side and kept watch over him.

Now the Agrons were led toward the crowd, their handlers controlling them with their leashes. They sniffed at legs and feet and sleeves. Tam tried to show no fear as one drew near him and paused. He hadn't touched the girl, or the Grand Consul, but he'd been in their presence. He knew that the Agrons were better than bloodhounds, and these were clearly on another level entirely, but he held his breath, and his nerve, as the Agron snuffled at his clothing, seemed to consider what it was picking up, and then moved on. Meanwhile, the Securitats collected the biometric identity cards that citizens were obliged by law to carry with them at all times. The cards were handed to Vena, who leafed through them with a bored expression on her face, as though they were someone else's holiday snaps that had been forced upon her. She offered them to Sedulus, but he waved them aside.

"We believe that more than one person here knows the whereabouts of Resistance operatives in this area," Sedulus continued. "We want the names of those operatives."

Nobody moved. In the past, the Military had tried bribes and threats in an effort to force the villagers to betray the Resistance, but with no result. Durroch had even sacrificed some of its sons and daughters to the Illyri legions before those remaining had the good sense to make themselves harder to find. Everyone in the square knew the nearly as ruinous consequences for betraying the Resistance: at best they would be exiled from the village, their names dirt, forced to lose themselves in one of the cities to the south, hoping that their reputation for treachery wouldn't follow them. Worse, in some places those who informed on the Resistance simply disappeared, especially if their betrayal led to loss of life. The Highlands had no shortage of bogs and marshes, and bodies that sank in them, weighted by stones, tended not to resurface.

But the villagers of Durroch stayed quiet now not out of fear of the Resistance, but out of loyalty to their own. They were human beings first, and they would not give away those who fought in their name.

Sedulus did not seem surprised by their lack of cooperation, merely disappointed. He turned to Vena.

"Pick ten," he instructed. "Make sure there are children among them."

Vena, with half a dozen Securitats at her heels, moved through the crowd and chose ten people randomly, tapping them on the shoulder with her electric baton. They were escorted to the northern end of the square, where the ruins of an old Catholic church stood, now little more than low walls with the remains of the ornate lancet windows still visible. The ten villagers consisted of five children—three girls, two boys, none older than ten or eleven—and five men and women, none of them younger than fifty. Among the chosen was False Ed, the pub landlord. He, like the other adults, tried to keep the children calm, even though the older villagers were just as frightened as the younger ones. There were cries and sobs from among those who had not been chosen as parents, husbands, and wives waited to see what might happen to their loved ones.

The door of the transporter opened again to reveal four mechanized support suits standing in the gap, unmoving. Tam squinted at the faceplates of their helmets. They appeared empty, but then the suits began to descend the walkway, and something like smoke swirled behind the glass as they made their way toward the ten villagers.

Don't do this, thought Tam. Whatever it is, don't do it. He felt an awful guilt. He could give himself up, but if he did, the Illyri would check his details and immediately head for the farm. He had to give Heather, Just Joe, and the rest time to get away, but at what cost? He could see some of the villagers glancing at him, willing him to do something, to stop whatever was about to occur, but he couldn't, not yet.

Sedulus lifted his right hand. It contained a small black device no bigger than a key fob. All eyes fixed on it.

"Do you know why we were so interested in this world, why we chose to colonize it?" he asked. "Simple: because you looked so like us. When the Illyri Empire began to search the universe for signs of advanced life, we thought of it in terms of our own form. We wanted it to have two arms, two legs, one head. We wanted it to be carbon-based, to have languages that we could interpret. We hoped it would think like us. In the end, we were as surprised to find you as you were to be found.

"Because the truth is that there are all kinds of life-forms in the universe: some primitive, a few more advanced, and some strange beyond all knowing. If you think the Galateans are unusual, or the Agrons, or even ourselves, prepare to be astonished. You are about to witness something that few humans have ever seen."

He pressed a button on the device in his hand, and the faceplates on the support suits slid up with the slightest of hisses.

At first, Tam thought that what came flooding out of the suits were swarms of black bees. They swirled in the air, creating complex patterns against the cloudy sky above, before compressing into four solid masses that faced the terrified villagers waiting against the ruined church. They still roiled and twisted, but now they resembled bodies covered in black insects, albeit bodies with only the suggestion of arms or legs, and heads without eyes or mouths. They were shadows given substance, a devil's mimicry of the human form.

"Let us begin," said Sedulus, pressing his thumb to the device for a second time.

The shapes fell upon the chosen villagers, circling them like tornadoes, their darkness forming coils that closed around the bodies of the ten. The villagers began to disappear; first their foreheads, then their eyes, then their gaping, agonized mouths. It was like a magic trick performed by conjurors from hell itself. No, Tam realized, they weren't vanishing—they were being consumed from the head down, but so quickly that they barely had time to bleed, yet bleed they did, faster and faster, until they were reduced to red pools on the ground, and then the dark beings consumed those too, every molecule, until there was nothing left of the villagers but the memory of them, and a few pieces of inorganic matter: plastic belts, metal buttons and badges, a single pacemaker. The beings became four swarms again, hovering beside their suits, waiting.

Waiting for more.

A woman in the crowd screamed a child's name over and over and over again. Others joined in, swept on a wave of horror, and the Illyri and Galateans brought their weapons to bear to keep them at bay.

"Another ten," said Sedulus, and Vena again stepped forward to make the choice.

"No."

It was a woman's voice. She stood between a boy and a girl, each of them strikingly similar. Her name was Morag, and her twin children were Colin and Catriona. Now she looked at Tam, and he gave her an almost imperceptible nod. He had been about to step forward anyway. He could not allow this atrocity to continue.

Sedulus looked at Morag.

"Well?" he said.

"If we tell you, will this end?" she said.

"Yes," said Sedulus. "But I want a name. Now."

It was Tam, not Morag, who spoke next.

"I'm the one you're looking for," he said.

"Take him," said Sedulus, and Vena led the quartet of guards that pulled Tam from the crowd. "Put him in the transporter."

Tam was led to the nearest of the transporters, away from the scene of the slaughter. As he walked, he heard Sedulus give his final instruction.

"Kill them all," he said. "But spare the stonemason."

Tam turned back as he heard Morag scream, "No! You promised! You said it would be the end of it!"

"And it will be." Sedulus took the identity cards from Vena and handed them to the stonemason. "To help you remember the names."

And before the crowd could react, the roiling black mass descended upon them all.

Tam watched it happen. He tried to pull away, but he could not. More Securitats surrounded him, forcing him to retreat from the carnage, as he was dragged backward to the troop transporter. Already he was almost at its door. As he struggled, the sleeve of his coat tore in the hands of one of the Securitats, revealing not padding but a patch of high explosive, one of more than a dozen sewn into the garment.

The guard reacted, but not fast enough.

Oh well, thought Tam. I was hoping to take Sedulus and Vena with me, but you lot will just have to do.

He closed his right fist, and yanked at the threaded fuse.

And he, and everyone around him, ceased to exist.

# CHAPTER FORTY-SIX

There was chaos in Durroch. The explosion had vaporized those closest to Tam, and reduced many of the Illyri in the immediate vicinity to pieces of meat. The angle of the heavy transporter had shielded the villagers from the worst of the blast, but some of them had also been injured, although the black swarms quickly put an end to their suffering. Some villagers had escaped in the confusion, and were now being hunted through the streets, but they were fighting back. The sound of pulsers was met with scattered gunfire, and Sedulus knew that he risked losing control of the situation. He did not have time to battle humans from house to house.

The explosion had also severely damaged the transporter: the big armored vehicles were particularly vulnerable when their doors were open, and this one had been gaping wide to receive Tam when he activated the device. It was now useless, but the inconvenience of its loss was reduced somewhat by the fact that most of its former occupants were now dead or seriously injured.

Of more concern to Sedulus was that a piece of shrapnel had blown apart one of the support suits. The three undamaged suits had been resealed, and their occupants pressed darkly against the faceplates, watching one of their kind dying. It circled uncertainly around the useless suit, its energy gradually dissipating, until at last it assumed the form of a kneeling, armless figure. The shape of a mouth opened in agony, and the creature came apart like ash rising into the air, the wind blowing all trace of it away.

Sedulus felt a mix of anger and grief—and fear. The creatures he had unleashed on the villagers—the "pets" of which Meia had her suspicions, and which had entirely wiped out villages in the past—had no name. Sedulus had found them marooned on a moon of Sarith when he was part of the Scientific Development Division—an innocent name that disguised the elite division's true purpose, which was to seek out alien life-forms and technologies that might be used as weapons—and hence the creatures were known only as the Sarith Entities.

His ship had picked up signs of life on the barren moon, but they were difficult to pinpoint; at moments there seemed to be millions, at other times only five. When he led a team down to investigate, they tracked the life signs to a cave system. Outside the cave lay five shattered pods of alien design, unfamiliar to the Illyri and destined to remain so. Their origin had never been ascertained.

The three-member Illyri exploration team entered the caves warily. Their lights caught swirls of dust, but there was no wind to cause such a disturbance: the Sarith moon was a still, dead place. The dust began to thicken, assuming shapes that mimicked those of the Illyri in their spacesuits. There were five in all. One stepped forward and approached Sedulus.

Interesting, he thought. They identify me as the leader.

Later, back on the ship, he would wonder at what happened next. He reached out a hand, and the dark form simply restructured itself around it, so that it appeared as though Sedulus's arm was buried in its chest. In that instant, he had a flash of what he could only think of as understanding, a revelation of the nature of the thing before him. They were five, but they were many in five; each a single consciousness formed of countless smaller entities. He sensed rage—incredible, boundless rage—and loneliness, for they had been marooned on this world for so very long.

But most of all he felt their hunger, and as the other four coiled around the members of his team, he knew what he must do. He carefully drew one of the small laser cutters designed for the collection of mineral samples. He stepped back and used the beam to slice through the scientists' suits, exposing the man and woman who had been unfortunate enough to join him on the expedition. The entities poured through the holes in the material, and Sedulus had watched, enraptured, as they fed.

After that, they were his.

Now, in Durroch, two of the surviving Entities turned away from the empty suit and prepared to return to their transporter. One remained, and Sedulus saw himself reflected in the blank visage of its faceplate, giving him the uncomfortable sense of being trapped inside the support suit. The Securitat's head was bleeding from the scalp, and his right cheek had been cut deeply by a fragment of stone. A medic approached to seal the wounds, but Sedulus waved him away as he faced down the Entity. A sacrifice would be required, Sedulus knew. The Sarith had already lost only one other of their kind since they had allied themselves to him; it was in the early days of the occupation, and the technology of the support suits was still in the process of being perfected. On that occasion, a malfunction had led to the Entity's suffocating inside its suit. Sedulus had given the surviving Entities the small Norwegian town of Fagernes as recompense. He had wanted to make an example of it anyway, and the mystery of the disappearance of its citizens had suited his ends on that occasion.

But Durroch was different, for Sedulus wanted witnesses to its annihilation. It was why he had left the stonemason alive, and why the deaths of its inhabitants had been secretly filmed by the lens worn by Vena. Sedulus would ensure that the film was leaked to the Resistance, and not only on these islands. He wanted it to circulate. He wanted to sow terror, and the desire for vengeance. He wanted the Resistance to grow bolder, to be goaded into committing further atrocities against the Illyri.

He wanted Earth to damn itself.

He spoke to the Entity. "You will have revenge for this," he said.

The Entity briefly produced the shape of a head. Two eyeholes appeared, and a mouth. The mouth silently repeated one word.

*Revenge.*

• • •

The Illyri dead and injured were placed in the undamaged transporter to be taken to one of the other cruisers, for Sedulus did not want the dead stinking up his personal craft. Time had been wasted, but the delay had been relatively minor. The bomber's biometric identity card had revealed the location of his home. Even without it, the Agrons already had his scent.

Sedulus gave the order to attack and seize the farm.

# CHAPTER FORTY-SEVEN

The drone came in low, scanning for life-forms. It detected the heat signatures of four humans in the main house, but no signs of life elsewhere. The drone remained close to the house while the three cruisers roared out of the clouds. Two landed in fields just outside the walls of the farm while the third hovered above the main farmhouse, scanning the entire area for movement, a skimmer beside it. The Resistance were known to use tunnels as escape routes and hiding places, and Sedulus did not want his troops on the ground to be taken unawares as they moved in on the farmhouse. The hovering skimmer spat out dozens of tiny seismic detectors, each of which penetrated the dirt with probes as soon as they hit the ground. The probes were capable of detecting evidence of excavation, as well as human speech patterns and any movement larger than that of a small mammal. They revealed no sign of human activity. Meanwhile, the figures in the house remained motionless.

A squad of Securitats moved in on the farmhouse, the cruiser and the skimmer now hovering barely a few feet above its roof. All pulsers were set to hard stun. Sedulus desired information, and dead Resistance operatives were of no use to him. Gas grenades were fired through the windows of the house, and a hover ram fitted with a camera broke down the door and entered the building, just in case the entrances had been booby-trapped.

The hover ram reached the farmhouse kitchen in which the heat signatures had been detected. Its camera revealed four battered metal frames in vaguely human form leaning against the exposed brickwork, each heated by a network of elements that glowed redly in the dim light.

At that moment, the entire farmhouse exploded, taking the hovering cruiser and skimmer with it.

On a hillside nearby, Heather paused and looked back as a cloud of smoke rose up from the farm that she had loved. Beside her, Alice gripped her hand tightly.

"Uncle Tam?" whispered Alice.

Heather shook her head. She was trying not to cry for her daughter's sake, but she couldn't help herself. They had faintly heard the earlier explosion in Durroch, and she had feared the worst. The destruction of the farmhouse confirmed it.

"He's gone, darling," she said. "Uncle Tam's away to argue with God."

# CHAPTER FORTY-EIGHT

Syrene's image appeared in Sedulus's lens. Even in the midst of the disaster that constituted the last couple of hours, he knew better than to ignore the Archmage's incoming communication, but he would have given anything not to face her at this precise moment. He had, in the space of little over an hour, lost one cruiser, one skimmer, one transporter, one drone, twenty Securitats either dead or injured, along with a handful of Galateans and Agrons, and one Sarith Entity, although the latter was more personal than any of the other losses. Already the light was fading, and with the darkness the rain returned. The Agrons might have been able to function despite it, and even pick up the trail—for they detected particles in the air as much as on the ground—had the land around the farm and its surrounds not been sprayed with a chemical-based compound made from hot peppers, which attacked the Agrons' sensitive scent glands, rendering them useless for hours. Sedulus had fed two of them to the Sarith Entities in an effort to suppress the Entities' growing wrath.

Their anger was evident as he approached them in their sealed compartment, the Agrons desperately trying to escape from their harnesses as they understood what was about to befall them. This time, the three Entities had risen to face Sedulus, even ignoring the cowering Agrons for several long seconds, until their insatiable hunger finally got the better of their anger.

Sedulus turned his back on their feeding. Usually he enjoyed watching them eat, entranced by the purity of their hunger. He did not want to destroy the Entities, but he would if he had to. It was he alone who controlled the support suits, and he had made sure that they had a self-destruct mechanism built into them as part of their design. Whatever race had marooned them on Sarith had devised a particularly cruel torment for the Entities. Sarith was a barren, brutal environment, entirely without life and with an atmosphere poisoned by carbon monoxide, and yet the Entities were able to survive there unsupported. In an oxygen-rich environment like that of Earth—or even Illyr—they would die within minutes, but only on such planets would they be able to feed, and so Sedulus had designed the support suits, and in that way had made the Sarith Entities his creatures.

But what the remaining Entities did not know was that the death of the first of them shortly after their arrival on Earth had not been caused by a suit malfunction, not in the truest sense of the word. The suit had done just what it had been programmed to do, which was to kill the Entity inside it on Sedulus's command.

The test had been necessary, for Sedulus had no illusions about the nature of the Entities.

The same could have been said of his relationship with Syrene, except that, while he thought he had some inkling of how the Entities functioned, the Archmage remained a mystery to him. Even her image in his lens radiated a compelling authority.

"Report to me," she said. "What news of my husband?"

"We picked up his trail, Archmage," said Sedulus, "but we encountered some . . . *obstacles* to further progress."

If medals had been given out for understatement, Sedulus thought, he would have been weighed down with metal.

"Explain."

He had been hoping that it wouldn't come to this, but there was no point in lying to the Nairene, not unless he wanted to die painfully in the very near future.

"We've taken casualties," he replied. "The Resistance has proved more resourceful than anticipated."

"Or you have proved *less* resourceful. How close are you?"

"We are only hours behind them, but we've temporarily lost their trail. I have drones in the air."

A lie, but a small one. He had *one* drone in the air, mainly because he had only one drone left. He might as well have tried to find a fish in a vast lake by trailing a single, unbaited hook.

"I have lost contact with my husband," said Syrene.

Sedulus frowned. This was news.

"Could he be . . . ?" He did not say the word, but he thought it: *dead*.

"No, but he has closed himself off."

"Why?"

"To spare himself pain. To protect himself, and his cargo."

*Cargo*. Such a careful word to use. Even here, in a secure communication with the Diplomat's head of security and, by extension, Syrene's own head of security, she was cautious.

"I will find him, Archmage," said Sedulus.

"I know you will. I have confidence in your sense of self-preservation, because you know that if you don't bring my husband safely back to me, you should probably throw yourself on the mercy of the Resistance. They will be kinder to you than I will."

Sedulus bowed in understanding.

"One final thing," said Syrene. "It appears that you might have been incautious in unleashing your pets and leaving survivors. There is already radio traffic. Andrus knows that you've breached the First Protocol. He wants you summoned back to Edinburgh. In fact, he wants you to be arrested for war crimes."

The First Protocol had been determined at the start of the great Illyri conquest. It stated that hostile organisms should not be introduced into advanced alien ecosystems in order to avoid contamination. Sedulus, and many like him, regarded it as something of a joke; after all, what were the Illyri themselves but hostile organisms? Similarly, Galateans and Agrons were hostile within the restrictions imposed on their behavior by the Illyri. The Protocol politely ignored such an obvious hypocrisy, preferring to concentrate on the potential for disease and infection, or, in the case of something as unknowable as the Sarith Entities, the capacity to annihilate an entire civilization.

But then the Protocol could not even begin to grasp the reality of the Illyri mission on Earth, and what lay behind it.

Nevertheless, there were those like Andrus who tried to adhere to all of the Protocols: the First; the Second, which forbade the killing of civilian noncombatants; and the Third, which denied the Illyri the right to kill child combatants or even to use enhanced interrogation methods on them, and which had already been dispensed with by the Grand Consul. All of these restrictions had led Sedulus, as a young officer, to doubt the conduct of the Illyri conquest of Earth, until the truth had been revealed to him, and he had learned patience, for the rewards would be great.

"What should I do?" he asked. While Andrus had no authority over Sedulus on Earth, he could create difficulties back on Illyr.

"Do exactly what you're doing now. Search for my husband, and bring him back safely to me. Send one of your officers to me with a full report of all you've discovered so far, and all that you've lost. Andrus will be dealt with, in time."

And the Archmage's image vanished from his lens.

# CHAPTER FORTY-NINE

Hidden in the undergrowth, Meia watched the comings and goings at Eden. Her entire body was encased in a camouflage dark-suit that altered its color to match not only her surroundings but also the fluctuation in natural light. Her keen eyes recorded all she saw: the changes of the guard; the movements of the Illyri scientists and technicians who had taken over the facility; and the security procedures that were in place, all controlled by Securitats. The problem for Meia was that entry to the facility appeared to require both a retinal scan and a fingerprint test, for like humans, the Illyri had distinctive prints on their fingers.

Eventually, as daylight vanished and a light rain began to fall, Meia found her victim and made her move. She had already created a hole in the fence large enough to slip through, and the descent of night aided her. The female scientist wore the seal of the Securitat-controlled Scientific Development Division on the left breast of her coat, and a hood shielded her from the drizzle. Meia considered trying to take her alive, but thought better of it; there might be a struggle, and while she would undoubtedly prevail, she could hardly drag the scientist's unconscious body across the parking area to the entry door. Anyway, Meia hated the Securitats, scientists or otherwise, and the SDD was notorious for the cruelty of its experiments. These were scientists whom other scientists disowned.

So it was that minutes later, Meia approached the entry door wearing the scientist's lab coat with the hood covering her head and shielding her face. She moved fast; she had very little time. It was not the fingerprint that concerned her, but the retinal scan. Retinal scanners used a low-intensity light source and a sensor to scan the pattern of blood vessels at the back of the retina, as each eyeball, like a fingerprint, was entirely unique; the error rate for retinal scanning, however, was only about one in ten million, while for fingerprints it was one in five hundred.

There was no guard on the door. There was no need for a guard, for the scans did everything.

Meia placed the scientist's severed right index finger on the fingerprint reader, and received a green light in return.

"Ready to commence retinal scan," said a voice.

She glanced around quickly to make sure that no one was approaching, then held up a single eyeball, extracted from the skull of the dead scientist and impaled on a spike of inorganic matter at the tip of Meia's left little finger. The scan commenced.

Retinal decay occurred fast in a corpse, and the Illyri scanners were sensitive enough to detect not only the retina's minute array of blood vessels but also signs of life, so while the scanner examined the blood vessels, it also shot a rapid series of light beams at the eyeball. A dead eye would not respond to them, but a living one would.

Unless, of course, the dead eye was under Meia's control. Her fingertip twitched the dilator pupillae, imitating the nerve action that caused the pupil to expand and contract.

The voice spoke again: "Welcome back, Dr. Sidis. Please proceed to sterilization."

The sterilization room wasn't difficult to find; it was mere footsteps from the door. A series of instruction diagrams on the wall indicated what was required, including an order to leave all weapons outside the area. Meia had anticipated as much, and had left her blast pistol back at her interceptor. She stripped down to her underwear and placed her clothing in a locker, but not before activating a small incendiary device, timed to explode and destroy everything in the locker within two hours if she did not disarm it. If for any reason she had to make a swift escape, she didn't want any traces of her identity to be discovered. She passed through a sterilization chamber that bathed her body in ultraviolet light as it cleansed her of potential contaminants. Beyond the chamber were racks of loose white suits, each with self-contained breathing apparatus. It was better than she could have hoped for. The suit wouldn't conceal her features entirely, but it would help.

Meia had chosen this time to enter the facility because, from her observations, it seemed to operate on a mostly daytime schedule. She had seen a lot of Illyri emerge over the hours, and they had not been replaced by a similar number. Nighttime, therefore, was quieter.

Sealed pathways linked the various parts of what had once been the Eden Project. They all looked identical to Meia, but they clearly looked identical to many of those who worked there too, for at each junction was a map display showing the location of the junction and identifying the surrounding areas. There was a restaurant, assorted labs, a gymnasium, and various rooms marked only with numbers and letters. Meia didn't know what she was looking for, and was considering trying to find someone to ask—possibly in a painful and probably fatal way—but decided that the place to start, in the absence of someone to torture, was one of the geodesic domes, which towered above the other buildings like the eyes of some great buried insect.

She had begun tracing her route on the map when a hissing from behind her announced the opening of a door. She risked a glance over her shoulder, to see two white-suited Illyri emerge from a dark, low-ceilinged room behind her. She glimpsed glass cases, and unfamiliar forms within. The Illyri didn't even seem to notice her as the door closed behind them.

When she was certain that they were gone, Meia swiped the

late Dr. Sidis's identity card through the locking device. The door opened immediately, and the same voice as before welcomed her by name. She wondered if Sidis's ID provided unrestricted access or if an attempt to enter a restricted room or area would provoke some form of alert. She didn't want to have to fight her way out of Eden. She favored a stealthier approach to her trade.

Her entry caused low overhead lighting to click on, illuminating a corridor formed by two parallel lines of glass cases, all filled with what appeared to be preservative fluid. Each case contained a mammal, arranged in ascending order of size. The smallest was a cat, the largest a horse, but all were horribly mutilated, their bodies swollen and distorted, as though their bones had been broken and improperly set, their musculature deformed by disease. The damage to their heads was worse; the skulls were split or, in some instances, entirely fragmented. Meia examined each one closely, and decided that the injuries had been caused by something erupting out rather than by any external force. At the back of the room she found smaller jars, all containing animal fetuses in various stages of development. Again there was severe damage to the bodies, although some were so small that she couldn't identify the species concerned. She tried to find records of the procedures, surgical or otherwise, that had left the animals in their ruined state, but there were none. The room was nothing more than an archive, a storage space for a series of apparently failed experiments, but what had been their point?

At the back of the room, a little window looked out on one of the smaller geodesic domes. Inside, she saw what appeared to be fertilizer bags with plants growing from them. She focused, and realized that they were not bags at all. What she was seeing were bodies; human bodies that had somehow been "seeded," although with what she was unable to tell. She returned to the main door and hit the EXIT button, then operated the CLOSE button almost immediately. A group of four Illyri passed, briefly visible as the gap narrowed. An electronically operated gurney hovered between them, and on it lay what was clearly a live human male, strapped into place.

Meia waited a few seconds, then left the room and followed them.


The operating theater had an observation gallery, masked with smoked glass, and it was there that Meia watched what was occurring. Clearly something had gone wrong; there was a sense of controlled alarm about the four Illyri as they prepared the human for surgery. A mask was placed over the human's face, and a scanner overhead revealed the entirety of the man's internal workings on a screen to the left of the operating table. His skull was shaved bare.

"We're losing vital signs," said one of the surgeons.

Yet to Meia, the man's life signs seemed stable: his heartbeat was a little fast, but otherwise he was in no immediate danger that she could see.

"He's prepped for craniotomy," said a nurse.

"Turn him over."

The patient was expertly flipped, revealing the back of his skull to the surgeon, who traced the first incision, a long vertical cut from the crown of the head almost to the base of the neck.

Meia changed her position, the better to view the operation and the screen that displayed the man's system. Something was wrong here. She craned her neck, and more of the screen became visible. Until now she had not been able to see the reproduction of the man's skull, but suddenly its interior was revealed to her. She gasped.

Just then, the door behind her opened, and two male Illyri in blue scrubs entered the room. They too wore the insignia of the SDD.

"Dr. Sidis," said the first. "We noticed you were in the building. We hadn't expected—"

He stopped as he saw Meia's face.

"Wait a minute, you're not Sidis. What are you doing here?"

"I might ask you the same thing," said Meia.

She was already moving as the second medic dived for an alarm button. His fingers brushed it, but it was his last act before he died, a kick from Meia cracking his skull. The first medic was luckier. He used the distraction offered by his colleague to spring at Meia. She saw a flash of steel, and then felt a burning pain as the scalpel slashed across her right arm, but before the medic could strike again, she caught him a glancing blow to the side of the head that sent him sprawling against a table in the corner of the room. The scalpel spun across the floor and was lost beneath a console.

Meia was now between the medic and the door. He stared at her. His eyes found the tear that the knife had made in her suit. Blood dripped from the wound, but there was also a spray of thick yellow fluid, and a piece of damaged tubing poked through the material.

"No," he said. "That's not possible. You were all destroyed."

"Not all," said Meia. "Not I."

She knew the medic was going to spring. She knew before he knew himself. She saw it in his face, in his eyes, so that when he made his move, she was ready for him. Her fury surprised her. She never forgot her own nature, but the way the medic had spoken—his obvious horror of her, his knowledge of the ordered genocide—had awoken dormant feelings. As he sprang, her left hand shot out, the fist bunched tightly. The force of it caught him in the chest and pinned him hard against the wall, his toes dangling six inches off the floor.

He gurgled, spraying blood from his mouth. He shuddered, his eyes staring horrified at his own rib cage. Meia's left arm was buried in it halfway to the elbow. The medic tried to speak, but no words came. Meia didn't need to hear them anyway. Whatever he said would be meaningless. He was dying, and the dying always tried to cry some variation on the word no.

Meia withdrew her fist as the life left the medic. His body slumped to the floor, and his blood dripped from her fingers and onto his face. Somewhere in the distance, an alarm sounded. It was time for her to leave. Below her, the surgical team had evacuated the theater. Only the body of the human remained, his life signs now extinguished. His skull had been opened, and the cerebellum lay exposed.

But the thing that Meia had glimpsed on the screen, coiled like a worm around his brain stem, was gone.

# CHAPTER FIFTY

Governor Andrus paced furiously in front of the captain of a recently arrived skimmer. The black craft had attempted a landing in the inner courtyard, but had been refused permission. The governor's personal transport vehicle had quickly been driven into the courtyard and left parked there, just to make it clear to the Securitats that this was still Andrus's residence, and not theirs. The officer had been intercepted at the castle gates and brought, under protest, into the governor's presence. He had, Andrus suspected, been on his way to report to Syrene.

The Military was closely monitoring all flights coming from the Highlands; the fiction that the governor was a concerned parent worried for his daughter's safety was a role that Andrus had no difficulty in playing. While he knew that his daughter and Ani were in the hands of the Resistance, that didn't mean they were safe. Andrus didn't share Meia's faith in the Resistance; he was aware that there were those within its ranks who would dearly love to hold Syl hostage—and those were the good ones. There were others who would happily kill her and send her back to her father piece by piece.

The situation was further complicated by rumors of the destruction of at least one Securitat vessel, and the deaths of an unconfirmed number of Securitats and Galatean troops. Andrus desperately wanted to know what was going on, but so far the tense, fidgety captain had given him little more than his name and rank. Andrus glared at him afresh.

"So, whatever your name is—"

"Beldyn," said the man. "Captain Beldyn."

"I don't care who you are. I'm telling you for the last time: I want a full report of progress in the search for my daughter, or I'll lose you in the castle dungeons."

"And I can only repeat what I've already said. My orders are to act as liaison between Marshal Sedulus and the Archmage Syrene. The rescue operation is a matter of the greatest delicacy. Your daughter's life is not the only one at stake. The safety of the Grand Consul must be our primary concern."

Andrus slammed his fist against his desk. "*Must* be? As the father of a missing child, you'll forgive me if I beg to differ."

Beldyn gave a small, strange smile. "My lord, I can reliably inform you that we are searching for both your daughter *and* her friend. The Archmage Syrene was adamant on that score. Most adamant. Otherwise, the situation is under control."

Andrus couldn't help but laugh.

"Really? I hear stories of exploding ships and dead troops. It sounds to me as if you have an insurgency on your hands, Captain. Perhaps it's time for the Military to intervene."

"I'll pass on your concerns to Marshal Sedulus, Lord Andrus. Now, I must insist that you allow me to seek out the Archmage, or—"

"Or what? I'd be very careful how I finish that statement if I were you, Captain."

Beldyn closed his mouth and stayed silent.

"Get out of my sight," said Andrus.

He watched Beldyn stride away, resisting the urge to help him on his way with a good kick. The desire to lash out was almost beyond endurance, his frustration so great that he felt it as an ache through his teeth and neck and spine.

He turned to Balen, who was sitting at his desk sifting through papers, as usual, but clearly not concentrating, which was most *un*usual. Syl had always been a favorite of Balen's, just as her mother was before her. In fact Andrus had often suspected that Balen had something of a schoolboy crush on the Lady Orianne; when Orianne died, the secretary seemed to have transferred the best part of that affection to her daughter. As she'd grown, Syl had been a regular visitor to her father's office, and Andrus had often found her sitting behind Balen's desk doing her homework under his caring tutelage. Balen would have forgiven Syl anything, even treason, and the depth of his concern for the girl's safety was clear. For a moment Andrus almost shared the truth about the crash with him, but decided against it. Balen tended to wear his feelings on his sleeve, and was regarded by many in the castle as a barometer of the governor's moods. For now, it was better that he knew as little as possible: that way, he wouldn't have to act.

"Why don't you go to your quarters and rest for a while?" said Andrus. "You haven't slept since the crash."

"With respect, Governor, neither have you."

"That's the point: one of us needs to have a clear head about him. Get some sleep, Balen. You'll be more use to me fresh than exhausted."

Balen rose. He was so tired that he swayed on his feet.

"Go to bed," said Andrus. "I'll make sure that you're woken if needed."

Balen did as he was told. Andrus remained standing, now uncertain of what to do to occupy himself. He had not heard back from Meia. He should never have let her go to Eden. He needed her here. She was his point of contact with the Resistance, and the only assurance of his daughter's safe return.

An hour passed. He was sick of doing nothing. It was time to act. He summoned Danis. When the old general arrived, Peris, the captain of the castle guard and one of the governor's most trusted veteran soldiers, was with him, just as Andrus had instructed.

Within the hour Peris, acting on orders from the governor, had assembled a Military squad ready to move into the Highlands.

# CHAPTER FIFTY-ONE

While Andrus fretted, the objects of his concern continued their hard, damp march across the Highlands. They were nineteen in all, including Ani, Syl, and Gradus, who walked along much like a zombie, his eyes unseeing, his footfalls automatic. Syl had now learned all the humans' names. There was Heather, of course, and young Alice, who spent much of her time walking with Syl and Ani while her mother mourned the loss of Tam. Alice had wept for him too, but she did not blame Syl and Ani for the crimes of other Illyri, which made her very different from some of the others, such as the vicious Duncan and the sinewy woman named Aggie, who had declined Syl's help earlier in the march. Their animosity toward the Illyri had not lessened since the truth of the events at Durroch began to reach them. Just Joe had used a shortwave transmitter to send and receive a series of Morse code messages, and the story of what had taken place in the little village had roused fierce reactions.

"We should kill them," said Duncan, pointing at the three Illyri. "We should leave their bodies on spikes for their mates to find. That'll send them a message for sure."

"Those were innocent people in that village, Joe," said Aggie. "You knew their names. You'd eaten in their houses, and played football with their bairns. Most of them are dead now—and their kind killed them," she added, pointing at Syl.

Not my kind, Syl wanted to say, but she knew better than to interrupt. Paul and Steven, along with Mike and Seán, had taken up positions close to the three Illyri. Steven had even been entrusted with a gun by Seán, much to Paul's unease. They were there to show that no assaults on the Illyri would be permitted, that they were still under Just Joe's protection, although Joe had made it clear that there was to be no shooting, not unless he gave the order. Three others stood behind Just Joe: a woman named Kathy—who had appeared at the farmhouse shortly before they left, bearing a fresh battery for the shortwave radio—and Joe's closest lieutenants, the grim-faced Logan and the small, lithe Ryan.

Siding with Aggie and Duncan were two men, Frank and Howie, who looked like twin brothers but were actually cousins. They had never been particularly hostile to the three Illyri until now, but they had an uncle who lived in Durroch, and nobody could find out if he was among the dead or the handful of survivors.

Heather and Alice stood apart from both factions, as did a muscled young man who called himself AK, and Aggie's husband, Norris, a massive figure more ox than man, who regarded his wife with a mixture of frustration and admiration. Syl couldn't imagine what kind of argument the couple were likely to have later over the fact that he didn't appear to be supporting her.

"I know that, Aggie," said Just Joe. "Don't think I don't feel for them, and for Tam most of all. But it doesn't change the fact that these two young females put their lives on the line for two of ours, and I don't remember them killing anyone at Durroch. Slaughtering them for revenge will get us nowhere, and will make us no better than the ones who murdered our friends. We'll get those responsible, and we'll make them pay, but I won't let you spill blood here."

"And what about the other one?" said Duncan, pointing at Gradus. "Who has he saved?"

"He's important," said Just Joe. "Maybe more important than any of us can imagine."

"All the more reason to leave his head for them to find," said Aggie, and the two cousins shouted their agreement.

"We have to take him to the Green Man," said Just Joe. "Those are my orders, and they apply to you as well. If you don't like them, you've no business being here. Do you want to leave, Aggie? And you, Howie and Frank? You've always been loyal. Don't let me down now. And you, Duncan: I understand your anger, because it's in me as well, but we'll find another outlet for it. For now, though, I need you all to stand with me. We're still being hunted, and the greatest hurt we can do the Illyri at the moment is to keep them from getting their hands on the three who are with us. Am I clear?"

There were some rumblings from the four malcontents, but the challenge to Joe's authority had been dealt with for the present. Aggie went back to her husband and scowled at him so hard it seemed her face might crack, while his own remained impassive. Howie and Frank shared some whisky from a small bottle. They looked secretly relieved that the argument hadn't ended in violence. They were followers, not leaders, and in the end they would always rally behind the strongest in any group; in this group, that was still Just Joe.

But Duncan sloped off, and they did not see him again until Just Joe announced that they had all rested long enough, and it was time to be moving on. Syl was sorry to see Duncan reappear, zipping his trousers, an apple stuck in his mouth. She had hoped that he might have deserted.


They marched long into the night. Syl and Paul walked together, sometimes with Alice between them. When she became too tired to walk, they took turns at carrying her on their backs, and eventually she fell asleep against Paul. In soft voices they talked, discussing details from their respective childhoods, which had been so different, sharing their interests before they were drawn into this brutal war—Syl's passion for art and books, Paul's fascination with all forms of music and his attempts to play the guitar. Eventually Paul told Syl about the death of his father, and she in turn shared the details of her mother's death, and although each still felt the old lingering hurt, there was something peaceful about their conversation, and the words flowed with ease.

With little other choice, Ani and Steven had begun to walk together, each keeping an eye on the other, and lending a hand if one got into trouble when climbing, or wading through soft, muddy ground. If the truth were told, Ani had never spent much time talking to humans—or at least not as herself, as an Illyri. She was on nodding terms with some of those who were trusted enough to serve the Illyri at the castle, and she liked to think they were not actively hostile toward her. Most of them were friendly enough, but she was not so naive as to ignore the fact that deep down they resented the very fact of her existence.

But she had learned to mix with them outside the castle walls. In the beginning, she would sit disguised in dark corners of safe coffee shops, sometimes pretending to read so that she could keep her head down and not attract attention. Later, as her awareness of her powers grew, she was able to engage some of them in conversation, clouding their minds just enough to prevent them from recognizing her as an Illyri. Old people were the easiest, children the hardest to fool. They seemed to see her for what she was, no matter how hard she tried. Ani had decided that this was because children had not yet begun to engage in the kind of deceptions so integral to adult life, and it was easier to fool those who were already fooling themselves.

Sometimes she could see the doubt surfacing as a human began to suspect that all was not quite right but could not manage to pinpoint the source of the unease. When that happened, she would concentrate harder or, if she felt there was nothing further to be gained from the conversation, simply give up on it. It was all practice, a further honing of her developing skills. In a sense, she was as much a confidence trickster as a psychic; she understood that humans and Illyri alike wanted to believe certain things about the world. Her role was to discover the nature of those beliefs—or desires—and satisfy them. An older human may secretly want to believe that this was a pretty young girl seated before him, fascinated by the stories he had to tell, and in that case, much of Ani's work had already been done for her. Similarly, a lonely woman with a jerk for a boyfriend wanted a sympathetic ear, wanted to be understood. Ani had learned to make very slight changes to her personality in order to temporarily fill these gaps in the lives of others, and once she had managed to get beneath their defenses she could start to understand much more about them. As Meia had recognized, she had the capacity to become a very good spy.

But Ani had no desire to be a spy. She had discovered for herself the great and terrible truth about spies: that they spent so long adopting disguises and pretending to be something they were not that eventually they lost their own identities entirely and became shadows of themselves.

Steven walked with Ani shyly at first. After their awkward conversations in the truck on the long journey north, he still seemed somewhat in awe of her. It made her feel a little less jealous of Syl, for when she was reunited with her friend and saw her with Paul, it was instantly apparent that a deep bond was forming between the two of them. They were still circling each other, uncertain of their feelings, unsure if it was even possible for any relationship to exist between them. They had both been captors and captives, and years of enmity lay between their species.

And that was another thing: as Ani had reminded Syl, she and Paul were of different species—perhaps not all that different in many ways, yet different enough. Then again, Ani's views on such matters had begun to alter subtly. She had seen Althea with the human named Trask, and now she was watching Syl and Paul commence their tentative romance. Maybe males and females were *always* strange to one another, and the relationship that was developing between Syl and Paul was simply a more complicated variation on an already complex theme.

And so Ani did not spurn Steven's small kindnesses as she might have done before. They were all on the run together now, and were likely to share similar punishments if they were caught. What began as exchanges of no more than a couple of words—a thank-you for help scaling rocks, his hand warm against hers, his grip suprisingly strong; an enquiry as to whether she was cold, or wet, or hungry, followed by an effort to solve the problem—quickly became longer conversations, and she found herself happy to have him as her traveling companion. He was quieter than his brother, and more inclined to listen than to talk. Still, she noticed that he would occasionally offer some quiet suggestion to Paul, or even to Just Joe himself, and the older men would often nod in agreement, or pause to consider what they had just been told, as though Steven had caused them to see the situation in a new light. He was more sensitive than his brother, but with that came a kind of cleverness; his sensitivity meant that he was more open to experience, and that openness brought with it understanding. Steven would never be a leader, and he did not want to lead, but he would grow up to be the kind of man upon whom leaders relied.

"Do you like him?" Syl whispered to her as they lay shivering in the ruins of a farmhouse, waiting for a sudden downpour of hard, icy rain to ease so that they could cover a few more miles in the darkness.

"Yes," said Ani. "I do. Not the way you like Paul, but I like him."

Syl smiled at her. "Maybe that will come too, that other kind of liking."

"No," said Ani, and there was no uncertainty in her voice. "And he's young."

"He will be older soon enough."

But Ani did not reply.

# CHAPTER FIFTY-TWO

They stopped to rest shortly before dawn. Even Syl, with her sharper eyesight, was able to distinguish relatively little of the landscape around her, and the stars above were lost behind the clouds. She wished she could see the night sky; she was a child of the larger universe, and she was more aware of her place in it than the humans with whom she was marching. Their species had been no farther from Earth than their own moon, but Syl had been conceived in outer space, her cells splitting and developing in her mother's womb while her parents crossed the universe, and it gave her comfort to see those flickers in the darkness, even if the light she saw came from stars that no longer existed.

She watched as Howie separated from the group and walked a short distance to relieve himself against a rock. Then Duncan got up and headed into the bushes. She could hear Howie urinating, and soon others started to do the same thing, men and women. It was gross, but it reminded her that she needed to go herself, and that Paul was reluctant to let her out of his sight after the events at the farmhouse and their aftermath.

"They should be more careful," she said to him.

"What?"

He sounded tired, and irritable. He was aware of the continued whisperings of Aggie and Duncan, saying he was getting too close to the alien girl, that he favored her above his own kind. If Duncan and those who felt like him about the Illyri captives ever succeeded in drawing enough of the others to their cause to take over the leadership from Just Joe, Paul knew there was a good chance that they might kill him and his brother alongside the Illyri.

"When they pee," said Syl. "They're not careful. They just go anywhere and don't think about it. They need to dig a hole, and then cover it over when they're done. You know that my people will be using Agrons to track us on the ground, and Agrons can see in the ultraviolet spectrum. Urine will show up as bright yellow. All those people who slipped away to pee while we were walking? They'll have left a trail to be followed. Even I can see faint traces of it."

"Why didn't you say something before?"

"Because I didn't *think* of it before. Because I've never been hunted before! Now I need to go too, but I *will* dig a hole."

Paul reddened. "I'll go with you," he said.

"What are you going to do, hold my hand? Read to me?"

"I'm not supposed to let you out of my sight."

"Where am I going to go? I'm in the middle of nowhere, and you keep forgetting that as far as the Illyri are concerned, I'm a criminal and a traitor. They hate me and, although your people hate me too, for now I think my chances are better with you than with the Illyri. If that changes, you'll be the first to know. Now, if you'll excuse me . . ."

She rose and stomped off. She passed Ani along the way. Steven was seated next to her, and they were sharing a bar of chocolate.

"Well, aren't you just the pretty couple?" Syl said.

Ani stared at her, a block of chocolate halfway to her mouth.

"What did we do?" she asked. "And where are you off to in such a temper?"

"I am going to *pee*, if that's all right."

"Do you want some company?"

"No, I do not! The *last* thing I want is company. I want a couple of minutes alone, and if anybody else offers to come with me, I'll have to start selling tickets!"

"Right," said Ani. "I won't come, then."

"Isn't Paul supposed to stay with you?" said Steven.

Syl raised a finger of warning at him.

"Don't," she said. "Just don't."

She turned her back on them and stalked off, ignoring the looks that the humans gave her, heedless of whether they were hostile or merely curious. She passed Gradus slumped against a stone. He was still little more than a walking zombie—not that she had tried to speak to him, but she knew from Paul that he was still unresponsive. Duncan had even stubbed out a cigarette on his arm, with no result. He had received a punch in the stomach from Just Joe for his troubles.

"You leave him be," Just Joe had warned. "We'll deal with him when we get to the Green Man."

"If he lives that long," Duncan replied.

"If something happens to him, you'll be keeping him company in the next world. For now, you stay away from him, you hear?"

But Duncan just smiled as he slunk away. He had caught Syl watching him, and the change in his features made her shiver. There was hatred in them, but also hunger, and that frightened her more than anything else.

She found a quiet spot in a small hollow, and when she was sure that she was alone, did what she had to do. She took her own advice and carefully dug a small hole with her hands first, then covered it over when she was finished. She used some of the water in her backpack to clean her hands, and poured a little on her face in an effort to wake herself up. She was so tired, but she knew that Joe might well decide to continue to march. They were on the outskirts of some woodland, which would at least provide shelter, but Joe was anxious to keep putting miles between them and their pursuers for as long as possible. Paul had told her that they were about a day away from the Green Man, but when she tried to press him about the identity of this person he simply shrugged and looked away. Syl suspected that he knew no more about the Green Man than she did.

She wiped the water from her eyes and drank what was left in the bottle. She could hear a stream flowing nearby. It sounded as if it was just over the other side of the hollow. She could refill her bottle from it, and it would save her having to ask for some of Paul's, or forcing him to ask Norris for more. Norris was the quartermaster, so he was in charge of their supplies, and functioned as a kind of human packhorse, carrying extra water, food, and ammunition without complaint. The only time he did complain was when someone asked him for any of it. He lived in constant fear of running out of something, and the easiest way to ensure that he always had supplies was by not giving any of them away.

Syl found the stream, filled her bottle, and drank deeply from it. The water tasted fresh and pure. It made her feel a little better but she was reminded that, unlike the water, she was distinctly unfresh, and very dirty. She sank down on the grass, pulled her knees to her chest and rested her forehead against them, lost in thought, trying to make sense of the series of events that had led her to this situation, beginning with her decision to skip classes for her birthday and head out into the city. That was her mistake, she decided. Had she not done that, everything would have been different. She and Ani would never have met Paul and Steven, and her safe, sheltered life in the castle would not have been disturbed.

Would Paul and Steven have died, though, had she not ventured beyond the walls? Would it have mattered to her if they had? She liked to think that it would have, and that she might have tried her best to persuade her father to spare them, but she would not have involved herself in any harebrained rescue plan. Perhaps Meia would have found another way to save them. Perhaps, perhaps, perhaps.

But not to have met Paul . . .

She was too weary to examine her feelings for him in any great depth. She knew only that she felt something, and he in turn felt something for her. She didn't want to call it love. It was too early for that. The only thing of which she was certain was that she was glad that their paths had crossed, whatever the consequences might prove to be.

She heard footsteps behind her, and because she had been thinking of Paul, she looked up expecting to see him there. Instead a stranger peered down at her from the rise. He wore filthy camouflage clothing, and he held an old bolt-action rifle fitted with a bayonet. It gleamed darkly in the slow-dawning light. Syl guessed that the man was in his thirties or forties. The dawn shadows, and the woolen hat pulled down almost to the level of his eyes, made it difficult to tell. The muzzle of his rifle was pointing directly at Syl.

"Open your mouth, you little alien whore, and it'll be the last thing you ever do," he said.

Slowly Syl got to her feet, her heart thudding in her chest. She considered trying to run, but then another man, dressed similarly to the first, appeared to her right, and two more popped up on her left, younger than the others. The fast-moving stream cut off her escape to the north. She was surrounded.

"She's pretty," said one of the younger men. He was probably in his early twenties, and his face was hard and cruel. He made the word *pretty* sound unclean.

"She's Illyri," said his companion, and he made the word *Illyri* sound like an insult. He was smaller than the other man, and his face was softer, but in an unpleasant, effeminate way. Syl suspected that he might even have a crueler nature than his friend.

"Doesn't bother me," said the first.

"She's not to be touched," said the man with the rifle. "Not yet, anyway."

The man to Syl's right was closing in on her. He was bald, and his right eye was white and dead. Syl backed away from him until she felt the water of the stream on her feet. The man with the rifle raised it to his shoulder and got her in his sights.

"No further," he said. "I'll drop you where you stand, I promise you."

Suddenly a small figure sprang at him, forcing the barrel of the gun upward while landing a fierce kick to the man's right knee. Syl was so relieved to see Steven coming to her aid that she took her eye off the bald man to her right, and instantly he was upon her. The force of impact sent her tumbling into the shallow stream, the bald man going down with her, but he recovered more quickly than Syl. He bent down to grab her by the hair, but her right hand came up fast, a rock held firmly in its grasp. It caught her attacker on the side of the head. His eyes rolled up, and he tumbled unconscious into the water. Now both of the younger men were advancing on Syl. They came at her simultaneously. With a furious growl, she struck one a blow to the left arm with the rock, but it did little damage, and then he and his friend pinned her arms behind her. Syl tried to scream for help, but a hand clamped down over her mouth, muffling the sound.

Meanwhile, on the rise above, the gunman had recovered from the shock of Steven's assault, and with a swing of his rifle he slashed the boy across the chest with the tip of the bayonet, drawing blood. Syl heard Steven cry out to Paul for help, but his voice seemed impossibly small against the sound of the stream, and the pumping of the blood in Syl's head. Harder and harder it pumped, louder and louder, until her entire vision filled with red. There was a growing pressure in her skull, as though her brain might explode.

And then Steven was sent sprawling on the ground, and the rifle rose above him, the bayonet poised to descend and finish him off. Syl bit hard into the hand against her lips and tasted blood in her mouth. There was a yelp of pain, and the hand was pulled away.

Later Syl would try to recall what happened next, but it was unclear in her own mind. Only the dead and the dying proved that it had occurred at all. A great rage coursed through her, starting from somewhere deep in the core of her being. It was like a flame igniting, turning from red to white, scorching everything that it touched, but its focus was the man with the rifle. Syl held him in her sights as though it were she, not he, who was pointing a weapon, except now Syl herself *was* the weapon. There were no longer hands holding her, and she was vaguely aware of bodies falling into the rushing stream. She uttered one word—"No"—and in the aftermath she would recall how quiet it sounded, how calm and controlled. It was not a shout or a scream, but the solitary syllable denied the possibility of any outcome other than the one she pictured in her mind—the rifleman's death.

He jerked upright, and in a single fluid movement spun the rifle so that it was no longer pointing at Steven but was aimed at himself. Then, without hesitation, he balanced the butt of the rifle against the ground, the bayonet toward his own chest. He paused for a second, and on his features there seemed to appear the realization of what he was about to do. He looked at Syl, and there was a question on his lips that was destined to remain unasked, for the force of her will compelled him to finish what had been started. He slumped forward, and the bayonet pierced his heart. His body shook once, and then was still.

From the camp came shouts, and a short exchange of gunfire, but Syl barely heard it. She fell to her knees, all strength leaving her in an instant. She stared at the dead man on the rise, his body and the rifle in perfect balance so that they formed a triangle against the dawn. She looked to her right and to her left. The two younger men lay stunned in the water, but they were still alive. The bald man was facedown in the stream, blood flowing from the wound in his head. Somehow Syl managed to turn him over, but his face was pale, and she felt sure that he was dying.

The mist cleared from her vision, the sound of the blood in her head growing fainter. Steven came splashing to her, calling her name, his shirt red with blood. He put one arm around her waist, wrapped her arm around his neck, and pulled her to her feet.

"Don't tell them what I did," she whispered. She was crying. "Please don't tell them. I didn't mean to do it, but he was going to hurt you, to kill you. I didn't mean it. Please, please . . ."

"I won't," said Steven, and he was crying too. "I won't tell them anything, Syl, I promise."

Now there were more people approaching, Paul and Ani among them. Syl tried to say something, but no words would come. Her vision blurred, and the world went away.

# CHAPTER FIFTY-THREE

Syrene had left instructions that she was not to be disturbed, not while she was meditating, but now her principal handmaiden Cocile stood before her. Cocile functioned as an extension of the Archmage; she spoke with Syrene's voice, and was the only one permitted to intrude upon the Archmage at any time, yet still Syrene felt irritated by the interruption.

"You bring news?" she asked.

"Yes, Your Eminence. Marshal Sedulus sends word that he has crossed the trail of the Grand Consul. The Agrons have his scent once again."

Syrene breathed a sigh of relief. Her beloved husband was not safe yet, but this was progress.

The handmaid lingered. She looked unhappy.

"Is there more?"

"A breach of security at Eden."

Syrene could not disguise her anxiety at this information.

"What kind of breach?"

"A scientist was killed. An intruder gained entry using her . . . *remains*. Two more scientists died during the incursion. It seems that the intruder may have witnessed a procedure. A human procedure."

Pain lanced through Syrene's brain. *Panic. Alarm.*

"Do we have any idea of the identity of the intruder?"

"They were disguised throughout, but an injury may have been inflicted. Material was recovered at the scene."

"Material?"

"ProGen skin, and internal lubricant. Your grace, the intruder was an artificial life-form."

Syrene could barely fathom it. An artificial, a Mech, here on Earth? They had all been destroyed. The order had been given.

To Danis.

To Andrus.

Were they capable of deceit on such a scale?

"Summon Vena from the hunt," she ordered. "Send her to Eden. Tell her to access every surveillance system, every secret camera. I want to know the identity of the Mech."

Meia's intention had been to return to Edinburgh and tell Governor Andrus of what she had seen at the Eden Project, but a call from the castle had forced her to alter her plan. Anyway, she was uncertain of what precisely she *had* seen at Eden: an infestation of some kind, an infection? An organism had clearly been introduced into the human, and it had spread through his system, but what was the point of introducing it to begin with? Furthermore, it seemed to Meia that the host body was fighting the intruder and was, in fact, in the process of rejecting it. That seemed to tie in with the preserved remains of mangled animals that she had discovered. The only conclusion she could draw was that the parasite had been rejected by an array of Earth's species, leading to the death of the host body, and the human was simply the latest of those unfortunate creatures.

Perhaps it should not have concerned her as much as it did. The Diplomats and the Military were forever examining, and experimenting on, the new life-forms they found, but it was a core belief among the Illyri that such experiments should not be carried out on advanced races, even if Securitat scientists were known to quietly ignore such niceties. Humanity was more advanced than any other race yet discovered. What was being done to humans at Eden was not just unethical, it was illegal.

But then the call had come, and Eden was put aside for a time. Meia was a spy, and spies in turn relied on spies: she had a network of informants both inside and outside Edinburgh Castle, some of them under the governor's nose. The news that Peris had been dispatched to the Highlands with a strike team created problems. The Resistance had Syl and Ani—and, indeed, Gradus, which must have been quite a bonus for them—and Meia had heard nothing to indicate that the three of them were anything but alive, and safe. She knew their final destination; it was reasonably secure, as long as they could make it there without being intercepted by Sedulus and the Securitats.

Gradus's decision to take the same flight as Syl had been disastrous for Meia. Had the Illyri female been alone on the shuttle, all would have been well, and Sedulus and his Securitats would have had no reason to involve themselves in the subsequent search. Andrus and Meia could have ensured that the hunt went nowhere near them, and they could have kept Syl and Ani hidden until some form of negotiation ensured that they would not be grievously punished for what they had done. If necessary, Meia could have hidden them for years—even offworld, if the Diplomats proved unwilling to bend on the issue of punishment. Instead, Gradus had become the focus of the search, and Sedulus's future was dependent on his safe return. Sedulus was dangerous and ambitious, but he was not a fool, and the Highlands were not limitless. If he persevered, as Meia knew he would, he would close in on his quarry, and he would corner it. It was also widely known that Sedulus hated both Andrus and Danis, and Meia believed that were their daughters to die in the Highlands, Sedulus would sleep as soundly as he had ever done.

Now Peris and the strike squad had complicated the situation still further. Meia knew what Peris would do. He was an experienced soldier, clever and resourceful. From what she had heard, Sedulus's efforts to carry out a quick, successful rescue of Gradus had resulted only in carnage. To find him, all one would need to do was follow the trail of bodies. Peris would shadow Sedulus in the hope that he could snatch Syl and Ani from under his nose, but if Peris started killing members of the Resistance as part of some ridiculous rescue plan, there were those among the Resistance who would happily put bullets in the Illyri girls' heads in reprisal.

Meia could not contact Peris. He was maintaining radio silence for fear of any communications being intercepted by the Securitats. Her best hope was to get to Syl and Ani before either Sedulus or Peris, and move them out of Scotland. As for Gradus, well, she would happily leave him to the Resistance, but it might make more sense to extract him too. Who knew what vengeance Syrene and the Diplomats might wreak if some harm befell him?

Her shuttle display told her that she was well past the remains of Hadrian's Wall.

Before her, the Highlands loomed.

# CHAPTER FIFTY-FOUR

When Syl regained consciousness, she was seated upright supported by a backpack, and someone was gently offering her water. She was struggling against nausea, and every muscle in her body burned, as though she had been stretched on a rack. The first thing she saw was Paul.

"How do you feel?" he asked.

"Groggy. What happened?"

"You fainted."

"No, I mean what happened to the men who tried to attack me?"

Another voice spoke. "That's just the question I wanted to ask you."

Just Joe appeared over Paul's shoulder. He was looking at Syl in a new way; there was respect there that she had not seen before, but doubt too. Syl gathered her thoughts: she saw a man impaled on his own rifle, and the life from another bleeding into a rushing stream. And she was responsible; she had taken care of one with a rock, but the other . . .

She wondered what story Steven had concocted to explain what had happened. Whatever he had said, she had to be sure that their descriptions of the incident matched. She had to protect herself. What she had done was terrible. She had killed; worse, she had made a man kill himself by the sheer force of her will, by the depth of her rage.

Already, as her head began to clear, she was making connections, identifying small moments in her past that suggested the power she had tapped into had always been present. She had never previously recognized it—or been willing to recognize it—because its use had been subtler, and had not been fueled by anger. Her father always remarked upon how easily she could bend others to her will and escape the consequences of breaches of discipline: homework left undone and classes missed; illicit trips beyond the castle walls that were smiled upon indulgently by guards who should by rights have reported her to their superiors or to her father. Once Althea had found a hand-rolled cigarette sprinkled with cannabis, given to Syl by a boy in a coffee shop, its presence in a drawer forgotten after only a couple of puffs made her violently ill. Althea had been furious. Cigarettes were considered bad enough, but illegal drugs of any kind were forbidden in the castle. It was a matter for parental intervention, Althea had told Syl; she had no choice but to report it to Lord Andrus. But in a matter of minutes, Syl had persuaded her that no such report was necessary, and by the end of their conversation it was as if the joint had never existed.

Now these seemingly unconnected incidents began to form a pattern, and Syl thought again of her father's fond tale of her conception—the one she'd always squirmed away from in disgust: of how she and Ani were formed as their parents' ship passed through clouds of illumination like nothing the Illyri had ever glimpsed before in their travels through the universe, rippling phantasms in which the spectrum of visible light was twisted and re-created in new forms, the glow bathing the fleet and causing those on board to feel light-headed to the point of giddiness, even though the ship's instruments could detect nothing in the void. The display and its effects had lasted for a day and a night, and no more, but it was during this unsettling time that the travelers had reached for their beloveds, seeking comfort and solace amid the strange new rays, and Syl and Ani had been conceived as the light from without bathed their makers' skin and danced in their eyes.

Just Joe's voice brought her back.

"Did you hear me?" he said. "I want to know what happened back at the stream."

Syl bit down on her own lips, swallowing. The water she had taken in was trying to come back up, along with whatever was in her stomach. She was determined to keep it all down.

"I don't remember," she said. "I can recall swinging a rock at one of those men. After that, it's all a blank."

Just Joe didn't appear to believe her, but he had little choice for now.

"Are they dead?" asked Syl.

"One is," said Just Joe, "and another soon will be. His skull is smashed in, and he was near drowned when we pulled him from the stream. He might have survived the blow given proper treatment, but the water did him in. He won't last out the hour."

"And the others?"

Syl tried to keep the fear from her voice. What had they told Just Joe? She wasn't sure what she'd done to them. She had simply visualized herself freed from their grip, and it had happened.

"They have massive bruising to their chests, like they've been punched by a pair of big fists, and there's damage to their throats too. They can barely croak, never mind speak. You sure you remember nothing?"

"It's as I said: all blank."

Just Joe regarded her thoughtfully, but said nothing more before he walked away. Paul continued to hold Syl's head as he poured a little more water into her mouth. She liked the feel of his hand against her cheek, and his arm around her shoulders. She wanted to stay that way. She—

She pushed the water bottle from her lips, turned to her right, and vomited on the grass. There wasn't much in her stomach, but it all came out anyway, until she was just dry-heaving, her body spasming and her throat aching. Paul held her hair back from her face so that it would not be soiled.

"Oh," she said. "Oh."

She began to cry, ashamed and embarrassed that he had seen her like this, but Paul simply pulled a T-shirt from a backpack, soaked it with water, then handed it to her so she could clean her face.

"Hush, now," he said.

"I'm sorry."

"Don't be."

"Is Steven okay?"

"He's shaken up, and they're going to have to stitch his chest, but he's alive, though I suspect he wouldn't be if it wasn't for you."

"What did he tell you?"

"Nothing, except that you fought those men and distracted them for long enough for him to turn the tables on Alex Ritchie."

"Who?"

"The man who died on the bayonet. His name was Alex Ritchie. According to Steven, Ritchie stumbled as they fought, and he fell on his own blade."

It sounded unlikely, which was no doubt why Just Joe had been so anxious to hear her version of events. Then again, was it any less likely than the truth: that an alien girl had willed a man dead, and the man had obliged? Syl examined Paul's face; it remained studiedly neutral. If he doubted his brother's tale, he wasn't prepared to let anyone know.

"What does Just Joe think?"

"He searched you for a weapon while you were unconscious. He was convinced that you'd concealed something, some kind of alien technology that allowed you to blast those two in the chest. Mind you, it still wouldn't explain how Ritchie ended up impaled, but Steven's story is the best that he has, for now."

He let the last two words hang. It was an implicit warning. Just Joe wasn't going to let this lie. He would be back to question her again.

"Can I see Steven?"

"In a while, once they've finished working on him." Paul winced. "We're low on anesthetic, and Heather doesn't want to give him anything too strong while we're on the move. Steven's had a dram to ease the pain, but it's still going to hurt like hell. I suspect he'd prefer as few people as possible to see what happens, and that includes me. Once Heather has finished with him, I'll make sure that you have a few minutes alone together. Until then, you can rest here, or you can come and hear what the prisoners have to say."

"I thought Just Joe said they couldn't speak," said Syl.

"Not those two," said Paul. "The rest of them."

Syl remembered the sounds of gunfire and shouting just before she fainted.

"How many of them were there?"

"Nine," said Paul. "It seems that they wanted Gradus, and they wanted you."

Five men sat on the damp grass, their hands fixed behind their backs with plastic cable. Some of them were bleeding from the beatings they'd received. They were surrounded by Just Joe's group. Nearby, four bodies lay on the ground, a fine mist of rain falling on their faces and their sightless eyes. One of them was the drowned man; he had died while Joe was talking with Syl and Paul.

"Two were killed in the attack," whispered Paul as he and Syl drew nearer to the group. "Norris was also injured in the exchange of fire. They shot him in the shoulder, but he'll be okay. Norris is hard to kill."

Ani, dismissed from Steven's company while his wound was being tended to, came over to join them. The captives looked at Syl with hostile eyes and, in the case of the two men who had been injured at the stream, a degree of fear. That pleased Syl. They would have hurt her badly, she knew, and she shivered as she recalled the dark appetite in the youngest man's leer and the way he had used the word *pretty* about her.

Just Joe was standing before a big man with white hair and pale skin, his eyes tinged with the red of albinism.

"This is a bad business, McKinnon," he said.

"That it is," replied the pale man.

"You're lucky Norris and the boy are still alive, or I'd kill two more of you for each of them."

"We didn't want to hurt anyone," said McKinnon. "We just wanted your prisoners."

"And why would that be?"

"They'd make good hostages. The Illyri have a dozen of ours. They're to be sent to the Punishment Battalions. We want them back. We're fighting the Illyri, just the same as you are."

Just Joe laughed.

"You're nothing like us," he said. "You're bandits. You're thieves and rapists. You steal from your own people at gunpoint, but not one of you has used a weapon in the service of the Resistance. At the first sign of a fight you melt into the Highlands and leave others to die. I'm glad Ritchie ended up spiked, otherwise I'd have been forced to kill him myself, sooner or later."

Just Joe squatted so that he was on the same level as McKinnon. He took a knife from his belt and held it meaningfully in front of the pale man.

"Well, I suppose with Ritchie dead, that leaves you in charge, doesn't it?" he said. "And if you're in charge, that makes you responsible for all this mess. It's the price of leadership, McKinnon. What are we to do with you, eh?"

McKinnon kept his eyes on the knife. With his strange, washed-out features, he already resembled a man who had been cut and drained of blood.

"How did you track us?" said Just Joe.

"You left a trail a blind man could follow," said McKinnon.

"Not true, not true," said Just Joe. He used the tip of the knife to lift the end of McKinnon's pants from his left leg, exposing his shin. The knife pricked the skin, and a bubble of blood appeared. "There isn't one man among you who is capable of doing what the Illyri and their Agrons could not. You're not trackers. You don't even belong out here. You should be tucked up in bed at home, with your mother feeding you cocoa from a spoon."

Syl saw Paul tense. His hand dropped from her shoulder, where he had been supporting her in case she felt wobbly again. She turned to him, wondering if he was going to object to what Just Joe was doing, but Paul was not watching their leader. Instead, his gaze was fixed on Duncan, who slowly circled the group, closing in on where Just Joe squatted before McKinnon. Duncan's hand slipped inside his coat, and as Syl watched, it emerged holding a pistol. He sidled closer to Just Joe, seemingly unnoticed by all except Syl, and Paul, who moved quickly yet silently to intercept him.

"So," Just Joe continued, "how did you manage to get so close to us without giving yourselves away?"

Duncan was now behind Just Joe. He raised the pistol, but Syl could see that he was aiming right past Joe. It was McKinnon he wanted to kill.

There was a loud *click* as Paul materialized at Duncan's side, his gun pointing at the smaller man's head.

Just Joe didn't even turn around.

"Do you have him?" he asked.

"I have him," said Paul. "Not a muscle," he warned Duncan. "Let it drop."

The gun fell from Duncan's hand. Mike, who was standing closest to it, picked it up, checked the safety, and tucked it into his pocket. The crowd distanced itself from Paul and Duncan as Just Joe got to his feet and faced them both. He looked more sad than angry.

"I thought it might be you," he said to Duncan. "I was hoping it wasn't, but every time you made an excuse to wander off, I wondered, and eventually my doubts became near certainties. I just couldn't figure out who you were in league with: the Illyri? But no, you hate them almost as much as you hate yourself. So it had to be Ritchie and McKinnon, or someone like them."

Just Joe gave McKinnon a wink.

"You should have picked a more trustworthy ally," Just Joe said.

"Duncan was going to put a bullet in you before you gave him away. We might just have saved your life."

McKinnon didn't reply, but he regarded Duncan with a killer's gaze.

Logan appeared carrying Duncan's pack. He emptied its contents on the ground. Among them was a small portable CW transceiver, with a lightweight wire antenna and a switch press for Morse code signals.

"Let me guess," said Just Joe. "One of this lot was following close to pick up the signals, while the rest kept their distance until the time was right."

Duncan's face was a picture of barely contained fury.

"McKinnon is right," he said. "We have hostages, and important ones too. I've heard you talking to your pals. We have a governor's daughter, and a Grand Consul! You didn't share that with us, Joe. You kept it quiet. We could demand almost anything in return for their safety. We could demand that the Highlands be kept free, that the Illyri retreat below the wall, all for the promise of keeping these three alive. And what do we do instead? We *guard* them. We *feed* them. We keep them safe, even at the cost of the lives of our own."

Just Joe put a hand on Duncan's shoulder. "You don't understand. This is about more than hostages. You should have trusted me. You should have kept faith."

Then his right fist slammed into Duncan's gut, and Duncan dropped to his knees. Just Joe patted him on the shoulder again, and adjusted the collar of his coat, as though trying to make him look respectable for an important appointment. He turned to Aggie, Frank, and Howie.

"Were you involved in this? Tell me true."

"No," said Aggie. "We might have disagreed with you, but that doesn't mean we'd betray you to the likes of these cutthroats."

Joe seemed to believe them, although Syl saw that Logan and Ryan had been lurking behind Aggie and the cousins just in case Joe had decided otherwise.

"What are we going to do with him, and with the rest of them?" asked Paul.

"Take away their weapons—and their food too—then let them go."

There were gasps from the group. Even McKinnon looked surprised, but Just Joe raised a hand, silencing any possible objections. Only Paul showed no emotion.

"What would you have me do, kill them?" asked Joe. "I've told you before: we're not murderers. We're not like them, and we're not going to do the Illyri's work for them either. We'll send them on their way, and godspeed to them.

"They came across the loch," he said, turning to Paul. "Logan found their boat. Cut them loose, and send them back the way they came. Use my field glasses to watch them for as long as you can, then rejoin us."

"I will," said Paul.

"You did well," said Just Joe.

"Thanks."

"Don't let it go to your head," said Just Joe. "I still don't entirely trust you."

He stared hard at Syl.

"And her neither."

But before anything else could be said, Syl had her final shock of the day. An Illyri strode into the camp, and nobody batted an eyelid. Even Aggie barely glanced at him before returning her attention to her husband, who seemed about as troubled by his injury as he might have been by a midge bite. Syl thought she must surely be hallucinating, but the Illyri, tall even by the standards of their race, appeared to be real. She could even hear the sucking sound the mud made against his boots. His clothing was entirely terrestrial in origin: a long wax jacket over an old sweater, and waterproof trousers tucked into lightweight walking boots. His hair had been shaved to within a quarter of an inch of his skull, and he wore a small silver hoop in the lobe of one ear.

"You took your time," said Just Joe. "You missed all the excitement."

The Illyri took in the prisoners, and the wounded. His eyes lit on Duncan.

"I never liked him," he said.

"I never liked him either," said Just Joe.

"No loss, then."

"None at all."

And Just Joe embraced the big Illyri, and the Illyri hugged him in return.

"It's good to see you," said Joe.

"And you, my friend."

The Illyri stepped back, and Joe pointed to Syl and Ani.

"Safe and well," said Joe.

"And the other?"

"Still alive, but he doesn't talk much."

The Illyri shrugged.

"He won't have to talk to tell us what he knows."

"If you're right."

"Yes, if I'm right."

The Illyri raised a hand in greeting to Syl and Ani.

"My name is Fremd," he said, "spelled with a D but pronounced with a T: *Fremt*. I'm going to be looking after you for a while...."

# CHAPTER FIFTY-FIVE

McKinnon slouched in the front of the van, brooding, while Craven, the group's driver, revved away from the battered jetty where they'd tethered their forlorn boat after guiding it to shore without the aid of oars. Thankfully their van was still parked where they'd left it beneath the copse of scraggly trees, unremarkable and untouched. They weren't concerned about being stopped by the Illyri. They had no weapons, and they had been interrogated often enough to know the routine. There was light in the sky, or as much of it as could filter through the clouds and the rain, and it lifted his mood. He had traveled often before the arrival of the Illyri; his father had worked for a big bank, and McKinnon's early years had been spent in the Far East, and Australia, and the United States. He'd seen many beautiful places but he loved the Highlands most of all, although even he sometimes wished that it would rain a little less.

Duncan sat in the back with the others, lost in his own grievances. He would be another mouth to feed unless McKinnon could get rid of him, which he planned to do as soon as they reached the next town. Duncan could find his own way in the world now, because McKinnon didn't want him around. A man who betrayed one master would betray another even faster because he had the taste for treachery in his mouth. McKinnon had enough trouble keeping his own men in line. He had no desire to add Duncan to the mix, especially after Duncan had seemed all too ready to put a bullet in him in order to ensure his silence.

McKinnon was surprised that Just Joe had let them go so easily. Joe was a hard man, and McKinnon had always respected him. It was why his words had cut him deeply. He *was* a bandit. He'd started out as something better, but he'd just lost faith somewhere along the way. Ritchie had changed him. Ritchie believed that in hard times, the strong preyed on the weak, because the strong should survive. But now Ritchie was dead, and McKinnon was the leader of their less-than-merry band. Perhaps he could change, but what would be the point? He doubted that the Resistance would have him even if he wanted to join them, and the only reason he remained alive—let alone free—was because enough people feared him and his men. No, the die was cast now, and there was no turning back.

Damn, but he'd wanted the Illyri captives for himself. The Grand Consul and a governor's daughter could have bought him a lot: freedom for his imprisoned men, but maybe also a chance at another life. He could have handed them back to the Illyri in return for a fresh start: money, a new name, a decent home. Painful though it might have been for him, he would even have been tempted to leave the Highlands and build a fresh existence somewhere else. He was still dreaming of lost opportunities when he heard the skimmer approach. It drifted down from the east, swooped over the van, then rose behind them in a lazy arc.

"What should I do?" asked Craven.

"Just keep going for now," said McKinnon. "If they want us to stop, they'll let us know soon enough."

The usual procedure was for the Illyri to illuminate any vehicle they wanted to investigate using searchlights, but this skimmer seemed content to shadow them without forcing them to stop. They could hear its whine above the van's engines, and McKinnon could see it flying low to the east. It was black, and it gave him an ominous feeling.

"I don't like it," said Craven. "Why haven't they just stopped us?"

"I don't know," said McKinnon. This wasn't typical Illyri behavior.

Any further questions were curtailed by a deep roar, and a pair of black cruisers burst from the clouds. One of them came to rest half a mile from the van, blocking the road. The second stayed directly above them until Craven pulled over, whereupon it landed nearby and began disgorging Securitats and Galateans. The van was surrounded before Craven even had time to kill the engine. More Securitats poured from the carrier on the road. For the first time, McKinnon was truly grateful that Just Joe had deprived them of their guns. If he had not, they would now be living their last moments on Earth. The Securitats wouldn't have bothered with trials and exile to the Punishment Battalions; they would have killed them here and dumped their corpses in a bog.

"Stay calm," said McKinnon. "Keep your hands where they can see them, and say nothing. If they ask where we've been, we tell them we're laborers heading back home. We have nothing to hide. Remember that."

A voice boomed from a speaker in the nearest carrier.

"Out of the van. Keep your hands held high once you exit. Do not disobey. Any sudden moves will be treated as a hostile act, and you will be shot."

The men in the van did as they were told. Once they were outside, the Galateans took over, forcing them to their knees while a pair of Securitats searched the vehicle. As they did so, an Illyri dressed in a smart black suit approached McKinnon, heedless of the rain. The only clue to his identity and position was the gold badge on his lapel, but McKinnon knew who he was, for his picture had long been circulating in the Highlands and elsewhere: Sedulus, the Securitats' torturer in chief. Maybe, thought McKinnon, I won't live out this day after all.

The two males, human and Illyri, watched each other carefully but said nothing while the van was torn apart. Eventually the two Securitats climbed out. They looked puzzled.

"It's empty, sir."

Sedulus frowned.

"You're certain?"

"We removed the panels and the flooring. There's no question."

Sedulus pointed to the kneeling men.

"Scan them."

The Securitats moved behind the six humans, each holding a small circular scanning device. They both stopped when they came to Duncan, who looked nervously over his shoulder.

"What? What is it?"

One of the Securitats moved closer, the scanner now almost touching Duncan's clothing. After a moment's hesitation, he put his hand into the pocket of Duncan's jacket and came up with an Illyri tracker.

McKinnon started to laugh. He had underestimated Just Joe.

The others looked at him as though he was mad. Only Sedulus seemed to echo McKinnon's amusement. His face broke into a faint smile.

"Let me guess," he said. "You were unwitting decoys."

McKinnon's laughter faded. "I don't know what you're talking about."

"Well then you're no use to me," said Sedulus. He drew his pulser, and shot McKinnon dead. He did the same with four of the other men, leaving only Duncan alive. Duncan cowered, his face almost at the level of the ground, his hands curled over his head, waiting his turn to die, but Sedulus simply tucked his pulser back into its holster, its work done for the time being. His smile returned as he regarded Duncan.

"Now," he said, "perhaps you'd care to tell me how you came by that tracker. . . ."


Duncan made a halfhearted effort to resist the interrogation. He tried explaining that the coat had been given to him on a farm when his own had simply fallen apart due to wear and tear. Unfortunately for him, the tracker had been sending its signal ever since Paul removed it from its lead box and slipped it into Duncan's pocket as he manhandled him into the boat. The initial transmission had come from nowhere near the location of the fictitious farm on which Duncan claimed to be working with the others. Joe had entrusted Gradus's tracker to Paul when he placed him in charge of the prisoners, and Paul had known just what to do.

Duncan's story instantly collapsed, and he was taken into the larger of the two cruisers and strapped to a chair. In a pen at one end were what appeared to be three empty mechanized space suits, until one of them moved its head and Duncan saw what looked like oily black smoke swirl behind its visor. He might have been tempted to ask what they were had Sedulus not administered the first of the electric shocks, quickly followed by a second and a third. Within minutes, Duncan had told them of the finding of the wreckage, the survival of the three Illyri, his own attempted betrayal of the Resistance to McKinnon and the rest, and the arrival of the Illyri deserter named Fremd.

"Where are they taking them?" asked Sedulus.

"I don't know," said Duncan. "Only Just Joe knows."

"You're lying."

"I'm not, I swear it."

"Then why should I let you live?"

Duncan considered the question. He saw McKinnon's body slumping lifelessly to the ground once more, and the others that followed, blood leaking from their mouths and their ears.

"You'll kill me either way," he said.

"I will not kill you," said Sedulus. "You have my word."

"The word of an Illyri," said Duncan, making it clear how much he felt that was worth.

"That would hurt more if it did not come from the mouth of a traitor."

Duncan conceded the point with a shrug.

"I can't take the Punishment Battalions," he said. "I wouldn't last a week. I'm too old."

"You will not be sent to the Punishment Battalions. Again, you have my word."

Duncan swallowed. He looked to the pen. All three of the suits were now in an upright position. Whatever moved behind those black visors seemed to be interested in him.

"What are they?" he asked.

"They are the Sarith Entities."

"I don't know what that is," said Duncan.

"Frankly," said Sedulus, "I'm not sure that I do either. You were saying?"

Duncan hung his head. "Only Just Joe knows the destination for sure, but I heard him tell Logan and the others that they're going to turn northeast, and there has been talk of a Green Man."

"Who is the Green Man?"

"It's a code word for a Resistance leader, but I've never met him. That's all I know, honest."

Sedulus nodded. "I believe you."

"What's going to happen to me?" asked Duncan.

"Why, you're going to die," said Sedulus.

A pair of Securitats appeared. They undid the straps on Duncan's arms and legs, and helped him to his feet. He staggered, weakened by the shocks.

"But you promised!" he said.

"I promised that I wouldn't kill you, and I won't," said Sedulus. "They will."

He pointed at the three mechanized suits. The black clouds swirled behind the faceplates as Sedulus gave the order.

"Feed him to the Entities."

# CHAPTER FIFTY-SIX

Syl could not resist stealing glances at the strong, graceful Illyri named Fremd. She had already learned a little about him from Alice, who was in awe of him. He was an Illyri deserter, one of the first to change sides, and the Securitats had placed a price on his head that grew every year. Alice didn't know why he'd abandoned the Illyri for the humans, and Heather, when she joined them, would say only that he had his reasons. The Resistance had imprisoned him for a long time before they began to trust him.

"Now he's at the core of the Resistance," said Heather. "Him, and Maeve."

"Who's Maeve?" asked Ani.

"You'll meet her," Heather had replied. "He's taking you to her."

There was a ruddiness to the gold of Fremd's skin that spoke of long days spent battling the elements in Scotland. He had wrinkles around his eyes and mouth, astonishing for one who was still comparatively young. Even her father had barely a line on his face, and he was considerably older than Fremd. What struck Syl most about him was the sense of a spirit liberated, a being at peace with himself. In a strange way, this hunted man had found the place where he was always meant to be. If he died in the Highlands, he would die happy.

He in his turn seemed curious about Syl and Ani. After all, they were in a similar situation. He had turned his back on his own people, at the risk of his life, to live among the humans, just as Syl and Ani were now being pursued for their own treason.

After twenty minutes spent talking in private with Just Joe, Fremd fell back to join the little group comprising Syl and Ani, and Steven and Paul. Alice was with them too. Her mother had entrusted her to them, for it had been made clear that the group of Resistance fighters was going to split up. Already the others were preparing to leave without them. Only the lad named AK stood apart from the rest, holding one end of a rope that was wrapped around Grand Consul Gradus. Gradus's jaw hung open, and his eyes remained blank and lifeless.

"You're all coming with me and AK," Fremd told them.

On the small rise above them, Just Joe let the rest of the Resistance pass him, then paused and raised a hand to Fremd in farewell before rejoining his group. There was something sad about the gesture, as if he feared that he might not see Fremd again.

"Why are they leaving?" asked Syl.

"Because Joe has to play a risky game now," said Fremd. "He's had his suspicions about Duncan for a while, and he's been feeding him tidbits of false information about his plans. If all has gone well, Duncan is now in the hands of the Illyri, and is telling them what he knows, or thinks he knows. That will lead them away from us, and toward Joe."

"And what will Joe do then?"

"He'll fight them."

Syl looked back at the rise, but there was nobody to be seen. They were so few. How could they hope to take on their Illyri pursuers and prevail?

"You've done well to avoid them so far, by the way," said Fremd. "To tell the truth, I thought they might catch you within a day, but it seems the old gods are smiling on you."

"Old gods?" asked Ani. "What old gods?"

"You can't live out here for long and not start to believe in spirits, both good and bad," said Fremd. "They're in the stones, and the air. You don't want to go messing about with the old gods, but if you treat them right, they'll keep their part of the bargain."

Ani looked at him as though he were mad.

"Do you drink?" she asked.

"What, like whisky? Of course."

"Well, maybe you should consider cutting back."

Fremd laughed. "Have you ever heard of Pascal's Wager?"

Ani shook her head.

"It's a philosophical position," said Fremd. "Pascal was a Frenchman who argued that it made more sense to believe in the existence of God than not, because you had nothing to lose by believing. So I take the view that if I act like there are old gods, and they don't exist, then there's no harm done, but if they do exist, then by treating them with respect I'll avoid any harm to myself. I win either way."

Fremd began walking, and they all followed, AK leading Gradus the way a drover might lead an obedient mule.

"That woman back at camp, Aggie, she hates me, but she barely looked at you when you came into camp," said Syl.

"Do you hate all humans?"

"No, of course not."

"Aggie doesn't hate all Illyri," said Fremd. "She hates what the Illyri represent on Earth—conflict, repression, captivity—but she's slowly learning that we're not all alike. She doesn't know you. To her, you and Ani and the Grand Consul are all the enemy. She'll learn the truth about you as well, in time."

"Your name," said Syl. "It's not Illyri."

"No, it's German. It means 'strange' or 'foreign.' Or in my case, 'alien.' One of my first captors was a German. He gave me the name, and it stuck."

"What's your real name?"

"It doesn't matter," said Fremd, and for the first time Syl saw the steel beneath his placid nature. "That's not who I am anymore."

The conversation ended, and they continued walking for an hour or more. They moved through places where there was a little cover, although Fremd was more concerned with making progress than reducing exposure to their hunters, until at last they came to an area of new-growth pine. Once upon a time, the ancient Caledonian Forest had covered the Highlands, but primitive tribes had begun its destruction, and the Vikings had helped by burning large parts of it. Farmers and fuel-gatherers finished the job. Even before the arrival of the Illyri, efforts to restore the woodland had begun, and now millions of trees were growing in the Highlands; not just pine, but alder, birch, holly, hazel, and mountain ash. Fremd had led them to the outskirts of one of these new patches of forest, and allowed them to refill their water bottles from a small stream.

Syl winced and limped a little as she felt a blister burst on her heel.

"Sore feet?" said Fremd.

"Very."

"I have something in my bag that might help, when we stop to eat."

"Dry socks? Boots that fit?"

"You never know; miracles do happen. But you have my sympathy. Just Joe walks a hard march."

"Sometimes we seemed to be going around in circles, or at least taking the longest route between any two points," said Syl.

"Joe didn't want to leave a straight trail, or an obvious line," explained Fremd, "because that's what the Agrons look for. It's in their nature: why go around something when you can go through it? They'll assume that we'll do the same. Their sense of smell is incredible, but their logical processes leave a lot to be desired, and their handlers are at their mercy. They go straight, we take the scenic route, and the Agrons get confused. By taking one step back, we take two steps forward."

"And how long are you planning to keep making us take these miraculous steps?" asked Ani.

"Just for another couple of hours. There's a ruined bothy by a loch with a supply dump nearby. We'll let you rest up there properly before the final push."

Ani frowned at Syl. "What's a bothy?"

"A cottage," said Fremd. "You really don't get out much, do

you? You've been in Scotland most of your life, and you still don't know what a bothy is."

"I never *had* to know what a stupid bothy was," said Ani.

She paused to watch AK tear a strip of fabric from his T-shirt and tie it around his forehead before he squatted down and artfully smeared mud across his face.

"What is that idiot doing?" she said. "Hey, idiot, what are you doing?"

"Don't call me idiot, idiot," said AK.

"Great comeback," said Ani.

AK grunted.

"Camouflage," he said, and he stamped his muddy boots meaningfully on the ground and squinted at the horizon.

Syl bent over the water and began muddying her own features. When she turned to face Ani, she'd daubed a rough *L* for *Loser* on her own forehead in mud, and they started to laugh. It was the first time Syl had laughed in what seemed like weeks. For a moment she forgot the pursuit, and how much she missed her father, and Althea. She even forgot Ritchie impaled on his bayonet, and the drowned man in the stream, and the gift, or curse, that had caused their deaths. Her laughter took on an edge of hysteria, but she kept laughing because she was afraid that if she stopped she might start crying instead. Eventually she got herself under control. She wiped her eyes. There were tears, but they were of mirth, for now.

"You know, it wasn't that funny," said Ani.

And Syl started laughing again.

Fremd shook his head in puzzlement, and set off again. Behind him, the laughter faded, and the little group recommenced their slow, painful trudge.

Syl slowed to take a few minutes to talk quietly with Steven, who was walking carefully for fear of taking a tumble and bursting his stitches. He confirmed that he had not said anything of what had happened—not even to Paul—in part because he wasn't sure what had happened himself.

"How did you do it?" he asked.

"I'm not sure," said Syl. "I got angry and I just willed it. I was afraid too. I think that was part of it. I couldn't control it. I was so frightened, and so furious. It was like a storm inside me."

"Have you done it before?"

"No, not like that. I don't think I even realized I was doing it in the past. Looking back, I can see how I might have made people do something because I wanted them to, but it was subtle. I talked them around, mostly, but I'm starting to think that if they resisted, I might have given them a little push. You understand why nobody must know, don't you? They'd think I was a freak. They'd do tests. They might lock me up."

"No," said Steven. "They'd use you, like a weapon."

The truth of it made Syl stop in her tracks. He was right.

She saw Paul and Ani staring back at her when they noticed she was not following. She stomped her right foot on the ground and stretched her thigh, like someone fighting a cramp, then waved to let them know that she was okay.

"So it's our secret?" she said to Steven.

"Yes, it's our secret. It would be even if you hadn't used it to save my life."

"Thank you," said Syl.

"It's nothing," said Steven, and Syl wished that were true.

# CHAPTER FIFTY-SEVEN

For the next hour Syl walked beside Paul and told him stories of places that she'd never been but wished to see, describing things she'd only ever read of in books or glimpsed on screens or in virtual-reality constructs, and some even that she might simply have dreamed: the curlicue insects of Illyr, like musical notes moving through the air; great lakes that shone not blue, but gold and yellow, while the sky above constantly swirled with ferocious clouds tinged with blue and red as storms raged high in the atmosphere even while all was calm and humid on the ground. She told him of towering plants that grew to the sky and sucked rain from clouds, and of the strange creatures that spent their entire lives atop these highest flora, winged and scaled with bright red skin as tough as canvas to protect them from the storms, their bodies only descending at last to the ground upon their deaths. She told him of the moons that fought over the waves, and the lazy arc of the planet's bright star—Illyr's sun—that gave a sense of near-endless days and deep, dark nights. She told him of the luminous creatures that followed the night so that they were always in the dark, and camouflaged day creatures that stayed always in the sun, their bodies so perfectly adapted to their environment that they were visible only as a blurring against the clouds, a ripple in the fabric of the sky.

In return, he answered her questions about his life. He talked of his decision to join the Resistance. He spoke of a sister who had lived for just a few hours after her birth, and whose presence he sometimes felt near him, as though her ghost had remained with them and continued to grow, reluctant to be separated from her brothers. And he told her of his mother, who, on the death of her husband, had somehow found it within her to love her boys twice as much to make up for his absence.

"She sounds marvelous," said Syl.

"Well, she drives me mad sometimes, but then I do the same with her. Anyway, you know mums."

"No," said Syl. "I don't. But I've got Althea."

"Oh Syl, I'm sorry. That was thoughtless. But tell me more about Althea."

And she did, spilling feelings she'd never shared before about her formative years, about the hole she felt inside that never went away and how Althea had filled at least part of it, speaking words to a near stranger that she had never shared with a friend. Paul had heard that there was an Illyri from the castle who was friendly with Trask—and perhaps more than that—but he had not known her name until now, and he thought how strange it was that even in this he had somehow been connected to Syl without knowing it. As Syl grew forlorn at her separation from those in the castle who loved her, Paul cheered her with upbeat tales of his life and his extended, oddball family, of cousins and aunts and uncles so bizarre that she thought he must surely have invented them, until she came to the conclusion that nobody could invent a family so strange.

Then he had more questions about where she came from, about her homeworld, so she told him of marvelous fabled cities: of Olos with its castles of ice; of the magical Arayyis that spilled elegantly into the sea; and of splendid, spired Tannis, the birthplace of her mother, the most glorious city of them all.

At last they came to a small loch in the heart of the woods, its waters still and cold, reflecting the mountains in shades of icy blue and green, and Syl sighed with pleasure, smiling at Paul and saying, "But of course, this is beautiful too."

He took her hand and squeezed it, smiling too, and she felt his touch tingling all the way up her arm and catching like a sigh in her throat. She squeezed back, and he lifted her fingers to his mouth and pressed his lips to the back of her hand. Just then Fremd started to bark instructions and, blushing, they both let go before anyone could see them.

Fremd announced that they would rest here. As AK pointed out, there was also the possibility of catching some fish for supper.

"With your bare hands, no doubt," said Ani.

Her dislike of AK, unreasonable and instinctive, had not decreased during their walk, and she seemed to take pleasure in baiting him. AK gave her a funny look before he wandered off to "survey the terrain," only to return a little later with four plump silver fish on a hand-hewn wooden spear. Ani spluttered with surprise when he handed her his prize.

"You've got to be joking," she said. "What am I meant to do with these?"

"Cook 'em," he said. "Or stick 'em where the sun don't shine."

"Cooking them might be better," said Steven.

"And tastier," said Syl.

Paul was sitting on a boulder keeping watch while Fremd went to the bothy for whatever supplies he needed. Syl had thought about joining Paul, but then decided to give him a little time alone.

"I'll help you," Alice told Ani. "I know what to do."

"Right," said Ani, staring doubtfully into the glassy-eyed faces of the dead fish. Alice dug about in her small backpack, pulled out a penknife, and gave it to Ani, who gamely set to work gutting the fish on a flat stone, wrinkling her nose with distaste as she followed the little girl's instructions.

"Do you think," she said, "that we dare to make a fire, or is it to be sushi for dinner?"

"Neither," said Fremd, as he stepped from the woods.

From his pack he produced a pair of small gas camping stoves, and a battered metal plate.

"These should do the trick."

He also had two tins of baked beans, a small pot, some bars of chocolate, a jar of instant coffee, sachets of creamer, and paper cups.

It was to be a feast.

They shared the fish as it cooked, stuffing the hot food into their mouths with their fingers. Ani offered the first morsels to AK, and he pronounced it to be very good indeed, and a thaw in their relationship began. When they'd eaten the last of the beans, Fremd rinsed out the pan and filled it with water to boil, spooned the coffee into the cups, and shared out the chocolate. Syl had lost all track of time. There was still light in the sky. That was all she knew for certain.

"I have a sudden desire for toasted marshmallows," said Paul.

"I'd settle for soap," said Steven, sniffing theatrically at his armpits.

"As if by magic," said Fremd, and from his pocket he produced two thick bars of yellow soap. Steven grabbed them.

"And on that note, I'm declaring it bath time," he said.

He got to his feet, and with a whoop hurtled down the slope toward the water.

"C'mon!" he shouted, tearing off his clothes until he was down to his boxers. "Last one in is a chicken."

Paul and AK took off after him, Alice at their heels, but the Illyri girls hung back. Syl pulled a face. "A chicken? Why is the last one in a chicken?"

Ani shrugged, frowning.

"I don't understand either."

But now Paul was shouting to them from the bottom of the slope as he too stripped down to tartan boxer shorts. His body was pale and lean, his stomach taut, his limbs held together by obvious sinews and tight knots of still-bruised flesh, and Syl felt a tingling in her thighs and an odd weightlessness in her chest.

"Syl?" Ani said. "Earth to Syl."

"Sorry," said Syl. "I was just . . ."

Ani waited, one eyebrow arched like a bird taking flight. "Yes? You were just what, exactly?"

"Never mind," said Syl.

She took her friend's hand, and together they loped down the slope to bathe in the icy water. It was freezing—so cold that Syl thought she would only be able to stand it for a few seconds—but she was desperate to clean herself. She moved away from the others, who were playing piggy-in-the-middle with a bar of wet soap, Steven and Paul squeezing the bar in their hands to propel it over Ani's head. Syl was in no mood to play. Instead she scrubbed and scrubbed with the second bar of soap, as though she could wipe away not just the filth and the mud but the memory of the blood she had spilled. When she could stand the cold no longer, she ran shivering from the water. She came to their camp and saw that Fremd had built a fire in the lee of a boulder, shielding it on the exposed sides with raised banks of earth.

"Don't worry," he said from nearby. "It's not dark yet so it would be hard to see even without the rock and dirt, and it'll do you all good to warm yourselves by it. We can cook on a gas stove, but we can't dry ourselves with one."

He produced a small tube of ointment and gently tended to the blister on Syl's foot. He was bare-chested, for he too had taken the opportunity to wash. Syl saw scars and burns on his skin. When he was finished, he turned his back to her to shrug on his shirt, and Syl glimpsed a great tattoo that stretched from his shoulders to the base of his spine. It was a bearded face made up of leaves and vines and young branches, all of them bright green. It was a face from ancient myths, the face of an old god.

It was the Green Man.

# CHAPTER FIFTY-EIGHT

They warmed themselves, then dressed again and tried to sleep for a time while Fremd kept guard. Syl lay awake, watching the fire die and thinking about the great tattoo on his back. Could it be? Could an Illyri be at the heart of the Resistance? What was it that Heather had said about Fremd?

*He is at the core of the Resistance.* But Fremd, it seemed, was much more than that.

And Syl fell asleep and dreamed of old gods.

Fremd woke them while it was dark, and they marched for the rest of the night. The rain returned just before dawn, heavier and colder than any they had yet experienced. The ground turned to swamp, and even Fremd struggled to make headway. Eventually they were forced to camp by a bank of rocks, the largest of them looming like a gray cliff face over the trees. There was a fissure at its base where Fremd lit another small fire, certain that it would be shielded from any watchers above. It was too deep in the rock face to give off much warmth to those outside, but he instructed them all to remove their shoes and socks so that the fire might dry them out. He again produced the container of ointment from his bag, and tended to those whose feet were blistered. He did so unselfconsciously, as if it were the most natural thing in the world for him to hold and heal the filthy, battered limbs of strangers. Only AK declined.

"I'll do it myself," he said. Fremd shrugged. If he was offended, he gave no sign.

They sipped water and nibbled on protein snacks and muesli

bars, more treasures from Fremd's store at the bothy. Ani set about diligently breaking her two bars into squares and making them into sandwiches, muesli hugging the brown gunk of the protein. Steven took her cue and molded his protein bar into the vague shape of a dog, then promptly ate it. Ani consoled Alice, who was missing her mother, until the child fell asleep, then started a silly game that entailed scrawling shapes on each other's backs and guessing what they were, but AK ruined it by drawing a pair of crude oversize breasts on Ani's back, which earned him a punch that deadened his leg, while Syl found herself flustered and unable to reply when Paul drew a heart on her spine.

"I didn't mean anything, you know, weird by it," he whispered over her shoulder. "It just seemed like the easiest thing to draw." She wasn't sure if she was relieved or disappointed, but she liked the tickle of his warm breath on her ear. She shivered happily.

"You're cold," he said, taking off his thick waterproof jacket and wrapping it around her shoulders.

"Don't be silly," she said, shoving it back into his hands. "Then you'll be cold."

"How about you sit right here then, between my knees, and I'll wrap it around us together? Then we'll both be warm," he said. His legs curled around her, making a chair, and he pulled his oversize parka around them both, snuggling her between his arms. Syl was too embarrassed to shuffle away, but too aware of her own weight to lean on him, too awkward to relax.

"That's warmer," he said next to her ear, pulling her closer and leaning his head on her shoulder. "You don't mind, do you?"

"No. No, not at all. It's definitely better," she heard herself say, and she had to admit it was, even when she saw Ani watching them, grinning with wicked amusement. She was too engrossed in making Syl feel awkward to notice the look of longing that Steven directed at her, but Syl caught it. She wanted to tell Ani to be careful, for Steven was clearly falling for her. Ani could hurt him if she wasn't careful.

But then she was aware that she too was falling for someone who could hurt her.

"Do you like what you do?" she asked Paul.

"What do you mean?"

"I mean all this. The fighting. The Resistance."

She moved in his arms so that she could see his face as he answered. He looked down on her, and she thought that she had never seen such tenderness in the eyes of one to whom she was not bound by blood or the passage of years.

"There's nothing to like about it. But I dislike the occupation even more."

"Why, though? I'm not trying to be flippant or anything; I just can't understand why it's so abhorrent that you would rather die fighting the Illyri—I mean, us."

Her choice of words betrayed the strength of her growing feelings for Paul, and the confusion they were causing her—the Illyri weren't something other than herself; they were her own people— but Paul did not pick up on it. Instead, he noticed that she had placed her emphasis on the word *you*; it was his safety, and his life, of which she spoke.

"Do you hate us?" Syl continued. "I mean, you personally, like Duncan did?"

"Sometimes," said Paul. "But honestly, I just wish you'd go away. Just bugger off back to where you came from."

She looked at her feet, her face burning.

"Right," was all she managed in reply.

"I don't mean you!" He gripped her shoulder, turning her toward him. "I mean, you're . . . It's . . ."

He struggled to find the right word, then settled for "You're different."

"Different? Is that the best you can do?"

"No," he said.

His lips touched hers now, briefly, sweetly, another stolen contact gone before the rest of them could notice. Syl smiled, her cheeks pink. Paul's eyes were shining as he stared into her face, and he grinned broadly.

Finally Syl found she could relax against him. She dozed in his arms as if it were the most natural thing in all the world, until a high-pitched whine roused her, and she saw Ani and Fremd responding to it just as she had. Seconds later, the humans heard it too.

"Skimmer," said Fremd.

They looked to the brightening sky, lit by the first tentative rays of dawn. It was Ani who picked out the fast-moving craft first.

"There," she said.

A pair of black specks fell from it, as though the craft were slowly disintegrating.

"What are they?" asked AK.

Fremd looked unhappy. "I don't know, but if they're good news, I'll be surprised."

He rose to his feet.

"AK, keep watch. If I'm not back in an hour, kill the fire and go to Maeve. Just Joe will join you there soon enough, all being well." He pointed at Gradus. "But make sure you don't lose him!"

Fremd grabbed his gun and was lost to the pines. Syl wriggled away from Paul, the spell broken. They were all silent now. There were no more laughs, no more teases, no more games. They could only wait for Fremd to come back and tell them what new turn the hunt had taken.


An hour passed, and Fremd did not return.

"AK," said Paul. "We should go."

But AK just shook his head.

"We wait."

"But Fremd told us—"

"We wait!" repeated AK, and Syl could see how scared he was. For all his bluster, all his bravado, he was still only a boy. He didn't want to make decisions. He didn't want to lead. Fremd should have left Paul in charge, thought Syl, but then Fremd didn't know Paul. Now, seeing the fear in AK's eyes, Syl suspected that Fremd didn't seem to know AK very well either.

They remained as they were, AK's eyes fixed hopefully on the forest, willing Fremd to appear.

"Syl," whispered Ani.

"Yes?"

"Do you hear it?"

She did. It was a soft whirring, but it was there.

"It's coming closer," she said.

"What?" said AK. "What's coming closer?"

Then they saw it: a small hovering black object, little bigger than a football, a single red light blinking at its heart. It moved about four feet above the ground, altering its course to avoid the trees. Closer and closer it drew to them. AK began to get to his feet, his weapon pointed at the approaching threat, ready to fire, when they heard Fremd's voice from nearby.

"Don't move!" he said. "Just don't!"

They all froze, AK poised uncomfortably between kneeling and rising. The object approached him, and Syl could see that its surface was a mass of sensors and antennae. It was only a few feet from him when it stopped moving forward. It paused for a moment, as though thinking, then dropped until its blinking red light was level with AK's head. The boy trembled, partly in fear and partly because he was trapped in an agonizing position. Syl could see it in his face. His brow was contorted with pain as he tried to remain still. She willed him to hold on. *Just a few seconds more, AK. Do it for us. Please.*

As if her plea had been heard, the object rotated in the air, its red light turning to the forest, and began to move away. AK sagged to the ground in relief.

And the orb spun back in his direction.

AK panicked. As he started to run, Fremd cried a single word: "No!"

The young soldier only managed to take a few steps before a dart whistled from the body of the object and hit him in the back. He stumbled and fell to the ground, just as Fremd's blast rifle blew the sphere to smithereens.

Syl was the first to reach AK. She stretched out a hand to him, but instantly Fremd was beside her, pulling her back.

"Don't touch him," he said.

AK was writhing on the ground, as though being tortured with electric shocks. At least two inches of the dart still protruded from his back. A series of green lights along its length slowly began to blink out.

"What's happening to him?" said Syl.

"The dart has determined that he's human, not Illyri," said Fremd.

"And?"

"Nanobots," said Fremd. "It's flooding his system with nanobots."

Inside AK, millions of tiny self-replicating robotic forms were reproducing. Technically, such weapons had been outlawed as part of the restrictions placed on the Illyri artificial life-form program, for nanobots had proved more difficult to control than expected. The most advanced bots, used to target defective and diseased cells in Illyri, had turned upon their patients, having identified all flesh as inferior and flawed when compared with machines, killing those whom they were supposed to cure, although the problem had since been solved.

But the Securitats were not concerned with restrictions, and had seen the weapon potential in the rogue nanobots. These particular bots were designed to target essential organs in humans—the liver, the lungs, the heart and the kidneys—and tear them apart. Blood bubbled from AK's lips. His eyes widened, his body jerked one final time, and then he lay still. Inside him, the nanobots, their work now done, shut down their systems and died along with their host.

# CHAPTER FIFTY-NINE

Vena stood in the control center at the Eden Project. She had been there many times before. While her base of operations was Edinburgh, Sedulus had entrusted her with the task of discreetly overseeing security procedures at Eden, even though there were already senior Securitat operatives in place to take care of such matters. It was all wheels within wheels: spies watched people, other spies watched the spies. It was enough to make one doubt one's faith in everyone, human or Illyri, assuming one had any faith to begin with, which Vena did not.

She had examined the bodies of the dead scientists. Sidis, the one in the car park, had been killed with a single stab wound before losing a finger and an eye. Her body had been tested for trace evidence. Fingerprints were found, but they did not match any on the Illyri databases. Vena was not surprised; if, as suspected, the attack had been carried out by a Mech, then the fingerprints could be changed at will by the simple application of some newly patterned ProGen skin. The other bodies had revealed little, although the clothing taken from Harvis, the scientist who had wounded the Mech, had been sprayed with both internal lubricant and blood. The blood contained no identifiers, confirming that the intruder's flesh was laboratory-grown, an artifice.

That was interesting. The Mech was, in a sense, biomechanical: it had added a thin layer of real tissue over its mechanics and hydraulics. Why? Vena supposed that, in the event of a minor injury, it would be seen to bleed like an Illyri. A deeper wound, such as the one Harvis had inflicted, would cause more problems, but only if there were others around to witness it.

Perhaps the Mech simply wanted the tissue in order to maintain the illusion that it was an Illyri so it could hide itself more easily, but why stop there? Vena wondered if the Mech could feel pleasure or pain. After all, Illyri who had suffered major injuries requiring amputation, and for whom replacement limbs could not be created for genetic reasons, usually had regrown tissue applied to the artificial limb and then linked to their nervous systems so that no sensation was lost. One of the problems with the Mechs was that they began to believe that they could *feel*. But to truly experience the world required more than a cyborg's brain and a series of complex artificial systems. How could one love if one could not enjoy the touch of a lover's skin? How could one feel pain without the vulnerabilities of flesh?

No, thought Vena, this was not just a Mech with delusions. This was something more special, more dangerous. This was a Mech in the process of transforming itself: not completely artificial, and not yet Illyri, but an entity in between.

This was an abomination.

Pieces of video appeared on the screens around Vena as the system collated all sightings of the intruder. The Mech had been careful—a hood raised here, a head down there, always conscious of surveillance, seen or unseen—but gradually the system began to assemble a face from the brief glimpses of features that the cameras had picked up: an eye from this one, a cheekbone from another, a corner of a mouth from a third.

After an hour, Vena had an image. She almost laughed when she saw it, for the identity of the Mech came as both a shock and an unexpected gift.

Meia.

It would give Vena nothing but pleasure to terminate her existence.

# CHAPTER SIXTY

Sedulus stood in the command cabin of his cruiser, a relief map of the Highlands on the screen before him. To his right was the Galatean sergeant; like all of his kind, he had no name—or none that the Illyri could pronounce. The Galateans called each other "Brother" or "Sister" according to gender, although in reality there were no family or clan loyalties among them, and as far as the Illyri could tell, they had little time for complicated emotions such as grief, or guilt, or even love. They mated, they bred, they lived, they died, and, in the service of the Illyri, they killed. It seemed to be enough for them. Sedulus was content to address the Galatean as "Sergeant." When this one died—as he assuredly would soon, for the Galateans had a life span of only twenty years—he would be replaced by another who looked, sounded, and smelled just the same.

To Sedulus's left was Beldyn, recently returned from briefing Syrene in person. Sedulus trusted Beldyn as much as he trusted any of his staff, which wasn't very far at all, Vena excepted. He could have spoken to Syrene himself via his lens, but he was concerned about this particular exchange being intercepted, and there were times when a whispered conversation was better.

Syrene had replied as he had hoped: it was unnecessary for the Illyri traitors, Syl and Ani, to be returned to Edinburgh alive. She remained curious about the one called Ani, for she had powers that could be of use to the Sisterhood, but, as with Syl, it seemed that attempting to entice her to join the Sisterhood would be more trouble than it might ultimately be worth, assuming that Gradus, once he was safely back in her arms, could be persuaded to spare their lives. Andrus and Danis were powerful men, even as the Corps and the Sisterhood worked to limit that power, and they would not give up their daughters without a fight.

Equally, unwilling apprentices were useless to the Sisterhood. Syrene's predecessors had learned that hard lesson a long time before. Girls forced to join the Sisterhood by their families, or recruited in the hope that they might be molded to the sisters' desires, invariably proved difficult and untrustworthy, and sowed discontent among the rest. In the past, to save their families distress, the Sisterhood had usually informed them that these novices were unsuited to life in the Marque and had instead been sent to new worlds, there to seek knowledge that might prove useful to the Sisterhood.

In reality, they had been quietly and painlessly killed.

But that was all in the past. The Sisterhood was now a haven only for the willing, for those who had elected, freely and without pressure, to give their lives to the pursuit of true knowledge.

Much of this was known to Sedulus, and what he did not know he suspected. It did not matter to him. The Sisterhood had given the Corps real power, and what was good for the Corps was good for him, but it was a delicate business. The continued difficulties in restoring Grand Consul Gradus to his wife seriously threatened Sedulus's thus-far smooth ascension through the ranks of the Securitats, not to mention his life. If Gradus died, Sedulus would follow him into the void.

Now, though, they had a possible lead, courtesy of the turncoat Duncan. Sedulus had dispatched the second cruiser and his last skimmer in that direction. Galateans and Securitats would soon be on the ground. The net was closing on the humans and their Illyri prisoners. Sedulus was simply waiting for confirmation of a sighting, and then he and the remaining cruiser would join the hunt. Two red lights indicated the positions of the craft on the display before him. The Securitats on board were represented by the smaller white lights of their trackers. The Galateans were not fitted with trackers, an indication of their dispensability.

The cruiser touched down. The lights spread out as the Securitats began to disperse. Then, as Sedulus watched, one of the white lights vanished, followed by a second, then a third. Behind him, the aide monitoring communications turned in his chair.

"Sir," he said, "we have contact!"

---

Just Joe had known that they would come. It had been merely a matter of time, and he had made a calculated gamble by having Paul slip Gradus's tracker to Duncan. He or McKinnon would inevitably have betrayed them to their Illyri pursuers, although Joe's money was on Duncan. McKinnon was a thug, but he would have died before giving the Illyri more than his name and the time of day. No, Duncan had been the weak one.

Just Joe had baited the trap for the Illyri: a fire, a handful of sleeping bags stuffed with rocks, and fighters moving around and giving a semblance of life to the camp. Theirs were the riskiest roles, and he could only hope that the Illyri wouldn't open fire on them from the air but would wait to tackle them on the ground. He reckoned that it was about 70:30 in the Resistance's favor that the Illyri would land rather than shoot; they probably wouldn't risk blasting them from their ships for fear that the Illyri prisoners might be among those sleeping in the camp. Actually, 70:30 didn't seem like bad odds, but Just Joe still didn't care much for them. The people below mattered, and Just Joe had already spent too much of his life informing men and women that their loved ones would not be returning to them.

The land was uneven, and scattered with rocks. There were only two places where the Illyri could land safely while still being within quick striking distance of the camp. In an ideal world he would have mined both sites, and as soon as a ship touched down it would have been blown to pieces. He had no mines, though, so guns and grenades would have to suffice. Neither did he have enough bodies to cover both sites, so he had made another gamble: that the Illyri would send a cruiser, not simply a loaded skimmer. In that case, only one potential landing site was big enough, and he had concentrated all his firepower on it. If he was wrong, there might still be time to move fighters into new positions, but they would be forced to break cover to do so, making them vulnerable to pulser fire, and the element of surprise would be lost.

Just Joe lay beneath a camouflage blanket. Around him, the rest of his band of fighters were similarly disguised. He had positioned his best shots on the high ground, armed with high-powered rifles capable of penetrating Illyri body armor even at long range. Closer to the landing site, two fighters lay hidden, each armed with a grenade launcher and a single grenade, the last in Joe's arsenal.

Joe thought about Fremd, and the two Illyri with him. They had entrusted so much to Fremd, and now some of Joe's people were probably going to die on little more than one of the Illyri's hunches. Hell, they'd risked members of the Resistance already because of his suspicions, most recently at Birdoswald. But Gradus was too valuable a prize to surrender without a fight, and if Fremd was right, the knowledge he might yield was worth dying for.

He didn't even hear the cruiser before it appeared. The pilot must have been ordered to glide down, a dangerous maneuver for such a big, heavy craft. Flanking it was a single skimmer, which had probably picked out the fire and the people from above and guided the cruiser in.

Just Joe took a deep breath. His hands shook. They always did before a fight. Only a fool wasn't frightened of dying, he told himself, and there was no bravery without fear.

The cruiser touched down. His people at the camp grabbed their weapons and ran for cover. The skimmer flew over them, and a pair of black spheres dropped from its belly, homing in on the nearest fleeing humans. Joe heard the hiss of the darts deploying, and watched as Kathy and Howie were felled.

The cruiser's doors opened, and the enemy appeared.

Just Joe aimed his weapon, and he and his fighters rained vengeance upon them for the dead of Durroch.


Sedulus watched as more and more of the white lights blinked out.

"We need to help them," said Beldyn.

"No," said Sedulus. "We wait."


The first of the grenades struck the side of the cruiser and exploded harmlessly against its heavy armor. A flurry of blasts from the Galateans' guns blew the grenadier's position apart. He died instantly, but the distraction was enough to give the second grenadier time to aim. From her position behind a massive moss-covered boulder, Heather steadied the launcher and tightened her finger on the trigger.

"For Tam," she said.

The grenade shot away and vanished into the cruiser's gaping maw. Seconds later it exploded in the enclosed space, crippling the cruiser and killing or injuring all of those left inside. Splinters of rock erupted around her as the Illyri opened fire, but a barrage of covering shots allowed her to break for safety. She was terrified, but she remembered to hold on to the launcher. There would be more grenades somewhere, and they couldn't afford to lose weapons. She made it to where the first line of Resistance fighters lay, then threw herself to the ground, drew her high-powered pistol, and started shooting.

Meanwhile, Just Joe and Norris were trying to take down the black orbs. They had already watched three of their people die, and they were determined that there would be no more. Norris winged the first with his shotgun, destroying its guidance system. It responded by firing its array of darts aimlessly, although one still struck close enough to Norris's head to produce sparks from the rock behind him. A second shotgun blast put an end to it, and its remains dropped to the ground and fizzled harmlessly.

Just Joe drew the second orb to him by waving his coat at it from behind a tree stump. It was, he considered, as the first dart smacked into the wood, just about the dumbest thing he'd ever done in a lifetime of doing things that were not very smart. As the orb approached, he stepped from behind the stump, his backpack strapped to his chest, and prayed. He felt the impact of the dart as it struck the pack, and he sprayed the orb with bullets even as he kept praying, until the magazine was empty and the orb was no more, until all that was left was his own voice calling on some god, any god, to protect him.

"We've lost contact with the cruiser," the radio operator informed Sedulus.

Sedulus could see that for himself. The red light blinked rapidly, indicating catastrophic damage. Only six white lights remained intact, and one of those vanished as the operator spoke. Sedulus remained outwardly calm. This was a disaster, but he could not allow his men to see him panic.

"It was a trap," said Beldyn. "The human lied."

"No, I don't think he did," said Sedulus. "He was simply lied to by someone cleverer than him. Recall the skimmer."

"And the Illyri and Galateans still on the ground?"

"They're dead," said Sedulus. "They just don't know it yet."

Now the radio operator spoke again.

"Sir, we've lost a hunter orb."

"Are you insane?" said Sedulus. "We've just lost a *cruiser*!"

"No, sir, not there. To the west. It deployed a dart, and then went down."

Sedulus stared at him.

"Give me its last known location on the map."

Before him, a green light flashed into existence.

"It's them," said Sedulus.

"How can you be certain?" asked Beldyn.

"I have to be," said Sedulus. "If I'm wrong, then we're all finished."

# CHAPTER SIXTY-ONE

AK seemed so small in death, so huddled and young. They had no time to bury him, no time to do anything except stare blankly at his remains until Ani—Ani, of all of them—began to cry.

"I just . . . I could have been kinder to him," she said.

And there was nothing that anyone could say to console or contradict her, because it was true, just as it was true that AK could have been kinder to her in return. Syl thought that Ani had never looker sadder or older. Later, Ani would come to look back on that moment as one in which she experienced true adult regret for the first time, and something of her childhood was washed away in the mud and the blood and the rain.

"We have to go," said Fremd. "They'll know they've lost a hunter drone, and they'll come looking to see why."

But Ani did not seem to hear him. Instead, she dropped to her knees and brushed the damp hair away from AK's face. Steven crouched beside her. His left hand hovered uncertainly over her, like a bird fearful of alighting, and then rested itself gently on her shoulder. Ani leaned into him, and their bodies shook in unison as he absorbed her grief. Alice joined them, stroking Ani's hair.

"Ani!" said Fremd. "I said we have to go."

"What's the point?" said Ani. "I'm tired of running. We just keep running and running, and we never get anywhere. Let them take me back. I don't care."

Fremd grabbed her arm and yanked her to her feet. Steven seemed about to intervene, but Paul restrained him.

"Listen to me!" said Fremd, and he gave her a little shake. "They're not going to take you back. Don't you understand? They're not interested in you. It's Gradus they want. If you and Syl die out here, it will be easier for everyone. Once Gradus is secured, you'll be killed. They'll blame the Resistance, or crossfire, or whatever it takes, but the end result will be the same: you'll end up like AK, dying in the dirt, but there'll be no one to weep for you because we'll all be dead too."

"You're lying!" said Ani. "You don't know that!"

"I do. I know it because I know Sedulus. I know it because I was once like him."

Ani stopped struggling.

"Tell us," said Syl.

"I will," said Fremd. "I promise. We're close to our destination. Just a couple of hours, and when we reach it I'll tell you. I'll tell you everything."

The four youths exchanged glances, and a silent agreement was reached.

"All right," said Paul. "What about him?"

He jerked a thumb at Gradus, who remained seated in the mud, his eyes like the eyes of the dead.

"Get him to his feet."

"He's slowing us down!" said Paul. "Without him, we'll move three times as fast. Just let the Illyri have him."

"No," said Fremd.

"Why?"

"Because if I'm right, he holds the secret to all of this."

"And if you're wrong?"

"Then I'll kill him myself before I hand him back. Now move. Move!"


Syl thought she would surely collapse. Every muscle in her body ached, her legs most of all. They felt so heavy that she could barely put one foot in front of the other, dragging them through the mud. She was hot and clammy despite the cold, but she found herself shivering and her teeth chattered painfully in her mouth. Ani and Steven trudged ahead of her, their heads down, stumbling more than running. Paul was beside her, but he did not speak. Like the others, he barely had strength enough to keep himself going. He had precious little left to share, but he still found it in himself to take turns with Ani to carry Alice.

Fremd forced the pace, leading Gradus on the rope. Sometimes the Grand Consul slipped and fell, and once he struck his head so hard in falling that he drew blood, but he made no sound. Each time, Paul and Steven helped Fremd to haul the heavy Illyri to his feet, and they moved on.

All the time they waited for the sound of a skimmer breaching the clouds, for the roar of a cruiser, but none came. Yet as her fever increased, Syl grew more and more paranoid. She looked to the sky, trying to pierce the banks of gray and black. They were watching her, waiting for their chance to strike. They would swoop down and pluck her from the ground, and then they would hang her from the gates of the castle, her legs kicking at the air, the blood congesting in her face. She felt the rope tighten around her neck as she walked, and so real was the sensation that her hands rose to her throat and she clawed at her skin, raking it with her nails until Paul stopped her, gently forcing her arms down and holding them at her sides, pulling her to him and walking with her.

"Almost there," he said. "Almost there."

Now she saw Ritchie impaled on his bayonet, but he was still alive and somehow he forced himself from the blade, the metal separating from his flesh with a damp sucking sound. He came toward her through the rain, his hands outstretched before him, the palms facing up and colored red with his own blood.

*I killed you.*

*I killed you, and I am glad.*

She saw Illyri warships passing through washes of illumination, and heard a baby cry as it left the womb. And she was that child, but now it was no longer simply a child but a collection of billions of atoms, and the light corrupted each and every one, altering them, mutating them.

Mutating her.

She was an alien, not simply to the people of Earth but to her own kind as well. She did not belong. She was different. Only Ani might understand, but even Ani was not like her. Ani could blur minds, making others see what she wanted them to see, but she did not take lives. Maybe she could if she tried hard enough, but Syl was not sure, and the fact remained that she was the one who had looked at a man and forced him to turn his weapon on himself. Again she remembered the look in Ritchie's eyes before he positioned the blade to pierce his own chest: the terror, the desperation, the knowledge that a part of this alien girl had entered him and turned him against himself. In that final stare was a plea for her to save him, to spare him, and she had refused. Her own fear had been too great: her fear, and her rage.

"I'm sorry," she whispered, but even as she said the words they sounded hollow. No, she thought, I am not sorry. I am glad. He deserved to die, he and the one I struck with the rock, the one whose face I pressed into the water. Because she had done that too, she finally admitted to herself. Even as Ritchie was dying, she had felt the man in the stream trying to rise, but she had held him down, willing the water to enter his lungs, willing him to suffer, just as he would have made her suffer had he been given the chance.

"What am I?" she said. "Who am I?"

And while Paul said her name over and over, trying to calm her, she thought that she was imagining things as she saw flashlights in the distance, and heard the voices of men and women. She saw a wall with battlements, and a castle keep rising above it. Gates opened in the wall, and she glimpsed people camped inside, and fires burning. She smelled smoke, and roasting meat, and heard the lowing of cattle. A small hand gripped hers, and she looked down to see Alice smiling up at her.

"It's okay, Syl," said Alice. "We're safe."

But it was not okay, thought Syl. They would never be safe again.

# CHAPTER SIXTY-TWO

The castle was called Dundearg. It had been built during the reign of James II of England, and the same family, the Buchanans, had occupied it throughout its existence, but only one of their line remained. Her name was Maeve, and she was a short, dark woman in her early forties, most of her hair already turned to gray, yet still pretty and youthful. She looked on sternly as Syl, Ani, and Gradus were led into the huge fortified keep, watched by the hostile eyes of those who dwelt within the castle walls in makeshift dwellings, or containers that had been converted to homes. The inhabitants had created a narrow channel down which the new arrivals passed. Even with the protection of Fremd, they were still jostled, and someone spat in Ani's face. Although Syl felt for her friend, she was glad that it had not been directed at her. Even in her fevered state, she saw herself turning on the offender and wishing harm upon them. The consequences of that might have been fatal for all concerned.

"No," said Fremd, and at first Syl thought he was talking to her, warning her not to react, until she realized that he was addressing the crowd. They obeyed him, and there was no more jostling, and no more spitting.

At last they were safe within the walls of the keep, and the doors closed behind them. It was cold inside—but still warmer than it was outside, and at least it was dry. To their right, a great fire burned in a room filled with overstuffed chairs and couches.

Syl did not know what to expect next, but it was not to see Maeve

Buchanan take Fremd in her arms and kiss him full on the lips. She held him close to her, and breathed in the scent of him.

"I smell," he said.

"You smell of mud and grass and sweat."

"And blood," said Fremd. "We lost AK—young Alan."

Maeve's eyes squeezed shut in pain.

"His father and mother will have to be told," she said. "They're in Perth."

"It'll be done, and gently."

"He was troubled, and angry, but he would have changed. I could see it in him."

"So could I."

Maeve disengaged herself from Fremd, and turned her attention to Syl and Ani.

"My God, these young ones are frozen." She touched her hand to Syl's brow. "And this one has a fever."

She called out a name—"Kathleen!"—and a stout woman wearing carpet slippers and an apron appeared on the stairs above.

"Yes, ma'am?"

"Bring towels, and warm clothes, and a basin of whatever hot water we have left."

She guided Syl and Ani to the fire.

"Now get out of those clothes. All of them! You can wrap yourself in some of the furniture throws while you wait for Kathleen."

She began to close the door behind herself and Fremd in order to give Syl and Ani a little privacy, but Syl rose and stopped her.

"Remember," she said to Fremd. "You promised. You promised you'd tell us your story."

"And I will," he said. "Get warm and dry first. When you're done, come find us, for what is about to happen here concerns you as much as it does the rest of us. But if I'm right, my story, and what you may see in this castle, will just leave you with more questions, and you won't be the only one."

Behind Fremd, two men she had not seen before were holding

on tightly to Gradus's arms. Maybe it was the comparative warmth of the castle, or a slow recognition that his situation had changed, but Gradus seemed to be coming out of himself. He was still dazed, but he was taking in his surroundings.

"Clean him up, but keep him restrained," Fremd ordered.

"I'll wake the technician," said Maeve. "Everything is ready to go. We just need to prep the generator."

"Do it," said Fremd. "We don't have much time."

The woman named Kathleen, assisted by her two daughters, Marie and Jeanie, brought Syl and Ani not just towels, clean clothes, and basins of hot water, but huge mugs of broth thick with chicken and vegetables. She also fed Syl two small pills to help bring down her fever.

Low cheers rose from outside their door. Syl opened it slightly and peered out to see Just Joe arrive, along with Logan and Aggie and Norris. Heather was there too, holding a delighted Alice in her arms. Maeve came to greet them.

"Where are the others?" she asked, but Joe simply shook his head.

"Dear AK's gone too," said Maeve.

"Ah," was all that Joe could say. "Ah."

Syl closed the door.

The food and the change of clothes had made Syl feel a bit better, but she was still weak and her brow was hot to the touch. Nevertheless, she did not want to remain in the room. She needed to find Fremd.

"Will you take us to him?" she asked Kathleen upon her return, and she and Ani were duly led into the bowels of the keep, where an infirmary had been established. One of the beds was now occupied by Norris, whose shoulder wound had become infected. He had been sedated while the wound was cleaned and dressed, and stared woozily at Syl and Ani, as though unsure of whether he was seeing or dreaming them.

Finally they came to a smaller chamber, and Syl was surprised to see that it contained an array of both human and Illyri medical equipment, most of it new and apparently in perfect working order. The room vibrated with the hum of generators, and Fremd was methodically working with another Illyri—who looked barely older than Syl and Ani—to check the wiring and make sure that everything was in sync. Maeve watched over them, gnawing at her lower lip the way a dog might worry at a bone.

"Okay," said Fremd. "It looks like we're ready."

He noticed Syl and Ani for the first time.

"Ladies, let me introduce you to Lorac," he said, and the young Illyri smiled uncertainly at them. "Lorac, this is Syl and Ani."

"Hello," said Lorac, rising from a crouch to his full height. He was especially good-looking, even for an Illyri, but he gave the impression of being uncomfortable in his own skin, and he walked with a slight limp as he approached them. Syl saw that he was a little older than she had first thought, probably in his early twenties.

"Are you hurt?" asked Ani.

"It's an old injury," said Lorac.

Fremd had gone to Maeve, his arm curled protectively around her waist.

"Lorac made the same mistake that I did," said Fremd. "He looked too long at a beautiful woman, and was lost."

Maeve slapped him gently on the chest, but the compliment still brought a blush to her cheeks. Ani looked slightly disappointed at the news that Lorac was taken by another. Syl was just glad that Steven wasn't there to see her face.

"You've met her," said Lorac. "Jeanie, Kathleen's daughter."

Ani seemed decidedly unimpressed, and even Syl was a little surprised. Jeanie was pretty enough, but not spectacularly so; Lorac had left his own people and thrown in his lot with the Resistance to be with *her*? Whether he was Military or Corps, desertion was punishable by a lifetime sentence on a prison world, and lifetimes on prison worlds tended to be short and brutal, although Syl suspected that few deserters ever made it to the prisons and instead were simply killed by the Securitats. Truly, she thought, the ways of love were very strange indeed, but then, was she not also falling for Paul? What future was there for the two of them? Not for the first time, she felt that her life had become extremely complicated in a very short space of time.

At the mention of her daughter, Kathleen straightened and glowed with pride. She had hardly spoken before except to fuss over Syl and Ani, but now she said, "You won't find a better girl from here to Land's End."

Ani appeared on the verge of disagreeing, but Syl carefully but forcefully stepped on her foot, just to make sure she didn't end up with it in her mouth.

Lorac tapped his right leg. "My comrades in arms found out about us. To discourage me, they shattered my foot with their rifle butts. I deserted that night, but my foot was so badly damaged that there was nothing to be done but to amputate it."

The words came to Syl's mouth before she realized that she was speaking them, never mind thinking them.

"Was it worth it?" she said.

Lorac answered as if he was surprised that anyone could ask such a question. "Of course it was," he said. "I love her. Haven't you ever been in love?"

Syl could see Ani grinning at her. This was all getting a bit personal, but having asked the original question, she felt duty bound to give some kind of answer.

"Not like that," she said. "At least, I don't think so."

"You'll know it when you are," said Maeve. There was a skeptical expression on her face, and it struck Syl that the older woman did not believe the answer Syl had given. For that matter, Syl wasn't sure that she quite believed it either. She was, after all, in this mess because of a young man. She had put her life on the line for a human male, just as Lorac had put his on the line for a human female. Syl wanted to tear her hair out; she felt like she was drowning in a vat of emotions. She turned to Fremd in the hope that he might yank her from it for a time.

"You promised you'd tell us what's happening," she said.

"I did," said Fremd, "or as much of it as I know."

He patted Lorac on the shoulder.

"Bring our esteemed guest, the Grand Consul. We're ready for him now."

And while Lorac went to get Gradus, Fremd told them his tale.

# CHAPTER SIXTY-THREE

The first surprise was that Fremd was not just a member of the Diplomatic Corps; he had been a junior Securitat, and Sedulus had once been his adjutant.

"I believed," said Fremd. "I believed in the great expansion of the Illyri Empire. The wormholes had opened up the universe to us, and I was young and wanted to explore its vastness. It was about the discovery of worlds and not the conquest of them, although I admit that was part of the mission. Yet we were to be gentle rulers. We would not ravage societies. We would not rape planets for their resources. What was good for the Empire would be good for the new races we found, and the opposite would also be true.

"But humanity was different, for this was a species very like our own. The Empire had monitored the human race's development for decades. There were debates about whether or not conquest was the appropriate response to humanity's growing resourcefulness, but the Corps overruled the Military's hesitancy. And to be fair, there were strong reasons for subduing humanity. They were hostile to one another, so the violence of their reaction to an alien civilization could only be imagined. Their history was one of brutality and warfare, and they allowed whole nations to starve while others stored food in barns until it rotted. It was felt that they could not be reasoned with.

"So Earth became a planet of conquest, but it was decided that care was to be taken with its inhabitants, for we had yet to discover any race as similarly advanced. But then, as you know, humanity proved more difficult to control than had been hoped, and the occupation became less gentle. There were those of us who started to believe that we should not be on Earth at all, and a new approach to humanity, one of cooperation and peaceful coexistence, needed to be implemented.

"But I was not directly involved in such debates. My posting was four and a half light-years away in the system the humans named Alpha Centauri, monitoring the mining of the diamond world 55 Cancri e, and the harvesting of methane from larger planets in the system."

The harvesting of methane meant that Illyri ships traveling without using wormholes did not have to carry as much fuel for their flights. Instead, they could be refueled from methane bases scattered throughout galaxies. Within Earth's solar system, the Illyri had planted harvesters on Jupiter, Mars, and Uranus, but the largest harvesting operation was on Titan, one of Saturn's moons, where it literally rained methane and the surface was dotted with rivers and lakes of it.

"The mining was being carried out by Illyri prisoners and, I'm sorry to say, by Punishment Battalions from Earth," said Fremd. "It was near the end of my deployment there. I didn't care for it—I was little more than a prison guard, and I spent too much time wearing a Lethal Environment Suit for my liking—and so I requested a transfer to Earth. In addition, there had been disciplinary problems, and prisoners had attempted to hijack a shuttle and escape. The Corps sent a senior consul—an uncle of our friend Gradus—to Alpha Centauri to investigate the problem. I was to finish my deployment when he arrived and travel on to Earth, but the pilot made a docking error as he approached the station at Cancri, and the ship was damaged. There was an oxygen leak, and most of the crew died, but we were able to rescue the consul. He was badly injured, but we brought him to the surgery and the medics went to work on him.

"And that was when I was called, because the scans revealed something living inside the consul's head."

Fremd could still clearly recall the moment; the "first sighting," as he thought of it, the first glimpse of the Other. Wrapped around the consul's brain stem, embracing his cerebellum with wispy tentacles, was a parasitic organism of some kind.

"When we made an attempt to remove it, the organism tightened its grip on the cerebellum, and those whiplike tentacles made further inroads into the consul's brain. His body began to convulse, and the medics decided that no further investigation of the organism should take place for fear of killing its host. We sent a coded message to Gradus, informing him of the discovery, and the consul was placed in an isolation chamber. The message that came back was simple: nobody was to leave the station for fear of contamination, and there was to be no further communication about the consul or the organism until a team from the Scientific Development Division arrived.

"But further unrest erupted on Cancri," said Fremd, "and I had no choice but to leave the station and travel down to the planet to deal with it. I had to wear a full LES kit on Cancri, anyway, so there was no danger of my passing on any infection."

He paused then, as though the memory of what came next was still painful for him.

"The scientists arrived while I was on Cancri, but with them came Securitat death squads, and the slaughter began. I stayed on the planet while everyone on the station was being killed. I had left a communications channel open with my second in command, Seval, in case I had to explain my absence, and I heard him die. I heard them all die. They were murdered by our own people. Seval's last act was to excise all record of my trip to Cancri. As far as the Securitats were concerned, I was missing, presumed deserted.

"Then they blew up the station and left everyone on Cancri to die. The prisoners saw the station exploding, and there was a rush for my ship. I had to kill to save myself, and I abandoned the remaining miners on Cancri. That's my burden. I carry it with me every day."

"How did you get to Earth?" asked Syl.

"I hitched a ride through the wormhole on the coattails of a Corps ship," he said. "Eventually I made my way here, to Scotland."

Syl couldn't help but be impressed. Hitching was an incredibly risky maneuver, relying on the gravitational force of the larger ship in the wormhole to pull the smaller craft through. If the hitchhiker miscalculated even slightly, or if the main ship was bounced around either entering or leaving the wormhole, then the other vessel would be destroyed.

"It took a long time for the Resistance to trust me, and for me to trust them," said Fremd. "They kept me in a cell for two years. I barely saw daylight. Eventually I met Maeve, and things started to change. But I said nothing about what I'd seen on the station, not until a few months ago, when I started hearing rumors of human bodies going missing, and of secret facilities set up on Earth by the Scientific Development Division. We also learned from our spies of a flood of Corps officials arriving on Earth, all of them related, or loyal, to Gradus, and all with links to the Scientific Development Division. What happened at Cancri station suggested that there were those at the highest levels of the Corps and its Securitats who wanted to keep the existence of the organism, the Other, secret. But what if it wasn't the only one? What if there were more of these things infecting the Illyri? And perhaps the relationship between the organism and its host wasn't merely parasitic, but symbiotic."

"Symbi-what?" asked Ani.

"Two organisms of different species operating in unison, to the benefit of each," said Fremd. "Like, for example, the pilot fish that feed from the mouths of sharks and clean away decaying matter, or even dogs and humans, except in the case of the Other and its host the relationship is obviously more, um, intimate. So we decided to target newly arrived Corps officials, especially those with a familial relationship to Gradus, in the hope of capturing one, but we had no success—until Gradus himself fell into our laps, thanks to you two."

At that moment Gradus appeared, struggling between two men,

Just Joe close behind. He was no longer the pathetic figure who had trudged through the Highlands at the end of a rope. Now he screamed and swore, and his eyes were filled with panic. He saw the medical equipment, and he seemed to intuit its purpose: there was a small X-ray machine, and a lightweight Illyri magnetic resonance imaging scanner, capable of producing immensely detailed images of the interior of a body. Alongside them stood a tray containing scalpels, calipers, and dressings.

"No!" said Gradus. "You can't do this."

"Place him facedown," said Fremd.

The men laid Gradus on a gurney, firmly securing his hands, feet, and head with straps.

"Sedate him," said Fremd, and Lorac slipped a needle into Gradus's arm. The Grand Consul grew calmer, but he remained conscious.

"No," he repeated. "No, no, no . . ."

"Come," said Kathleen to Syl and Ani, guiding them toward the door. "Maybe you should leave."

"No," said Fremd. "Let them stay. If I'm right, they should see this."

On Fremd's order, they placed protective masks over their noses and mouths. Lorac powered up the MRI scanner. Fremd looked upward, his lips moving in prayer to his old gods, and said:

"Begin."

# CHAPTER SIXTY-FOUR

The rain had ceased, but in its place came a mist that was just as drenching. It seemed that each tiny particle of moisture was visible in the light streaming from the castle, but then the artificial illumination dimmed as power was diverted to the machines in the basement of the keep. A handful of emergency bulbs continued to glow brightly, but battery-powered lights were pressed into service, and even, here and there, oil lamps.

The guards at the walls watched the mist, and the inhabitants behind the walls watched the guards. The castle's occupants were those who had fled their isolated homes because of bandits, like the late McKinnon and his associates; or those with family members whose involvement with the Resistance had been discovered, and whose houses had been destroyed in reprisal—for the Illyri's tactics north of the wall were often more brutal than in the cities. These people had found a haven at Dundearg, and Maeve Buchanan had almost bankrupted herself taking care of them. But she was of an older order, one that recognized a duty toward those who lived on the land owned by the castle, and extended even to land that had once been owned by the castle long before. They were her people, because they had always been her family's people.

But everyone within those walls knew what had taken place in recent days: the pursuit of a precious prize that the Resistance had defended to the death. Now that prize was inside the castle, and they feared that the pursuers would soon be at their door.

And those fears were about to find form.

• • •

Four guards stood on the battlements above and flanking the main gates. Two were still in their teens, and two were older and more experienced. That was the way with the Resistance in the Highlands: there was an abundance of fresh water up there, and so, unlike the city dwellers, they had remained relatively unaffected by the contamination of the water supply with chemicals that subdued the instinct to fight, to resist. Yet at the same time, the struggle against the Illyri was more overt in the North, and harder fought. The casualty rate was higher as a consequence, so it was important that the younger ones learned quickly from the older fighters, because those more experienced fighters might not be around for long.

The gates were fortified by a truck packed with bags of cement and sand. Once the gates closed, the truck was driven into place and only moved when friendly parties were trying to enter or leave. Machine-gun posts occupied each of the rounded turrets, and mortars were in place behind the walls.

The youngest of the guards, Jack Dennison, had just turned seventeen on his last birthday. He could easily be identified by the green-and-white Celtic scarf that he wore around his neck whatever the weather. The Illyri had long ago tried to clamp down on the most vicious of sporting rivalries by disbanding certain teams: the Red Sox and the Yankees in baseball; Real Madrid and Barcelona in Spanish football; and a whole list of teams in England, including virtually the entire English Premier League. But a particular target had been the Rangers and Celtic teams in Scotland. The two had long been at each other's throats, a consequence of religious conflict that had hardened into pure hatred, but the tipping point for the Illyri had been a Scottish FA Cup Final during which violence had broken out between not just the supporters, but the teams themselves. When the Illyri tried to intervene, they succeeded in doing what centuries of efforts by priests, pastors, and politicians had failed to do: they united the rival supporters, if only against a common enemy. The ensuing riots against Illyri rule lasted for weeks, and added fuel to the ferocious Scottish Resistance that continued to that day. Even wearing the green-and-white of Celtic, or the dark blue of Rangers, was an arrestable offense.

Now Dennison stared out into the darkness, his eyes and especially his ears alert. They would hear the Illyri before they saw them. They always did, just before they screamed, or roared, out of the air. But all was quiet. Dennison shivered. Beside him, Phil Pelham huddled into his waxed jacket. Pelham was from Manchester, and where Dennison wore green-and-white, Pelham favored blue-and-white, the colors of the former Manchester City. He and the younger man had found a point of contact in teams that no longer existed.

"All right, lad?" said Pelham.

"Yeah, all right."

"Experiments in the basement." Pelham jerked a thumb at the keep behind him. "Maybe they're making Frankenstein's monster."

"They'll need lightning for that," said Dennison. "And dead bodies."

He realized what he had just said, and shuffled with embarrassment.

"Well," said Pelham, "best we make sure they don't have any of them then, right?"

"Right you are, Phil."

The mist rose before them. Dennison hated mist. It made him see figures where there were none, merely phantasms of his imagination. He wished the main castle lights would come back on. At the very least, the wall lights made it easier to distinguish between what was real and what was unreal. They had lit torches on the walls, as much to keep them warm as to provide more light, but they only helped a little.

A form appeared in the haze, then vanished. Dennison narrowed his eyes against the damp and the dark.

"What's wrong?" said Pelham.

"I'm not sure. I thought . . ."

There it was again, except it was closer now, and to the left. But how could it have moved so quickly?

"There's something out there."

Pelham eased the AK-47 from his shoulder.

"I don't see anything. Where? Are you sure?"

The first of the Galateans appeared, and he had his answer. A massive blast struck the gates even as Pelham sounded the alarm. The heavily laden truck shuddered on its axles, but remained in place.

For now.

The assault on Dundearg had begun.

# CHAPTER SIXTY-FIVE

Peris and his strike squad were carefully monitoring the progress of Sedulus's remaining cruiser, staying far above it in the hope that the attention of the Securitats would be focused on what was happening on the ground below them, and not on the skies above. When the cruiser eventually landed, apparently miles from the nearest village, Peris called up a map of the surrounding area, and found Dundearg Castle at the center.

"That has to be their destination," he told Aron, his second in command, as their shuttle circled high above cloud level. "There's nothing else nearby."

"Then why have they landed so far from it?" asked Aron. The cruiser had come down more than a mile from the castle, and the last of Sedulus's skimmers had joined it.

"He wants to have troops at their walls before they know it, and the mist will hide his approach," said Peris. "Plus he only has one cruiser left: if that castle is defended with missiles or heavy-caliber guns, they could blow him out of the sky."

"I don't understand why he hasn't called for reinforcements."

"Because it would be a final admission of failure on top of the loss of most of his force," said Peris. "Above all else, he wants to bring the Grand Consul back to his witch wife and reap the benefits. Pride will be Sedulus's downfall."

He pointed at the on-screen map.

"That looks like clear ground. Glide us in."

Aron sighed. "It could be a bog, for all we know."

"Well," said Peris, "at least we'll have a soft landing."


But Peris's progress was also being tracked, although not by Sedulus. Meia had Peris's strike squad and both the recently landed cruiser and skimmer on her monitor. She could see what Peris was trying to do: quietly land closer to the castle than Sedulus's Securitats, and try to get inside to rescue Syl and Ani before Sedulus made it to the walls. He had to be stopped, because right now Meia knew that she, and she alone, was Syl and Ani's best hope of getting out of Dundearg alive.

Peris's shuttle glided down on what was, thankfully for his squad, firm ground, the engines only kicking in at the final moment to soften the landing, just as Meia had anticipated. Her skimmer differed from Peris's craft, and indeed, those of the rest of the Illyri fleet, in two crucial ways: its software was faster and its engines quieter. She had used all her skill and knowledge to make the improvements, and had shared none of them with others. In war, every advantage was crucial, but especially so for Meia and those who fought in the shadows.

Most useful of all, her skimmer was virtually invisible to radar. In addition to having its infrared exhaust emissions altered by coolant and its internal and external structures replaced by radar-transparent diametric composites, it used ionized gas to form a camouflaging plasma cloud around itself. Its shielding had enabled her to reach, and escape, the Eden Project without being blown out of the sky, and now it allowed her to land next to Peris's shuttle, its wake buffeting her slowly as she dropped gently behind it.

Thus it was that the first thing Peris saw as he and his squad disembarked was Meia, wisps of mist swirling around her like angry ghosts. Peris figured that he should have been more surprised, but then he had been dealing with Meia for long enough to learn that the usual rules of behavior didn't apply to her. He took in her battle armor, and the heavily adapted blast rifle that she carried. The twin-barreled weapon could rain depleted uranium ammunition on its targets, along with dragon-breaths of fire. It looked huge as it hung from Meia's slight frame, but the weight didn't appear to trouble her in the least. A belt of high-explosive grenades was strapped around her waist. Meia, it was clear, was ready to wage war single-handedly.

"I don't suppose there's any point in telling you that I'm in charge here," said Peris.

"Oh, be in charge if you like," said Meia. "I don't mind."

"The fact that you can say that means my authority is largely illusory."

"Yes."

"Well, I always was better at just being a simple soldier. So what's the plan? Are we going to fight our way into that castle, or sneak in?"

"Neither," said Meia. "They're just going to admit us without hindrance."

"And why is that?"

Meia smiled.

"Because the world is a lot more complicated than a simple soldier like you could ever imagine."

Lorac had just activated the MRI scanners when the sound of the first explosion reached them. It shook the castle, sending dust and small pieces of masonry cascading from the walls and ceilings. Seconds later, Paul came running in.

"They're at the gates!"

"How many?" said Just Joe.

"I don't know. The mist is too thick. But we're taking fire."

Just Joe grabbed his rifle. In the infirmary, those who were strong enough to fight began to rise from their cots. Even Norris was on his feet, although swaying slightly.

"Go back to bed," ordered Just Joe.

"Hit me," said Norris.

"What?"

"Hit me!"

Just Joe gave Norris a massive open-handed blow across the right side of his face. It would have felled a lesser man, but in Norris's case it served only to clear his head.

"That did the trick," he said. "Right, where's my shotgun?"

He found the gun and his backpack under his bed, and began to fill his pockets with shells. When they were sufficiently bulging, he joined Paul and Just Joe.

"We need time," said Fremd.

"I know," said Just Joe. "We'll buy you as much as we can."

Syl caught Paul's eye. She wanted to say so much to him, but all she could come up with was, "Be careful."

"I will," he said. "You do the same."

"Yes."

Before he could say any more, Norris had picked him up by the scruff of the neck with one meaty paw and carried him over to where Syl stood, Paul's toes dragging along the ground.

"For God's sake, kiss the girl," he said, setting Paul down. "It may be the last chance you have."

Paul did as he was ordered. He kissed Syl, softly at first, then harder. Her arms rose to embrace him as his hands settled lightly on her waist, before he was suddenly yanked away from her again.

"That's quite enough of that," said Norris, hauling Paul toward the fighting. "I said kiss her, not marry her."

Fremd touched Maeve on the shoulder.

"You have to start the evacuation," he said.

Maeve nodded. A tear fell from her right eye.

"We knew this day would come," said Fremd. "We couldn't be lucky forever."

"Just a little longer would have been good," said Maeve.

"We're not dead yet."

"No," said Maeve. "Not yet. And pray God we stay a long way from it."

She kissed the tall Illyri, rising to her toes as he leaned down to her, and then left the room. Only Syl and Ani remained, along with Fremd and Lorac, but then Ani turned and began to follow Maeve.

"Where are you going?"

"To help," said Ani. "You stay here. You're the smart one!"

Syl wasn't sure about that. She moved as if to join Ani, but Fremd put a hand on her shoulder.

"Stay," he said.

"Hey, aren't you going to tell me to be careful too?" asked Ani.

"Be careful," said Syl, and she hugged Ani to her.

"Thanks," said Ani. "I don't need the kiss, by the way."

She laughed, and was gone.

Paul was racing to keep up with Just Joe and Norris when Steven joined him. He had an AK-47 assault rifle in his right hand.

"Where did you get that?" asked Paul.

"Dunno," said Steven. "I just picked it up."

"Well put it back where you found it. You stay where it's safe."

"No," said Steven, and his voice sounded deeper and more serious than before.

Paul stopped.

"Steven—"

"I won't," said Steven.

He looked so stern, so certain. He reminded Paul of their father, but Paul could still see the child in his eyes.

"You can't keep protecting me like this. I have to learn. I have to know how to fight." Steven swallowed hard. "Because you might not always be around, and then I'll have to look after myself, and Mum, and . . . and maybe Ani."

Norris gave him a hard look.

"Ani?" he said. "Not you as well."

He turned to Just Joe. "My God, they're all at it. They're like rabbits."

Just Joe gestured impatiently as gunfire rattled from the walls outside, but he did not interfere. This was between the brothers.

Paul gave in.

"All right," he said, "but stay close to me, and try not to shoot yourself in the foot with that thing."

The truck was still in place behind the gates as they emerged from the keep, though gunfire, blasts, and pulses rang out from the battlements and beyond. A steady stream of women, children, and old men were moving in the other direction, all of them carrying bags of their most precious belongings. Paul saw Maeve and Kathleen, along with Kathleen's daughters, directing the flow.

"Where are they going?" asked Paul.

"There's a network of evacuation tunnels under the castle," said Norris. "One of them goes back to the time of King James, but the rest are new. They come out well beyond the walls. These people know what to do."

Above the gate, a man twisted as he was hit by a blast, and tumbled to the ground. He landed on his back, a blue-and-white scarf covering his face like a shroud. Just Joe grimaced, and Norris racked the slide on his shotgun.

"Come on, then," he said. "There's killing to be done."

The Galateans formed the first line of attack troops, and half of them had already fallen. Sedulus's intention had been to force the gates open with a massive blast from the last of his heavy weaponry, but he hadn't reckoned on the cement-laden truck. Now he called in the cruiser. The men and women on the walls heard its approach before it roared overhead, its red approach lights blinking in the dark.

"Clear the gates!" called Just Joe. "Take cover!"

A pair of missiles struck the gates, blowing them and the truck apart. The force of the explosion shook the walls and knocked their defenders to their backs. Paul was thrown against the castle walls and left with his ears ringing. The air filled with dust and dirt, mingling with the mist to create a curtain of gray. Paul's eyes stung, and he could barely keep them open. His first thought was of Steven, but his brother found him first, pouring water into Paul's eyes to clear them.

"Are you okay?" asked Paul. "Are you hurt?"

"No, I'm good."

Beside him, Norris, Just Joe, and the rest were struggling to their feet. Shapes appeared in the gaping hole where the gates had once been, the remains of the truck flaming around them.

"They're coming through!" said Just Joe.

The machine gun on the top of the keep opened up, and the invaders began to fall beneath its fire, but some of them made it inside and took up positions behind rubble, twisted metal, and undamaged bags of cement. The cruiser soared above the castle again, and its heavy cannon ripped into the machine-gun post, silencing its fire.

"That thing will tear us all apart," said Just Joe, as a figure appeared on the battlements, struggling beneath the weight of what looked like a long metal tube.

"That's Heather," said Paul.

"Heather, and a Stinger," said Just Joe. "Go on, my girl!"

Heather hefted the launcher onto her shoulder, took aim, and fired at the thrusters of the cruiser, one of its few vulnerable spots. The missile shot away, hurtling toward the big vessel at seven hundred miles per hour. From such close range, Heather could not miss.

The cruiser seemed to bounce in the air as the warhead struck, and flames spewed from its starboard exhaust. The huge vessel veered sharply as it fell, striking the ground nose first. Its fuel tanks ignited, and darkness turned daylight-bright as the cruiser was blown to pieces. The castle's defenders cheered, but then the battlements were raked by pulses from below, and Heather disappeared in a fury of debris and smoke and fire. A handful of Resistance members ran to see if she could be helped, but Paul feared there was little hope.

A heavy pulse hit the wall beside him, the shock waves bouncing back and giving him a sick feeling in the pit of his stomach. Beside him, Steven started firing, the assault rifle bucking in his hands, but Paul could see that he held it firmly against his shoulder, his body relaxed despite his fear. A Securitat twisted as one of Steven's rounds struck home, and the stricken Illyri disappeared in the mist.

You're tainted now, little brother, thought Paul. You're as lost as the rest of us.

# CHAPTER SIXTY-SIX

While the battle raged outside, the first basic MRI scan of Gradus's skull appeared on the screen in the infirmary, revealing a small, dense formation of matter, about three inches in length, squatting at the base of the cerebellum. It reminded Syl of an insect larva, with legs that curled around the consul's spinal cord, anchoring it in place. It appeared to have no eyes or mouth. How does it feed? Syl wondered. Is it even alive?

Fremd and Lorac crouched over the image on the display, with Syl peering between them.

"Is it the same as the one you saw at Cancri station?" asked Lorac.

"I think so. It's bigger, though. Can you improve the definition—maybe get in a little closer?"

"We're just getting started," said Lorac.

Behind them, Gradus was moaning as the scanner made a series of passes around not only his head, but his entire body. Illyri technology had made the devices lightweight and portable; the massive tubes of old had been replaced by thin low-radiation screens capable of producing images so detailed that it appeared as if the internal workings of the body were being projected onto the exterior; the pumping of the heart, the twitching of muscles, even the flow of blood through the brain, all were visible on the screen. The machine beeped, and a digital readout on its side began counting down from ten, indicating that a full imaging sequence was almost complete. Gradus, now silent, twisted his head slightly under the restraining band so that he could watch what was happening with one eye. Syl thought it looked like the sedative might be wearing off. She was about to say something to Fremd when the countdown reached zero, and what the display revealed wiped all other concerns from her head.

The organism in Gradus's head, the thing that Fremd had described as the Other, appeared to be breathing, its body slowly inflating and deflating as though drawing air. Its head was a mass of twitching tentacles, probably only a few millimeters long, beneath which was what looked to be a sucking mouth. Syl could see its organs now, although most were unfamiliar. There were small organs that looked like lungs, and what might have been a series of lateral hearts, almost like those of an earthworm, but much of the rest of its physiology was strange to her. On closer examination, what had appeared to be legs were actually more like gripping tentacles, more developed versions of the ones on its head, or thicker versions of the threadlike filaments that seemed to protrude from most of its body.

But that was not the worst of it, for what the scan revealed was that the organism was not isolated in Gradus's brain; those filaments had extended throughout his entire nervous system. They were growing as the Illyri watched, like wires moving through the Grand Consul's body.

"It's like nothing I've ever seen before," said Lorac. He spoke not with horror, but with fascination. "How is it feeding? It must be absorbing nutrients from his system, perhaps through those filaments. But they're so much more extensive than they need to be."

He tapped one of the screens, to focus on an enlarged image of Gradus's cerebellum.

"There seems to be a concentration of filaments here, at the reticular formation," he said. "I'd say that it's wired to his consciousness, but there's little contact with his thalamus, only marginal connection with his frontal lobe, and none at all with the temporal or parietal lobes."

"Meaning?" said Fremd.

"Meaning his bodily senses—hearing, sight, memory of nonverbal events, spatial perception—are mostly cut off from this thing. The frontal lobe deals with motor responses, creativity, and emotional reactions; the link looks stronger there. This thing may experience the world partly through the emotional responses of its host. It's also hooked into his cerebellum, so it may be able to stimulate certain muscle responses."

Fremd squatted close to the gurney. He spoke in Gradus's right ear.

"What is it?" he asked.

Gradus's voice was almost clear. It should be more slurred, Syl thought. We drugged him.

"It is . . . God."

He began to laugh. Lorac examined the computers hooked up to the scanner.

"The data is saving," he said. "It's slow, but we're getting there."

Fremd poured disinfectant on his hands before walking to the tray of surgical equipment beside the scanner. Gradus managed to move his head just enough to follow his progress.

"What are you doing?" he asked.

"We're going to take a sample from your 'god'," said Fremd.

He picked up a packet marked "BD Spinal Needle," and removed from it a long, thin instrument. Syl winced involuntarily.

"No," said Gradus. "You mustn't."

He began to struggle again, wriggling against his restraints like a great maggot.

"Give him more sedative," said Fremd. Lorac hit Gradus in the arm with a smaller needle. It didn't seem to have much effect, appearing if anything to make Gradus more agitated.

"Again!" said Fremd. He reached between the MRI screens and pushed the consul down in an effort to still him. He put the tip of the lumbar puncture needle against the skin of Gradus's neck.

"Lorac!" said Syl. "Fremd!"

"In a moment," said Lorac.

"No, I think you need to see this," said Syl, who was staring at the screen. "I think you need to see this *now*."


Meia and Peris watched the chaos of the attack on the castle with growing frustration. Smoke and mist masked much of the fighting, but they had seen the cruiser go down, and had watched as Sedulus pulled back his troops after the apparent failure of the initial assault. Their Illyri loyalties meant that they should have announced their presence to Sedulus and fought alongside his remaining forces, but that would have been to ignore their suspicion that Sedulus did not have the best interests of Syl and Ani at heart. Sedulus too might well have had them disarmed at gunpoint rather than allow them potentially to interfere with his efforts to secure Gradus. In addition, Meia had no desire to begin killing members of the Resistance, not after they had helped to rescue Syl and Ani in the first place, not while she still had her fragile truce with Trask.

Peris and the strike squad were growing impatient.

"I thought you said we could just walk in," said Peris.

"Unfortunately, Sedulus beat us to the walls," said Meia. "Or hadn't you noticed?"

"We can't stay out here forever. Sedulus won't give up until he's inside, and he won't care who he kills once he's in there as long as he gets the Grand Consul back. And if he doesn't get the Grand Consul—"

"Then he'll kill *everyone*," Meia finished.

"Including—"

"Quiet!" said Meia.

Her hearing was even more acute than that of the other Illyri. She was, in every way, a more advanced creation. Now she picked up footfalls on grass, and the whispers of women and children.

"Do you have signal flares?" she asked Peris.

Peris produced a pair of the self-igniting flares from his belt.

They were lightweight tubes, barely six inches long. Meia took them from him.

"I think I may have found another way into the castle," she said. "If you don't see one of these flares go up within thirty minutes, you have my permission to blast your way in and get Syl and Ani, and I don't care who you have to kill to do it."

Meia left the squad. She shouldered her weapon and approached the sound of fleeing humans. She could see shapes appearing from beneath the ground, like the dead rising. When she was almost on top of them, she dropped to the grass and shouted out:

"My name is Meia. I'm alone, and I'm unarmed."

The voices rose in panic, and then were hushed.

"We are not alone, and we are *not* unarmed," a female voice replied, but it was immediately interrupted by another calling Meia's name, this one younger and instantly familiar to her.

It was Ani.


Paul was reloading his semiautomatic when the Illyri pulled back, the mist embracing them as they retreated, temporarily abandoning the castle to its defenders. The Resistance fighters advanced to the walls. Men began dragging sandbags and undamaged sacks of cement to the gates to create a barrier behind which to fight when the Illyri returned, as they surely would. Cries for help rose from the wounded, and demands for ammunition and water from those still unharmed.

Norris and Just Joe, along with Paul and Steven, remained by the castle keep.

They were too weary to move. Unlike most of the others, they had walked for days to get to Dundearg, and their bodies were approaching exhaustion.

"What now?" asked Steven.

"They'll regroup and try again," said Just Joe. "They've probably already called for reinforcements."

"We should abandon the castle," said Norris.

"We will, just as soon as we get the signal. For now, we need more time to evacuate, and for those in the infirmary to finish their work."

"Do you know what they're looking for?" asked Norris.

"Aliens," said Just Joe.

"Right," said Norris. "It's not like we don't have enough of those."

It was Steven who noticed the change in the mist.

"They're back!" he said, rising to his feet, but what appeared beyond the gates were not Securitats or Galateans. A mechanized suit materialized before them, followed by a second, then a third. The torchlight flickered upon the faceplates on their helmets so that they seemed to be lit within by fire, but even behind the reflected light of the flames Steven could have sworn that he could see movement. Not a face, exactly, but something that was trying to be a face.

Sedulus had given the Sarith Entities only one order: to scour the castle of every trace of humanity. Now, from his hiding place in the mist, surrounded by the last vestiges of his troops, he unlocked the suits and unleashed his demons.

# CHAPTER SIXTY-SEVEN

The changes to Gradus's system were being revealed on the MRI display. The filaments were extending faster and faster through his body, so fast that Gradus screamed in agony, his back arching high in pain, stretching the restraints, and Syl could hear the metal of the buckles scraping against the gurney. Sections of the consul's brain began to light up on the scans, exploding into angry oranges and reds. The real-time images lost their focus with Gradus's thrashing, but Syl caught a glimpse of the tip of the needle moving down, drawing closer and closer to the organism in Gradus's head.

The restraints burst. Gradus pushed himself from the gurney with so much force that Lorac was thrown back against the wall and Fremd fell to the floor, the needle still clutched in his right hand. The MRI screens shattered. Syl instinctively grabbed the first weapon that came to hand: a scalpel. Lorac drew a revolver from his belt and trained it on Gradus.

But he could not shoot, not yet.

For Gradus was changing.

At the castle walls, the defenders responded to the new threat. A volley of gunfire struck the suits, but they were heavily armored, and the bullets succeeded only in striking sparks from them. The firing ceased as Just Joe called for grenades, and in the silence that followed they all heard the hissed release of compressed gases as the suit helmets were unlocked, and the visors rose.

For a moment, all was still.

Columns of black smoke began to flow from the suits, each taking the form of a dark mockery of man, before the smoke became a swarm, and the Entities commenced their feeding. A boy who looked about Paul's age was the first to be surrounded, the Entities encircling him, consuming him from the head down, his clothing—even his green-and-white scarf—vanishing as they took him. Two more members of the Resistance, a young woman and an older man, were the next to go. Paul and the others could not fire for fear of hitting their own people, and the black forms moved so *fast.* . . .

"Get inside!" cried Just Joe. "All of you."

The survivors retreated to the keep, but now the Entities separated, each seeking its own prey. Three more people died, but more slowly now as the Entities' first surge of hunger was quelled by their feeding. It gave the rest time to make it to the keep, but it was Paul who realized that they would still be at risk inside its walls. The doors were old, and imperfectly sealed. Even when they were closed, drafts came in underneath them and around the sides, and these things moved like dark vapor, or a swarm of black bees. This is it, he thought: we can't fight them, and if we can't fight them, we die.

Suddenly he was pushed aside. An Illyri female stood beside him. From her right hand dangled a belt of grenades.

"Who are—" he began, but it was Just Joe who answered.

"Meia!" he said.

"Joe," she replied. "You need to get out of my way if you want to live."

"What are those things?" said Joe.

"Sedulus's pets."

"How do we kill them?"

"You can't. But I can."

Meia walked down the steps of the keep as the Entities finished off their latest victims and looked for new blood. They swarmed together, forming one great cloud, as if in response to the approaching female. They descended on her, swirling and biting. Paul could see fragments of tissue disappearing from Meia's head—a piece of her cheek, the tip of her right ear—but then the creatures pulled back. He could see that she was bleeding, but drops of a yellow milky fluid also leaked from her wounds and pooled on the seals of her armor. He thought that he could see hydraulics moving in her face. The Entities seemed to realize the threat that she posed, but they could not consume her. Whatever she was, whatever she was made from, they could not eat it.

"What is she doing?" said Steven.

"I think she's going after their metal suits," said Paul.

Meia began to run, arming the grenades as she did so. The first two went through the open visors and into the bodies of the suits, but she threw the entire belt into the third. She hit the ground, and the men at the keep threw themselves flat as the grenades exploded. When Paul looked up, two of the suits were still standing in place, but they were riddled with fissures and leaks. The third suit had split above the waist, and lay in two pieces on the dirt.

The black swarms combined to form a face, with long eye sockets and a gaping mouth. It screamed silently, and then vanished into the mist.


The Grand Consul, or some version of him, stood in the center of the room. His arms were extended from his sides, and his whole body trembled. Specks of blood appeared on his exposed skin, flowing from his face and scalp until he wore a mask of red, and his hands looked like those of a murderer. The shaking increased in intensity. His mouth opened, and he cried out in agony as his head and hands began to blur, the outline of his features becoming less clear as though seen through fog. Syl's screams joined with his, even as she realized that it was not fog but filaments that were emerging through the pores of his skin, waving in the dim light, testing the unfamiliar air. Syl could see them moving beneath his clothing, pushing at the material, their tips hardening to points as they finally tore through.

All trace of Gradus's features was now lost. The Grand Consul was a swirling mass of yellow filaments moving to a tide felt only by them, like a marooned ocean creature remembering the sea. His body swelled, and his mouth opened wider still, so that Syl heard the bones in his skull cracking as his jaw dislocated. From his lips poured a stream of particles, like pollen being expelled from a plant, and the room filled with the sickly sweet smell of corrupted flesh. The particles struck the unfortunate Lorac straight in the face. He had lost his mask in the chaos, and now collapsed choking on the ground. Almost immediately filaments exploded from his nose and his ears. They covered his mouth, and his eyes, and his face, slowly suffocating him, even as his belly started to bloat rapidly, and Syl could almost picture the filaments spreading through his system, infecting him, preparing to send forth another deadly cloud when his stomach burst.

Gradus turned toward Fremd, the Grand Consul's body now nothing more than a weapon to be used by the organism inside him. Another spray of particles poured from his mouth, but Fremd grabbed one of the broken MRI screens and used it to shield his face as he scuttled to where Syl stood, frozen in horror by the wall.

"Run!" he told her. "Run now!"

He grabbed her by the hand and pulled her toward the door, but Syl's hand slipped from his. She could not move any farther. She looked to her feet and saw the filaments wrapped around her ankles, tightening on her. Suddenly she was yanked backward so hard that she fell facedown on the floor. She stretched out her hand to Fremd, but another burst of particles sprayed toward him, and it was all he could do to protect himself with the screen and try not to breathe, for even a mask was little protection against this.

"Help me!" cried Syl. She was being dragged back now, toward the thing that was once Gradus, her own mask slipping from her face, leaving her entirely unprotected. Fremd's fingers reached for hers and their fingertips touched. There was movement to Syl's left, and she saw that Lorac's entire body was now swollen almost to its limit. Already puffs of particles were being blown through the pores of his skin like the water spouts of a whale. The whole room, perhaps the whole castle, would be infected by him when the last wall of skin finally broke.

A pair of shadows fell across Fremd, and Meia's voice shouted, "Stay down, Syl! Stay down!"

She felt a weight on top of her. A torrent of searing heat from Meia's blast rifle roared above her as Paul whispered, "I'm here, I'm here," and Gradus and Lorac began to burn.

Sedulus stood before the last of the skimmers. If everything went wrong, it would at least allow him to escape. Around him stood four Securitats and half a dozen Galateans, all that was left of the three platoons that he had led into the Highlands. The mist was slowly clearing, and the distant shape of the castle was now visible. They were waiting for the Sarith Entities to finish their work when they heard the vague sound of three explosions in quick succession, the final one louder than the rest.

"What was that?" asked Beldyn.

"What does it matter?" replied Sedulus.

The mist billowed before them. Something was emerging from it, something big and fast. Beldyn stepped forward, his gun at the ready. The rest of the troops did likewise.

Beldyn saw them first. He turned to shout a warning, but the Entity entered through his open mouth, pouring itself down his throat and consuming him from within. The others descended on the Galateans and the Securitats, pursuing them as they ran, their hunger made sharper by the fact that they were dying. Only Sedulus remained in place, and watched his troops fall.

Two of the Entities began to weaken, the intensity of their feeding dwindling, their essence coalescing into a single roiling mass that beat like a human heart until it turned from black to gray, and then to nothing.

But one remained. It took human form before Sedulus, and Sedulus thought that he had always known this day might come. He had never truly understood the nature of these beings. He had used them, but they had used him too. He feared them, but they hated him. They were like birds of prey; they were his only for as long as he could keep them fed, and they had no loyalty to their master, especially not one who had abused his power of life and death over them.

"Finish it," he whispered.

The Entity fell upon him, and they died together.

# CHAPTER SIXTY-EIGHT

All that was left of Gradus and Lorac was burnt remains. Some of their limbs had fused with the melted equipment in the heat of the fire, but the old stone walls of the keep contained the blaze.

The clothing had been burned from Paul's back, and his skin was raw and blistered. Part of his hair had been singed down to his skull. Syl was unharmed. She sat on the old flagstones of the corridor, her face against Paul's chest. She did not hold him—although she wanted to—for Maeve was working on him, salving his wounds prior to applying the dressings. Ani and Steven watched all that was taking place. They stood together, their shoulders touching companionably.

Heather and Alice waited outside, along with Just Joe and Norris, and what was left of the force in the castle. Heather was wounded, but Fremd had done his best for her. She could walk, and she would survive. Now he turned his attention to Meia.

"We have to tell everyone," said Syl, as Fremd tended to the damage inflicted by the Entities. "They have to know."

"Who do we tell?" asked Meia. "And what proof do we have? It's gone, all of it."

She told them of what she had seen at the Eden Project while Fremd patched her with ProGen skin. It was routinely used to heal battle wounds, even burns, and it was possible that some of it might be grafted on to Paul's back if his injuries proved severe enough. Meia showed signs of pain as the work was done. Had she known of Vena's discovery of her true nature, she might have agreed with at least one of the Securitat's conclusions: flesh gave feeling, and once one could experience pain, emotions were no longer illusions. With pain came rage, regret, loss.

Love?

The biggest surprise about the truth of Meia's identity was how little Syl and Ani were surprised. In a way, it made perfect sense to them, given their growing awareness of their own gifts.

*I should have known,* thought Ani, *for Meia only ever revealed what she wanted me to see.*

*I should have known,* thought Syl. *Meia was the only one I could never bend to my will.*

"My father will believe us," said Syl.

"We don't know who has been infected," said Meia.

"The Corps!" said Syl. "It's just the Corps officials and the Securitats. It has to be. My father isn't like them."

Fremd and Meia exchanged a look. Syl caught it.

"What?" she said. "It's true."

"We don't know that," said Fremd. "And even if it is true, by sharing what you know you put everyone you tell at risk, yourself most of all. Think of the panic we'll create if this gets out. No Illyri will be safe: you'll have every lunatic from here to the South Pole beheading Illyri to find out what's living inside their heads.

"No, we need proof, and on a vast scale. We need to try to understand the nature of the Others. Until then, we have to remain silent while we find out what's happening. This isn't just about a handful of Corps officials carrying some kind of life-form. We know from what Meia has seen that they've been experimenting on humans. They've been implanting, and they've also been seeding the dead with these things. We have to find out why."

"And then there is the Sisterhood," said Meia. "The Corps does the Sisterhood's bidding. If the Corps is involved, then so too is the Sisterhood. We must be silent, all of us. We must be careful."

"She's right, Syl," said Paul, and for an instant Syl wanted to hate him.

"You don't know my father," she said.

She tried to pull away, but he held her gently.

"I know you," he said. "If you trust him, so do I. But everyone who knows about this is at risk. If you tell him, you put him at risk, too. Whatever these things are, it's my people—humans—who are being experimented on. I'll do whatever I can to stop it, but it has to be planned, and it has to be successful once we start. For that to happen, we have to know what we're dealing with—all of us, human and Illyri."

"And it would mean returning to Edinburgh," said Meia. "You and Ani are still fugitives. That hasn't changed."

"So, what should we do?" asked Ani. "Keep running?"

"I can hide you," said Meia. "In time, we can get you out of Scotland, maybe even offworld. I can keep you one step ahead of them always."

"But then that will be our lives forever, won't it?" said Syl. "It will be like our time in the Highlands, except stretching on and on. We'll always be hunted, and that's no life at all."

There was silence, for Meia could not disagree. It was left to Ani to speak, and what she said broke Syl's heart, for it was Syl who had got them into this mess to begin with.

"Syl is right," said Ani. "We should go back. I'm tired of running."

Paul and Steven shouted the same word simultaneously: "No!"

The arguments began, but they were interrupted by Peris, who gestured for Meia to join him. She followed the soldier out of the keep and into the courtyard, where they stood beside the ruined gates. In the distance Meia heard the sound of incoming craft: skimmers and shuttles. She also picked up the dying drone of a cruiser's engines powering down; it had already landed nearby, and would soon begin disgorging troops. The engine suggested a Military craft, she noted, not the Corps or the Securitats. That, at least, was good.

"I'm sorry," said Peris. "I tried to keep them away for as long as I could. And you must know: my orders are to bring Syl and Ani back to their fathers."

"It's all right," said Meia. "They want to return."

Peris looked at her solemnly.

"I have to take the boys back as well," he said.

"They're under sentence of death."

"Not anymore. With Sedulus and Gradus both dead, Governor Andrus is once again in control, at least for the present, and the Corps and the Securitats will be out of favor after this whole mess. The governor has already abolished the death penalty; he says that he'll deal with the Council of Government himself if they object. And the medic who took DNA samples from the boys testified that he believes the same samples were used to contaminate the evidence from the explosions."

"On whose orders?"

"He says on the orders of Sedulus, and Sedulus alone."

"Always blame the dead," said Meia. "The cover-up has already begun."

"It's easiest that way. But the boys remain guilty of membership in the Resistance."

"After all this slaughter, and the death of Gradus, the Corps will press for them to be sent to the Punishment Battalions."

"Yes."

"Perhaps they'll survive," said Meia, but she sounded doubtful.

"I am aware that there is an escape tunnel in that room we've just left, you know."

"For a simple soldier, you are unusually complicated," said Meia. "But I suspect that those young men will want to return too. Paul will not abandon Syl, and Steven will follow his brother's lead."

She watched the reinforcements draw nearer, marching in double time toward the castle. They were only minutes away.

"I should have guessed that you were a Mech," said Peris.

"Why is that?"

"You never fell for my charms."

"I was aware of your reputation."

"And I of yours," said Peris. "I should tell you that a second order came through. Highest priority from Vena herself, who is now the ranking Securitat following the death of Sedulus. You are accused of treason and murder. You are to be arrested on sight and handed over to the Securitats. If you resist, you are to be shot."

Meia turned to face him. His finger was already inside the trigger guard of his blast rifle, although the weapon was not yet pointing in her direction.

"Are you guilty of the offenses?" asked Peris.

"The treason I deny, but yes, I have killed."

"Why?"

"Because there are forces at work here that you don't understand. None of us do—not yet. But humanity is at risk, and I think the Illyri race is in danger too."

"I've told you before, I'm just a simple soldier," said Peris. "I merely follow orders."

"So what will you do?" she asked.

"Follow my orders," he said. The slightest of smiles softened his features. "But if I can't see you, I can't arrest you, and I certainly can't shoot you."

"I can't leave them," said Meia. "I have to help them. I have to help them all."

"You can't help them if you're dead. Or decommissioned, if you prefer."

Meia's right hand reached out and touched Peris gently on the arm.

"These boys are important," she said. "The older one in particular has grown close to Syl, and she to him. There are those who may try to hurt her by hurting him, but he has also seen things in this castle, things that, for now, I can't share with you, but that will affect the future of our race. Believe me: the Kerr brothers must be protected. They must be kept alive. Do what you can for them, until I return. Please."

"I will."

He turned his back on her. When he looked again, she was gone.

•  •  •

When Peris returned to the room in the keep, Fremd and the Resistance survivors were no longer there. Peris sighed. He was not sure how he was supposed to explain the fact that the entire Resistance force in the castle had disappeared from under his nose. There were those who would undoubtedly describe him as not just a simple soldier, but a simpleton.

Yet four faces still looked up at him. Syl and Ani had been crying. Peris thought the boys might have shed some tears too. They had all linked hands, like children presenting a united front.

Peris felt a rush of conflicting emotions, but not least of them was admiration.

"Time to go," he said.

# CHAPTER SIXTY-NINE

The message from Peris came through to Edinburgh Castle. Syl and Ani were safe, but Marshal Sedulus was missing, and a single surviving Securitat had given a disturbing description of his possible fate. Grand Consul Gradus, Peris reported, had been burned alive during Sedulus's assault on the castle.

As Meia had noted, the dead made useful scapegoats.

Syrene's screams of loss echoed through the castle. Her handmaids flitted helplessly around her like moths drawn to the flame of her grief. Responding to the flood of emotions, the organism in her brain tightened its hold on her cerebral cortex, and the intensity of her shrieks increased.

In the silence of her quarters, Vena mourned for the lost Sedulus, but she did not weep. The heat of her rage evaporated her tears before they could fall from her eyes.

*I will watch as every creature on Earth is consumed.*
*I will continue my lover's work.*

# CHAPTER SEVENTY

Syl and Ani were returned to Edinburgh in the same shuttle as Paul and Steven, all under the watchful eye of Peris. The boys were cuffed, but the two Illyri were not. Peris kept them all separated for appearance's sake, and they were silent throughout the journey, but it seemed to him that the older boy never took his gaze from the governor's daughter, and the young Illyri held the human fast in her eyes.

Upon landing, Peris opened the shuttle door and peered out. He saw a platoon of Military to the right, and a line of Corps and Securitats to the left. For now, the scales favored those on the right, but it would shift again. The game was always being played, and the four youths were simply pawns on the board.

A quartet of Military guards approached, ready to receive the prisoners. With a raised hand, Peris instructed them to wait. He turned back to the occupants of the shuttle, and with a curt nod he uncuffed the humans. He watched awkwardly as Paul embraced Syl, and they kissed deeply, hungrily. At a loss, Ani gave Steven a hug too, and an awkward pat on the back. It was clear from the look on his face that Steven would have liked more, but Ani did not have more to give him.

"I'm sorry," said Peris. "I truly am."

They separated, and Peris cuffed the boys once again. The members of his strike team surrounded the prisoners as they were led from the shuttle. Paul and Steven could feel the hatred directed toward them from the Securitats. Their numbers in Scotland had been decimated during the preceding days, and they had lost their leader on Earth. These two boys were the only ones left to blame. If they could, their enemies would have executed them in the square.

The brothers were taken to a pair of comfortable but secure Military cells, there to await their fate. Syl and Ani were brought to the governor's office. They were both experiencing similar thoughts: that being locked in a cell might be preferable to the storm that was about to break over them.

Balen was seated in his usual place. He rose from his chair as the young Illyri entered the room. They looked filthy, he thought, and tired.

And older. These were not the same girls who had left the castle mere days before. They had been tested in fire, and changed by the experience. Balen was no longer looking at youths, but young adults.

"Welcome back," he said.

"Are we?" asked Syl.

"You will always be welcome here," Balen replied. "Both of you. Remember that, in the hours and days to come."

Syl tried to smile at him, but she could not. Being back here made her aware of all that she had sacrificed, and all that she might yet have to sacrifce. Whatever happened, nothing would ever be the same again.

The door opened. Seated inside were Danis and his wife, Fian. As soon as the girls were led in, Fian ran to her daughter and embraced her, even as her husband tried to stop her. Andrus stood behind his desk, his face severe. He did not approach Syl. It was only as the door closed behind her that Syl saw why.

Syrene was waiting in the corner of the room. She had exchanged the red robes of the Sisterhood for the deep blue of a widow's weeds. Her face was uncovered, and so pale that the tattoos of the Sisterhood were like wounds upon her skin.

"Fian," said Andrus, and there was a warning in his voice. Reluctantly Fian released her hold on her daughter, and returned to her chair.

Andrus regarded the two Illyri. He loved them both, daughter and near daughter. There would be time later for him to take Syl in his arms and tell her how much he cared for her, and how glad he was that she was safely returned.

Time, but only a little.

For now, Syrene filled the room with the jagged edges of her grief. Her pain was a weapon waiting to be used. If they were not careful, she would tear them all apart with it.

"You are unhurt?" Andrus asked.

Syl and Ani nodded dumbly.

"Good," he said, and he tried to fill that single syllable with all that could not be said. "Now, I want you to tell the Archmage of her husband. She has the right to know the manner of his death."

Andrus and Danis had agreed upon this with Syrene. They could not deny her. She wanted to be there when the girls were brought to their fathers. She wanted there to be no secrets. She wanted to be told.

Syl and Ani had prepared their story. Peris had coached them while the boys listened. Fire from the troop carrier; damaged fuel stores; a leak.

Flames.

Syrene probed for the lie, both openly with her questions and insidiously with her mind. They experienced it as an itch in their skulls, a bug crawling on their brains, but Balen had been right: these were changed young people, and their control of their gifts was growing. Perhaps Syl's, though newly recognized, were greater, for Syrene's testing betrayed no sign of her abilities, while Ani's brain twitched like a stimulated muscle. They, in turn, felt Syrene's pain seeking an outlet. There was a part of Syrene that wanted to see them both burn, just as her husband had burned.

When she was done, she turned to face Andrus.

"They're lying," she said.

Syl opened her mouth to protest, but her father raised a finger in warning, and she stayed quiet.

"I heard no lie," said Andrus. "Their story matches that of Peris, and he is an honorable man."

"He is one of your lackeys," said Syrene. "I do not trust him, or them. I do not even trust you, Lord Andrus. My understanding is that you harbored a Mech on your staff."

Andrus's face gave away nothing.

"I did not know of her true nature."

"I don't believe you. Even if I did, I wouldn't care. She is a renegade and a killer. She will be found and terminated."

"Regardless," said Andrus, "I have requested more information from the Securitats about the crimes of which she is accused, and have received nothing in return. On a similar matter, we have reason to believe that the bombings in Edinburgh might have been the work of dissidents within the Illyri, possibly even the Corps itself."

He knew that Syrene was on dangerous ground. To speak of Meia's crimes was to speak of Eden, and Syrene did not wish to do that. Neither did she care to discuss the bombs on the Royal Mile. Andrus just wished that Meia could have reported her findings before she went to ground.

"None of this helps to avenge my husband, or eases my grief at his loss," said Syrene.

"I do not know what more we can do," said Andrus. "Your husband's remains are being returned to Edinburgh. His death is a blow to us all. We will mourn with you."

"I do not want your mourning!"

Syrene's body coiled in fury. Spittle shot from her mouth and flecked the pink of her lips and the blue of her gown. She drew a breath, calming herself. She repeated the words, this time more calmly. "I do not want your mourning."

"What *do* you want?"

"A punishment to fit the crime. Your daughters are guilty of treason. They helped the humans to escape."

"The boys were innocent."

"Perhaps, but only of the bombings. They are members of the

Resistance. They have killed Illyri. Your daughters colluded with them."

"They were foolish. They are young."

"Not so young. Had they not acted as they did, my husband would still be alive. I invoke the Widow's Wish."

The tension in the room increased. The Widow's Wish was a relic of older times, an age when Illyri females had less power and were dependent upon their husbands for their wealth and security. A crime against the husband was viewed also as a crime against the wife, and a husband's murder was the worst crime of all. Before the death penalty had been eliminated on Illyr, the Widow's Wish allowed a woman to decide whether those responsible for the death of her husband should be imprisoned or executed. In later years, it could be used to increase or reduce the severity of a penalty, but it was mainly a weapon of the poor and was rarely used by the privileged. It remained enshrined in law, though, and could not be ignored.

"And what is your wish?"

"That my husband's final decision on the fate of these two traitorous Illyri should remain in force."

From the pocket of her dress, Syrene produced a note. She unfolded it carefully, and handed it to Andrus. He read it silently. When he was finished, some of his confidence was gone.

"The Punishment Battalions," he said, and Danis tensed in his chair at his words.

Syl wavered on her feet. That was a death sentence.

"They have not yet been tried," said Andrus.

"Then let them be tried," said Syrene. "The evidence against them is overwhelming. It was my husband's recommended sentence, and it is mine. No court will stand against it. If you try to deprive me of it, if you try to take these daughters of Illyr from here and hide them away, I will bring down the wrath of the Sisterhood and the Corps upon you. There will be civil war, I guarantee it."

Fian stood. She seemed ready to spring at Syrene, but Danis held on firmly to his wife.

"Then let there be war," he said. "I will not doom these children to the Battalions."

"I warn you—" said Syrene.

"Wait," said Syl. "Wait."

And though she spoke the word softly, so softly, there was still something in her voice, in the certainty of it, that quieted them all.

"We wish to give ourselves to the Sisterhood," she said.

"*What?*" shouted Andrus. "No! I will not permit it!"

Now Danis was roaring, and his wife was crying.

Syl looked at Ani, and Ani understood. She swallowed hard before she spoke, but when she did, it was with almost as much confidence as Syl had managed.

"We wish to give ourselves to the Sisterhood," she said, then added, so that only Syl could hear, "I think."

All shouting ceased. The room was quiet. If the Widow's Wish was an old law, rarely invoked, the pledge to the Sisterhood was older yet, and even more serious. It could not be refused, not by the family of the one making the pledge or by the Sisterhood itself. If the novice did not prove worthy, an alternative solution could be found, but any Illyri female who was prepared to offer herself as a Nairene had to be given a place in the Marque.

"I accept," said Syrene. All grief was gone from her face, and in its place there was only triumph.

And in Syrene's words, Syl heard the sound of the trap snapping shut.

# CHAPTER SEVENTY-ONE

C onsternation reigned. The shouts even drew Balen from his desk, and caused a pair of the governor's guards to come running with their weapons at the ready. Andrus dismissed them, assuring them that he was safe, but the debate raged on. It was all for nothing, though. Even in her grief, Syrene had played them all expertly. She had Ani, whose powers she believed she could turn to the Sisterhood's benefit, and she had avenged the Sisterhood for the loss of the Lady Orianne to her husband, Andrus. If they could not have the mother, they now had the daughter instead.

But Syl had her own secrets. As the arguments raged around her, she saw again a man silhouetted against the Highland dawn, a bayonet buried deep in his chest. Syrene was not the only one who could play vicious games.

"What of Paul and Steven?" Syl asked, her voice again silencing the adults. "They helped us after the crash. They kept us safe."

"For their own ends," said Syrene, and her tone made it clear that she was aware of the feelings at work between the humans and the young Illyri.

"They kept us *safe*," Syl repeated, and she held Syrene's gaze for so long that it was the Nairene sister who was forced to look away first.

"Have them brought here," ordered Andrus. He was glad of the distraction. It would give him time to think. He did not want his daughter in the hands of the Sisterhood. He wanted her to remain close to him. There had to be a way.

Eventually Paul and Steven appeared, accompanied by Peris. They no longer wore their own clothes, but had been given gray prison overalls. Steven's were too big for him, and he had been forced to roll up the sleeves and cuffs. It made him appear very small, and very young. The two boys barely glanced at Syl and Ani. It hurt Syl at first, until she realized that they wanted to do nothing that might get the Illyri into more trouble by exposing their true feelings.

Too late, thought Syl. Syrene knew, and she believed that her father might have some suspicions too. He was watching Paul as though he didn't trust him a single inch. Syrene no longer looked triumphant, but simply vindictive. These boys were among those who had taken her husband captive. Had they not done so, he would still be alive.

She wanted their heads.

Andrus stood. He towered over the two boys.

"It appears that you were not responsible for the bombings on the Royal Mile," he said.

Paul and Steven exchanged a look. Hope shone briefly in their eyes, but was quickly extinguished by Andrus's next words.

"However, you are guilty of membership of the Resistance, and of the murder of Illyri."

"We didn't murder anyone," said Paul. "We fought. We're soldiers."

"You are terrorists!" said Syrene.

"Quiet!" said Andrus. "All of you."

He waited until he was sure that he was being heeded before he continued. Where was Meia? he thought. He wanted to consult with her. He had colluded with her to place his daughter and Ani with the Resistance in order to prevent them from being taken offworld. Now he was being forced to punish these two boys for essentially doing his will.

"The sentence for those guilty of Resistance activities is exile to the Punishment Battalions for life," he said. "Given your age, I commute that sentence to five years."

Paul and Steven looked shocked. Five years in the Punishment Battalions was still a virtual death sentence. There was a small chance that Paul might survive, if he was strong enough, and lucky, but Steven would not. He was too young. Starvation and brutality would kill him within months.

"No," said Syl softly. "Not that."

The sentence she and Ani had avoided had passed to the Kerrs instead. Ani took her hand and squeezed it.

Then Peris stepped forward.

"If I might speak, Lord Andrus."

Andrus nodded his permission.

"I in no way condone the activities of these two young men," said Peris. "They are members of the Resistance, and they fought the Illyri at Dundearg. But I believe they were protecting your daughter and the daughter of General Danis, as well as the women and children sheltered in the castle. Marshal Sedulus, in his desire to rescue the Grand Consul, was guilty of using undue force, of the slaughter of human civilians, of endangering the safety of Illyri and human alike, and of introducing hostile life-forms into a protected environment.

"In their position," Peris concluded, "I might well have fought Marshal Sedulus too."

"Do you have an alternative proposal for punishment?" asked Andrus, and his voice betrayed his hope that it might be so.

"They are brave, and strong," said Peris. "They could be useful to the Empire. If you send them to the Punishment Battalions, they will die. But if you place them with the Brigades . . ."

The Brigades were different. This was where the one-in-ten of conscripted human youths were placed, and those who served in them were treated well. They were given proper food, and the best of training. They were soldiers, not prisoners. It was still dangerous, but the survival rates were many times higher than in the Battalions.

"It is not usual," said Andrus. "It may even be dangerous to place members of the Resistance in the Brigades. They could sow unrest."

"I will vouch for them," said Peris. "I will train them myself. And I will personally deal with any attempts to foment rebellion."

Andrus and Danis could not hide their surprise. What Peris was proposing was that he should leave his comfortable position in the governor's personal guard and return to the active Military. A place in the guard was a well-earned reward for loyal service. Nobody went from there to the Brigades. The traffic was always in the other direction.

"Are you sure this is what you want?" asked Danis. He and Peris had served together for a long time, and the captain was one of his closest comrades in arms.

"Yes, General," said Peris. "I am a common soldier, and a soldier's place is not in fine palaces, but in the field."

"I object—" began Syrene, but Andrus cut her off.

"Your objection is noted, but the decision is made. The prisoners will join the Brigades, and Captain Peris will take responsibility for them. It is done. Captain, prepare for your departure."

Peris saluted, and the boys were led away. This time, Paul risked a look back at Syl, and she managed a small smile. He winked at her in return.

There was hope after all, if only a little.


Once they were gone, Danis and his wife asked permission to spend some time alone with their daughter, for she was now the property of the Sisterhood. Their request was granted by Syrene, although she insisted that Corps personnel be positioned outside Danis's quarters to ensure that no attempt was made to remove Ani from the castle.

"And none of your tricks," she warned Ani in a whisper as she moved to join her parents. "If you cross me, I'll destroy your father and mother."

Ani departed, her head bowed low.

That left only Syl, Andrus, and Syrene.

"May I request the same kindness?" asked Andrus.

"You may," said Syrene, "although I would like a moment alone with you first."

Andrus didn't seem particularly happy about it, but he had little choice in the matter. He asked Syl to step outside, and she did so. She took a seat across from Balen, but she did not speak. She remembered her conversation with Meia and Fremd, and their warning to say nothing of what had occurred during Gradus's final moments. She had to tell her father something, though. He was a clever, careful man. He would know what to do.

Andrus stood before Syrene. He hated her now, and did nothing to disguise it. He had once viewed her as a potentially dangerous enemy, but one who could be handled and contained. That situation had changed. She had his daughter, and she had Ani. But he would find a way to get them back, even if he had to wage war to do it.

"Say what you have to say," he told her, "and then leave. I begrudge every moment I spend away from my child."

"She will be well cared for," said Syrene. "She will make a fine addition to the Sisterhood."

Not for long, Andrus thought. I will not lose her to the Marque.

Syrene stepped toward him. She placed a hand on his sleeve.

"What do you want from me?" asked Andrus.

"A kiss," said Syrene. "A kiss for a grieving widow."

Andrus laughed.

"I would sooner kiss a serpent," he said.

The tattoos on Syrene's face grew more vivid, and Andrus believed that, just for an instant, he saw them move independently, writhing like snakes. He looked into Syrene's eyes, and the flecks in her irises were like the light from distant dead stars. He tried to pull away from her, but he could not. Her mouth fixed upon his. He felt something probing at his lips, forcing them apart. He thought at first that it was her tongue, but then it began to separate, and there were tendrils in his mouth, probing at his palate and gums, moving inexorably toward his throat. He tried to pull away, but more tendrils were pouring from Syrene's jaws, wrapping themselves around his head, holding him in place.

Syrene's back arched. She breathed deeply into him, and his mouth was filled with dust.

# CHAPTER SEVENTY-TWO

T he door to the governor's office opened, and Syrene emerged. She barely looked at Syl as she pulled her veil down, masking her face.

"Go to your father," she said. "Say your goodbyes, for we leave tonight."

Syl entered the room. Her father was seated at his desk. He looked dazed, but he smiled as she appeared.

"I have to talk to you," said Syl. "I have to tell you something important."

"Syl," he said. He stood and raised his arms to her. She came to him, and he held her tight.

"Syl," he repeated. "Everything is going to be fine. You understand that, don't you?"

She looked up at him. His breath smelled spicy yet sickly sweet, like the corrupted air in Dundearg as Gradus had begun to change.

And she knew.

"What was it you wanted to tell me?" said Andrus.

Syl began to cry. She tried to stop the tears, but she could not. She wrapped her arms around her father and buried her face in his chest. She cried and cried until she had no more tears left to shed, until her throat was raw and her body ached. She stepped back from him and knew that she would never allow him to hold her like that again.

"Just that I love you," she said. "And I'll always love you, no matter what."

With that she left him, and went to her room to gather her belongings.

# CHAPTER SEVENTY-THREE

Paul and Steven were seated side by side in the Military shuttle. Around them were other young men and women, most of them press-ganged into the service of the Illyri. They were as much hostages as recruits, and most looked frightened. There were others, though, who had clearly joined up willingly, anxious to escape their lives on Earth. Those who knew one another laughed and joked, or spoke too loudly about how hard and tough they were in order to impress the rest, but Paul could detect the tension behind their bravado.

Paul and Steven's mother had visited them earlier that day. Saying goodbye to her had been the hardest thing either of the boys had ever done. Their parting had shaken Steven badly, and he had spoken little since then, retreating into himself. Paul wasn't much better, but he kept a brave face for Steven's sake.

At the back of the shuttle sat a transformed Peris. He wore military green, and the return to his old uniform seemed to have changed him. He was no longer the slightly soft-in-the-middle castle guard of old; he had cast off that identity completely. He seemed at once more relaxed yet more threatening, as though this were his true vocation—to train, to fight—and he was comfortable in this skin. He caught Paul watching him, and gave a single swift nod.

Paul looked away. For reasons best known to himself, Peris had signed on to mentor them, and Paul was not sure how he felt about that, or even if he could entirely trust the tough soldier. His instinct said yes, but the Resistance fighter in him said no. There would come a time when he might have to turn against Peris, for Paul was intent upon returning to Earth, *his* Earth, and freeing it from the Illyri.

The Illyri, and the Others. The true aliens.

He thought of Syl. His fingers tensed against the armrests of his chair. This parting was only temporary. He would not relinquish her to the Sisterhood. They were meant to be together.

Steven startled him from his thoughts by speaking.

"What's going to happen to us, Paul?" he asked. His voice was very soft, and very frail.

"We're going to become soldiers," whispered Paul. "We're going to learn weapons, and tactics, and the art of war."

"And then?"

"We're going to take what we've learned and use it to fight the Illyri," he said. "We're going to fight, and we're going to win. . . ."

# CHAPTER SEVENTY-FOUR

In a darkened cellar in Glasgow, far from prying eyes, Meia sat before a mirror and prayed. She could no longer be who she was, not if she was to aid Syl and Ani and discover the truth about the Others. She had injected herself with anesthetic, but what was to come would still be immensely painful, both physically and psychologically. She tried to tell herself that it was not important, that what mattered was what lay within her.

What mattered was her soul.

She took the scalpel from the tray, placed its blade beside her right eye, and slowly began to cut off her face.

# CHAPTER SEVENTY-FIVE

The Sisterhood's shuttle passed through Earth's atmosphere with a shudder and entered the vastness of space. Syl and Ani stared at the lights of the stars and the lights among the stars, watching as one speck grew bigger and bigger until the lineaments and dimensions of the great ship were revealed. It was the *Balaron*, newly arrived through the wormhole, now waiting to take them to the Marque.

Syl and Ani wore the yellow robes of novices. All their carefully assembled possessions had been taken from them on Syrene's orders, and they were certain that they would never see them again. Syl had managed to find a moment to whisper to Ani of her suspicions about her father, although Ani seemed to have no such fears about Danis. She had told him nothing, though, just as they had agreed.

The horrors of the day of departure had produced only one bright spark of goodness, one reason for them not to feel entirely alone: Althea had returned, and just as Peris had offered to take Paul and Steven under his wing, so too Althea had announced that wherever Syl went, she would go too. Syrene did not object. Why would she object to Syl's pathetic, needy nursemaid coming along? Anyway, it was not unusual for the wealthier novices to bring a handmaiden with them to the Marque, and it often made the transition to the life of the Sisterhood less traumatic for all concerned. But Syl had found one more use for Althea on Earth before they left, for Ani had told her all about Althea's part in her escape from the castle.

"Can you get a message to the Resistance?" Syl had asked, as Althea helped her to pack.

"Yes," Althea whispered, "if you give it to me now."

"Tell them to contact Meia," said Syl. "Tell her not to trust my father."

And Althea, reluctantly, had passed on the message, even if she did not understand the reason for it.

Now she leaned across the aisle, and together she, Syl, and Ani took in the immensity of the *Balaron*.

Syrene sat at the front of the shuttle, her widow's clothes already replaced by the red robes of the Sisterhood. The Archmage had not moved or spoken during the voyage. Ani risked a peek at her, and whispered to the others that Syrene's pupils were constricted, her irises blank. She was meditating, although she herself would have called it "communing."

Meditate all you like, thought Syl. You think you've won, but this is simply the first battle. Just as an infection has spread through the Illyri, just as an unknown threat has anchored itself to the collective spine of my race, so too the Sisterhood is about to be infected by a secret enemy.

And I am that enemy.

# ACKNOWLEDGMENTS

The authors would like to thank Emily Bestler, Judith Curr, Megan Reid, David Brown, and the staff at Emily Bestler Books/Atria Books; Jane Morpeth, Frankie Gray, Samantha Eades, and all at Headline; our agent, Darley Anderson, and his team, particularly Jill Bentley; and Clair Lamb and Madeira James.

*Physics of the Future* by Michio Kaku (Doubleday, 2011) and *The Singularity Is Near* by Ray Kurzweil (Viking Penguin, 2006) were among the books that proved particularly useful and thought-provoking during the research and writing of this novel.

And special thanks to Cameron and Alistair for their comments, and their patience.

READ ON FOR THE NEXT ENTRY IN
THE CHRONICLES OF THE INVADERS,
*EMPIRE* BY JOHN CONNOLLY AND JENNIFER RIDYARD

# CHAPTER ONE

The predators circled, each taking a turn to snarl at her, some more vicious than others, but every one determined to take their piece of flesh.

"Stupid, shabby thing."

"She never learns."

"She's too stupid to learn."

"Why are you here?"

"You don't belong in this place."

"Why do you even exist?"

"Elda. Even your name is ugly."

"Look at yourself!"

"She can't. She shuns mirrors. She's afraid they'll crack at the sight of her."

And then the leader, the alpha, came to bite, the pack parting, their faces turned admiringly upon her, her radiance reflected in their eyes.

Tanit, beautiful young Tanit: cruel, and worse than cruel.

"No, that's not the case," said Tanit. "She stays away from mirrors because there's nothing to see. She's so insignificant that she's barely there at all."

It was the way that she spoke, the words tossed carelessly as though the object of her disdain were unworthy even of the effort involved in crushing her. She looked down on Elda—Tanit was tall, even for an Illyri; it was part of her power—reached out a hand, and let it slip through this lesser Novice's mop of dark hair, the strands falling from her fingers in tousled clumps.

"Nothing," said Tanit. "I feel . . . nothing."

Her victim kept her head down, her eyes on the floor. It was better that way, easier. Perhaps Tanit and the others might grow bored if they couldn't provoke a reaction, and seek other prey to torment.

But no, not this time. Elda felt a prickling on her skin. It began at her cheeks, then slowly spread to her nose, her forehead, her ears, her neck. Warmth became heat, heat became burning pain. What Tanit was doing to her was against all the rules, but the rules did not apply to Tanit and her acolytes as they did to others. After all, this was merely practice for them. They were like disturbed children encouraged to torture insects and rodents so that they would not falter when told to inflict pain on their own.

And they had no fear of being caught. This was the Marque, the ancient lair of the Nairene Sisterhood, and held no shortages of places in which the weak could be tormented by the strong.

The burning grew more intense. She could feel blisters forming, her skin bubbling and lifting. She put her hand to her face in a vain effort to shield herself, but her palm immediately started blistering too, and she snatched it back in fright. She tried not to scream, determined not to give them that satisfaction, but the agony was becoming too much to bear. She opened her mouth, but it was the voice of another that spoke.

"Leave her be!"

Tanit's concentration was broken. Immediately, Elda's pain began to lessen. There would be marks, but no scars. That, at least, was something.

The Novice looked up. Syl Hellais was pushing her way through the pack—a well-placed elbow here, a knee there. Some resisted, but only passively. There was grumbling and confusion, but Tanit alone merely tossed her head and laughed, folding her arms across her chest as if settling in to see what Syl planned to do.

Now Syl stood by Elda's side.

"Elda, are you all right?"

Syl helped her to her feet, looking anxiously at the girl's face, then turning her hand over and inspecting the injury on her palm. Elda appeared badly sunburned, and her hand was red and sore, but the blisters were small and unbroken.

"Is it awful?" whispered Elda.

"It will fade," said Syl, which wasn't quite answering the question. Anyway, there was no time for that now. They had more pressing concerns. The pack was brave when in numbers, but still only ever as strong as its leader. Tackle the leader, and the pack would slink away. In theory.

But this was Tanit, and Tanit did not back down easily. She was watching Syl closely, her face set in a mask of amusement.

"What did you do to her?" said Syl.

"I simply told her she was pretty," said Tanit. "I made her blush."

"What is it to you anyway, Smelly?" said one of the braver females, bristling on Tanit's left. Her name was Sarea, and she and another Novice, Nemein, were competitors for Tanit's favor, and the floating post of her best friend. Tanit enjoyed playing them off against each other. Each would deny Tanit nothing for fear that she might turn instead to the other.

Now Syl and Tanit exchanged a look, a brief flash of ice-cold understanding between deadly rivals. Sarea was trying to score points by baiting Syl. Tanit gave Sarea a barely perceptible nod, giving her permission for the entertainment to begin.

Sarea stepped forward. She was graceful and almost delicately pretty, all fine bones and sparkling eyes. However, Sarea's prettiness hid a near-psychotic lust for violence. Her particular skill was the application of pressure with the power of her mind, from the merest sensation of tightness on the skin to the breaking of bones and the crushing of skulls. She had tried it on Syl once, shortly after her arrival at the Marque; a little welcoming bruise, that was how Sarea had described it.

Syl broke Sarea's nose in reprisal, and it didn't require much mental effort at all on her part. It was mostly physical.

Mostly.

Now Syl smiled, though her stomach felt weak and empty, her hands shaky. She balled them into fists.

"You're brave when picking on those weaker than you, surrounded by your friends," said Syl. "Would you be quite so mouthy if it were just you and me?"

She could feel Sarea itching to hurt her: a little pressure and she could burst some of the blood vessels in Syl's nose, or in her eyes. Slightly more, and a finger might snap, a toe break. And then there were all those lovely internal organs: lungs, bowels, heart.

Oh, the heart! Sarea yearned to crush a heart. And already what she was envisaging was becoming real. Syl felt the faintest squeezing behind her ribs, a pressure on the beating organ, and knew that it was Sarea's work, even though Sarea was banned from using her skills out of class. However, Sarea was just a Novice too, and not completely in control of her dubious talents, not yet. Or perhaps, she merely chose not to be.

Now Sarea opened her mouth as if to reply, but then her eyes glazed over and she shook her head, seeming to have no words. She stared hard at Syl before looking to the rest of her group, bemused. Syl watched her, her heart released again, freely pounding in her chest. She waited for the pack to attack, but then Tanit spoke once more.

"I'm sorry. We meant no harm."

"Excuse me?" said Syl.

"It was nothing, Sister. Nothing. We're sorry. No harm."

Tanit stepped away, turning to leave, and the others moved after her while Syl and Elda watched, slack-jawed with surprise. But one of the pack remained, staring at Syl, unmoving as the rest of Tanit's creatures melted away. She was half obscured in the shadows, a reedy, dark-haired figure in rich blue robes. Her name was Uludess, but her friends called her Dessa. As Syl looked into that intense, furrowed face, a bead of blood slid from the older girl's nose, and she shrugged and gave a rueful little grin. Syl opened her mouth to speak, but Dessa shook her head ever so slightly then spun away, wiping the blood on her sleeve as she hurried after her pack.

A tutor in the red garments of a full Sister approached.

"What was all that about?"

It was Cale, who was responsible for the junior Novices like Syl. She was young for a senior Nairene. Her family had died in a shuttle crash shortly after her birth, and only Cale had survived. The Sisterhood had taken her in and raised her, so Cale's progress through the ranks had started earlier than most.

Syl and Elda stared at the floor.

"Do either of you want to explain to me what was going on there?" said Cale, but it was only for show. She knew what Tanit and her pack were like, just as she understood that Syl and Elda would tell her nothing of what had happened. Even if they did, Cale could only go to the Grandmage Oriel to complain on their behalf, and Oriel, who supervised the training of all Novices, would only ignore her. Oriel had a fondness for Tanit and her kind.

"I tripped," said Elda. "Syl was pulling me to my feet."

"And the others?" said Cale.

"They were queuing up to help too," said Syl.

Cale gave Syl a peculiar look. She seemed about to smile, but thought better of it.

"Get back to your duties, both of you," she said.

They did as they were told. Cale watched them go, but so too did another, unseen. The Grandmage Oriel remained in the doorway for a moment, and then was gone.